Born in Guildfor[...] radiographer, Ian [...] in the early years of his education. After National Service in the RAF, he worked as a broker, an artists' colourman and a salesman before trying his hand at small business. Later he found more satisfaction in teaching drama at a Wiltshire comprehensive school, but now writes full time. He is currently working on his second novel.

Cathedral

Ian Maitland

First published in 1992
by HEADLINE BOOK PUBLISHING PLC

First published in paperback in 1993
by HEADLINE BOOK PUBLISHING PLC

A HEADLINE FEATURE paperback

10 9 8 7 6 5 4 3 2 1

ISBN 0 7472 3958 4

Phototypeset by Intype, London

Printed and bound in Great Britain by
HarperCollins Manufacturing, Glasgow

HEADLINE BOOK PUBLISHING PLC
Headline House
79 Great Titchfield Street
London W1P 7FN

To Jean and Jane
Thanks for the ride

Comes at last, and with a little pin
Bores through the castle wall, and farewell king!

CONTENTS

Boy Bishop

1

'I look at the floodlit Cathedral and see flames. The tower and its turrets are flames leaping up, and the blazing Cathedral is a wonder and also it is terrible. It is a body on a pyre, and the twin towers of the West Porch are its feet and the feet are on fire, and the tower at the centre is the dick pointing to heaven and the dick is burning and the arms of the transepts and the great dome of the Martyr's Chapel – which is the head of the burning body – all blazing up into the blackness above like a frozen bonfire to a mole or a hydrogen bomb to an Abbo.'

The bald man looked up, removed his spectacles and leaned his forearms on the lectern. He stared at his audience. The spectacles swung from a livermarked hand.

Fine rain hissed against the windows while the electric wall clock whispered the passing seconds. The bald man returned the spectacles to his nose, pushed them up with one plump finger and lowered his head. '. . . a hydrogen bomb to an Abbo . . .' he repeated, smiling at the page. This time when he raised his head it was just far enough to pan the stiff, silent rows over the gold wire frames. His milky eyes dwelt on each tight, unresponsive face. 'Well?' he said, 'ladies and gentlemen of the sixth form?'

I felt pain in my fingertips and consciously relaxed my grip on the chair edge. I would answer if I could, but for

3

me the shock had been so much greater.

The boy beside me shifted in his seat, making it creak.

The teacher's question hung; he nodded, settling on his stool, willing to wait out the silence. Sooner or later someone would break, and it wouldn't be the wily Doctor Sopworth, D.Phil, Cambs.

Beside the partition a nose was blown. Loudly. A joke of sorts. Someone else – a girl – cleared her throat. A little round of coughing came and went and for a second I felt the class had become like a colony, one organism risen against him, maybe even capable of holding out, forcing him to speak first giving clues to what might constitute a 'right' response.

Wrong.

'Someone?' said the teacher, seeming careless of the rules of the game yet giving away nothing whatever. The drizzle hissed in waves like static. 'Tamsyn?'

One row left, one forward, a shapeless girl in a huge black cardigan with dandruff and Doc Martens failed to clear her throat. 'Good, sir,' she croaked.

The teacher stared, waiting, eyebrows arched.

Tamsyn cleared again. 'Different,' she managed. Someone coughed a half-laugh, embarrassed for her; probably Monro attempting to support his girl without personal risk.

Doctor Sopworth shook his jowled head, looked down, picked up a small square of paper, waved it and said, 'Yours, Bishop?'

'Yes, sir.' It was my daily report (they call it a *Satisfecit* here, the snobs).

Speaking as he wrote, he said: 'Punctuality and Behaviour . . . Good. Classwork/Homework . . . Excellent.' The report came to me, hand to hand down the row. He gathered the sheets of A4, tapped them together on the lectern, waved them and said:

'I've given this an Alpha, Bishop. That's topgrade for the assignment.' He placed my work in its folder, loured

4

round the group then stepped down and, with the folder under his arm, hands in the pockets of his baggy grey flannels thrusting the dusty black gown behind, began to saunter between the desks. 'The rest . . . were boring. Utterly *boring*, ladies and gentlemen of the lower sixth. And in case any of you is still unaware of the fact, I will tell you one last time: the cardinal, unforgivable sin for a student of "A" level English is to *bore* teacher to death. Teacher is obliged to *read* whatever mindless drivel the student brings up.' He whipped out a hand and slapped a table hard, making the two occupants jump, 'That, Patterson, is the English teacher's cross! And some of you . . . some of you – Messrs Patterson and Barns in particular – are making it very, very heavy. Very heavy indeed.'

Doctor Sopworth now stopped beside my desk. He drew the folder out from under his arm. 'Would you care to read these boring persons a couple more paragraphs, Bishop?' he inquired. 'Before we move on to discuss one or two of their own banal and *boring* contributions?'

I shook my head, feeling the wave of spite wash over me. Why was he doing this to me? He must know how they hate me already.

The teacher turned quickly with a grunt, seeming to read my thoughts. He returned to the lectern, opened the topmost folder, extracted more sheets of A4 and began to read from them.

To me the words quickly became mere sound as meaningless as the rain on the glass. Mental static. My mind was furiously sorting and discarding options as one possible explanation after another failed to survive the test of logic. Doctor Sopworth loves a metaphor – known fact. The juicier the better – fact. My essay begins with a metaphor – fact. It just happens to be somewhat gross – error – fucking gross – correct. Further in, the essay progresses – fact. To utterly grotesque – fact. And after that: moronic,

5

puerile, delinquent. FACT, FACT, FACT!

So . . . what was the old man up to?

I began to feel that I'd been mistaken in my initial assessment of the good doctor; maybe he was not as I first imagined the only halfway-human being among the staff of this place. Maybe he was playing the same game they all tried with Shag and me – divide and rule. Well, if that was it he'd shit out; when you've only one so-called mate in the school you learn to shy away from creeping teachers. And yet . . .

And yet, was it really likely? There was no denying the man's intelligence; he had to have read the rest of the essay; he knew what it was like. Had he scented a conspiracy? Was he just calling their bluff? *Pretending* he liked it, *pretending* to give it top grade, *pretending* he was prepared to allow me to read more of it out loud? Knowing I might do so, but gambling I had brain enough not to.

If only I had destroyed it, burned it when I had the chance instead of just hiding it under the floorboards . . .

Someone knew about my secret cache, that was obvious now. Whoever it was had found the essay, read it then handed it in for the crack. My guts told me that that someone was sitting at the desk right next to me; I'd no *proof* it was Shag, I just know him.

Shag's proper name is Rodney Arthur Lawrence. If you saw how he walks – feet splayed, arse tucked under, crotch stuck out like a walking inseminator, you'd know why they call him Shag. He's a thief, a pervert and a total animal. And, like I say, he's the only mate I've got.

Shag and I emigrated from different comprehensives straight into the sixth form of what they claim is the oldest public school in England. Shag got in on the Assisted Places Scheme, and I'd won a scholarship, so neither of our parents pay full fees. Apart from that we have nothing in common, except we're both yobbos with brains, which is something these hoorays can't hack. Everyone here hates our guts though they're mostly too slimy to say so. The slimiest ones even act friendly just so they can feel superior. It's worse for me because I'm clever. Shag's clever too, but I'm cleverer. That's why I never should have trusted him. I'm on my own here; that was obvious from the very first day.

The Bishop family landed among the dreaming spires like a big tin alarm clock going off. Talk about your culture shock. Talk about a show-up. Christalbloodymighty!

I briefly re-tuned to the lesson. The doctor was still reviewing essays; I heard the words 'cliché', 'quotidian', 'dismal'. His voice rose and fell only gently, it merged with the rain and the clock and the humming strip lights now supplementing the grey light of winter outside, then even the hum was gone, and the classroom with it.

The journey from home had been a grim affair with no one talking, each of us locked up inside our own skulls. Ma, still dopey from the effects of the morning tablet, silently staring out of the van window at the autumn countryside flitting past (though not seeing a single orange leaf if her frown was anything to go by), Pa humming hymns loudly no doubt to cover the silence and show us all how cool he was about the impending meeting with the born-leader brigade, and, slumped between the pair of them, me in a blue funk wondering whether or not that very night I'd be sleeping in the same dormitory as Lawrence or bedding down with a roomful of total strangers. And no one to share my miserable emptiness with but the voice of my own thoughts.

I really believed I could trust Lawrence then, that he was my mate. I'd only met him once, nearly a year before at the entrance exam, but that's how I felt. The exam was in November; it's the same for all sixth-form entrants whether you're after a so-called commoner place, an assisted entry place or trying for a scholarship like me.

There are only five scholarships to be won each year and the competition is fierce. You have two days of written papers and interviews to endure.

Also there is the 'conduct' lecture, during which the Registrar goes through a thing called the Code of Conduct – sometimes referred to as the 'contract'. This is an official-looking document which everyone entering the sixth form must sign. It means that, if accepted, you have agreed to abide by certain rules. Once signed, if you break those rules you lose points. Small misdemeanours – like smoking or cutting a lesson – cost you one point for the first offence. Then there are the biggies like 'The Possession or Use of Illegal Substances', and two brand new ones: 'Sexual Harassment' and 'Gross Sexual Misconduct'. Any of these cost the maximum, that is, four points in one go, and that means you're out, or, as the Registrar put it, 'We assist your parents in choosing a more suitable school.'

Shag and I had shared a bedsit in the new block. I was so uptight about the exams and sleeping away from home for the first time in my life and the way they treated you, so polite and formal, that even Lawrence's crude and ugly form seemed wonderfully reassuring. He was a laugh. Nothing seemed to bother him. He was always himself, Shag Lawrence, and everyone else – the Registrar included – was 'mate'.

Of course I knew there'd been changes in the public school world since the days of Billy Bunter and *If*; for a start there were going to be girls in the sixth form for the first time in the school's thirteen-hundred year history, but it was still going to be a whole universe away from what I'd been used to. And I was scared, despite the strong, silent front I was putting on for Ma. The biggest irony was that I'd spent my last year at Comprehensive wishing I could wave a wand and make disappear the whole falling-down, prefabricated, spray-painted slum together with all of the Philistines, bullies and morons that

8

infest it, and transport myself to the place we were now approaching. I suppose then I was still seeing the Cathedral and the school within its flint-walled precincts through the eyes of childhood – precisely through a single memory of my one and only former visit, one magical night way back sometime before all the horrors began.

When the day arrived I had felt horribly tense and nervous. I could see serious problems looming; the first would be the family transport, the Bishopmobile. How many of the other young gentlemen, I wondered, would be unloading their trunks from an eleven-year-old six-wheel transit. Whatever passed for 'street' within those hallowed walls it wouldn't be ancient Ford vans.

It was silence that pulled me back now to the classroom; Doctor Sopworth was no longer speaking. Outside the light was failing fast, putty sky turning to pewter above the Greencourt elms, rain drying slowly on the small square panes. Sitting by the window, I could see my own reflection, John Lennon spectacles, thin, miserable lips, brillopad hair; not a picture to dwell on. I turned away.

The doctor rose from his stool and handed the pile of folders to a black-gowned scholar whose name I did not know. The boy began to distribute them. The process was slow; he had to ask names as if he might be a new boy like Shag Lawrence and me, though I didn't recall his face at selection. I felt a touch on the thigh; Lawrence offering gum under the desk. I shook my head noticing his thick fingers and dirty, hard-bitten thumbnail. I looked out of the window again, seeing nothing, drifting back to memory.

When the high flint walls of the precincts had come into view, I quietly suggested to Pa that he might find it more convenient to park in the street. Still humming, he shook his head, said the single word, 'Trunk,' and carried on humming. Minutes later we arrived at the big oak gates which were wide open; Pa shouted something stupid about

9

the Groves of Academe, heaved the van round like a racer and swung it under the pointed stone arch into the square of tarmac surrounded by tall flint and stone buildings known to the inmates as the Mint Yard.

I glimpsed a flat-hatted security man as we rocketed past his wooden hut. He had time to open his mouth and raise a hand but no more, then we were squeaking to a halt between a Volvo Estate and a dark green SJ6. I glanced at the initialled cases and the cabin-trunks with the wooden hoops and the reinforced corners, the brass locks and hinges, and I moaned a great internal moan. Mine was a tin trunk. In rust-brown with dents.

'Chins off of chests. We're as good as the best,' said Pa too loudly. I glanced about. Pa leapt from the cab, flung back the rear doors with a clatter and clang, jerked my blue metal toolbox on to the tarmac, leaned in and dragged the trunk squealing to the back edge. For the first time I realised that everything about us Bishops was metal, from the wire frames on our specs to the steel toecaps in our boots. (Though I was wearing stout black brogues today, brand new.) I grabbed the other handle – desperate to be rid of him I'll confess – and backed rapidly towards the side entrance of School House, towing him after.

The weight of the trunk caused his chin to lift and I noticed with dismay that he'd missed all the whiskers underneath and down one side of his stringy neck. It was clear he'd been saving razorblades again, using the old ones till they couldn't cut jelly, but the sight of his grizzly gizzard accelerated me to near running speed.

A bunch of laughing boys passed us coming out. They looked like second or third years; none was in uniform. Only me. They were cool in hacking jackets and tracksuits and I was stiff in new wing collar, black jacket and pin-striped trousers. Shit!

Reversing up the steps to the white painted door I felt a dig in the back. It was Lawrence. I was pathetically pleased to see his grinning face. Then I noticed that he too was dressed casually in grey tracksuit and trainers.

With an amused twitch of the lips, he took in Pa's ensemble, the dull heavy boots, the two-tone Sue Ryder suit, the frayed blue collar. I forced a grin.

'Allow me,' said Lawrence, taking a grip on Pa's handle. Pa hesitated. 'Sir,' said Lawrence. Pa grunted, looked pointedly towards me and shook his head. It was typical of my father to play the devoted parent the moment he'd found a way to get rid of me. But it soon became evident that he'd met his match in Lawrence.

'Cheerio then, Mr Bishop,' said Shag locking eyes with Pa.

Pa shifted his weight, tightened his lips and pulled down the corners. He also appeared to shrink just a fraction. The moment seemed suddenly charged way out of proportion – after what felt like an age Pa said, 'Well then. All right then. Manners maketh man. Manners maketh man. Good boy. Good boy.' He yielded the handle to Lawrence and patted his shoulder. 'Good boy,' he repeated; to me he said, 'I'll fetch the box, Jim.'

'Don't you worry about that, Mr Bishop, sir,' said Lawrence, 'that's why we have fags.'

I started to say '*Fags*? What *fags*?' but already he was shouting instructions to a group of small boys in uniform, standing stiff and lost-looking by the library steps. 'Blue toolbox, Simunec. School House, study seven. Move!' I gaped at him; he could only have been here an hour – two at most – before me and already he was ordering the first years about. What's more they were quietly obeying, not telling him to get stuffed! Lawrence winked at me and said, 'Treat 'em mean, keep 'em keen, Jim.' Then he actually patted my father on the shoulder and said, 'We can manage now thank you so much, sir.'

Pa's arm flapped three or four times as if he wanted to shake my hand but was fazed by them both being occupied

11

with the handle, then, for a ridiculous moment, I thought he was actually going to hug me but the spasm passed and he settled for the old cliché, 'Take care then, precious boy, and don't forget—' at which point Lawrence gave the trunk a big tug and off we trotted, he and I, with the tin trunk containing my worldly possessions jerking between us and Pa bawling through the open door after us stuff about not forgetting to write to my Ma and all that shit. I love my Ma, but, Jesus!

It may seem a small matter, but to me it wasn't. You see, I would never have stood up to my father like that; so I do admire Shag in some ways. The thing that really divides us is what I call simple decency – conscience, if you like. I don't want to sound priggish, but Shag just cannot compute things like conscience and personal responsibility. What's one thing to do with another? That's his attitude. It's his upbringing, of course. Not that I blame him for that. But Shag insists that people are only 'moral' because they haven't the guts to do what they really want to. I'll grant him one thing: he's true to his principles, Shag is, a genuine fuckpig, snout to arsehole.

And it's pointless to argue. Arguing with Lawrence is like fencing with an orang-outang; while you're poncing about with the feints and parries he clubs your fucking head off. I think he hates me, deep down, but I find him fascinating, like the inside of an anaconda, even if he is a moral and ecological illiterate with boils on his neck from too many holidays with the carcasses in the slaughterhouse earning bloodmoney to pay for his Japanese whale-butcher motorbike.

I reckon deep down Shag is jealous of me because his pa really is boracic – broke, that is – whereas mine's just a miser who pretends to be. But for all he's a rebel, Shag likes to be top dog. It's his way of paying the world back for giving him a slaughterman for a father. And, like I say, I'm cleverer and I get the better marks.

12

Which is why I was watching my reactions as the work was handed back. The way the good doctor had drooled over my essay, well, there could have been trouble coming my way. If it *was* Lawrence who had found the essay and handed it in then his nasty little scam had backfired. Badly. And there's something about Lawrence that strikes me as not quite stable – something hard to define that you might call an aura of ruthlessness. Anyway it seemed a good idea that, as the folders came round, I should take care to appear uninterested, and so I turned once more to the window.

Last dregs of daylight; rain beginning to fall again on the Greencourt. In winter even when the sun does shine it barely clears the ridge of the nave roof. Some days the shadow of the tower sweeps slowly along this segment of the perimeter drive, but today the tarmac below the classroom window was uniform grey and gleaming like wet lead. Everything grey – earth, sky, flint and stone buildings, even the shine on the grass oval big as a football pitch and pocked with worm casts and fallen leaves – except for the Deanery windows which, having their backs to the failing light, were black, and the three giant lime trees tracing black arteries across the Cathedral.

The Cathedral . . . I had no wish to dwell on the subject of my distress but my eyes were drawn upwards as if by some hypnotic force first to the flint arch of the Dark Entry then right and up to the ruined half-arches of the old monastery library standing like a copse of blasted oaks, then up and up inevitably to those cliffs of sculptured stone which form the north flank of the Cathedral.

Questions crowd in. Contradictions. Facts to be sifted from illusion, fantasy, *craziness* (please God not that!). What possible connection could exist between that huge, dark whale of a building and the strange words in the essay? Essay? Hardly an 'essay'. Those images . . . weird, and so alien to me? Could they have come from me –

13

perhaps from a nightmare or some trauma from the deep
distant past, some shocking event I was too young to
remember, consciously? 'Repression'? Is that it? What
Doctor Keylock calls the septic dungeon of the unconscious, full of pus, in need of a good lancing to prevent
it poisoning the whole system? I've never gone for that
kind of stuff. Maybe it's possible, could just possibly be,
but that isn't *me*. No way. In any case, it wasn't just the
images . . . there was the whole middle section . . . the
style . . . completely different, unrecognisable. And the
ending, that handwriting. And that spelling! I could see
it now, the exact line where it ceased to be my own
handwriting and the infantile scrawl began, flecks of ink
where the nib dug in, half the ds and bs the wrong way
round. Where had that come from? No answers. None!
What could have triggered off a thing like that? There
was nothing that I could remember. Think! What came
before? Supper. Anything freaky there? Did we have anything dodgy like mushrooms or red beans? What *did* we
have? What day was it? It was, let me see, five days ago,
a Wednesday.

'Breaded fish and green bullets. Yum, yum,' Lawrence
had said in his normal loutish voice just as everything
went dead quiet. The whole refectory must have heard his
Yum, yum, including the Top Table where the Masters
and a selection of School Monitors sit on the raised
platform.

Immediately to my right, at the head of our own long
oak table, Vidal-Hume, Captain of School House, School
Monitor, King's Scholar and Captain of Shooting, shushed
and frowned and pressed his trigger finger to his small
pink lips. Lawrence grinned, shrugged and put his slaughterman's maulers together in mock reverence as the Head
Boy, now standing at the Top Table, launched into grace:

'*Benedicat nobis, Omnipotens Deus*

14

Et tuis donis datis ad Henrico Rege
Caeterisque benefactoribus nostris
Per Iesum Christum Dominum Nostrum
Amen.'

'Amen,' responded five hundred voices, and the clatter of steel on china commenced.

'Honestly, Lol,' said Vidal-Hume with a shake of the head and what was supposed to be his you're-a-bit-of-a-rascal-but-I'm-a-broad-minded-guy-and-I-love-you-deep-down smile (yes, Vidal's the slimiest of all and he really does call Lawrence, Lol!). 'We're pretty old fashioned here, I suppose. Even so, old man . . .' another shake of the head, pushing the leathery fish around his plate with his fork like it might be a fishy skateboard, 'quite how a fellow can get excited about uneatable tack like this I'll—'

By which time Lawrence had eaten his, skin and all. 'That's OK, mate,' he said, lifting the house captain's plate, sliding the entire contents on to his own, 'No worries.' Big wink, sideways nod and he's packing it all away.

Vidal was furious, you could see that just for an instant before the smiley mask came back and he settled down without a word to the brown bread roll and the little curl of marge as though that was all he ever really wanted. That's something else about Lawrence – the speed. He's like Richard III in the Shakespeare play, sudden. Yes, that's what Shag is, he's sudden.

But all this is by the way; the real point is, apart from that one small incident, like I say, nothing unusual about supper. The fish course came and went after which it was apple, orange or banana for those who wanted it, the usual mugs of brown tea straight out of the big enamel jug, a couple of notices for the First Fifteen and the Drama Society, then, immediately after supper, prep.

15

Prep is from 7.00 to 9.00 every night. From the refectory the boarders filter back to the six houses scattered around the precincts. The sixth-form girls are farmed safely away in what was once the Abbey, where lairy sods like Lawrence can't get at them – they even have breakfast there so we don't see them again until morning assembly in the Chapter House. The rest of us – apart from years one and two lumped together in the biggest houseroom known simply as Hall – file away to our bachelor studies inside our bachelor houses.

There are two boys besides Lawrence and me in study number seven, School House. The room is a tatty old garret with a sash dormer window, low, wedge-shaped ceiling and bare board floor. The door is peppered with small round holes, apart from a circle at head height where the dart board hung before being confiscated after the accident with Musslewhite's fag. It now bears a badly torn centrefold of Jane Fonda, repaired with sellotape and re-hung by Shag (having been ripped off the wall by Vidal in the second week of term).

The study gets pretty stuffy what with the electric pipes and the broken sash cord; it would be easy to fall asleep – I know, I've done it – and at first I thought maybe I'd just dreamt it all. Looking back now I know different.

Everything that happened after that evening proves it was *her*. I know now that *she* was the true author of those words; the 'essay' was just the beginning, but at the time I thought I was going potty. I really should have known of course – it is, after all, quite typical of her to pick on the one thing that mattered to me more than anything, and cynically use it to wind me up. Bitch!

The fact is I wasn't thinking as straight as usual; I was worried about this particular piece of homework. Like I say (bollocks to modesty) I'm bright, and work doesn't normally bother me, but this did. One reason was that there'd been a big fuss about my course here – what

16

subjects I should take, what went against what on the timetable et cetera. Pa being a late working-class, socially mobile, materialist Philistine by nature naturally wanted his only son-and-heir to take all three Sciences plus Maths and sod the Arty Fartys, as he calls the Arts. 'Science and Technology is where the future lies, precious boy,' that was always Father's cry, whereas the report that came with me from Elizabeth Barton comp emphasised particularly my prowess at the English Language and Lit. That's what *I* wanted, too. And when Pa left, I said so.

At the comp they would, without question, have arranged for me to do both by fiddling things around, swapping teachers for certain lessons and so on. In that kind of way it was a good place to be. There they would always bust a gut to help individuals; everyone was a 'person' at Lizzy's, not just a pupil like here. The teachers automatically did their best to stretch what little talent came their way. The system there was designed to be flexible, whereas here it's mostly either or – Arts/Classics or 'The Sciences'.

Nevertheless, Pa being Pa, after a great deal of fuss they made a special provision for the son of Edward Bishop the scrap-metal magnate of Marshside; I was granted my own, unique timetable involving splitting my Maths between two different teachers, dropping 'A' level Theatre Studies (which pissed me off) in favour of a single Drama-for-Interest lesson and adding one period of so called General Studies as a filler just to stop me having too much 'private study' time. (GS is useless, which is why I cut it.) The rest of my timetable was filled with the inevitable 'Three Sciences'. And, of course, English.

And that is why this essay was so important to me. It was also the group's first Creative Composition. 'You may not all be Shakespeares,' Doctor Sopworth said, 'but when you're writing your own, original stuff you are doing what Shakespeare *did*.' The assignment was a test for all of us,

17

a way of seeing if we could spell and punctuate as much as anything, but more so for me. After all the letter writing between both schools and Pa, and the meetings between Pa, the 'Master', and each of the staff concerned, and on top of that the hype raised by my old English teacher's report, I felt obliged to lay 'em out flat with my English genius.

I had chosen 'Cathedral' from the list of four titles simply because of the fascination the place held for me; I thought I could do a real job on it. We'd been told that it could either be a descriptive or imaginative piece; I had decided to make it the former with a touch of the latter to bring it to life. I expected the words to flow as usual, but, that evening, something was wrong.

I must have sat for the best part of an hour without a single idea coming into my head. The boy Musslewhite, house prefect, house sacristan, fanatic desk tidier and quite the most miserable person I've ever encountered, was huddled over Latin translation with this real drongo Clemetson-Hogg – known universally as 'Common-entrance Clemmo' – as if they only had one half brain cell apiece. Clemetson-Hogg's speciality is sniffling and snorting in both directons, ie both inhaling *and* exhaling, for hours at a time without missing a single respiration. But tonight even this pair of animated arseholes was relegated to the status of minor irritant. What really got me was Lawrence.

The sound of Lawrence's pen scratching away behind me rapidly developed into a Chinese-type torture. I got to the point where I was convinced he'd selected an especially scratchy nib and rough paper, and was writing any old rubbish simply to get me going. Just when I thought I could stand no more and would have to go down to the common room to make coffee or kick the furniture into matchwood, I had this idea of shutting my eyes and trying to *picture* the Cathedral as clearly as possible in my imagination. I decided to start with one particular detail, to bring

18

that right into focus, then, having bust through the block, work my way out to the rest of the pile. Great theory. Unfortunately, when I shut my eyes expecting to see a single gold pennant on top of the south eastern turret of the tower, what I actually saw was *flames*!

My Graduate Cartridge Pen by W. H. Smith plc was poised over the page, and, for a moment or two, nothing happened, then suddenly – down plunged my hand and away it raced, darting along line after line like a thing possessed. 'Shit!' I exclaimed.

'What's up, mate?' said Lawrence, looking across from the desk behind my right shoulder.

'Nothing. It's OK.'

'Don't forget it's the final draft,' said Lawrence, staring at my scribbling pen.

'It's OK,' I said, trying to smile casually, control my breathing, and, at the same time, slow the thing down. *But the pen would not be slowed. Neither could I control it in any way!*

Lawrence shrugged and turned back to his work, but after a moment he looked up again with a suspicious frown on his face. 'Going mad, aren't we?' he said.

My heart was beating wildly. 'Got to get the ideas down while I can remember them,' I offered, but Lawrence was already rising from his seat.

'Let's have a butcher's,' he said.

Suddenly the pen stopped. Thank God, I thought, quickly covering the page with my folder and putting my hand on top. I had now read some of the stuff the pen was producing and had begun to feel sick.

'Come on,' he said, taking hold of my wrist, 'what's the big secret?'

'Nothing. I'm not ready to publish, that's all,' I said, forcing a grin.

He began to pull harder, but at that moment the bell went for the end of prep. Lawrence gave a final yank and my hand broke away but I managed to slam it back down before he could snatch away the folder. 'Please yourself,' he said, following the others to the door. 'I wouldn't be late for assembly if I were you, Piggie's in one of his moodies again.'

'Can't hand this mess in!' I shouted after him. 'Answer my name, will you?'

His voice called back from halfway down the stairs: 'It's due in tomorrow, Jimbo. Get your arse in gear if you don't want another month on report.'

Prayers. The drone of Vidal-Hume's voice drifting up the stairwell. He's reading from the bible, '. . . where moss and rust doth corrupt . . .'

I slowly lifted the manila folder and stared at the smudged paper beneath. The handwriting was mine – the ink still wet. And my pen lay, uncapped alongside the final fullstop.

My chest felt hollow as I skimmed the words. I seemed to *recognise* what was written – the blood, the fire, the rivers of molten lead – but could not imagine where the ideas had come from.

I felt a strange excitement, half terror, half wonder. What now? The writing was crude, and hideously violent – it would need re-drafting, certainly but . . . well, it *was* after all, a start, some basis on which to build.

Even at that point, without any attempt at analysis, I guess I knew in my guts it wasn't *my* creation. But my excitement was such I felt almost drunk – the only question in my mind being, Dare I ask for *more*?

I re-tuned to the sounds coming from the stairwell; the bible reading was still not finished. I drew a deep breath, and, feeling like I imagine a man who swaps his immortal soul for knowledge might feel, I reopened the pad. I stared at my pen as if it might be a live creature – little black snake, gold fangs, black venom. Seeming to make no decision, I watched my fingers take hold of the barrel. It felt ice-cold and my fingertips seemed instantly welded to

20

it. The nib hovered above the page. Suddenly it trembled, jerked to the first empty line . . .

I became aware that my chest was heaving dangerously, the tips of my fingers tingling – both signs I recognised as signalling the onset of one of my panic attacks. I fought for control but, as always the struggle simply made things worse. Too late to draw back now.

The Lord's Prayer came through the half open door in hissing waves as if chanted by a chorus of snakes. A stable corner of my brain registered urgency: hymn next, then notices, then they'll be coming up the stairs.

I felt the pen kick and wriggle. The flames were back (when had I closed my eyes?) and there was something else . . . something moving . . . something dancing in the centre . . . a young girl dancing . . . naked in the flames, her body glowing red, orange, purple like the flames, her hair flowing upwards, like the flames, her eyes filled with . . . what *is* that look? Is it pity? . . . or *hate*?

No hands! She has no hands, just stumps gleaming in the firelight!

'Don't go! Come back! Where are your hands?'

Gone.

The flames are still there, but she's gone.

It seemed to me no time had passed. My eyes were open, and the page . . .

The page was full!

New, wet writing. Scrawly, childish, not mine. Nothing like it.

Voices below singing . . . hooting . . . waves of sound like a stretched tape recording . . . 'The darkness deepens, Lord . . .'

Get a fucking grip, cock. You've got thirty seconds, maybe less. They already talk about you and tap their foreheads. Who can blame them?

That was the voice of my thoughts – my headvoice, as I call it.

'Shut it!' I shouted, making myself jump. My heart was

21

still pounding but the breathing had steadied and my fingers felt normal. I opened the desk drawer, took out my steel ruler, levered up the ten-inch length of loose floorboard under my desk, fished out the half-full bottle of Vat 69, swigged, returned it, gathered the two sheets of A4, shoved them into the hollow between the joists as far as my arm would reach, replaced the board, lit myself a Capstan, put my feet on the desk, and waited, dragging hard, burning it down fast.

My hand was shaking, but the fag they would. understand.

Lawrence entered first. He put his fists on his hips, then took the cigarette from my lips, placed it between his own, rolled it from one end of his mouth to the other, and, in a fair imitation of PG's voice said, 'I wish to see you in my office immediately, young man.'

'What, really?' I asked.

Lawrence nodded. '*Really*. Tougho nuttos, Jim lad.'

'Someone's been pulling your leg, young man,' said PG, rolling his cork tip from one corner of his mouth to the other and back without moving his lips. Percy Gardener is a professional smoker – number one seed – yellow fingers, yellow lip, permanent one-eyed squint. And crafty.

The other eye narrowed. I knew what was coming.

'But while you're here, Bishop, you'd better tell me what you've done. Hmm?'

I stared at the inch of drooping ash, wondering when it would fall on his ashy, wrinkled tie. (Why do they all wear little screwed-up ties in navy with maroon zigzags?)

'Take your time, Bishop. We don't want . . . ah, *mistakes* creeping in.'

We both knew I'd say nothing, however long he waited, but the ritual had to run its course. Next would come the smile, then the arm round the shoulders, the pat on the bottom that's almost a stroke but not quite, the little squeeze, the jokey finalé.

'That's one I owe you, Bishop,' he chortled. And the ash fell.

Outside the door, this struck me as a peculiarly tame trick for Lawrence, not at all his usual brand of 'fun'. I was still wondering about this as I climbed the iron staircase to the dormitory.

I hardly slept at all Wednesday night. As Lawrence had gleefully pointed out, I was already on report for cutting GS, the problem was I'd told porkies about having permission and Mr Ward had delighted in shopping me. Failure to hand in my English was likely to stitch me up for another fortnight, but that wasn't what really upset me; what upset me and kept me awake was the whole queer business with the writing and the pictures in my head, plus thoughts I've been having for months now about Ma and me. Me being like my Ma in so many physical ways. Why not *mentally* as well, then? was the thought that nagged me on and off all night.

Being on *satisfecit* didn't help either of course. By dawn the next morning I'd made up my mind I would have a last try at the essay during lunch hour and hand it in late – better late than never, I thought. I never did though. I couldn't. Just the thought of it set my pulse racing. So that's where it stayed, under the floorboards, at least, so I believed.

Now we'd arrived at Monday. Crunch day. And me sat right next to Shag Lawrence silently rehearsing my excuses for not having handed in the work, when all of a sudden the good doctor starts reading it out! He's well past the burning dick before my head would believe what was happening. It was real, though – the first paragraph anyway.

Dark outside now. The four fancy iron streetlights have just lit up. Fifteen minutes to the bell for the end of English, then it will be a quick walk across the dark and misty Mint Yard to the Bio Lab for the last hour of the afternoon session. We're filleting out the sciatic nerves of frogs, from their *filum terminales* all the way down to their little flipper feet.

The boy who doesn't know his classmates' names even after five whole weeks in the group was still faffing about with the last few folders.

'Atkinson? Atkinson?'

'Here,' growled a black lad with a nearly moustache and shaved parting. (How could anyone forget Big Akki?)

'James Bishop?'

'Yes. Over here.'

I heard the folder land on my desk. I was aching to see if anything had been added (or subtracted), but I ignored it.

Doctor Sopworth was back behind the lectern reading to the class from a book of poems some morbid piece about rats' feet and broken glass. Lawrence was busy decorating the desk edge with Tippex swastikas and had so far made no move for my folder. After a moment, I casually lifted the flap. Near the bottom of the second page was an A in a circle, underneath this a comment in green biro:

What do you expect on a bone fire site? was what it said. Then in brackets, *Talk to me, James.*

'Talk?' I thought, 'About what?' I glanced up. Doctor Sopworth was staring at me with his soft, wet eyes. And damned if the old bugger didn't wink!

I looked down quickly, feeling the blood surge up my neck. What was the man trying to pull? I dropped my eyes, partly from embarrassment but also to re-read the spidery, ink-splattered final paragraph, at the same time moving my left shoulder forward to shield it from Lawrence's gaze. I really believe I expected it to have become something else or perhaps even that it might vanish altogether as my eyes passed along each line. But the words were exactly as I remembered them – spelling, writing, everything:

Theirs this sab doy standing on top of the green hill he is look at the church far away. The big church is in the middle of the city. Up come the sun and the birds degun sing. The skye behind is all black and bark dut in front its lovely pink and red and gold. The church look just like it on fire but isnt rely not rely but the boy like fire and start fel hapy and he want go down so he run dow the windy yello path bown to the churchs front gate wen he get to the church the doy is sab because there int no fire but then he look up and see his frend waiv to him from the window at the top of this big big tower then he fels pleasb and the black dirds start sing come and play come and play some body up hear want play with you

The thing made me shiver, even in that hot stuffy classroom. It was madness, nightmare in the late afternoon. I looked again at the doctor's comment, felt my teeth grinding together fit to splinter. No way was I talking to any teacher about this stuff.

When Shag made a grab for it, I was ready and hung on tight. He got a corner. The rest I screwed up and ate.

2

Next day I managed to avoid Doctor Sopworth altogether apart from one narrow escape when he beckoned me from across the Greencourt. I was still trying to blank the whole episode out of my mind and the last thing I wanted was a head to head with the doctor, so I pretended I thought he was waving, waved back and scooted up the library steps.

It seemed that Shag Lawrence was avoiding me in turn, thereby adding weight to my suspicions about his role in the affair. I first noticed this at breakfast which is self service between 7.30 and 8.00. I'd been late for the start as usual. By the time I arrived there was only the sawdust-like muesli left and no sign of Lawrence. Lawrence always eats a giant breakfast and is normally first there and last to leave so his absence a mere twelve minutes after kick off was odd to say the least.

It turned out the first I saw of him that day was bedtime, and then I got the feeling that was only because he happens to inhabit the space on the other side of my locker. He managed to grunt, 'All right, mate?' but immediately turned away, dropped his pants, pulled on his flash, yellow pyjama bottoms and without so much as a glance in my direction, flipped back the covers and hopped into bed. He sat up just long enough to pop his front stud, loosen his tie and yank off his top clothes – string vest, shirt, pullover all in one lump, then he chucked the bundle on the floor, snatched up a magazine from his locker and hit the pillow with his back towards me. All this was executed at tremendous speed as if by a man in a fury.

This bugged me. *I* was the injured party, not him. 'Yes ta,' I said, sarcastically answering his earlier inquiry. But his nose was already buried in the five-month-old copy of *Psychic News*.

At that point there was a big burst of laughter from the far end of the dormitory, and the sound of someone counting: '. . . forty-six, forty-seven, forty-eight, forty-nine, *half-century*!' Up went a great roar, and the counting continued. I looked across to the huddle of half-dressed boys. Fat Marcus Hunt, whose father owns a hotel in the Canaries and who likes to tell you juicy details about the Canarian prostitutes his dad has financed for him (spoilt brat), was kneeling at the foot of his bed, dressed only in his pyjama top. Between the roars and guffaws, the sound of many farts.

I sat on the edge of my bed and began to untie my laces. I'd seen this performance a dozen times; The Big Match they call it: Marcus and David's party piece, non-stop farting, double farting in fact, farting that, like Clemetson-Hogg's sniffing, somehow contrives to operate both inwards and out. Hunt and his pal, David Fisher, have an ongoing competition, very elaborate with prizes and forfeits, and there are side bets et cetera – big money – pound coins all over the bed. It's not genuine fart, of course, only air, but impressive enough. The first time.

School House is among the oldest of the eight buildings that make up the school's living quarters. There are no trendy 'bedsits' for the senior boys in School House as there are in most other houses, (including – needless to say – the Abbey where the new intake of girls is housed). Eight boys share the senior dormitory in School House. Of that eight, only I saw the door swing open and the Captain of House come in (which is hardly surprising, the fart-count having reached the eighties, and the century, as

28

they say, being on). Vidal-Hume stood in the open doorway, arms folded across his chest, small mouth pinched
tight, face a study in moral outrage.

I glanced down at Lawrence, certain he must have heard
what was going on, but he was slowly turning the next
page of his old magazine. He must have sensed my gaze
or something for, without looking up, he muttered, 'The
gross Potty Humour of fartarse Hunt.'

'Absolutely,' I whispered – maybe I was trying to show
solidarity, to meet him halfway, I don't really know – but
Shag offered nothing further. When I looked back at Vidal
he was white in the face and visibly shaking.

'You disgusting animal, Hunt!' he shouted above the
laughter and counting and farting. The noise subsided, six
faces turned towards the door, six boys stood together,
forming a wall of bodies between Captain and betting
money. Marcus struggled with his pyjama bottoms, tangled and fell with a crash and a flash of bare buttock. His
freakish anatomy must have been, as it were, loaded, for
in struggling to untangle his legs a last, monstrous fart
broke forth rising sharply in pitch as Marcus tried to stifle
it with muscular pressure; it finally died with a forlorn
flubber. No one laughed. All eyes switched to the Captain
who was now standing, head bowed, scribbling on a small
yellow pad. As he wrote, he said, 'I'm giving you a chit for
obscenity, Hunt. Report to Mr Gardener in the morning.'

'It's a crime to have wind, now is it, Vidal?' muttered
Fisher, the fart-antagonist and mate of Hunt.

The Captain ignored this. 'The rest of you, it's gone
ten-fifty,' he said, without looking up. 'Five minutes.'
With that, he spun round and stomped away down the
corridor.

Marcus was now sitting on the bare boards solemnly
pulling up his pyjama bottoms. Fisher said, 'Hard tit,
Marcus; ninety-seven.' Marcus shook his head and gave
the closed door the V sign.

One of the gamblers wandered glumly round the bed

spaces returning cancelled bets, others resumed their undressing or made their way towards the ablutions. I looked at Lawrence's back. I knew what he thought of our Captain of House; I could surely expect some reaction, some comment at least. But there was none.

In the winter the upper dormitories are close to freezing if not actually freezing. The authorities – the Old Boys or the Governors or whatever – seem to consider these spartan conditions necessary for the raising of born-leaders, as if cold bedrooms and cool determined heads were somehow magically connected. I tried to reason that Shag had probably got the hump about it being so cold, but I wasn't convincing myself. Lawrence and I always had a mutual moan session at the end of the day. Never missed. And it always seemed to help, just a little. The feeling I had now was not so much loneliness – although that was part of it I'm sure – tonight it was more chronic peculiarity. I really did find the type of behaviour we'd just witnessed childish, not to say distasteful. I could never myself be part of the 'rugby song' set, I thought and yet, what exactly *was* I part of? Nothing, it seemed. It wasn't the first time in my life I'd experienced this sense of not-belonging, but tonight it felt as though I'd made some stupid mistake on my application for membership of the human race. I'd been misfit enough at Elizabeth Barton, here it was a hundred times worse. And as for home . . . as for home, well. 'I keep being turned down. Why? WHY?'

On the far side of the still-reading Lawrence, Musslewhite whispered something to his neighbour. Both boys looked at me, grinning. The word 'why' was still echoing in my ears. I knew then that I'd spoken aloud.

I felt myself redden but managed to stare back until they turned away. I began to undress myself, feeling angry and foolish, focusing with absurd ferocity on the simple task of folding my grey flannels down the creases. I tried to see Lawrence and me from the outside. What was that

30

phrase they use in parliament? I spy strangers? I spy
aliens, more like; foreign bodies; weirdos . . .

Bollocks to them, said headvoice, **it's you! It's no good
muttering to yourself. He's pissed you off. Tell him!**

True, I thought. Anyone watching the two of us tonight
would think it was *me* who'd played dirty with Lawrence
rather than vice versa . . .

An amazing thought struck me at that moment. Could
it be guilt? Could this churlish performance I was being
subjected to actually signify Lawrentian remorse? *Does the
beast have a conscience after all?*

Still grappling with these almost-too-astounding-to-be-
seriously-entertained propositions, I gathered up my towel
and sponge bag and headed for the iron staircase.

The ablution block has white tiles all over like an old-
fashioned urinal. Along one wall is a row of white basins
and against the opposite wall a row of eight white baths.
At the far end is a large, metal-framed window with frosted
glass permanently running with condensation. And it's
cold.

By the time I arrived there was only one boy left, and
he was busy scraping a little fine down from his chin and
lip with an orange plastic razor of the female kind. Obviously saving himself time in the morning, I thought, clever
boy.

Standing with the hot water up to my wrists, palms
pressed flat on the bottom of the basin, watching my hands
turn slowly from white to blotchy red, I began mentally
to sift through a number of possible statements I might
make to Shag Lawrence on return to the dormitory. It
would have to be something not too intellectual sounding,
something concise without being unduly heavy, something
like, Nicked any good essays lately, mate? I tried a few
more out, but finally – my hands now looking like they
were sporting a pair of red Marigold gloves – settled on
precisely that.

The bathroom was empty now. I rinsed my face and

began to dry. Without a thought for the passing of time, I allowed myself to fantasise that my effort at open and honest communication might be all the encouragement Lawrence would need to bring forth an apology – maybe even a heart-felt one. And, who knew, maybe in turn that might even lead to a better understanding – even the prospect of *true* friendship in place of the phony friendship that existed between us now.

Such was my speculation during the warming of the hands and the subsequent drying thereof. The subtle but telling epithet would be launched over the top of Lawrence's magazine immediately on my return to the dorm. And then? Well, then we would see.

In the event, when I finally strode back into the dormitory, I found Lawrence totally absorbed in the slagging off of Musslewhite, who it seemed had had the temerity to interrupt Shag's reading merely to complain about the Lawrentian socks and underpants landing in his bedspace.

I held fire, awaiting the moment, determined to give it my best shot. But as I stooped to stow my things in the locker, still revising the line, I spotted the empty spec case. I'd left my glasses on the bathroom shelf. Everyone else was in bed.

Sprinting down the spiral steps three at a time I passed PG coming up but kept going, giving him no time to react. By the time I'd retrieved the specs and sprinted back upstairs, the dormitory was in darkness. PG was standing in the doorway, tutting. He tapped his wristwatch with a yellow-stained finger then put that finger to his lips. I thought about the Code and the Silence After Eleven p.m. rule – penalty one point. I stopped running, bobbed my head and proceeded on tiptoe.

'You're late, Bishop. Bed. Double quick,' he said, looking stern, holding the door ajar just long enough to light my way across the dark floorboards.

The sheets were thin ice, fresh on, cracking with starch.

32

When the door closed I could still see the shadow cast by PG's feet making two dark patches in the strip of light underneath. PG was cunning, but not quite cunning enough to stand to one side of the doorway. Nevertheless, his presence outside was sufficient to make me abandon my dream of reconciliation and to lie instead with my legs crossed and my feet tucked under my bum, chewing over the events of the day; the things I *would* have moaned about to Lawrence if other things had gone as they ought to have gone this evening.

At morning break big Tamsyn had taken the trouble to fight her way up to me in the tuckshop simply to announce, between slurps of Slush, that she hadn't meant what she'd said about my essay in class and that, far from thinking it either 'good' or 'different', she really thought it a piece of gross adolescent drivel. It so happens I quite fancy Tamsyn even though she dresses like Giant Haystacks at a funeral, and is aggressively women's lib. Her attack might have caused me some grief had I not already noticed the weed Munro hunkered in the corner sniggering into his Wagonwheel, giving strong clues as to who was really at the bottom of the little pantomime. Anyway, I thanked Tamsyn with a kiss on the cheek, whispered 'Cunt' in her ear and gave Munro the finger, from which it will be gathered that I'd already given up on the idea of winning friends and influencing even the less brainwashed inmates of this Conservative stronghold. Apart from these peripheral incidents, nothing occurred that had any connection with either the essay or the Cathedral, at least, not during the day.

Tuesday happens to be my worst timetable of the week. It starts with whole-school assembly at 8.45, and assembly here is even more boring than it was at Lizzy's. It's always exactly the same: hymn, prayers, notices – there's never anything even mildly *nouvelle vague* like a Samaritan in sandals or a little 'morality' drama, and there's certainly nothing like the good old 'Tampax Lady' with the hilarious patter we had at Lizzy's, nor even a holy-type pop group to give us a giggle and break the monotony. It's straight Christian worship in the cold and ancient cavern of the Chapter House with its flagstone floor and painted wooden ceiling arching high above. Serious godsquad is what you get here, and lump it.

After assembly I have double maths, then it's break, then double chemistry – which is all atomic theory at the moment, and that's pretty damned boring too. Then there's one hour of GS and, in the afternoon, two hours of physics with Dumbo Haynes (who used to be a drummer with the Heath band, so he says, though he acts about as hip as a second cello with the LPO). There are no major games for the Upper School on Tuesday afternoon unless you're in one of the teams, so between lunch and afternoon session there's a couple of hours when you're allowed to do more or less what you like – including going into town if you happen to have an *exeat*, by which they mean, pass. After supper, it's prep, evening prayers and bed. No telly of course. And no talking after lights out, just cold sheets and silence apart from the snoring and the creaking of springs. (Which could be anything in a monastery like this. I mean, anything rhythmic of course.)

It's the little things sometimes. I'd not yet got used to the tall, curtainless windows of the dormitory, hard-edged, pointed arches, six in a row like the bars of a cage only bigger, and the way the light from the Mint Yard lamp-post spills through the dusty panes to fall in narrow bands across the rows of beds and daub silver-grey chevrons on the wall behind me. Nor the silence rule. Above all, that. On our very first night Shag and me were 'cautioned' by Vidal-pinklips-Hume for whispering after lights out. What neither of us realised then was that the inmates, almost without exception, submit to every rule and tradition in the place without question, no matter what manner of

34

creepo is giving the orders or whether the tradition is benign or malignant. It's as if they're all brainwashed – that's how it's set up, there's no future here for the rebellious spirit. If you're not the *sturmbannführer* then you're the mindless, broken Eloi vacantly obeying the Morlocks' dinner gong. No one seems to stop and say, Hang on a minute, mate: Why?

That's something else I can't get used to: at Elizabeth Barton I considered myself, if anything, a touch too far on the side of the angels, whereas here I'm a tearaway. A tearaway, me! Another thing, the noise level generally in this place is amazingly low compared to Lizzys – in class, at mealtimes, everywhere – but what really gets me, as I say, is the silence of the dorm after eleven o'clock sharp every evening. That seems to rattle my busy little brainbox, and it winds me up like nothing else. And on Tuesday night, what with Shag bottling me the way he had plus the business with Marcus's bottom and my bloody awful not-belonging feeling, the silence got me even worse than usual.

About half an hour after lights out, it started. No, that's not quite right. To be accurate it started the previous night – the same day I got the essay back – I heard something then only it was so faint I could pretend I thought it was imagination or a fly or something and eventually got off to sleep. But this was different. This time it was not something that could be brushed aside. Not that the sound was continuous, far from it, but I kept waiting for it to come back, straining my ears at every little noise.

When the shadow of PG's feet finally disappeared – it must have been all of five minutes after he closed the door – I lay in my narrow, iron bed, harking to the dwindling traffic sounds beyond the wall. On this side of the wall the night watchman had just called the hour of eleven and chanted his nightly message of peace and safety, ten minutes late as usual. Shortly after that, a powerful motor-bike began tearing up the hills encircling the city, echoing endlessly around the bowl. Before that sound died a solitary diesel came chittering through, heading west on its way to London, and later came the rattle and clank of a goods train going the other way. Close inside the cage, the wheezing, sighing, rumbling breaths of seven slumbering bodies.

Half an hour after lights out my feet still hadn't thawed but my knees were aching so much I had to brave the icy regions and straighten them out. Just as I moved my feet, that's when I heard it. I stopped moving at once, with my knees still making a tent shape. Yes, it was certain now; the weird little sound I had succeeded in denying the previous night . . . it was back. Still softer than a bat's wingbeat it was, but undeniable. And relentless.

I can only describe the sound as being like a much speeded-up tape recording or, perhaps more precisely, like Donald Duck – maybe in reverse – gabbling nonsense at the bottom of an echoing wellshaft. Which might sound comical but I promise you it was anything but. It made my scalp wriggle and crawl on the bone. After five seconds or so, it stopped.

I held my breath, ears hissing, pulse thumping. Then I heard it again: quackwackywackitywackitywackwack-wack. It was the kind of sound I could imagine gremlins would make, if there ever were such things, while trying to converse in a state of wild panic. Of course, once I'd arrived at the idea it might be language of some sort I was straining at every imagined syllable trying to find meaning, and, at the same time, hoping and praying the sound would not return.

I found no meaning. And it did return.

At least when you're lying awake at night inside the Cathedral precincts you don't need a watch to tell you the time – the clock in the clock tower does that for you.

Round about half-past two, the random five-second bursts of hideous duck-speak settled to a regular interval of approximately three minutes; this I estimated by counting in my head: one-and-two-and-three-and-four et cetera. By half-past four the interval had increased to five minutes or so and the sounds had become so faint I could no longer be certain whether I was hearing *them* or my own metabolic processes.

Like I say, Tuesday night I hardly slept.

3

Come morning I was in a black mood.

When Matron called me into sick-bay I was on my way to breakfast and desperate for the soothing, nourishing, health-restoring live yoghurt they have on a Wednesday, if you get there early enough. (Which I almost never do but would have done on this occasion since I was practically up before I went to bed if you follow me – except for Matron – except for that female tomcat in the blue dress and starched apron with the big silver buckle on the broad, black elastic belt around her outgrowing waist that makes her look more like an all-in wrestler than a paramedic or whatever she's supposed to be. Jesus, she's an ugly piece of work, and thick – thick in a upperclass-sounding way that's so over the top and riddled with cockups you can tell straight away she's bottom drawer.) She wanted to discuss my 'somewhat limited list', she announced. Call yourself a Matron, I thought, can't you see when a person's dying? I *need* yoghurt.

Such was my condition, I could barely understand a word she said, and quickly felt myself becoming irritated beyond reason.

'Your pillowcase contains precisely *one* soft and *one* wing, James,' she announced, then stared at me, thick black brows arched, moustached lips a thin red line like she'd just made her mouth with a scalpel.

Soft what? Wing what? I thought. What the hell is she

on about? Must be in code, I thought, feeling the frustration knotting my stomach. I stared back, head thumping, mouth like a vulture's crutch (to borrow a favourite Shaggism).

She waited, grimly. Finally, she said, 'That's in a whole week, young man.' She waited again. When there was no response, she spoke slowly and very, very clearly, as if to an imbecile or foreigner, 'Where is the rest of it, James? The remainder? Where, James? Hm?'

This was hurting my head quite a bit now. Remainder? What remainder? I puzzled. I shrugged, shook my head, shrugged again.

'The soft collar is most likely beyond reclamation, James—'

Ah, I thought. Cracked it. 'Soft' equals Soft collar. 'List' equals laundry list.

'—it is absolutely filthy,' she was saying, 'ditched, probably ruined. How in the name of heaven did you manage to get it in that frightful condition?'

I inspected a snag on the toecap of my left brogue.

'Come here,' she commanded. 'Let's have a look at that one.' She reached forward and took hold of the top edge of my detachable collar at the back of the neck with her ice-cold fingers, twisting it, turning it over, nearly choking me. 'Honestly,' she said with a theatrical sigh. 'And why only two pairs of briefs—?'

While she was casually cutting off my air supply, I'm thinking, Briefs? Does she take me for Rumpole of the Bailey?

'Where are they?' she demanded. Then, even more slowly, leaving a ridiculous gap between each word, 'Where . . . are . . . your . . . other . . . undergarments, child?!'

Undergarments? Ah! *Knickers*, she means. I raised both hands, palms up.

She stared in blank incredulity. 'Good golly, boy! Don't tell me you—'

Somewhere about then I switched off.

No. More than switched off. Inside my head, I left. While Matron pulled and prodded my vacant corpse, turning a cuff here, a waistband there, I hopped back a couple of months in time, and twenty or so miles in space. In a sou' sou' easterly direction, at a guess . . .

The dining room at home is almost completely filled by an oak-veneered table with sliding extensions, (not that the table is especially large, you understand). Above it hangs an ugly anodised shade in gunmetal blue on a black plastic rise-and-fall cable (another of Pa's jumble sale bargains). Normally the table is clear after tea. This evening it was covered in small piles of clean laundry. A printed list, bearing about equal numbers of pencilled ticks and crosses, lay on top of a pile of three shirts.

I was seated on the floor with my back against a wooden-armed utility armchair pretending to watch 'Songs of Praise' on TV. I was, if anything, in a blacker mood than the one I'd just switched from.

Pa sat in the big armchair – *his* chair – filing a fingernail with an emery board. Every so often he would bite the next nail – carefully nibbling round the curve – spit the sliver into a wicker waste-basket and file the chewed edge until smooth. There was no sound from the TV, I was not allowed sound this evening; this evening had been officially designated Preparation and Packing Evening, by my father. It was Sunday evening, 6.50 p.m. Term would start tomorrow, Monday. The preparations had already been going on for a fortnight, and the muted, half-hearted protests from my mother. Tonight was the climax. And the atmosphere was charged.

At this point, Ma was sitting, head in hands at the opposite end of the table to Pa in his armchair, her back to the screen, facing the pair of us. Suddenly she grabbed up the card on which the clothes-and-equipment list was printed, shook her head vigorously six or seven times,

41

tutted, sighed deeply, tutted again and returned the card to the pile. The sound of the emery board ceased. Ma held her head again. Pa spoke slowly and deliberately, as if to a child or simpleton:

'It's all right, Elizabeth. You're not to get yourself in one of your silly states. Everything is perfectly all right. You just don't understand, my dear. It's standard practice. The authorities always ask for twice what is needed; that's simply to cover themselves, that's all, it's insurance; then if something extraordinary happens – a fire or a flood or something like that – and someone does happen to run out of something – whatever it might be, say socks, if you like, as an example we'll say that it's socks – that person cannot complain, can they? Because – if they had any sense at all – they probably didn't go out and buy half a warehouse full of socks – or knickers or whatever – in the first place. That's how the powers that be cover themselves, you see, dear? That's how it's done. It's the same with the military. Same with these exhibitions they go on, to the Antarctic and that. Same thing exactly, Mother. All right?'

Ma was nibbling at her own nail now, not looking at him.

'All right, Elizabeth?'

Silence.

'Look, I know what I'm talking about, my dear. Three shirts is ample. More than enough. One on his back, one in the wash, one spare. That's all you need. Correct, James? Of course it is. That's all anyone needs. He's no different from anyone else.'

I knew I was not really supposed to comment. Ma looked desperate; she gave a small shake of the head, barely perceptible. I kept my eyes on the screen. After a moment Pa produced a small stage laugh:

'Look, you can't wear two shirts at once, you know, Angel. Not even at public school you can't; not even at a

42

posh school like that, my love . . . Eh, Elizabeth? Eh, m'dear?'

A soft tut from Ma, barely audible but evidently enough to provoke him.

He shot bolt upright in the chair, red cheeked, wide eyed. 'Good grief, Elizabeth, they're very nearly twenty pound apiece, those double cuff shirts. Twenty pound! That's a ridiculous price. Ridiculous! Then there's the two different sorts of collars. Then there's the cuff-links. Then there's the collar studs. And that's only his shirt requirements satisfied. Then there's the two different ties, the Sunday tie and the weekday tie. Then there's the jacket. Then there's the blazer. Then there's the two sorts of trousers. Then there's his gown thing . . . his scholar's gown. Then there's . . . the watchermacallems . . . the house shoes and the gymshoes and the walking shoes and the slippers and the dressing gown – he's got to have a new one of those of course, naturally, just because his other is a tiny bit short in the sleeve. But never mind. Never mind – we've had all that out, and I've agreed about that so never mind. It's paid for, and that's that. Where was I? Yes. Then there's . . .' He was waving the emery board now, and his voice had risen half an octave or more. 'Hells bells, woman . . . Then there's—'

Ma's head snapped up, her face transformed as if by a vision. She said, 'All right, Edward. It's all right. Forget it. Just forget it. I didn't mean it. It's perfectly all right. I know what you mean now. I'm so stupid. So stupid! *She* will provide.' She smacked her forehead with the palm of her hand and gave him a sweet, pathetic smile. 'How come I'm such an *idiot*, Edward?'

Pa stared at her briefly, a small frown twitching his crow's feet. 'Well,' he said, 'that's not quite what I—'

She stood quickly, and skipped across to sit on the arm of his chair, took his hand between hers, laid her forehead against his. 'How do you put up with me, dearest? I really

43

don't know. I really don't. I'm such a Doubting Thomas and you're so . . . so steadfast.'

'Elizabeth . . . I'm not saying you're—'

'No, Edward,' she cut in, wagging one finger then laying it on his lips, 'I *am*. I'm just a stupid, blind fool. When She gets back from the States things are going to be completely different, aren't they, dear? When She comes home we'll be quite well off; we won't have to be so careful, will we? It won't be long now. Then Jimbo can have the lot, can't he, Edward?' She was smiling radiantly now. She sprung up. 'I'll make some decaf. Who wants decaf?'

Pa stared for a moment, his cheeks returning to normal colour at chameleon speed. 'I'll have a drop. Thank you.'

I nodded at Ma.

Pa subsided into the depths of the chair. He called to Ma through the hatchway to the kitchen. 'To be honest, Elizabeth . . . I mean, quite honestly . . . The whole thing's—'

A gas ring popped. Sound of water rushing into the blue Swan kettle with the flip-up spout. Ma's cheerful voice called, 'I said it's *all right*, Edward. Let's just drop it, shall we? James will manage till then; won't you, dear? You'll manage all right, won't you, James? James, dear?'

I looked briefly at Pa. 'Mmm,' I called. 'Course.'

'. . . worse than a baby. Far worse. You haven't got gypsy blood in you have you, James? Didicoy blood . . . ?'

'Mmm,' I said. 'Course, Matron. The old chap's a horse thief and the old dear lives in a bender on Greenham Common. That's how come they got the money to send me here.' I said this quick and low without smirking, while Matron was still wittering.

'. . . it wouldn't surprise me if you had. No. Not in the least. You look greasy enough. You really are a wretched creature. And so . . . so, lackadaisical. Stand up. Stop

44

lounging against the door, boy. You just don't care, do you, James. You just— *What* did you say?!'

'Mm? Me? Nothing, Matron.'

'Don't be so . . . ! Come here.' She broke off long enough to wrench up my tie, completely wrecking my Boston knot. 'For heaven's sake, straighten yourself up. Oh, I give up. I give up. Go away. Get along to breakfast now. And get a move on; it's gone quarter to.'

As I shuffled away down the hall she called after me:

'I'll be asking Mr Gardener to write to your parents, Bishop. About your list.'

I did feel like a gypsy then – one who'd been 'moved on' a time too often.

So Wednesday morning I was late as usual, and the yoghurt was gone.

Live yoghurt is more than a food. Live yoghurt is a very special medicine. Very special. More special than, say, for instance, ginseng or royal jelly. For one thing live yoghurt cures hangovers. It's the equivalent of the old-fashioned raw eggs in milk, but a lot, lot nicer. I needed that yoghurt to calm my gurgling stomach and soothe away the ache in my head. And to give me the strength to survive another day in the wilderness.

That evening, Shag was talking to me again as if nothing whatever had happened. He wanted most of all to tell me about his clash with Harding; that was obvious by the way he burst into the dorm demanding to know whether or not I'd met 'the holy prick'. When I told him I knew the gentleman quite well, he said he'd save that story for last 'as it was special'. He then began to regale me with his experiences of the afternoon.

For Lawrence, the Wednesday afternoon activity is CCF – Combined Cadet Force – whereas I had opted for the alternative – Community Service. Apparently Shag and the other soldier boys had been fooling around with these antique Brenguns or LMGs, doing something called First and Second IA. Lawrence tried to explain all about 'gas regulators' and 'return springs' and suchlike, but it meant nothing to me.

Anyway, it turns out Lawrence had somehow got hold of a full clip of live ammunition (I didn't ask how – it seemed best not to know) and naturally, being Lawrence, he wanted to fire it off. So, at the end of the training session he waltzed up to the instructor, one Sergeant Major Campbell (known to all as Barch, because of the way he shouts, 'quick barch') and told him all about how keen he was to practise the IAs in his own time so that he might do really, really well in his Cert A Parts One and Two since his pater was frightfully keen on his gaining a commission in the regular armed forces and how his pater used to be an officer in the Buffs (knowing full well that was Barch's old regiment) and how he had to retire with shell-shock, trench fever and shrapnel in the spine and how he didn't want to let the old soldier down what with him having only a few months to live and all.

Well it turned out the sergeant was not that stupid. He refused to lend Lawrence a functional weapon, but said he might borrow one of the practice Brens until Monday.

'Because practice Brens have no firing pins,' said Lawrence.

'No firing pins,' I repeated, flatly. I stared at Lawrence. Lawrence was grinning. Then I remembered his *special talent*. I shook my head.

'What a decent chappy, don't you think?' said Shag.

'Where is it?' I asked.

'In my locker. Downstairs. If you're not doing anything Sunday . . .'

'You're a bugger,' I said.

'Think about it. Could be a laugh. Anyway, what about you? How've you got on today? You look a bit knackered. What's up?'

46

'Oh, nothing. I'm OK. Did a spot of gardening this afternoon. Digging up spuds for some old mother in Deacon Street.'

'Sounds fun. Hope she paid you in kind.'

'Christ! Shut up, can't you.'

'Anyway. What about it, son? Fancy a bit of mutton, Sunday afters. Make a change from pigeon.' He laughed. 'Nice little barby? Down the marshes; we'll go on the bike. Mint sauce and everything. Loveleeee.'

'Lawrence, you're an animal!' I threw my slipper, and missed. 'What about Harding, then? Tell me about that,' I said, keen to change the subject.

Harding is a gentleman of the upper sixth, which means he may carry a black silver-knobbed cane. He is also a school monitor, which means he must wear a crimson gown on Sundays, and *may*, if he so wishes, wear it on other days also; being Harding, he does, all the time. Technically he may also marry and sport a moustache – neither of which he has done (nor can, I suspect). In addition to these favours, Harding is a sportsman of the highest calibre, having attained his 'first colours' in both rowing and athletics. Which means he may wear a special hatband on his straw boater, silver piping around the edges of his blue blazer or change it completely for a white one with blue piping should he prefer; he may sport white ankle socks with his pinstriped trousers in place of the regulation black or dark grey, also – and here's the rub – he may walk *across* the grass of the Greencourt, winter and summer, rather than plod round the tarmac perimeter like the rest of the *hoi polloi*. He is also the Sacristan of Maugham House (of which more in due course).

What Harding is not, is intelligent. This, presumably, is why he is pushing twenty and still at school, having – so it is rumoured – scraped only the one C and two Ds in his first attempt at GCSE, and thus being obliged to repeat the year to gain the minimum six GCSEs grade C or above required to qualify for entry to the sixth form, and which, in my view, is why he hates anyone with more than a hen's share of grey matter. Especially if that person can beat him over the high hurdles, as Shag can, and is an oik to boot, which Shag is.

So, for Shag, it was doubly unfortunate that the school monitor who caught him taking a quick shortcut across the Greencourt after supper, and under cover (so Shag thought) of darkness, was none other than the same Holy Harding. It seems Shag was trying to catch up with an extremely attractive sixth former called Laura Siebert, as he said, 'for a spot of Gross Sexual Misconduct in Pigeon Alley before she got banged up in that Abbey for the night. And, fuck me if this prick in a cloak didn't leap out the shadows like fuckin' Zorro or something. "Hi there," he said. "Come here, boy." It's the truth, mate. That's what he called me, fucking "boy". No shit. I said, "Who's that? Is it a Pinkerton's man in a duster?" Then he comes right up and says, "I know you. You're that new boy, Lawrence. What are you doing on the Greencourt, Lawrence? You know perfectly well that you're not allowed to walk across the grass. You've been here six weeks now. So there's no excuse, is there?"

' "Sorry, sir," I said, sarky like, "only I thought I saw that ghost, Nell Wassname; her who's supposed to be walled up in the Dark Entry, sir." We were right close to the Dark Entry, see, Jimmy. That's what gave me the idea, like. Only Prickarse Harding didn't seem to think it was so fucking funny coz he give me this little yellow chitty thing that says, Insubordination, *un* fuckin' *point*. I told him it was pathetic, and do you know what he said, mate? He said, if he had his way they'd bring back school beatings for types like me. You know about school beatings, don't you, Jim? Musslewhite's been telling me about them. They still had them when he first came – and proper fags, not this half and half, voluntary stuff. A school

48

beating was done by the school monitors themselves – that's what that vicious prick meant, he wanted to whack me himself, the bastard – they used to stick your arse across two chairbacks then line up at the end of the library, all eight of them, then they'd run down the length of the library and whack you as hard as they could with their canes. According to Musso they often drew blood. And if you yelled you got an extra one. So kids used to stick bits of rubber between their teeth and bite on them to stop themselves yelling. I tell you, boy, that Harding . . . I'll get him, though, never you mind. I will, mate. He's a bastard.'

He looked at me, shaking his head in disbelief at what had befallen him.

'It was a bit cheeky,' I suggested, cautiously.

He studied my face for a second then grinned and said, 'You're pulling my plonker, ain't yer, son. He's a prick. How can you be cheeky to a prick?'

Anyway, I slept like the dead Wednesday night, just hit the pillow and more or less passed out. If the noise did come back, I didn't hear it, which was a relief not only for my nerves, but because the next day promised to be really heavy going. Apart from maths and physics, I had double English with Sopworth in the morning, and the lunch hour would be swallowed up with the Chaplain's Confirmation class meeting.

Doctor Sopworth and the Chaplain are as different as chalk and flint. Example: at sixty years of age Sopworth is still collecting train numbers. Every day he pedals off on his copper-type bike – legs going slowly, slowly up and down like a stick insect with sleeping sickness because no one ever told him what the lever on the cross bar is for. He always heads for the same spot, the bridge where the games field track crosses the London line. Sometimes you see him standing on the pedals all red in the face just to bike up the High Street – which is about one in fifty at the steepest part – but mostly he sticks to the level road and the track to the big field. When he gets to that old brick bridge, out comes the notebook and there he stands like a grey heron with his big round body and stick-like legs till the sun goes down and he can't see to write any more.

I don't trust any of the teachers here, but I have to admit the worst Sopworth's ever done to me is hit me on the back of the head with a piece of chalk. Not like the chaplain. The chaplain doesn't throw chalk; the chaplain lets fly with the board-rubber.

Where Sopworth is soft and round and silver haired, The Reverend Shewring is hard, bony and black all over (apart from his collar, and his face which reminds me of diseased concrete being grey and pockmarked and giving the impression one smile would crack it beyond the power of healing). Where Sopworth wants to believe in a person and convince himself that their wickedness is only on the surface, Shewring believes in the wickedness and ignores the surface completely. Nothing gets past the man they call Creeping Jesus (CJ to his enemies, that's just about everyone). He gives me the shivers. The man sees all, even stuff that's still only in a person's imagination. Like the explosions, for instance. But I'm jumping ahead now, the explosions come later, after the Confirmation disaster; I haven't explained about that yet.

4

That a self-proclaimed atheist should volunteer for Confirmation struck me as odd – almost as odd as my own father's failure to have me Confirmed before now – but when I asked Lawrence about this over lunch, he said, 'Never provoke the enemy 'till you're ready, James,' and would answer no more questions.

Lawrence and I were embarking on Confirmation classes two to three years later than is normal here. So it is not surprising that, at precisely fifteen minutes after one o'clock, we found ourselves sitting awkwardly among a group of lower-school boys in the Chaplain's teaching room above the school tuckshop. As the group waited in silence for the Chaplain to sort out his notes, I glanced at Lawrence. He had not spoken since we left the dining hall. His grim mood unnerved me as much as the hard little priest, but the time for talking was past.

'Today is a new beginning,' said the Chaplain, somehow making it sound like the end of everything. 'This is the moment when each of you will begin to prepare himself to shoulder the greatest responsibility of his life—'

A dozen boys, each isolated. None whispering. None fidgeting. None glancing at his neighbour, or watch. The room seemed to darken.

'—vows made at Baptism; a responsibility until now carried on your behalves by your parents—'

Baptism, baptism . . . the word fills my mind with shadows.

'—promises? And what do they mean for you, personally? What actions must you take? Do you need to take actions, or is Christianity something that comes on its own, like hair on the chin or a low-pitched voice.' The Chaplain's eyebrows arched expectantly. He waited, elbows propped, one hand clasped in the other.

Silence, but for the clatter and buzz from the tuckshop below.

The Chaplain rose from his seat behind the desk, walked to the window, looked out.

Outside the sun was shining on the four gold pennants of the tower. The wind flicked them casually this way and that, making them gleam and glint as though signalling, while the Cathedral ploughed westward through flying cloud like some great flagship from another world. Inside the shadows leaned over me.

'Today is a new beginning, young people, and, yes, there *are* things to be done—'

The air isn't working. What's wrong with the air?

'—three positive *actions*; the first is to make a clean start. That means—'

The deeper I breathe, the worse it becomes.

'—and I'm talking about *real* repentance, not just *saying* sorry to God, but *meaning* it in your heart. So there's pretty hard thinking ahead.'

He turned to face us, silhouetted against a blue and white sky that dizzied the eyes with the speed of its passing. Above the long ridge of the nave and high into the air, the jackdaws wheel and dive and climb and wheel and dive again and again then vanish one by one but quickly, into the stone, as if on an order.

'The second action – if anything, more positive even than the first – is the action of turning to Christ—'

Open the window for God's sake, I'm drowning.

'—backsides and wait for Him to find us. Loving your neighbour, honouring parents, telling the truth, these things—'

Something's gone wrong with the air in here. It's all used up.

'—tackle this lunch time, is action number three, the action of *renouncing Evil*.'

He moved from the window to perch on the front edge of the desk, leaning forward, staring without blinking at each boy in turn. I felt my body tense in readiness.

'If anyone here doubts the existence of evil in the world today, if any of you is so blinded by science as to imagine that the Devil no longer has relevance to you personally—'

What's that shrill whispering sound in my head? That yittering quacking . . . ?

Oh, not in broad daylight, please, oh please.

'—a fairy-tale figure our grandparents dreamed up to frighten small children, like the "policeman", they'd be wrong. So don't underestimate him; he's no fool, the Devil. That is precisely what he wants us to think—'

My fingers dug into the hard plastic seat, I knew if I relaxed for an instant I'd go down. All the way down to the bottom of the tank.

Hark, someone talking. The words ring around me. But what do they mean?

'—awful vacuum, that great Black Hole of the soul, the Evil One leaps in and grabs the helm. To deny the Devil—'

chit chit spkqerrityquack quack sskity quer quer ssskitywack—

Let me alone, damn and blast you I'm off.

'—invite him into – Hi! Where do you think . . . ? Ah, Bishop. All right. All right the rest of you. It's nothing to do with— Go with him, Lawrence. Make sure he's— Sit down, Paul. Sit down!'

By the time Lawrence caught up with me I was sitting on the low wall outside the Bursar's office. The noises had ceased and the panic all but subsided.

'Bastard,' he said, sitting alongside me, laying a hand on my shoulder. 'Don't let the sanctimonious son-of-a-bitch get to you, son, he's not worth it. Anycase—' He broke off to lean forward and look up into my face. 'OK, Jim?' he asked. I nodded. 'Sure?' I nodded again. 'That's OK, then. Like I say, mate, don't let the bugger get you down. I've got something in mind for our Chaplain. We'll fix him, I promise.'

The afternoon session passed without incident. As did the next two days, more or less. Lawrence said nothing further on the subject of the Chaplain and naturally enough, by Sunday I'd forgotten all about his vague 'promise'. But at suppertime, as he whispered the details of his outrageous plan in my ear, the knowledge crept through me that the maniac sitting beside me meant every word that he said.

I lowered my fragment of bread roll untouched.

'Are you an atheist then or what?' I asked, more to buy thinking time than anything.

'Try Satanist,' he said. He was joking, I thought, but I wasn't even sure about that. He flashed me a disconcerting grin. 'It's a chance to try out my new formula and get shot of one dangerous bigot at the same time. At least it might make the bugger stop and think about what he's saying.' I shook my head, and Lawrence gave me a strange, searching look: 'Unless you've a better idea?' he said. I had the feeling that he really expected me to produce out of the hat some plan so diabolical as to make his own seem like trick or treat. When I shook my head again to say, No, he shrugged, and, switching to what I assumed was supposed to be his IRA voice, said, 'Roit, lad. We'll blast da slimey wee bogger to fock, so we will.'

At which point a server arrived with two plates of sausage and tinned tomato. I slid my food on to Lawrence's plate. He looked up and smiled. 'Sure dees posh fellas eat some filty bloddy garbage, so they do, Jimbo,' said he, cramming his mouth with filthy bloody garbage.

I nodded, but it wasn't the food that had lost me my appetite.

By the following Friday I had started falling asleep all over – at mealtimes, study periods in the library, during lessons – I just couldn't stay awake. Even in my favourite Drama I went off during a listening exercise; they told me after that I'd snored so loudly no one could hear anything else. Miss Brannon had apparently tried to wake me and couldn't so she and one of the girls dragged me into the props cupboard – still asleep, still snoring – and left me there the whole lesson because Miss said I looked so knackered. Saturday things changed. I stopped dropping off and walked about in a kind of coma instead. It felt like being under lukewarm water and was almost pleasant; nothing bothered me – not even the duck noise – and my head wasn't hurting anymore.

The duck noise had returned with vengeance. There was no proof of course, but even then I had the idea it might have been something to do with the meeting, for the fact is there had never been any hint of it during the day except on that one occasion. But the nights, the nights were terrible.

Friday night it seemed to me that I lay awake counting and struggling to make sense of the hideous, quacky messages until a pale lilac dawn made tall church-window cutouts in the black wall of the dormitory. At one point, just as the first shape became recognisable, I thought I heard a word – it sounded like 'murder' or 'murdered' – but in the end I put it down to the state I was in; nothing else came through that made any sense whatever.

Another thing, I kept getting this itch. Not the usual nervous tickle that keeps moving about, this was a real wriggly feeling at the base of my spine. Not on the surface either, under the skin. At least, that's how it felt.

Eventually I must have gone off despite the quacking for I woke sweating with a shout stuck in my throat and an image of smoking, blood-soaked buttocks riddled with black holes like something from a war film or bomb atrocity report. I didn't need a psychoanalyst to work that one out; it was all about Shag's insane scheme, no question.

I was desperate to tell someone my fears – that I really believed insanity might be hereditary and that things were happening inside my head that I needed some help with – but Matron was the last person I wanted to confide in, and who else was there? I felt that noises in the head was not the kind of thing Shag would understand. In any case ever since the revelation of his plans the previous Thursday I'd been avoiding Shag like the plague. Even at bedtimes I'd managed to time my return from the bathroom to coincide with the arrival of PG and lights out.

And so on Sunday, as the members of School House, pin-striped and black-jacketed, filed through the Dark Entry towards the Cathedral, and Lawrence grabbed my elbow and whispered that I was to cover for him, I found difficulty in answering, let alone thinking up an excuse on the spur of the moment. Next thing his ticket was in my pocket. And that was me lumbered.

Every other Sunday, Matins is compulsory for the whole of the school. Each boy (and girl now) is given a ticket with his school number on to be collected by the monitors on their way out of service so the authorities know whether or not you were there. I have a peculiar problem with church services, so for me it is, in any case, a fortnightly ordeal. On this occasion it would be even more so than usual, for mine would be the task of palming two tickets at once into the hand of the monitor, and hoping he would not notice. Apparently Lawrence was intending to cut Matins in order, as he put it, to work on his chemistry practical. If the experiment was successful, he gleefully informed me, he and I would shortly be laying an invisible minefield in time for our next Confirmation class that very evening. The *pièce de résistance* would be a pile of touch-sensitive explosive on the Chaplain's stool. He mimed the effect of the Chaplain sitting on this, no doubt expecting me to be amused. I was not.

I felt cornered. What I just could not understand was why this arch anarchist kept insisting on involving me and consulting me about his dangerous, lunatic schemes, as though I was some sort of wicked uncle or diabolical court jester. *He* was the mad Joker, not *me*; I was beginning to think he'd do murder for a giggle, and it scared me.

Suddenly all my ideas about preserving our peculiar, seesaw friendship evaporated. I blurted straight out that I thought he was mental and didn't want anything to do with his crazy games.

To my surprise, instead of losing his rag, he looked at me in that strange way again, as though he could see something ruthless or devilish in me, something I myself was totally unaware of, then he grinned as though I'd said, Great idea, Lawrence, I'm with you boy, let's go, and he gripped my upper arm even harder so that all I could do was walk miserably alongside, grunting distractedly while he poured out the details.

Gunpowder was the easiest to make but far too crude for this particular job, he explained. And fulminate of mercury was, he said, dangerous and unstable in production. 'NI_3, is the connoisseur's choice,' he said. 'The baby with the featherlight touch.' He lightly kissed his fingertips, then shouted, 'Bang!' in my face.

I jumped about a foot in the air. 'Bugger off, can't you?' I snarled.

'See you in the pavilion,' he whispered, dropping off the column of boys to disappear behind a pillar, 'After service, OK?'

Being late November the weather was turning cold. But

inside the Cathedral it would be warm; the Cathedral is always the same temperature – like they say caves are, but warmer. To my mind caves and Cathedrals have more than a constant temperature in common, but that is what I tried to focus on as we filed through the Dark Entry this particular Sunday morning. And that is what I intended to fix my mind on as soon as I entered the building. I have to focus hard on some aspect of the Matter if I'm not to disgrace myself, again.

Two monitors were stationed one either side of the entrance at the top of the Martyrdom steps. As we approached, both put fingers to their lips to shush the chatterers, then we were inside the great hollow with its still air and its awed and whispering throng. I tried hard to focus on the almost suffocating warmth, but immediately came the first stirring of the Problem. So I switched my attention to the structure.

The pillars and spaces of the nave made me think of avenues of giant beech trees, straight, strong and bare with the ten o'clock winter sunshine slanting down between them. Today that heaven-reaching space was filled with a dusty, colourless light. Peering east along the seemingly endless avenue, a hint of the rich, dark gloom of the interior – the more ancient, more mysterious part – was visible above the choirscreen and through the iron gate at the top of the steps. But today both school and public were together in the vastness of the nave.

To be accurate, my difficulty is not confined to churches; I'm the same in any situation where there's a crowd, and that crowd is silent. But churches are the worst; the bigger and more crowded and more silent they are, the more the obscenities well up inside me like a septic volcano: *that* is The Problem.

As soon as I settled myself on the rush-seated chair among the rows of black jackets, still and awestruck, and the whispering voices rose all around me, and the tuneless, meandering piping of the organ began filling time till the show would begin – I started to feel once more the whole huge mass of stone like an ageless mountain above, and I felt the otherworldliness of it all come down . . . the other hands . . . I felt the blood drain from my feet . . . and my ankles . . . and the terrible weakness creep upwards . . . **Fuck off you cocksuckers! You fuckpigs! You cunts!**

Oh no you don't, I said. And I bit my lip hard inside, focusing on the flavour of the blood. Warm yoghurt, I thought. In the nick of time a voice came loud and clear from the pulpit, and the blood returned, woosh, to my legs. 'Dearly beloved brethren, the scripture moveth us in sundry places – '

What made me look up I don't know, but I found myself staring out over the organ loft and up through the gloom of the quire. There was something disturbingly familiar about a triple arch high on the topmost balcony, close to the vault itself. The word Mission popped into my head, closely followed by a sharp sense of terror and shock. Suddenly I knew I was looking at the very place where, only a week or so earlier, Lawrence had almost killed us both.

'– to acknowledge and confess our manifold sins and wickedness,' said the preacher.

I closed my eyes and gave myself up to the warm air of the nave. And the Mission . . .

Two-thirds of the way up the ladder I stopped climbing. Rung twenty-seven to be precise. (I'd been counting to focus my mind. And not looking down. Obviously, not looking down.) The tower clock had just struck eight, and a cold wind was blowing. Lawrence had disappeared over the parapet above me. I should have been safe in my warm little study, finishing off an essay on *The White Devil*; instead I was standing, alone now, on an iron ladder fixed to the floodlit south face of the Cathedral.

59

By good fortune the ladder rose almost to the parapet within a narrow band of shadow cast by a buttress; even so, I could not believe that the headmaster, for example, or his wife could possibly fail to see my moving shape should they chance to glance out from any of their half dozen bedroom windows.

My feet began to wobble on the rung, rocking rapidly back and forth and me powerless to control them. At that point I would certainly have gone back down but for the problem that this maintenance ladder, like all the others, terminated a good fifteen feet from the ground. And the rope we had used to reach the first rung was now looped over Lawrence's shoulder. Even in daylight the jump would be dangerous. Up was the only way to go, and I dare not.

What if they caught us? What would they think? How would they know we were just curious schoolboys. What could I say? I did not even know why we were here myself – all my questions had met with the same sarcastic response: 'It's a missionary expedition, my son.'

One thing I did know was that fifty feet below and a hundred yards west of me was a small wooden hut. And I knew that inside that hut sat a security guard protecting the Christchurch Gate entrance, and that somewhere else, prowling the lawns and pavements of the southern precincts, crackling walkie-talkie in hand, was his mate. Those tough-looking men were put here for one purpose; to protect the Cathedral. Maybe that did speak of a certain lack of confidence in the Almighty's own abilities, but so what? Those guards wouldn't give a shit; why should they? For all they would know we could be two vandals intent on some act of mindless destruction, or terrorists looking to pull off one spectacular, anti-establishment coup like launching the tower into orbit. We could be a bunch of Satanists bent on black masses, desecration, defecation . . . *anything*!

So what are we doing up here? said headvoice.

Before I could answer, a voice from above hissed, 'Come on, Bishop. What the fuck's up with you?' I looked up and there was the pencil torch shining down like a middle-sized planet in the darkness.

'Coming,' I whispered. And I started on up again – shaking my head, but climbing nevertheless.

At the point where the iron handrails loop over the parapet the shadow ran out and I saw my own grey arms suddenly splashed with orange light. I folded at the waist and more or less fell into a huge lead-lined gutter, the bottom of which held a thick layer of stinking moss and slime. 'Ugh,' I said, kneeling up, wiping my hands on my tracksuit bottoms. I glanced over the parapet and was immediately blinded by two blazing centres of light shining up from below. I had an impression of orange-black sky, city roofscape, black branches, nothing else before a rough tug from behind pulled me down.

'Ssh. Down! Keep down!' hissed Shag. 'This way. Come on.'

I turned to face the voice. On my left, the parapet reached above kneeling head-height, in front, a huddled figure just discernible in the blackness, on my right, a two-yard band of shadow then the ribbed lead sheeting of the quire roof sloping up to the apex some thirty feet above. The wind was stronger up here. 'Where are we going?'

'Sssh.' The shape moved away from me along the gutter.

'Hey. Lawrence. Where are we going?'

'This way. Ssssh. Don't talk now; I'm opening the hatch.'

I heard the sound of a bolt being wriggled then drawn. The figure in front of me vanished through a small wooden doorway set, dormer like, into the slope. I followed. Inside I felt myself jostled aside, the door closed behind me and I stood in total blackness. I heard heavy breathing, nothing else.

Lawrence was whispering instructions now. He informed me that he had been this way several times and no longer needed the torch. That was the reason he gave for refusing to turn it on until we reached our destination; that and the Mambas, as he calls the Cathedral vergers. Lawrence would lead the way. I was to follow holding on to the tail of his tracksuit.

'Come on,' he whispered, 'grab hold.'

I reached out, felt his woollen jerkin and took a fistful. Immediately he moved forwards.

Underfoot seemed smooth enough to be polished stone. After less than ten paces, Lawrence jerked and stumbled violently. 'Steps,' he whispered. 'Down.' Then we were descending wooden steps, shuffling from tread to tread. I wafted my left hand hopefully, but there was no rail that side. My right hand was occupied. Only four steps down, then it felt like flat boards. 'Rail on the right,' whispered the leader. I quickly changed hands.

And so we proceeded in darkness, sometimes climbing, sometimes descending, sometimes dead level, sometimes on a gradient up or down, sometimes on wood, sometimes smooth stone, and sometimes – mainly, I noticed, on the slopes – on a surface that seemed rough like cement or hard plaster. Lawrence did not stumble again, but I did. Often. Suddenly his voice whispered, 'Hold it.' There was a pause with only the sound of loud breathing in the blackness, then he said, 'I'm not sure . . . I'm not sure . . . Hang on . . .'

When the pencil beam came on, I could see nothing beyond Lawrence but the beam itself chalking a shadowy line of dust motes in the blackness dead ahead.

'Fuck!' said Lawrence. The beam switched to point vertically downwards. I leaned left and looked past the broad shape in front of me. An edge of lit stone glowed in the small semi-circle of light; it wavered, and there was the toe of Lawrence's trainer – and beneath that . . . nothing. Empty black void.

Horrified, I jerked back, pulling him after, collapsing back on to the stone floor.

We quickly untangled, but each remained seated.

'Ooopsie. Wrong way,' said Lawrence. I could tell he was trying to sound casual, but he was trying too hard.

'Christ, Lawrence, one more step and you'd have—' I stopped short, numbed by the next thought; the thought that we had been hitched together like a tractor and trailer, and that we would almost certainly have stayed that way, at least for the first few yards as we went over the edge. 'You idiot! We could have been . . . We're having the light from now on,' I said firmly.

Immediately the light went out.

'Hey!'

'No need, mate. I promise you.'

'Lawrence!'

'It's OK, Jim. I know where we are. We're on the shelf that runs round below the roof of the quire. The room is along here, to the left. We can't miss it. We just go back to the wall and feel our way along. There'll be about four steps going down. That'll be it. Come on.'

'It is *not* "nicking",' said Lawrence, playing the pencil beam around the small chamber, 'I'm just *showing* you, mate.' We were standing at the centre of a flagstone floor surrounded by piles of books, most of which were very large and very dusty. The door of the chamber was closed.

Lawrence rested the little torch on top of a two-foot high stack of books. He adjusted its position so that the narrow beam fell on another, similar stack and illuminated part of two thick, gold edges. Two bands of reflected gold light fell across his waist and hands. His face glowed softly, lit from below. 'I thought you were into books, Jim. These books are like . . . watchermacallit . . . like conscience money. They're gifts to mother church – not just this church – every church; which means everyone is entitled to read them, aren't they? *Everyone*; all Christians, anyway; which means they didn't ought to be stuck up here in this poky attic where no bugger can see 'em. That's *wrong*, mate. It's bleedin' obvious it's wrong . . .' There was a pause. I said nothing. When he spoke again, Lawrence's tone had changed: 'Look, mate, I'm not kidding, they're bloody beauties.' He directed the torch back to the pile of books. 'Here, look at this one, Jim, this one's something else. Just take a look. No messing. Just look, OK?'

He unfastened a pair of dull bronze hinges, turned back the cover of the topmost book and tilted it towards the beam of the torch. Through a leaf of fine tissue paper I could make out an arch-shaped picture on the page beneath, but no details came through. The pages were a good eighteen inches tall. In the centre of the facing page were printed the words 'The Light of the World' in big red letters.

Lawrence carefully turned back the tissue paper. I stared down, stunned. It was a picture straight out of my childhood – off my nursery wall, if my memory was not playing tricks – except that in my memory the picture was crazed with dark lines. A jigsaw puzzle – that was it! – a jigsaw that someone had framed for me and hung up in my bedroom. It made me feel very strange and hollow inside my chest. At last I murmured, 'That's amazing . . . That's . . .' I shook my head. I was staring at a picture of Jesus knocking at a wooden door hung with weeds and creepers. In his hand he carried a lighted lantern, and around his head, showing up the golden crown all tangled round with sharp thorns, was a halo – or it might have been the moon behind his head. My knees had gone weak, I wanted to sit down.

'I told you,' whispered Lawrence, obviously mistaking the cause of my wonderment, 'she's got to be worth, I don't know, with pictures like that, and those hinges and all, could be fifty, could be a hundred and fifty smackers;

I just don't know.' He punched my shoulder. 'See. What did I tell you? I told you, mate, didn't I? We're rich, kid. And wait till you see some of the old ones. Some of the *really* old ones. I tell you, boy, they've even got colour decorations round the borders, some of them, and big letters made into like pictures. They look medieval to me. They're bloody amazing. Here, have a butcher's at this one.'

He picked up the torch and directed the beam on to a monstrous tome with a spine a good seven inches across. The cover was the colour of wax and veined like it might have been the skin of an animal, and the spine itself had eight pairs of raised ridges the thickness of sturdy string running round beneath the surface. The corners of the front cover were plated in what looked like silver, carved or stamped into the shape of angel heads, each having a pair of wings at right angles to follow the corner shapes. In the centre of the top cover were the words 'Holy Bible' embossed and painted in black and gold. The side opposite the spine was closed by a pair of ornate silver hasps and I could see that the edges of the pages were cockled and unevenly cut. Lawrence tried to open it but couldn't. 'This one seems to be locked,' he said, 'but most of them aren't.'

He picked up a green volume from another pile and blew a thick cloud of dust from the cover. The gold inscription read: Sacred Art. In a small, *art nouveau* panel at the bottom were the words 'The Bible Story Pictured by Eminent Modern Painters'. 'Hmm,' he grunted, 'Modern.' Then he seemed to notice the book which had been hidden beneath the first, put the first down and picked up the other. It too must have measured some eighteen by twenty-four inches but here the similarity ended for the cover of this volume appeared to be made of tooled leather embellished in deep blue, red, black and gold. There were no hasps or hinges nor any metal plates on it. In the centre was a bunch of what looked like lilies tied by a loose banner on which were the words 'The Parables of Our Lord', and under this, 'Designed, Illustrated and Compiled by Noel Humphreys'.

The book fell open between Lawrence's hands and two pages of heavy black script were revealed, around each a wide border of holly-like vines in red, blue and gold woven into a frame. The letters appeared to be much heavier and blacker than those of the first book, they were also old-fashioned looking – maybe the word is Gothic, I believe so – anyway, from the look of them I expected the words to be in Latin, but after a moment I could see that the pale blue writing at the top of the page said, 'The Rich Fool'. Underneath that it said, 'Luke 11. 16–21'. The first letter, built like a big brass weighing scales, was a T. As I decoded the first words I read them out loud: ' "The ground of a certain rich man brought forth plentifully. And he—" '

'Oh good,' cut in Lawrence. 'Trouble is, they're so fucking huge. We'd never get them down the ladder. Too dangerous. You know what I think? I think it's a rucksack job, an inside job; you know, we pretend to be tourists – Froggy students, anything like that. There's no problem; I know where the door is that leads to up here; it's down in the crypt; I watched a Mamba disappear through it one day. That's what gave me the clue. I've sussed out all the little slit windows; that spiral staircase goes all the way up. We'll need a key of course, but I reckon I know where we'll get one.'

I let the 'we' pass . . .

Somewhere in the margin of my mind I heard a congregation say, 'Amen.' I opened one eye, jerked in my seat, opened the other just as my Order for Matins card slid to the floor. The boy on my left grinned at me knowingly.

'. . . who has safely brought us to the beginning of this day,' said the preacher, 'defend us in the same with thy

66

mighty power; and grant that this day we fall into no sin, neither run into any kind of danger, but that all our doings . . .'

'Amen.'

The palming of the double ticket went without a hitch, thank the Lord, amen.

5

The old pavilion is at the far end of what's known as the Big Field. Being winter, the grass was wet and covered in worm casts. My feet were soon caked with mud and as heavy as a deep sea diver's. The door was ajar when I reached it, Lawrence had obviously not heard my approach. I stood for a moment with my eye to the crack watching him pack what looked like a plastic funnel and half a dozen jam jars into his games bag. There was a stink of horse piss (which I later found out was ammonia) and I could see a row of filter papers set out along the slatted seat to dry.

Perhaps it was careless of me to creep in on my soft muddy feet and sit down without taking more notice where I put my backside, but the brown powder on the white paper circles might have been coffee for all I knew. Anyway, that's what I did. The residue I sat on must have already been dry.

The explosion was a shock to both of us, but painful only to me. Even through tracksuit, shorts and Y-fronts it hurt like hell. While I hopped and skipped round the room, Lawrence, having recovered, began to roar with laughter. When I came to a standstill, he told me he couldn't have asked for a better contribution. Now he knew exactly what quantity would suit the Chaplain. Allowing for the thickness of cassock and tweed trousers, he reckoned a double filter load would sort the bugger out.

★ ★ ★

Some five hours later, having soothed the smarting circle on my backside with quantities of cold water, I found myself stationed at the Chapel door, my eye to the crack.

We had arrived before anyone so that Lawrence could prime the Chaplain's stool. That was the easy bit. Behind me now, in the gloomy little room, he was waiting to distribute the dark brown powder across the tiled floor between door and lectern. The slightest shock, even a careless tap with the plastic spoon, could send the lot up. Shag's problem would be to work fast but with sufficient care not to detonate the powder and sufficient cool not to arouse the suspicions of the others. For one thing was certain, on no account must any of them suspect the identity of those responsible for what was about to happen. And, of course, Lawrence could not begin this most dangerous part of the operation until the last member of the group had arrived and crossed the three yards between the rows of chairs and the altar. Three minutes later we were still waiting for the arrival of one first-year boy.

Latimer strolled up with less than a minute to go – it would be tight. Lawrence would have to work fast now; the Chaplain was never late.

I leaned against the door arch, trying to hold down my rising apprehension, at the same time straining to detect the first signs of the Chaplain's approach. I tried to calm myself by reasoning that since the Chaplain would detonate the stuff himself, and, since only a cretin could fail to evacuate the building the minute the first explosion took place, if he was stupid enough to sit down on his stool at such a time he'd have no one to blame but himself. Besides which, I told myself firmly, I'd taken no active part in either the planning or the execution of the operation – other than keeping *cave*.

It was foggy outside now, and pitch dark apart from the area directly underneath the flint archway linking Mint Yard to Greencourt. Here the fog glowed in the lamplight

like a fine net curtain, making it impossible to see beyond.
I heard a coin tinkle on to the tiled floor behind me and
guessed that Lawrence had started work.

At the first hollow note of the tower clock, the voices
behind me fell to a whisper. Precisely as the sixth stroke
died, a small black vertical appeared at the centre of the
lighthaze under the archway. It expanded fast, and
silently.

I closed the oak door and turned with pounding heart
to see that Lawrence was already seated with the others,
eyes shut, apparently dozing. Keeping close to the wall, I
hurried to my place at the opposite end of the row to
Lawrence. As I sat, the latch clattered up and CJ swept
in with a flurry of black gaberdine skirts and cold, wet air.
The whispering ceased. The door thudded shut. Silence.

CJ eyed us from the top step, counting his flock. He
had more the look of a man come to butcher sheep than
gather them to the fold. I thought of Lawrence's tales of
CJ's training sessions with the Colts XV, and was struck
again by the hardness of this priest. The Chaplain's demo-
tackles, which left boys stunned and gasping in the mud,
were legendary. I regarded the close-cropped head, the
lipless mouth, the jutting shoulders, and a soft, insistent
quacking commenced in my left ear.

The Chaplain stepped down. Despite my best efforts, I
felt myself cringe. The yittering in my head swiftly moved
to the centre, like someone adjusting the balance control
between my ears. Two paces in, CJ's foot hit the first little
pile of brown powder.

The Chaplain's eyes are like those knives that must
remain sheathed, or draw blood. In the nanosec before
the soundwave struck, those eyes flashed to mine. The
memory sometimes plays tricks, I know, but of this I am
certain: before the bang, I had time to think, *Why me?* In
my right ear the duck voice quacked the word 'murdered';

71

there was no denying it this time.

The first explosion was roughly like those high-power caps little boys use in their Smith and Wesson replicas for making grandad slop his tea. In that tiny Chapel, it was skullsplitting. I knew at once that Lawrence's estimate of a double filterpaperful for the Chaplain's stool was far too much. My ears were ringing and I was aware of a pulse bumping against the stiff wing collar around my neck. But the voice in my head had gone.

CJ, poised mid stride, glared down at his foot. A filament of ginger smoke snaked up the spotlight beam over the lectern. Stink of iodine. I dared not move my head, but, by swivelling my eyes, saw that the others were sitting bolt upright, eyes wide, mouths gaping. When my eyes returned to the Chaplain, he was looking at me again.

There are times when a person knows that, however innocent, fate is about to drop something on him from a clear blue sky – satellite, meteorite, tortoise or birdshit, it's rough but there's no escape. Right now, in this gloomy little Chapel, CJ's eyes were telling me that time had arrived for me. Whatever was coming was on its way down, and J. Bishop was smack on the spot.

I returned the look, knowing that if I dropped my gaze I was finished. As I strove not to blink, the wing-collar seemed to tighten almost to choking point. The Chaplain stared, I stared back. Suddenly he shifted balance as if to step forward, whereupon, not surprisingly, in anticipation of a second explosion, *I flinched*. Afterwards, CJ declared that that tiny, involuntary movement was all the evidence needed to establish my guilt. He took three steps towards me – bang! crack! bang! His jaw muscles rippled.

The class jumped higher at each successive explosion, but the Chaplain neither flinched nor hesitated. It was as if he were the subject of different laws. He halted at the far end of my row. I began to haul air like an asthmatic. Twelve heads turned to stare. 'Broom,' he snapped.

It wasn't an accusation, accusations can be denied, I was already condemned. In a very small voice, I heard myself murmur, 'Weren't me, sir.'

'Go,' he hissed.

The row stood to let me through.

In silence, I edged past him. Outside, I sprinted through the misty dark for School House and the broom cupboard. I felt sick.

When I got back to the chapel the air was so thick with pungent brown fumes that it took me a minute to discover the place was empty. I stared at the overturned chairs, the scattered shreds of paper, the scorched and smoking stool, and a horrifying vision came: the Chaplain, skirts round his waist, his shrapnel-pocked buttocks exposed in a pool of blood, stretchered in a howling, careering, blue lamp whirling ambulance, team of surgeons standing by in hope of saving maybe half a red raw testicle. I began to shake uncontrollably. On jelly legs I stumbled to the doorway. I meant to run. But where?

When in trouble as a child I would do a runner every time. Mostly not far, and generally only for an hour or two balled up on the backseat of one of the wrecks in the yard. Only in such isolated places did I indulge in the luxury of 'answering back'; I could kick and bite all I wanted – the seats took it all, for *him*.

When the Recovery arrived one stormy evening with an ancient Bedford ambulance hooked up to its stubby crane, I knew at once that I'd found a new refuge. As I knelt on my pillow, nose to the streaming window, I was praying, and my prayers seemed to me to be heard despite the thunder and the grinding of the Recovery's crawler gear below. Whatever the cause was, the fact is those two vehicles drove all the way down the concrete drive and on down the cindertrack, and they passed right on by the car

73

stacks, and they passed right on by the stack for vans and lorries, and they passed by the crusher itself. I lost sight of them then in the darkness beyond the pole light, except for short flashes when the lighting danced on the white roof of the ambulance, which, being angled directly towards my bedroom window, flashed like a blue-white strobe-lit doorway in the darkness. 'Please, Heavenly Father,' I prayed, 'please put it down by the tracks. Thank you, sir. Amen.'

Next morning I was up, dressed and down there at dawn. And there it was, slewed sideways among the ripped-up nettles and deep skid marks just inside the fence that skirts the embankment. And it was perfect. Even the smoked glass windows were intact, and the rear step, and the blue flasher only slightly cracked. But when I tried the back doors and they opened, and when I climbed up the step and went inside, and there was the long couch covered in maroon pvc which I immediately lay down on and closed my eyes and then, there was the other thing. I felt it. Something quite magical – a lot to do, it seemed to me, with growing up only faster, much faster – to do with me becoming someone else much much older, someone in charge of what happens, someone *in control*. It seemed to me something to do with the life the ambulance had led, and the things it had witnessed inside. I imagined I could hear the siren, feel the rocking and the sideways drag as we sped through shining wet streets and hurtled round corners on our way to The Scene. A matter of life and death, it was, oh yes, and who was in charge here? I was. And it was wonderful.

In the end I was running off to Bedfordshire so often it became like a joke; except I couldn't see it of course. The first few times I did it, Ma made some feeble attempt to stop me, but never my father, never Pa, and soon she stopped trying as well.

'Let him go, Mother,' he'd say. 'He needs peace and

quiet to pray to Jesus to make him a better boy.'

Ma never argued with Pa, never ever.

Shivering violently, I moved under the street lamp to look at my watch. The numbers showed 7.37. Supper was not over yet; perhaps I could go to my Aunt's then, I thought. It wasn't too late for that, the buses would still be running out there. What would she say, though? What would she do?

She'd help me. Of course she would. She'd helped me then, hadn't she? The time when I stuck it out down in that freezing hulk till after the milk train went through. That was all about slugs, I remembered, a load of nonsense really, but at the time it seemed more like the Nürnberg trials or something.

Standing in the foggy darkness, not knowing which way to run, I felt as though the incident had been yesterday, though it had to have been twelve years earlier, maybe even thirteen, before She arrived anyway, so I couldn't have been more than three and a bit. It must have been summer, because of the slugs. It had certainly been raining for weeks, summer or not. The garden was soaking, and I was out playing in my black plastic wellies. They were new, and about ten sizes too big.

What I was doing when Pa caught me seemed entirely innocent to me. I had taken off my clumsy boots and had half filled one of them with water from the outside tap. The other boot I was using to sit on in order to keep my bum off the wet grass by the lettuce bed. And there I sat happily baptising slugs.

Looking back, I believe I only wanted to make them good, so they'd stop eating our lettuces. I seemed to recall that some experiment Pa had been trying with a barrier of dried eggshell hadn't worked and the things were like a row of green lace, with slime. Anyway, I'd been at it some time before Pa came along, and I guess the boot must have been just about full to the brim with the drowned and the

the drowning. There were brown ones and white ones and black ones with ridges like blue whales but smaller and a whole lot of snails as well. Anything that came to the surface or crawled up the side got a firm shove down with the red plastic spoon from my teaset. Oh yes, it was full immersion.

He must have been standing behind me for several minutes – I was really too busy to notice – but as soon as he spoke I could tell by his voice I'd done something wrong:

'What *do* you think you're doing, James? You're drowning them, aren't you? Aren't you? Answer me, child.' Before I could turn to face him I was jerked vertical and shaken so hard I could not have answered even if I'd known the right answer, which I didn't. 'You *know* you mustn't do that to little animals. What does the Bible say, James? The Bible says, thou shalt not kill, doesn't it? Doesn't it, James? Those are God's little animals, James. You didn't *make* them; God did. And that means only God is allowed to drown them. Doesn't it, James? Answer me, please, this minute or . . . Very well then, James. You had better go down and have a little think, hadn't you. Go on. Quickly. Before Daddy gets cross.'

What made me say it, I'll never know. If it was inspiration from above, it was a dirty trick. Anyway, I said, 'Why did God make them, then? They *take* stuff. That's stealing. I was just—'

'That's enough! Downstairs. At once, please!'

I began to roar. It seemed so unfair that my very best answer – the answer he had demanded – brought down nothing but more anger and punishment. Through the tears of misery and rage, I saw Mother approaching, wiping her hands on a teatowel.

'What's the matter?' she asked as she came, shifting a wisp of mousy hair with a dough-covered finger. 'What's all the shouting?'

She stooped to look in to my face, but Father took her elbow, stood her up and said, 'Leave him, Elizabeth, please. He's been very, very wicked. Very wicked indeed.' Then into my bawling face, he said, 'Down you go, boy. Chop, chop. And ask gentle Jesus please to forgive you for the wicked thing you have done.'

And that's when I bellowed, 'No!' and I ran. And when I reached the palletwood fence I remembered the word Auntie used when the cat got the chop she was defrosting for supper – I knew what it meant, she'd explained, it meant, 'I don't like', which seemed about right so I turned round and yelled at him, 'Fuck Jesus! Fuck the Bible! And fuck you!' Then I scarpered.

Auntie came down in the end; much much later and against orders, I'm sure of that, but she's tough is my aunt. She must have been visiting and asked why I wasn't in my bed or something, and he must have told her what happened I guess; anyway, she came.

Which might be why I thought of my aunt's flat in Hambledown as I stood quivering in the doorway of the Chapel. But I'd barely set off through the mist towards the Dean's back garden – that being the stock route over the precinct wall – when I came to a halt, having remembered that Auntie was still in Australia.

At that moment, there came the sound of running footsteps and the voice of Vidal-Hume calling my name. A split second later he had me by the arm.

'Head wants to see you, Bishop,' he puffed. 'Right now, in his study. Come on.'

There was a note of glee in the house captain's voice which filled me with foreboding. He retained his grip on my upper arm as we made our way, rapidly and without speaking, through the saturated darkness towards the Master's red brick mansion. I wanted to ask about the Canon's mood – the Canon was renowned for his Jekyll and Hyde mood swings, it could make a big difference – but I could not bear to give Pink Lips the pleasure of laying it on me with his nauseous gleeful voice, as I knew he would whatever the truth of the matter might be.

Soon we had passed between the stone gate posts and were crunching up the drive. A chink of light was visible between the velvet curtains to the left of the porch but nowhere else in the big Queen Anne building. The security light switched itself on, lighting the steps and twin pillars, the ornate boot scraper, bay tree and white-painted door. I took hold of Vidal-Hume's wrist and removed his hand from my arm. 'It's all right,' I said, 'only a cretin would run.' He grunted, stepped forward and reached towards the brass lion's head knocker, at which moment the door opened and the tightly bunned head of Mrs Ramsbury appeared.

'Ah, Vidal, do come in,' she said with a tiny nod. As Vidal passed her she pushed the door back with her massive bottom. Not knowing my name, she stretched her lips at me and gestured towards the broad wine-carpeted hall. 'The Canon is in the study,' she said, 'third on the right. Just knock. He's expecting you.'

6

The Canon was still in his white surplice from Evensong
and at first sight seemed in Jekyll mode. As my head went
round the door, he removed his reading glasses and smiled
at me with his shrewd eyes from beneath a domed and
healthily tanned forehead. 'Aha, my dear. Come in. Come
in. You are Bishop. James. I remember; the boy who likes '
Wagner. Mm? Father in metals – quite big – yes, yes.
Come over here, James. Where I can see you properly.'
He rose from his easy chair beneath a large standard lamp,
an open book in one hand, an empty cut-glass goblet in
the other. I moved to the centre of the deep-shaded room.
Without taking his eyes off me, the Canon placed the
book face down on a large, mahogany desk. With the
pink-stained glass still in his hand, he strode round the
desk towards me. His free arm encircled my shoulders
and he cuddled me to him. I felt myself stiffen. Still
scrutinising my face, he drew me towards the pool of light
surrounding the lamp. 'We don't want to hide in the
shadows, eh James? We don't want to give folk the wrong
impression, mm?' He was smiling at me so warmly I found
myself shyly smiling back, so as not to give the wrong
impression.

He released me at the edge of the lamplight and walked
to the corner to replenish his glass from one of three
crystal decanters standing together on a small grey-marble
table. I glanced round the three walls of floor-to-ceiling

books, and a fourth of floor-to-ceiling plum velvet curtains. I was reminded of the quire of the Cathedral with its dark wood, rich light, deep shadow and the suggestion of hidden knowledge.

Decanting carefully, his back still towards me, the Canon said, 'We have only this minute bid farewell to young Rodney Lawrence, my dear. And already we are blessed with another visitor; young Master Bishop. That's wonderful.' He turned to face me with an amused smile and a goblet half filled with dark red liquid. 'Well now, James, I understand that you too are preparing for Confirmation this term?'

'Sir.'

'Uh-huh. Uh-huh. Wonderful.' He gathered an upright chair and placed it before the desk. 'Sit down, James. Sit down. And what do you think of our school, little Jamie?'

'Good, sir. It's good.' I sat on the chair, exactly opposite the Canon who was now perched on the edge of the desk, the glass of red liquid – too heavy and oily to be table wine – beside him, his black-skirted legs stretched out straight, his shining black toes almost touching the toes of my own dull brogues. The only light in the room came from the parchment-shaded lamp behind the desk and a narrow band under the door. The near edge of the lampshade was slightly raised and, from where I was sitting, I could see the bright bulb over the Canon's left shoulder, but little of his face.

'Uh-huh,' he said. 'That's wonderful. And what about our boys, mm? You're settling in all right? They're not such a bad bunch, really. You won't find any Flashmans here, James. We don't stand for bullying. That's a thing of the past. Even the fagging is voluntary now, and we're considering scrapping it altogether next year. Times are changing; we have girls in the sixth form, mm? – and a new high-tech language block – complete with satellite link – newscasts straight from Moscow, mm? And we have football in the Michaelmas term. We're moving with the times here, James, and we're jolly proud of our school.' He took a long drink from the glass, smiling at me over the rim. I smiled back. He set down the glass and nodded at me, thoughtfully. 'It *is* good; you're right James.' He glanced down at a note on the desk beside him, turned it and read for a second. 'Let's see, now, where were you before? Ah, Elizabeth Barton. That's right. Famous footballing school. Nothing wrong with that. Oh no. I'm all for team spirit. Absolutely.' He looked up. 'Now you're a sixth-form scholar, eh, James? Not bad going, that.' His eyes suddenly grew larger. 'Are you clever?'

'Sir?'

He leaned forward and took both my cheeks between his thumbs and first fingers and, with his face only inches from mine, gave them a little shake, not quite hurting. 'Come along, Jamie,' he almost whispered, 'which are you? Fool or knave? Knave or fool? It's one or the other, so why don't you tell me. Mm?'

'Don't quite know what you mean, sir,' I blathered while he enjoyed himself a little more with my cheeks. **Watch out**, warned headvoice, **he's altering states – could be the drink**.

'All right, little Jamie.' He released my cheeks and straightened up. The smile was still there, but it no longer reached to his eyes. 'We'll pretend you're a fool, if that's what you'd prefer.' For a long moment he stared into my eyes while his fingers drummed on the front of the desk. Then he said, 'Young Rodney has told me everything, James. The lot; sources, *modus operandi*, everything. Your friend Rodney is no fool; he's very very sharp, is young Rodney; he knows that the truth will out. *Always*, in this establishment. Because that is the way I run things. And he knows that, does Master Rodney. He knows that I won't allow anything to spoil the fine community spirit we have built here. We care for one another here. We are like a big family, a brotherhood, and he knows that. And he knows that it is wise to speak up. At once. And not wait until things become . . . unpleasant.' As he spoke the Headmaster was smiling with his lips and I knew that I was in big, big trouble. All of a sudden his forehead seemed to lose its roundness, his face to narrow to an angular wedge. I suddenly saw my father's face smiling with the smile I had learnt to fear. I blinked and the face of the Canon returned. '. . . spoken to the others yet, Jamie – the youngsters. But I will . . . if I have to, my dear. Mm? Alternatively—' he broke off, holding my eyes till I felt myself blinking despite my best efforts. 'Alternatively, you might think it . . . sensible to save me the trouble . . . and to spare the youngsters that unpleasantness . . . since you know that I already know the answers, little Jamie. Mm? Thanks to young Rodney. Mm?'

My brain was racing. What would Lawrence have said? If anything at all. Surely even Lawrence would not have stooped so low as to shift the blame on to me. I made a decision: 'If it's about the explosion, sir—'

'Yes, James?'

'I don't know anything about it, sir. Except what I saw tonight, sir. Mr Shewring sent me for the broom. When I got back, he'd gone. Is he—' I stopped dead, horrified at the blunder I had almost made; I had been on the verge of asking if the Chaplain was all right. The Canon leant forward.

'Yes? Is he what, James?'

'Is he . . . um . . . able to throw any light on the subject himself, sir?'

The Canon straightened up, his eyes narrowed, the smile gone. 'Well now, how civil of you to ask such an interesting question, my dear, though I must say I believe you were about to ask something quite different?'

'No, sir. I—'

'No, sir. I see, sir. Very well, then.' The Canon looked at his watch and stood up. 'It's late. You're tired, and not thinking very clearly, my dear. So what I want you to do is this. Toddle off back to School House. Sit down quietly at your desk, and write me a nice long letter telling me precisely what you know . . . everything, James. Everything. And then we shall see if what you say matches up correctly with what I already know. Is that fair, James? Mm?'

I nodded agreement, hardly able to believe that I was free to leave, free to confer.

The Canon's eyes told me I should rise. He took my elbow and walked me to the door. As he turned the black porcelain knob, he said, 'Bring the letter to me yourself, James, tomorrow lunchtime, 1.30 sharp. All right?' He squeezed my shoulder. 'Wonderful. Mrs Ramsbury will see you out.' He called past me, 'Veronica! Master Bishop is leaving.' He gave me a little push down the hall, himself remaining in the study doorway.

The door to the sitting room opened beside me and Mrs Ramsbury emerged. She slipped the chain and opened the front door. Behind me the Canon called, 'Good night, James.' I stepped on to the brightly lit porch. Mrs Ramsbury nodded good-night.

The door was half shut when the Canon called:

'Oh, Bishop!'

I turned. He was there in the doorway. 'One last thing, Bishop. You won't go looking for Master Lawrence, will you, my dear? I asked his father to collect him. He'll be on his way home by now. Off you toddle, then. I'll ring Mr Gardener. Don't forget to report in. Good night.'

By the end of morning break next day, the spare iodine crystals, ammonia and filter papers were at the bottom of Burley pond. Though they had never strictly speaking been my problem, my faith in 'natural' justice had taken a severe knock, and this action restored my confidence considerably. I delivered my letter to the Headmaster's house at lunchtime as instructed. The Canon being elsewhere, Mrs Ramsbury took it from me so I did not learn at the time how it would be received, but I wasn't in the least worried about that. Though I say it myself, it was a masterpiece of the art of saying not a lot at great length. In fact it added nothing material to what I had already said on Sunday night.

It turned out that, despite all manner of threats and the minute interrogation of the younger confirmees over a period of two days, nothing could be proved. One reason being that no one – not even the Canon with his supposed knowledge of all the answers – could deny that not only would it have been possible for *any* member of the Confirmation class to have planted the powder, but that anyone else in the school – or, conceivably, an outside agent – could have slipped in and laid it, *before* the class arrived. The Chapel was always open, after all. Pure chance could have spared the members of the Confirmation class from stepping on a single crumb of explosive *after* the dirty deed had been done. That was what we all of us tried to explain to the Headmaster – even the lower-school members agreed (after a spot of counselling) – and in the end the Headmaster could only accept our version of events.

Punishment had to be meted out to someone of course, so he cancelled Trip Day. Which, being a twelve mile coast-walk, pleased more than it upset.

During the next two days, things began to look up. I still had the gurgling stomach and the same odd little tickle at the base of my spine, but the duck voice had been silent since Sunday night. I was sleeping again and my school-work had already begun to pick up. Something else had improved; it was no longer only the creeps and hypocrites who spoke to me; the fart champion and his mate became quite sociable too. I wondered at first if this apparent change in attitude might be due to the absence of one Rodney Arthur Lawrence – maybe they had always wanted to talk to me and had been put off by his oafish presence – but it struck me later that Fat Marcus probably just wanted an audience for his Canary brothel sagas, and there couldn't be many who hadn't heard it all before. Nevertheless, I had my first laugh in the place, and I went to bed happy. Ish. And I slept right through – night watchman and all – and I slept through the next night as well.

Wednesday morning Lawrence returned in triumphant mood not having been expelled but merely suspended for three days, supposedly for having used 'Ungentlemanly Language' (two points on the Code of Conduct scale) in the course of his own interrogation. (The offending phrase might have been 'sod all', he said, but didn't seem too sure; he reckoned the Head just wanted him out of the way so he could concentrate on me. I found myself agreeing with this.) During his meeting with the Headmaster he had – with the utmost reluctance, so he said – decided against laying claim to his 'blow for freedom'; but neither, it seemed, had he told the man anything which might have implicated me. That idea must have come from elsewhere, he said. He'd been given the same spiel about fools and knaves as me, and his defence, like mine, had been ignorance. 'To put it another way, Jimbo,' he said, 'you and I both played the same card – the Fool.'

It evolved, therefore, that the 'Knave' and myself were treated to the same Headmaster's 'summing up' as the other members of the class – no more. Wednesday lunch-time the whole group was summoned to the Headmaster's study. The main objective seemed to be to play the incident down. We were quickly reassured that Mr Shewring had escaped unhurt, and that only his prayerbook had settled on the stool triggering the explosion, not his balls. (This explained the scorched and scattered pages I'd seen

85

in the Chapel.) The Canon informed us that his Chaplain would be off duty only for a day or two while recovering from the shock, but – and here he addressed Lawrence specifically, and with an odd little smile – he would be back in time for First Fifteen practice on Thursday. Lawrence managed to smile back, but I could tell he was less than delighted. The Canon then impressed on us the need to keep the matter to ourselves and not go blabbing it around the school or the town – particularly the town – because of the danger of public over-reaction and the discredit that might bring upon the school. 'Particularly if certain tabloid newspapers get hold of the story,' he said.

'Be very sure, my dears,' he went on, removing his horn-rimmed glasses and fixing us with a stare, 'outside these walls, the matter would not have been met with such a degree of understanding and restraint. The police have of course been informed, but they have been persuaded, on this occasion, to allow us some latitude to deal with the matter ourselves.' He paused, nodding slowly, staring at the semicircle of small boys standing silently around him, Lawrence and myself just behind. 'I doubt that you realise quite how fortunate you are, my dears. You are indeed most fortunate, most fortunate indeed. Such matters would normally come under the auspices of the Bomb Squad, mm . . . ? You've heard of the Bomb Squad, mm? But for the understanding of Chief Inspector Braintree, who happens to be a past member of the school, we would have been dealing with the Bomb Squad. And the Bomb Squad, I can assure you, my dears, goes about things quite differently to the way we do here . . . the way we do inside the precincts, mm? Quite differently, mm . . . ?'

Duly awed, we each of us promised faithfully to remain silent and be on our guards in the future, and to report at once any suspicious behaviour we might encounter, no matter how strange or unlikely it might appear. And that was the end of it.

At least, so I thought. But I'd reckoned without the Chaplain.

7

After prayers each evening the lower school, that is years one, two and the Removes, begins to make ready for bed and lights out at 10.00 p.m. The upper school resumes its studies or relaxes with quiet pursuits like reading, chess or model railways in the cellar. At ten o'clock a strictly no-talking-in-the-corridors rule comes into force. Whilst I could not imagine such a rule making the slightest difference at Elizabeth Barton Comprehensive, here it most definitely does. There's one very good reason for this: here they can expel you without having to go through great traumas with the local authorities, and everyone knows it. As the Registrar said at induction, 'You enter the sixth form here, we treat you as a responsible adult. You sign the Code of Conduct, you know the rules, if you don't want to keep them, fine, we ask Mummy and Daddy to come and see us and we help them to choose a more suitable school.'

If a teacher at Lizzy's said something like that you'd just know he was bluffing. Here they do it. And there's a lot of dough involved, and there's a lot of status to lose. That's the difference.

And I've got to say, it works. But it also makes me nervous – the quiet, I mean – I just can't get used to it. Another thing I've noticed; there's no graffiti – that's a form of silence too. And you never see a Coke tin or Quaver packet lying about; the kids are like miniatures of their mums and dads – pillars of society from the zygote. There are exceptions of course; one of them's Shag.

I don't object to this side of Shag too much; like I don't particularly object to his having locked the cellar door on his first evening back and turning the light off when he knew the Railway Society was down there (it's a deep, dark cellar with a door at the bottom of the steps and the top as well so it's pretty nearly sound proof, and those lads didn't surface until well gone beddybyes time), but, as I say, I don't really object to that sort of thing, that's just another of Shag's little contributions to the class war. But something else happened that same night, something I bloody well do object to. There again, I'd no *proof* it was Shag, but I certainly had my suspicions.

Unless I have work to do, I normally read in the study. Not that I'm the world's greatest reader, but I recently picked up a book by a man called Ballard all about car crashes, and I must say it stirred up fond memories of my own childhood. Consequently, on Wednesday night when Pink Lips poked his head round the door to say bedtime, I was reluctant to put it down. But I did. And then something – I don't know what it was, unless it was the book taking me back all those years – but something said to me, Better just check the old toolbox, Jimbo, make sure everything is in order. So I checked. And it wasn't.

I keep the box on the floor under my desk since it's too long to fit in the cupboard. It's a twin tray Toolmaster in metallic blue hammer finish, not new but strong enough. And the lock was a Union Combi with four number rings. For security reasons I'd refrained from writing the numbers down – there's no problem remembering a number like 4268 anyway – so whoever did it was good.

I would not say I'm secretive but I happen to be a believer in privacy. It is naïve to imagine that everything about one can be understood by others, friends or otherwise: some things cannot. Even between real friends there are certain matters best not discussed. Hence the safebox.

The lock was still locked, but as soon as I opened the two lids I could see that several items had been disturbed. There was no question about this. I keep my things neat. They were no longer as I had left them. Several of the photographs were out of order. The cap was off my jar of Vegemite and there was at least a fingerful missing. But the worst thing was that the items I keep in a sealed polybag in the bottom cavity were no longer in that cavity but up above in one of the trays. This discovery gave me a most unpleasant sensation and immediately set off my indigestion again. I had thought my toolbox one hundred per cent secure. Now I would have to remove certain items and keep them on my person, at least till such time as a more adequate lock could be acquired. I went downstairs in a foul mood and didn't even answer when Lawrence said good night. I also had dreadful wind in the night, which Lawrence complained about but I thought, Bloody well serve you right, mate.

One blessing, the duck kept quiet again so I slept on and off between the stinking farts.

Though bad enough, this episode was not the worst threat to my privacy that week; on Thursday morning came the *message* from CJ.

This shocked me. I had always believed the confessing of sins before a priest to be a uniquely Roman Catholic farce. This being an Anglican Cathedral, the school being in its precincts, I naturally assumed that such trivial sins as I might own were my private affair, unless, of course, my former, infantile belief in the Heavenly Father should miraculously re-emerge, in which case they would become a matter between me and Him. It never occurred to me that in either case would any so-called interlocutor be required. Ta very much.

Wrong.

CJ read the note out himself at morning assembly. To me he looked no different for his ordeal by nitrogen tri-iodide; if anything he looked meaner. I toyed with the idea of mentioning this to Shag who was standing next to me, but there seemed little point. Besides which the Chaplain's words were beginning to come through to me. '. . . of the Confirmation group collect their copies of the booklet, First Confession, from the Small Chapel today. The timetable for confession itself will be on the main noticeboard by lunchtime today. Thank you.'

End of message. End of ceasefire. End of peace of mind. The Chaplain was back. Cue for electronic organ: 'And Did Those Feet in Ancient Times', sung to a rumba beat, its synthesised jollity mocking my distress, the remainder of assembly wiped out by this mental picture of CJ and me alone in the windowless, sound-proof Chapel, lights dim, door shut, DO NOT ENTER.

Why the panic? said headvoice.

I had no answer. Why should Confession bother me? I had nothing to hide, did I? And even if I had, as far as CJ was concerned it could stay hidden. So, what then?

A soft tickling beneath the skin at the base of my spine was all the reminder I needed: it was the duck noise that frightened me, the thought of it returning to murder my sleep. Something inside of me, some corner of my mind that could not give a stuff about *reason* or *scientific logic* or anything like that was telling me that somehow the Chaplain and the minuscule, terrible yittering inside my head were related. And related like cause and effect.

All through the morning I could not stop thinking about it. Then, almost at the end of third lesson, which was Drama, something happened. It must have been some kind of a fit, they said, though I've never heard of a fit being *catching*. But it wasn't just me, that's the weird thing. I started it, yes – leastways, according to Tamsyn I did – but in seconds it had spread to half the class!

92

We'd been joined by the 'A' level Theatre Studies group which meant more pair improvisations on that mad Irishman's play. I was working with Tamsyn. We'd been given the bit where the blind cripple asks the servant if the stuffed toy dog is looking at him with adoring imploring eyes, begging for a bone or a walkies; and the servant says, Yes it is, even though the thing only has three legs and can't even stand on its own. Which they all thought was pretty damned funny. In our group, I was the one in the wheelchair, and I didn't find it funny, I found it hideously depressing; I mean the poor bloke's beside himself, just desperate for love . . . but that's by the by. For the last five minutes of the lesson Miss Brannon decided we should all calm down and take stock. And after that, all I remember is lying on my back on the carpet for the usual wind-down listening exercise, and that's when the yittering started.

Suddenly I could see nothing but a great blaze of red and I could hear nothing but what sounded like anti-aircraft fire or drum beats, very fast. Next thing I knew I was on my side with one knee drawn up and a sock between my teeth. My head was thumping and there was a vile taste of sick in my mouth. On the grey carpet in front of my face was a puddle of frothy yellow liquid, and I could still hear the drumming.

Right in front of me, almost touching my face, Tamsyn in her black leotard was flat on her back doing real pelvic thrusts quick and violent. Beyond the slapping, quivering pelvis, I could see Miss Brannon's purple-clad spine and freckled shoulders hunched over another thrashing figure who was beating the floor with his heels while she wrestled with his head and shoulder end.

I struggled up on one elbow, took the slimy sock out of my mouth and gaped round the room. I could barely believe what I saw. Half a dozen bodies in various corners of the studio, most, but not all, with a crouching attendant; all either rigid in some grotesquely contorted posture or writhing and lashing their limbs against the floor or the walls of the studio. I could hear sobbing and screaming and weird sort of hooting sounds and what might have been soothing words though I could not hear whether they were real words or not for the drumming and the cries all around. I wanted to call to the teacher, but something was stuck in my throat. I coughed and spat violently three times and finally out came a ball of what looked like matted hair about the size of a golf ball. And suddenly the drumming and screaming stopped, then the sobbing stopped too, then the words, and then there was silence and into the silence came the sound of the bell for lesson change.

Miss Brannon rose to her feet in the middle. She stood there a second then began revolving slowly, trembling like a wet dog, face a white mask, blood from her lip trickling down her white neck and into her white cleavage.

We were sent off in twos and threes to our respective matrons, each dazed little group escorted by one of the six members of the class who had somehow remained unaffected by whatever it was. By the end of break it was as if nothing had happened.

Other than Miss Brannon's lip, which had been caught by an elbow, there was nothing physical to see. No symptoms remained, nothing was broken, and, as far as I know, no one else had even been sick. Tamsyn is the only member of the group in the same house as me, and she told Matron she felt just fine. In fact she was starving, she said, and please could she go to the tuckshop. But Matron insisted she stay in sickbay until the doctor had seen her.

The school doctor eventually arrived at twenty to one with his stethoscope still round his neck from his previous call. He asked a lot of questions about what we had eaten or drunk during the past twenty-four hours, especially things other than those served up in the dining room. Although he didn't actually use the word 'drugs' or 'glue' he came close enough for us to know that was what was meant. Then he checked our pulses and temperatures, looked into our eyes and listened to our chests – Tamsyn's fine big chest unfortunately being displayed on the far side of a green cotton screen – then he shook his head, went into a huddle with Matron, pronounced us both fit for school and went away promising to look back after he'd had the chance to confer with the Ed. Psych. at the school Sanatorium.

I'd decided not to mention my little problem with the noises; he reminded me too much of Doc Keylock at the Child Guidance Clinic. I mean, he looked stupid.

Despite my flat feet, my name was on the 'B' team list for the afternoon practice match with the First Fifteen. The Chaplain's idea, no doubt at all. CJ himself decided to play at breakaway on our team, according to him just to even things up. But Lawrence, who, in spite of his fourteen stones is fast and plays centre, knew different. And he was right.

'Bastard!' he spat as we mounted up for the two-mile ride back to school. 'Creeping fucking Jesus set me up, the bony little fuckpig.'

I shook my head. I had to be careful. I'd never seen Shag so angry.

'Did you see him? Jesus. Every time, whack! Same bastard leg, same bastard muscle.'

He was hurt all right, I could tell by the way he was pedalling, using his left hand to push down on his knee, to relieve the left thigh muscle where the Chaplain had hit him again and again with his jutting shoulder.

I said nothing again, partly because I was puffed and having a job to keep up with him on the muddy track despite his injury, my old bike having two flat tyres, and partly because I hoped he might calm down enough for me to change the subject without him biting my head off.

As we turned out of the Big Field on to the track that leads over the railway bridge, I said, 'By the way, when's your appointment, mate?'

'What fuckin' appointment?'

'Confession.'

'Oh, that bollocks. I dunno. When's yours?'

'Sunday. I'm thinking of pulling out.'

'Good luck, son.'

The way he said it made me anxious to test the idea further, I suppose in the hope of a more optimistic reaction. It was my damned Soul, wasn't it? If we human animals have such refinements, which I doubted. If I wanted to take the chance it was up to me, wasn't it? There was no rule saying, Thou shalt be Confirmed. It wasn't on the Code of Conduct. Why shouldn't I just tell him: I'm pulling out, CJ, so stick it up your arse.

There's something about biking that helps me sort my ideas out. I often find myself telling the bastards what for while I'm shoving those wobbly old pedals around (which reminds me, I must get a new cotter pin, they don't cost a lot).

'So, what do you think, son?' I said.

It was Shag's turn to shake his head.

'Seriously,' I said, 'what do you reckon?'

No answer.

At the approach to the bridge, the track leaves the allotments behind and begins to climb between old hawthorn hedges. I stood on the pedals and heaved on the flat bars. Lawrence still managed to move in front on his new sports bike. As the brick parapets came in sight, I caught a glimpse of brown duffel coat past Lawrence's humping back. The colour and shape looked familiar.

'Fat chance,' said Shag. I'd almost forgotten what I'd asked him. Then I remembered.

I felt anger and frustration rise like a big red breaker. Push. Heave. Grunt. And I caught him, and I passed him. Well almost. 'We'll fucking see about that,' I gritted. Then my right-hand pedal flew round free and came off. Down I went on the crossbar, ball either side, and my eyes flooded.

'Look who it is,' said Shag. 'The train spotter.'

But right then I couldn't see pussy.

It seems the good doctor had not come to the bridge simply to train spot – though he did make us wait while he pencilled in the number of a coal train that passed beneath us heading west – but had also come with the intention of meeting Shag and me.

'Come to tea,' he said. 'Five thirty, Friday.' Lawrence, creeping for once, said 'Ta very much, sir.' I sort of groaned and like nodded (or doubled up), and that was that. The old boy stood on the pedals and wobbled slowly and sedately away down the lane with Shag and me gaping after. Before disappearing, he called back, 'Better bring a torch, boys.'

8

Lawrence decided to go his own way, preferring the motorbike to the bus. I, having accompanied him through a beech hedge only a fortnight earlier, declined his offer of a lift and boarded the 193 from the Castlegate depot.

It was almost dark as we left the bright orange outskirts of the city. Twenty minutes later the windows revealed nothing but blackness and broken reflections of the interior where my own hands had wiped away the mist of condensation. As soon as the engine began to slow, I clambered down the stairs and along the almost empty lower-deck aisle towards the cab.

'Is this Clout's Enclosure?' I inquired. The driver, a miserable woman with thin, scarlet lips (reminding me horribly of Matron) nodded and crunched the gearbox. 'The Barham end?' I persisted, boldly I felt.

'Yes,' she snapped, dropping her clutch.

Neither could I see anything after being thrown from the platform, apart from the double-decker itself and the little patch of lit verge it took with it up the hill. According to the doctor's map there was a lane right in front of me. I waited, listening to the dying drone of the diesel. The lights vanished first, then the sound. After a moment with just me and the wind, I began to see fir trees.

Clout's Enclosure is one of those forestry plantations that are too dense to pass through without bending double or getting down on your hands and knees to crawl over a carpet of dead needles and moss. As the moonless, starless sky gradually separated from the forest, I saw there was a gap in the black canopy that looked about cart-track width. Relieved, I thought, the map is accurate this far, then. I stepped forward, hands waving in front just in case.

The ground felt rutted and slimy underfoot. The air inside the wood was saturated and still. An owl hooted. In the silence which followed, my ears reached far out among the dark ranks of pine finding soft stirrings and flappings which multiplied as the seconds passed. Another owl hoot, further off, then a high-pitched small-creature-scream.

And I'd forgotten the torch.

By the time I reached the cottage I was cold and more than a little jumpy, but I hadn't looked behind me. Not once. It helped that, from at least a hundred metres back down the track, I'd caught glimpses of what I took to be a lighted window, despite its peculiar shape. Now I saw it was a sash window – three panes glass, one hardboard. I moved closer and peered in.

He was lying on a sack-covered sofa, apparently snoozing, with a white cat on his chest and a glass of amber liquid on the floor beside him. The bare plaster walls of the room were festooned with oil lamps of every imaginable shape and size, two more stood one each end of the mantelshelf, another on top of a paraffin heater at the head of the sofa. Half a dozen candles flickered on saucers and in various Wee-Willy-Winkie holders. Beside a smouldering wood and coal fire stood a new galvanised dustbin. Spread out around this on the hardboard-covered floor were three stained newspapers, each having at its centre a foil takeaway tray with evil-looking blackish chunks scattered around. Opposite the settee stood half a dozen galvanised buckets covered by a plastic sheet.

I stepped back from the window, strangely embarrassed.

The light on the ground showed a tangle of grass and what would have been nettles last summer. There was enough light now to show that the cottage stood in a small clearing which nature had already begun to reclaim with brambles and clumps of saplings rising from ancient stumps. Half hidden behind the wreckage of a corrugated iron shed, the white roof of a Land Rover glowed eerily against the black forest. I stood still, holding my breath, listening for the sound of the motorbike, praying for the sound of the motorbike. But I heard only the whisper of wind in the fir trees.

After a minute, I hit the door twice with my bare knuckles. It opened at once, just a crack. A draught of warm air came laden with paraffin vapour. A watery eye appeared.

'Oh shit! I forgot you,' said Sopworth. The door opened wider, 'Come in. Whisky, isn't it?' I glanced at his unravelling khaki sweater, the combat fatigues with torn pockets and riddled legs.

'Um, yes, sir,' I said, stepping on to the hardboard. 'Thanks very much, sir.'

He vanished through a doorway into an unlit room. A light came on in a third room showing the second to be empty – just bare boards, not even hardboard like this room. I heard a clatter and the pop of a gas ring. 'Tea won't be long,' he said reappearing with glass and bottle, 'teapot's always on the boil. Sit down, James.'

Whether the old boy really knew about the whisky I can't say, but that's what he poured me an inch of before disappearing once more into the third room. 'It's mashing now. Turf one of them out; make yourself comfy,' he called. 'Hope you like caraway cake.'

I looked around. What I had not seen from the window were the dexion racks full of books, these being against the window wall to either side, nor the once elegant claw-foot table beside which stood a pair of ragged armchairs, each containing a cat – one grey and fat, the other black and skinny. I tilted the fat cat's chair, but the animal clung to the brown velvet cushion so that both slid off together with a bunch of magazines hidden underneath. I saw the titles, *Liberator* and *Turning Point* over pictures of animals, among them a screaming monkey spreadeagled on a frame. I replaced the magazines and sat down.

The table was littered with books and old newspapers. *The Plays of Henrik Ibsen Vol. i* lay open, its margins covered in pencilled comments. I read the words, Daylight Coward, and what looked like: Greenwoman > Ingrid > guilt > Bogg or maybe it was Boyg, either way it made no sense. A black paperback titled *The Wasp Factory* caught my eye but I'd barely turned back the cover before the doctor called: 'If you want the lavatory it's up the wooden hill. First door. Take a lamp.' I picked up a blue tin lamp with polished reflector from the table. 'And watch the seventh step. There isn't one.'

The wick was uneven so that the glass chimney smoked and gave little light, though enough to show me the staircase leading off the empty room. The treads were bare wood and creaked loudly. When I reached tread five, the doctor called again: 'Better skip six and eight as well.'

Where the seventh step should have been was an unbroken view of the floor below. As I gripped the handrail and stretched for the ninth, I realised I was already beginning to feel strangely at ease in the doctor's house, especially considering that only minutes earlier I'd felt like legging it for the next stage out. Here was a man of obvious culture living like a UB40 in a squat. In fact the place made my own vulgar, sordid home seem luxurious. And that was *before* the bathroom.

No bath for a start, not a *real* one anyway but a galvanised trough on bricks. Beside this stood two more buckets and a chair with a maroon towel hung over the back. Cracked mirror. Pair of muddy boots. The yellow arms of a large bolt cutter peeping out from under a window curtained in green plastic hessian. A white, flushing toilet with no cistern, and – big surprise – pinned to the wall above the bath a huge poster (print, I guess) of a beautiful woman stretched on a bed or couch wearing only a black ribbon round her neck and one gold slipper on one foot crossed at the ankle over the other which was bare. She stared electrifyingly at me wherever I moved, as did the black cat at the foot of the bed, though not to the same effect, while a black servant holding a bouquet of chrysanths gazed at her adoringly.

Well then, thought I, perhaps he's not queer.

Two doors lead off the dark landing, the first ajar. As I headed for the stairs, the light from the lamp showed a corner of striped mattress and some clothing on the floor. Peeping in, I saw an unmade bed, what looked like a month's supply of dirty washing on the floor, candles in saucers, on plates, in holders, on tinfoil takeaway trays – mostly white candles but coloured ones also – and books. Books everywhere; on the bed, beside the bed, on top of a grey marble washstand, underneath it, piled in the corners, and, somehow strangest of all, filling the shelves of a fine mahogany book cabinet. I approached the cabinet and was surprised to discover that the leaded glass doors were locked. I stood still a moment listening to the pot and pan noises from below, then raised the lamp to the glass.

Many of the books were large and ancient looking, in fact not unlike those I had seen in the Cathedral with Lawrence. Some had titles which meant nothing to me, such as *Twentieth Century Thaumaturge* and *Naturopathy, Shamanism, Pranic-Energy and the Oath*. Others, like *Cosmic Consciousness* and three well-worn volumes titled *Materials Towards a History of Witchcraft*, meant more. And some, particularly *La Sorcière*, another called *Bible of the Undead* and a huge, white skin-covered volume called *Thesaurus Exorcismorum* frankly shocked me.

Before tiptoeing out I sneaked a look at his current reading on the bed; the first I picked up was a paperback titled simply *Feral Cat*, the second, more enigmatically, *Feline Neuroses and the Aura*, the third, another paperback, called *Candle Burning Rituals – a new guide to an ancient art*. This last fell open at a section headed, 'Part 3: Rituals for Protection'. There was blue wax on the page. I quickly scanned the instructions for the daily burning of blue candles when under threat, and a further instruction to repeat the following three times on each occasion:

> Thine power is great
> Around Me,
> My safety is sure
> My faith is Total
> My Earthly Existence Secure.

I shut the book quickly and crept out.

Downstairs the books on the clawfoot table had been pushed to one side; it now bore two enamel mugs of steaming brown tea, two tin plates and a badly mauled cake which looked home-made.

'What did you think of the Naked Maja?' asked Sopworth from an armchair, a cat on each knee and a third – a tortoiseshell I'd not seen before – on the chairback.

'Pardon?' I said. (I thought he meant 'major'.) I wondered which cat was the neurotic. They all looked well adjusted to me; the newcomer was stretched out full length, idly licking a paw.

'The picture in the bathroom. It's a prezzy from Dumpling. My niece. She's a tonic. She told me, You live like a pig in shit, Nunc, but you're not one, so here's a picture to show you what you're missing. She's one of those who thinks a man's not complete unless he's got himself lashed to some woman – preferably with a litter of kids, like her. But I've got my family.'

He laughed a little, making the fat cat flick its ear and look up. 'Get some,' he said, gesturing at the dark brown lump on the plate. I hesitated. 'Go on, grab hold; fingers were made before forks.' I pinched up some of the doughy cake. 'What d'y'call that? *Get some*, I said. Go on; boys your age are always starving. And don't look so worried, I didn't invite you here to talk English all night.'

I was hungry so broke off a large piece which I nibbled between sips of tea more like tar while the doctor talked.

'All I'm going to say about that essay of yours is, don't rein your horses in yet, lad – there's plenty of time for control and technique – let the buggers run. You've got passion, that's the treasure to be prized, not the bland pap we stuff into the young so that everything comes out like a *Daily Mail* editorial – not the bloodless, colourless crud the new wave's turning out. Everything's *manners* now – manners and *style*, there's no guts, no spunk.' He swallowed a mouthful of whisky and huffed, his wet eyes shining in the lamplight. 'Manners murdereth man, lad. Take care they don't castrate you. You *needed* to write like that, I could see the signs. The animal must come out to play some time in its poor, banged-up bloody life or it dies. Or it bloody escapes, *then* watch out.' He slopped whisky into his tea. 'And watch out for that shell of yours, James, it's too thick. I don't know what you imagine you've got to hide,' he shook his head slowly, 'but I don't like it; it worries me. Look at you. Look at the way you sit, straight up like a goddam secretary. Look at you nibbling that cake with your pinky stuck out – who the hell *taught* you that? Dammit, you're an animal, lad, like the rest of us. Give yourself a chance, for Christ's sake, let *something* hang out even if it's only your tongue.' He drained his glass. Reading the signs, both knee-cats jumped down. He stood up, poured himself another two inches and waved the bottle invitingly.

'Thanks, sir, but I haven't quite—'

What then landed on the back of the sofa struck me dumb.

Following my stare, Sopworth said, 'Oh dear, it's you, ST,' and stood still, bottle in hand.

It took me several seconds to recognise the creature as a white cat – the white cat I'd seen through the window, I guessed, but then it had had its back towards me whereas now . . . I felt myself shudder.

Besides the extreme emaciation, wild eyes and a terrible tension seeming to enervate its arching body, something truly horrific had been done to the animal's head. Between its ears, from the brow to the back of the skull, an oblong of fur had been removed down to the flesh. The flesh itself was white but bruised and scarred and cross-hatched with straight blue lines which looked to have been ruled in indelible ink. There were also four small holes, one at each corner of the rectangle, and a fifth, larger hole, at the centre. The central hole, about the size of a 1p piece, appeared to have pierced both flesh and skull, and something metallic in its depths gleamed in the lamplight. As I gaped, the creature leapt from the sofa and began to whirl round the room at insane speed.

The doctor quickly set down the bottle, shouted, 'Help, James,' and began to chase around as fast as his sixty-year-old legs could manage, lifting chairs, steadying lamps whose supports had been rocked, barring the way to the fireplace. Too late, I snatched up the dustbin, which rung with the impact and suddenly there were bloodspots on the hardboard. I watched open-mouthed as the blood-spattered beast rotated on its axis a dozen times in a blur of white and red, pounced, pounced again, threw two twisting somersaults in the air then bolted for the second room. I heard it thunder up the wooden stairway. It had evidently leapt the gap for immediately came the sounds of racing and pouncing and the crash of falling objects upstairs.

I looked at the panting, sweating doctor and started for the stairs, but he put out an arm and restrained me. 'No need,' he puffed. 'He'll stop in a mo. Same dream. Always. Same ending.'

'Pardon?' I said.

But sure enough, at that moment the noises stopped abruptly. 'Dream mouse,' said Sopworth, still wheezing but less violently. 'Always gets away.' He picked up the bottle, then, seeing my face, added, 'Poor St Tom, he's not well. Nothing to be done. Best to ignore it. In fact,' he stopped to pour a little whisky into both of our glasses, 'I'd like you to forget what you've seen if you would, James.' He looked into my eyes, and lifted his glass. 'Can you do that for me, James? Me and old Tom? There's a reason.'

I nodded, 'Of course, sir.' I raised my own glass.

'Good lad,' said the doctor. We both drank. The doctor sat down. I sat down.

'Thank you, James. I knew I could trust you. Perhaps later on—'

A loud thud came through the ceiling, then silence. 'That's it now,' said the doctor with a wry smile. 'Missed. It's gone. Finished. Tonight, at least. Thank God.' He took another sip of whisky. 'Now, what was it I was – Ah, yes, the essay. That essay of yours.' He shook his head. 'One thing I would like to know, Jim, is where'd'ya get the history from, eh?' He stared at me over the glass. 'The blazing tar barrels? The rivers of molten lead? The horned wildmen with the firebrands?' He lowered his glass, still staring.

What could I say? Could I say, The pen did it? Could I speak to him of those unspeakable horrors I was too terrified even to admit to myself? I toyed with the remains of the cake. I saw that he was nodding at me. After a second, he said, 'You know, that old church has been one long saga of death and destruction, Jim. It's seen three

107

burnings – excluding the Vikings – one earthquake, two murders, one suicide – and that's only what we *know* about . . . Still, if the Establishment will go sticking its Christian temples smack on top of old pagan fanes, they've got to expect things like that.' His eyes unfocused and his head shook from side to side making his jowls and dewlap wobble.

'That was policy in those days, you know, Jim; holy orders, straight from the Vatican by decree of the Bishop of Rome: "Do not, after all, put down the fanes," wrote his holiness, "but destroy the idols; purify the buildings with holy water, set relics there; and let them become the temples of the true God." That was the message Pope Gregory sent the first missionaries. I learnt it by heart; it's so priceless. I doubt whether you'd believe what came next . . . holy cow! talk about expediency; that fellow would have made our politicians look like a bunch of amateurs. This is how he explained it: hang on to those old pagan sites, he said – "So the people will not have to alter their places of concourse," – We learnt all this from the Bede, of course, James, you'll have heard of the Venerable Bede, I dare say. Anyway, it goes on: "and where, of old they—" they, that's your ancestors, boy "—were wont to sacrifice cattle to *demons* . . . thither let them continue to resort *on the day of the saint to whom the church is dedicated—*" '

The old man broke off to dab at his eyes, his whole body was shaking like a jelly, and I realised suddenly he was speechless with silent laughter. After a moment, he recovered and went on: ' "—and let them continue to slay their beasts no longer as sacrifice, but for a—" ' This time a great snort stopped him and brought more dabbing and shaking. ' "—but for a social meal in honour of Him they now worship!" ' He practically howled the last word and immediately collapsed in the depths of the chair where he sputtered and wobbled, quite unable to speak for several minutes. Meanwhile I smiled at him stupidly. At last he said, 'So, James, in my view, it serves them all bloody well right . . .' He wiped his eyes again, then leaned right forward, staring straight into my face, 'But . . . where did *you* learn the details, lad? That's what I want to know. And where did those images come from?' He picked up his glass again, then stopped in mid sip, staring at me over the rim, waiting for my answer.

I dropped my eyes, picked up the enamel mug nearer me and took a long drink, hoping it would look like I was thinking hard. How could I explain when my only idea was so utterly bizarre? What would he think of me if I blurted out what had happened that night in the study? Probably the same as Doctor Keylock thought when Pa took me to the clinic after the Accident, that I'd cracked up; only this time it might even be true. I looked up expecting to see puzzlement or irritation. What I saw was smug satisfaction.

'Just as I thought,' he beamed, 'straight from the horse's mouth: she talks to you, doesn't she, James. I knew it!' He slapped his thigh, making the grey cat jump and glare.

I nearly dropped my mug of hot tar. But as he went on I realised with immense relief we were thinking of two different Shes. 'What you've written is special, James. The Cathedral isn't a *building*, it's a *place*. It's not about fancy glass windows and regimental colours and carved statues and all that kitsch; it's not even about bishops and saints, however saintly. No, the power of any Cathedral as ancient as this – and I mean ancient before Jesus Christ was heard of here, or Bethlehem, come to that – is the place itself, the location, the *earth it stands on*. The closer you get to those foundations, the greater the power. Drink up, lad.

'It chose you to talk to, that's all, James. Nothing to worry about. Some folks can waggle their ears and curl their tongues longwise, others pick up vibes. You're one of the chosen. Don't look like that; it's a great gift, lad.'

He finished his sip now, still staring over the brim.

I was shocked. It was the first time anyone had said such things to me, and part of me wanted to yell out, Yes man! At fucking last! And that's not the only thing talks to me, you old bugger – there's a rusty old ambulance does just the same. But I didn't. I don't know why. I just didn't. Habit again, I suppose.

His wispy yellow eyebrows came together in a frown. 'Just one thing intrigues me, James. There's another voice comes into your essay, right at the end. It's quite different – style, lexicon, type-token ratio. It's not even your writing. Tell me, where did that voice come from, James?'

My brain was racing. I picked up the whisky glass this time and took a long swig, deliberately slurping to show I was relaxing like he said. The whisky made my eyes water but I kept going until the glass was empty, then I said, 'It was sort of an experiment, sir, that's all. Like you say, sir, just giving the old horses their head.' I was pleased with that, despite the slurring.

'Stop calling me sir, it makes me nervous, lad.' He stood suddenly, scattering cats. 'Leak,' he said, heading for the outside door. 'Saves water. I collect rainwater, see, Jim.' He waved at the buckets. 'Don't trust the buggering Waterboard – who wants dilute sewage in their tea, even if it is poisoned with chlorine. Not me. And not my boys.' With that, he picked up the fat grey cat, tucked it under his arm, lurched a few feet outside, not bothering to close the door. The 'leak' sounded like a carthorse.

He came back without the grey cat. Leaving the door open, he picked up the tortoiseshell, said, 'Killing time for cats,' launched it into the night, closed the door and drew the heavy army blanket back over the doorway. As soon as he sat down again, the old black cat hauled itself back on to his knee and settled to a hypnotic treading, claw-stretching routine. 'This one's too old,' said the doctor. 'No teeth. So it's chopped heart and Catkins for

Skelitor, ain't it boy?' He scratched the scurfy old head vigorously between the ears, then raised his eyes to the ceiling: 'St Tom has to make do with the cellar. He hasn't a clue about territory, poor little bugger. Only time I let him out he shot into the forest and made straight for the A2. Time I'd fired up the old Land Rover and got after him, he was past Bourne Park belting north on the hard shoulder like all the devils in hell were on his back.' His eyes unfocused and strayed towards the fire. 'It was only a guess too. I could just as well have turned left. God knows where he'd have stopped.' He shook his head at the memory and sipped more whisky. 'If he'd have stopped at all.'

I waited for the moist red-rimmed eyes to refocus, but they continued to gaze through the back of the smouldering, ash-filled grate. The treading Skelitor was now purring with a half inch of pink tongue poking out, eyes tight shut. Still looking through the fire, Sopworth breathed the word, 'Bastards.' Then, as if the sound had woken him from a dream, he looked at me and said, 'You've made yourself a bad enemy, James. You know that, don't you?'

It was my turn to stare.

'Can't say too much. Unprofessional. You understand?' He fixed me with eyes turned suddenly bright and clear. 'Course you do. Thing is that business in the studio. Madge told me about that. Madge Brannon, Drama,' he added in response to my blank look. 'If it wasn't for that . . . Well, never mind, let's just say there's more to our School Chaplain than meets the eye, son. Best keep clear.' He was nodding, his eyes locked on mine. 'Keep out of the way for a bit, James. All right?'

Dimly through the whisky haze I thought, Sunday. 5.15 pm. Me and the Reverend Shewring are due to meet. No getting away from it. Nevertheless, I nodded back to the doctor. 'Yes, sir. I'll try. Thanks, sir.'

He let the formality pass. 'No, James,' he said, 'I mean it.'

Lawrence never did show. Saturday I found out he'd gone to the pub with *our* girlfriend Lucy, the sod.

The rest of the evening was hazy. I remembered the old man asking about my family, what my father did, how I got on with my Ma, whether I had brothers or sisters, who I could talk to (I told him, Auntie, of course), whether my father was ambitious for me, what I wanted to do when I left school et cetera. And I remember waffling something about journalism and playwriting. Then he fetched the play, I remembered that, the one I'd seen the notes on, only a paperback copy, and told me to read it sometime – especially the bit about the vicar with the club foot and the butterfly net! I remembered that part because he said that although it was written tongue in cheek, it would help me to understand about the Chaplain.

After that . . .

After that, there were other things, important things. Things about the cat, things about CJ, things I needed to know. If only I'd drunk a bit less.

I remembered him talking on the phone. I was lying full length on the sofa with the old cat on my stomach purring like a football rattle and he was on the phone in the next room.

What the hell was that all about? He was phoning the school, that was it; some story about the Land Rover breaking down. I remembered him saying I'd be back in time for period one; I remembered wishing I was back at Lizzy's then; Saturday morning's for fishing, not physics.

When the lights went out on Saturday night, I lay in my cold bed planning how I would handle my problems in a determined and positive way. I was unhappy carrying my most private possessions around in my jacket pocket. It did not feel safe. It did not feel right. I knew that Shag had been engaging in . . . let us say, 'trade'; tomorrow I would ask him to lend me a fiver, and on Monday afternoon I'd buy myself a decent lock. That was number one. About the Confession, I'd already decided; nothing would be allowed to put at risk the run of silent nights and heavenly peace I'd enjoyed since the explosion. *Nothing*.

9

My appointment with CJ was for 5.15. By five o'clock I'd
drained the whisky, smoked my last Capstan in the tank
loft, brushed my teeth and was pacing the study rehearsing
my lines. I also had a headache and my guts were in such
an uproar I'd have opened the window if I could. Instead
I stopped pacing and stared out through the grimy pane
at the fading yellow light and descending fog. Already the
top of the tower had gone and the rest was a sepia fuzz.
I looked at my watch: five past.

As I pushed an arm into the sleeve of my jacket, I
heard stomping on the stairs and Lawrence burst in. He
grimaced and retreated to the doorway, swearing, then
stood there wafting the door back and forth. After remark-
ing coarsely on the state of my intestines, he said, 'I hate
that bastard; he's a sarky little shit. Do you know what
he told me, Jim, just because I made one poxy mistake?
He told me to go away and look up the word hypocrisy,
learn the meaning off by heart, then come back and see
him after supper tomorrow, tell him what it means, and
then we're to go through the whole bloody panto again. I
tell you, boy, I'm going to fix that Creeping Jesus if it's
the last bloody thing I do.'

I glanced at my watch; almost ten past. I wanted to get
going but Lawrence was still wafting, and I felt awkward.
Show token interest then scarper, I thought. 'Christ,' I
said, 'that's a bit rough. What was the mistake, mate?

What did you do, like?' Inside, I was thinking, Trust Lawrence to stir the man up just when I wanted him calm and reasonable.

'Sod all, that's what's so annoying. Look, you know in that booklet it tells you what to say, right? Well where it says, *I have done*, dot, dot, dot, so and so, and so and so *since my last Confession*, and you're supposed to fill in the so and sos – you know, like stick in whatever little naughties you think God might want to forgive you for, right? Well I weren't thinking, right? And instead of just putting in *my* bits, I said the lot, right? And fucking CJ goes apeshit, doesn't he. "What last confession?" he yells – he's got a fucking temper on him, the little shit – "You've never confessed before," he says, "have you?" I mean, so fucking what? I'd made half of it up anyway, so what's the fuckin' odds?'

I tutted sympathetically, shook my head, looked at my watch and said, 'Ten past. Better get going, mate. Talk to you later, eh?'

Outside it was almost dark and the fog was cold enough to glaze the tarmac and coat the black lime twigs in dripping, mould-like fuzz. The tower clock was chiming the quarter as I turned the twisted iron ring of the little oak door under the archway. Cold as it was outside, the interior of the Chapel was colder.

The Chaplain was alone, half lit by the lectern spotlight. He made no acknowledgement of my presence but remained on his stool, elbows on the lectern, his face hidden in sinewy hands between the fingers of which protruded two arms of an ebony crucifix. The black sleeves of his cassock were pulled short by his crooked elbows revealing white, hairless arms with a pulsing blue vein above the left thumb.

God's Adversary, said headvoice.

I hesitated on the topmost step; that was the phrase the good doctor had used on Friday night. I'd been squiffy

116

but I remembered it clearly enough. I suddenly felt under-rehearsed, like someone had moved the set around and changed the script while I was in the wings. He was supposed to be sitting on the chair waiting for me. That's how I'd pictured my entrance. And I was supposed to step boldly in and march straight up to him and . . .

Do something, said headvoice. **Anything. Doesn't matter. Just *something*. Take the initiative. Wrap it up quick, you've got to. Go on, then!**

I descended the steps and stood quietly waiting outside the circle of light. Immediately in front of the lectern was a chair with its back towards the Chaplain. On the floor in front of that, a hassock, I presumed for the confessor's knees.

I waited. Standing still. I had not come to confess.

After what may have been a minute but felt like ten, I said, 'It's about the Confirmation, sir.'

Silence.

I cleared my throat. I said, 'The, er, promises, sir . . . the baptismal vows . . .'

Silence.

Go on, go on, don't stop now, said headvoice.

'Well, sir . . .'

'Yes?'

There had been no movement from the Chaplain. The sudden sound made me flinch. My heart was pounding already. I took a deep breath:

'They're, er, they're very, very serious, aren't they, sir? I mean, a person should not make promises like that . . . um . . . without . . . er . . . without thinking pretty hard . . . sir. Must they, sir?'

Silence.

I shifted my feet. Damn him. To hide his face like that. How could I tell what the man was thinking? I swallowed, deafeningly. 'Well it's just that I have, sir. Been thinking, I mean, pretty hard and . . .'

'Yes?'

'Well, sir . . .'

The Chaplain slowly raised his head. Staring at the blank wall in front of him, he said, softly: 'Yes, boy? Go on.'

'Sorry, sir. I find this really really painful, you know . . .'

Cretin! said headvoice, **You've let him in now**.

The Reverend Shewring turned his cropped head. 'Bishop,' the emerald daggers unsheathed and glittered naked in the spotlight beam, 'before you say anything more, I had better inform you that your father wrote to me personally. Would I be right in assuming your father to be a religious person, Bishop? Yes?'

'Well—' I began, but he cut me off impatiently.

'Your father – quite rightly – is anxious that your baptismal vows be re-affirmed or "ratified", as he puts it, without delay. If I recall correctly, the phrase used was "immediate ratification imperative". And that this should take place in the "official church" in the presence of an "official vicar of Christ". I remember the phrasing; it struck me as being unusual, Bishop.' The Chaplain seemed to ponder the thought a moment before going on: 'Hm . . . Yes, well, your father's letter was quite emphatic, Bishop; he wishes you to be confirmed into the church of Christ Jesus with all possible alacrity. You are how old, Bishop?'

'Sixteen, sir. Last April, sir.'

'Precisely. You are more than a year overdue, Bishop. No one is blaming you – state transfers are frequently unconfirmed even at your age – but shillyshallying is not going to help. Correct? Correct. I am quite sure that, in your heart of hearts, you yearn for the protection of mother church and wish to become a full member in Christ.' He paused again, seeming to stare through me. 'So, if you are about to inform me that you do not feel ready—'

All my rehearsal seemed suddenly useless; abandoning the groundwork, I cut straight to what I felt was the main plank of my argument: 'I can't make those promises, sir. I can't be confirmed. It'd be wrong, sir. I'm a non-believer, sir. I'm an *agnostic*.' There. It was out. I hadn't been struck by lightning. And there was no answer to that, was there.

Silence. The Chaplain's eyes held steady, unblinking, piercing mine.

Was there?

Suddenly that main plank seemed wobbly, unsure. What had gone wrong? It had seemed so straightforward: I didn't *believe*; I could not be confirmed. End of debate. Now suddenly this seemed not enough. Other, more compelling reasons seemed to be required. But what could be more compelling than to declare oneself heathen?

Yet he was still just staring and staring.

Say something, idiot.

'Well . . . I mean . . . I just . . . er, completely, er . . .' I dropped my eyes, feeling physically sick now and ready to lump on anything that might remotely resemble a reason. But I could not think of a solitary thing.

Oh Jeeesus, moaned headvoice, **you really are crap!**

Crap's about right, I thought – why hadn't I done the same as Lawrence, just made something up and confessed, it would all have been over by now – then I thought, hang about, Crap, you said . . . maybe we've got something here. Crap is like dirty . . . dirty, unclean . . . unclean, nasty, bad . . . *evil*! That's it, I'm evil. I looked straight into those hard green eyes and said:

'Well, sir, what I mean is, I'm just too, er, too wicked. Sir.' The eyes seemed to light up. I knew then I'd made a mistake. 'I mean, I'm too . . . er . . . .' My voice trailed off. I felt sick.

You idiot! said headvoice.

The Chaplain continued to stare, then slowly his grim, inquisitor's face began to change, to twitch, the eyes to glitter, the brows to dance, the cheeks to crease like stiff paper that must finally, shockingly rip apart.

A *smile*?

Not a smile, but quite the most hideous *grin* I had ever seen, outside of nightmares, or in.

I was shocked dumb.

The Chaplain's look was scornful now. 'So young and yet so humble,' he said. 'How touching. Too wicked, is it? Well, well, well. In that case there is nothing whatever to worry about. You see . . .' He grinned again hideously, rising from his stool. 'That, young man, is precisely the purpose of Confession. Your part is only to repent. There is one who forgives.' He stood in front of me. God's Adversary. The Angel with Horns. And I was afraid.

He placed cold fingers on either side of my neck, pressing gently almost like a caress. 'No sinner is beyond redemption, Bishop, who calls on the Lord for forgiveness.' The words were a parody; he was toying with me now, mocking me with blatant insincerity. 'Despair not, Bishop, for the Lord is nigh.'

'But, sir . . .'

'Kneel, Bishop.' The fingers tightened slightly, urging me gently downwards.

I suddenly knew that, whatever the logic of my situation, I did not want to do this thing called Confession. And I knew that in some unfathomable sense my professed indifference was a lie; I was frightened beyond reason, in fact I was terrified. 'But I'm not prepared, sir,' I blurted, 'I haven't even read my . . .'

'Hushhh. Trust Him, Bishop. Trust Him.'

My mouth had gone suddenly dry and a wave of weakness was rising up my legs. I more collapsed than knelt, the result was the same.

'But . . .'

'Hush, Bishop.'

'But, sir . . .'

120

'Open your heart.'

In a last-second attempt to change tack, I closed my eyes and tried desperately to think of some token sin to confess; any little misdemeanour, just to get out of the place. But, no matter how hard I tried, nothing came. At last I said, 'It's no good, sir. I can't—'

'Oh,' said the Chaplain, 'but I believe that you can.'

I shook my head dumbly.

His tone changed. 'You see, Bishop, James, isn't it? You see, James, there's something I perhaps should explain to you. The fact is, James, I am possessed of a certain gift, a power, you might say. It is not something that comes from myself, you understand, but from beyond me. Put simply, I both see and read *auras*. Such gifts are not uncommon in my profession, but in my case the power is advanced. Your aura, James, is particularly—'

'Aura, sir? Sorry, I—'

'Which means that I *know* when a person has done wrong, James. Or when that person is *lying*, James, as you are lying now. Did you not wonder how I was immediately able to identify you as the culprit last Sunday?'

'But, sir, I—'

'It was easy. I have never encountered such an aura, such vibrancy, such brilliance . . . it was really quite shocking.'

'But—'

'No more arguments, please. Denial is quite pointless, undignified too. The evidence surrounds you now in a crimson rainbow, James. I see the sin-light shining, James . . . I *see* it rainbow clear no matter how deep inside your soul it tries to hide. Between us we will root it out, boy. *Confess* yourself. It is the only way—'

'But I never did it!' I wailed.

'Did, didn't. Do you imagine we are concerned here simply with *deeds*?' The Chaplain laughed mirthlessly. 'They say you're intelligent, James, I've seen your report

121

– but intelligence isn't enough, James, may even get in the way, in the spiritual realm. Oh yes. You speak a little Latin, I imagine?'

I shook my head. His eyes looked insane.

'*Mens rea*, James. Perhaps you've not heard the phrase, in spite of your intelligence? Well then, permit me to enlighten you, James: *Mens* – mind, *rea* – deeds. In law, it's the action that counts – "the thoughts of a man are not triable", as the saying goes, "for even the devil may not know them." But this is no temporal court, James, this is Almighty God's mansion, and I am his minister. Here it is *precisely* a man's intentions that count. Nothing else. Not actions. Not consequences. Nothing but the heart's intent, James Bishop, the *will*. Do you read me, boy . . . ? Well, do you?'

'Sir.'

The Chaplain spoke fast, his eyes widening until there was white all around the green pupils. 'What though the devil knows not the evil that dwells in your heart? *You* know it, James. Deny it at your peril.' I felt myself sway and looked down at my feet, but the Chaplain drove on: 'For when a mind is divided against itself, James, it cracks, and through that small fissure the Worm wriggles in. You understand me? The *Worm*, James. I'm talking about *insanity*, lad; you know something of that, I believe?' I looked up with a start, but the Chaplain's eyes were now tight shut, the lids fluttering like those of a person dreaming. 'I'm talking about real madness, the splitting of the mind which is hell on earth. Hell is madness, James, madness *is* hell. Yet . . . there is hope, James, oh yes there is hope, because there is One who forgives.' The fingers released my neck. The Chaplain was back at the lectern, half kneeling. I glimpsed hands held vertically in prayer. 'We are ready to hear you, now, boy. The evil is in your heart, James Bishop, and in your mind. You are engulfed in its unholy light. I command you, now . . .

'CONFESS!'

122

The great weakness flooded my whole body, my heart thundered and my guts began writhing as if I had swallowed a bucket of cold worms. Suddenly the terrible urge came on me that I must shout and scream filth and obscenities at this manGod. I bit my lips hard together. Almost at once came a different urge – even more compelling than the first – I felt as if I had to break wind, one end or the other, didn't matter which, but immediately, or my belly would explode. I belched. Saliva or sick ran hot down my chin. What came next seemed nothing to do with me, not my voicebox, not my will, not any part of me. As if it were speaking under water, but clearly and without a hint of duckishness, I heard a young girl's voice speak loud and clear – not from out of my mouth but from somewhere lower down – it said:

'James Bishop is the one who murdered his own baby sister.'

The Chaplain's face snapped towards me. 'What was that?'

Jesus Christ! said headvoice, **he heard that!**

Too late, I clamped a hand over my black-jacket pocket. 'Shut it!' I shouted before I could stop myself.

The Chaplain's eyes filled with fury. 'How dare you!' he hissed. I stumbled upright. The Ghost said nothing more, but the Chaplain sprang to his feet and snarled: 'Get out, Bishop! Get *out*! Go to your dormitory, and pray, boy. Pray! Pray for your miserable, ignorant soul. Go on, get out! Get out!

'*Get out!*'

He was still shouting as I blundered to the door.

Inside me I am a child again, the Chapel seems no longer this chapel but my father's church-in-a-caravan. I'm in such trouble as I do not deserve. I must go some place where I can be in control. Maybe for good this time. And they'd better not laugh, and they'd better not try to stop me.

★ ★ ★

Outside, the fog had gone and the stars were out. As I cleared the archway, there she stood – the floodlit Cathedral, my pantomime castle, so much larger than life. I began to trot.

The Castle

TRANSFORMATION SCENE:
UNIFORM OFF — JACKET, COLLAR, SHIRT, PINSTRIPES, BROGUES — SPIDERSUIT (OTHERWISE TRACKSUIT) AND TRAINERS ON.
KEY, GHOST, MONEY AND HALF A CUT LOAF IN THE POUCH-POCKET.
CHECK WATCH. 17.15? CAN'T BE! ABANDON WATCH.
WAIT A SEC FOR DUSK TO THICKEN — TICK, TICK, TICK — THAT'LL DO.
QUIET BELOW?
OK.
GO.
WINDOW UP BOTH FEET ON THE GLAZING BEAD FINGERS SPLAYED TO SPREAD THE LOAD CRACKED A PANE WITH YOUR KNEE CLUMSY TRY AGAIN GOOD JUMP RUN THE DEAN'S FOG-FILLED GARDEN CRACKED YOUR SHIN NOW WHAT THE FUCK A TRIKE STEADY COMPOST HEAP GARDEN SHED THE OLD FLINT WALL CITY WALL SOON BE WITHOUT IT CONCENTRATE READY HOW HIGH DON'T KNOW JUMP THEN WATCH THOSE KNEES TOO LATE BIT YOUR TONGUE RUN RABBIT RUN.

10

The back streets were dark, streetlights going by the clock not by the fog settling again like a soiled shroud over the city. The lifeless houses overlapped each other and me in the sodden alleys making me think of fungus around a rotting branch, but the darkness was welcome. I walked fast, in a hurry now knowing I'd shopping to do and knowing the crypt would be cleared and locked at 6.00 ready for Compline at 6.30. I scurried towards the offy on Stour Street, doubts crowding in like the houses:

Had CJ really heard the voice? I wasn't so sure now.

Does it matter? said headvoice.

Does it matter!? Of course it matters. If he didn't, it means . . . Wait a minute . . .

The realisation had struck me that here I was marching through the back streets talking to myself like it was a real conversation; I even had the impression that my lips had been moving though I was pretty certain no sound had emerged.

First sign of madness, jeered headvoice.

It wasn't you was it, you bastard? *Was* it?

No answer. I didn't need an answer. The voice I heard in the Chapel had been quite different from headvoice. It wasn't a voiced thought at all – I would have known if it was, I'd lived with them most of my life, hadn't I? (I touched the bulge in my tracksuit pouch pocket.) That voice had come from outside of me, no question, like the duck voice but louder, and slowed down so I could hear every word . . . shit! Hadn't I thought that I'd heard the word 'murder' or 'murdered' before, during the night when I couldn't sleep . . . ? So, could it have been some sort of audio-illusion then? Hardly. Not with the Chaplain hearing it too. If he did hear it! Unless it *was* the Chaplain! Throwing his voice. Stupid! It was a *girl*'s voice. That's it then: if *he* heard it; and *I* heard it; and it wasn't an illusion . . .

It was *real*.

Jesus! That's a bad thought, you know!

Don't get hysterical. It was a voice, OK? Call it an audio-illusion, call it a tapioca pudding if it helps. Look, if you *want* to cancel the whole operation, go back for another session with CJ, make sure he heard like . . . don't mind me, mate . . . I said—

Piss off!

Fairplay, but I think that's what we're doing, mate.

I switched off. There are times when these internal squabbles drag me down till all I want to do is get rotten and go to sleep. OK, I needed to sort things out, but why does it have to get so brutish and insensitive like some kind of ill-mannered animal in there? If I were to hit a real bad do with headvoice inside the Cathedral, it would take more than one slug of the old 'attitude adjuster' to see me through. I'm not an alki, far from it, it's simply a case of correcting the slight chemical imbalance that can happen to anyone. It's all chemical – everything is – no question; Ma's pills prove that. I'd find the answer eventually, and when I did, it would not depend on any Ouija boards or bogeypersons. The other voice had to have come from me, somehow, it *must* have, and the writing must have too. No other possibility existed. And if I had to spend a few nights alone in the Cathedral to prove that to myself, to *regain control* as it were, so be it. Not to let 'em spook you, that's the secret of life. Once you start looking over your shoulder – or not daring to walk through a certain wood or graveyard or under a ladder or whatever – you're on the way to somewhere nasty. Not me, pal. Self-sufficiency has always been my watchword.

I had six pounds forty left from the twenty Lawrence made on the last Bible deal (it was against my principles to accept money from thieving but he said it was a present so that made it OK). I would pick up a half bottle of Vat 69 at Mr Ali's, and a pack of Full Strength if the dosh stretched, then I'd head for the Shell and no looking back.

I felt pretty positive, like a jogger, I imagine, despite the flat feet. I began to jog.

11

I returned to the precincts via Christchurch Gate, knowing the great oak doors are not locked until 9.30 at night. Once inside, it only remained to get past the security man. Not looking at the wooden hut but horribly aware of it, I made straight for the noticeboard on the wall of the tourist office where the programme of services for November was displayed. I pretended to study this though the only light was that reflecting back from the Cathedral and this was barely enough to read by.

I found I was holding my breath while fighting a terrible urge to sprint straight for the sanctuary. But no challenge came. After what seemed to me a sufficient interval, I turned and wandered slowly across the empty forecourt towards the south porch, gazing all about me like I imagined a real tourist might. Underfoot felt slippery despite my trainers and I knew I'd been right to reject the ladder route. In any case, I had no rope.

As I approached the entrance I could see straight through the dark porch into the well-lit interior of the Cathedral. No one seemed to be guarding the entrance itself. Still, I made myself walk slowly.

For the first time I noticed that the outer iron gates – heavy black bars, huge slab of a lock – fitted the pointed archway perfectly. I tried to imagine the size of key needed for that lock; it wasn't at all like the one in my pouch. With a little thrill, I thought of the black-skirted figure locking up the castle gate later tonight. Floodlights off. Me inside; in charge of everything. *My* space. Me in *control*.

The gates were wide open now, as were the heavy oak doors within. Nevertheless I paused to inspect the floodlit saints and bishops in their fancy niches on either side of the entrance. (The man in the hut could still be watching, I thought, I must take no chances, not when I'm so close to home.) Although I was only pretending, I could not help but notice the eaten-away faces and the two vacant pedestals above the porch, and the thought came that if I was wrong and there was a God after all, how He (or She, sorry) must be laughing at these feeble attempts at permanence. The moss and rust get everywhere. Even God's place. However well built, sooner or later the set comes down. There's got to be a lesson there somewhere.

Cut the cod philosophy, Bishop. Get on with the fucking story.

I tutted and passed through the porch. Inside felt very warm. A thin woman sitting on a chair beside the leaflet rack said officiously, 'Excuse me. Services only. The Cathedral is closed for tourists. It opens again at nine in the morning.'

'I'm going to Evensong,' I said.

She looked me up and down. With the voice of scorn, she said, 'Evensong's finished. Tomorrow morning. Nine o'clock.'

'Sorry,' I stammered, 'I – I didn't mean Evensong, I meant . . .' I struggled to remember what the notice had said, wishing now I'd paid proper attention; there was another sort of service at 6.30 p.m., I was sure I'd read that. What did they call it? Sod the woman. This was supposed to be God's house, wasn't it? and you can't get in unless you know the password! What the hell was that word? Complex? Something like that. Wait a sec, got it! I smiled my most disarming, self-effacing smile, 'Sorry, I meant Compline, of course. The Chapel of Our Lady, I believe.' That's better; the more jargon the better for this bat, I thought. Still smiling, I said, 'The Dean is preaching tonight, is he not? I couldn't bear to miss that. Wonderful preacher the Dean. Perhaps you could tell me which chapel it is in? I'm not certain whether it is Our Lady Martyrdom or Our Lady of the Undercroft.'

As her crabby old eyes launched their poisoned darts, I turned towards the great nave and choirscreen dappled by spotlights in the distance. Without waiting for an answer, I walked away up the south aisle. A few squeaky paces later, I heard her say, somewhat ungraciously, I thought, 'Neither. It's in the Quire.'

When I arrived at the steps leading down to the crypt, two vergers were standing shoulder to shoulder by the iron gate at the top. There was only a handful of tourists left in the great echoing building and one of the vergers – a pretty young man with shoulder-length blond hair – began staring, so I pretended to scrutinise a tapestry in a glazed frame on the wall.

It was a gruesome scene showing a little family much like my own – mother, father, brother and sister – I feel certain it was the boy's sister though both have long, straight hair and she is too young for breasts – kneeling all together and up to their waists inside a cow or bull, its back open like a big cooking pot and a roaring fire beneath its belly. Squatting by the fire with a pair of bellows is a man in red tights and a pudding-basin haircut. Beside him, helping, is a Fool in cap and bells. A sort of playing-card king stands by. On his head is a crown topped by a snake-like dragon with wings. The king holds a sword. He too wears red tights, and ermine of course. Behind the king comes another Fool in a Punch cap waving a rod. Over the whole scene hangs a white pigeon or dove and a brace of angels.

I wasn't pretending interest any more, I had to find out

135

what was going on there in the name of the Prince of Peace. It looked like a clip from a medieval horror vid to me. Also the girl's face disturbed me; in a way it was like a small adult's, round and serious and pleading. With a start, I realised I was looking at an older version of our Cymbeline. At the same instant I felt a dreadful itching at the base of my spine. I glanced towards the vergers, they were no longer staring so I had a good scratch and turned back to the picture.

From somewhere above me the organ pipes delivered an avalanche of shivering chords. I switched my attention to the tapestry's caption neatly typed on card and hung in a small frame below: 'The Legend of St Eustace 120 AD – from a wall painting in the English tradition,' it read. Underneath the caption, more typed notes explained: 'St Eustace has become the victorious general of the Emperor Adrian who orders a great sacrifice to the gods to honour his victories. Eustace and his family refuse to offer incense. We see them being roasted to death in a brazen bull while the Emperor looks on, sword in hand. At the top of the painting two angels hold a sheet containing the four souls. The Spirit of God in the form of a dove descends to receive them into heaven.'

I was pleased about the Spirit of God coming down as a beautiful dove making everything all right in the end so to speak. I could see by his face that the Saint was in raptures, but couldn't help wondering how the other three members of the family felt and whether or not they received sainthoods too, posthumously as they say. In the midst of these thoughts, I smelt it.

At first I thought someone must be standing behind me eating a pork sandwich or a burger or something, but when I looked round there was no one, except for the vergers still nattering together, their backs to me now. But the smell was undeniable – powerful and sickly, like roast pork but not quite – beginning to burn now. What

136

turned me round though was the sizzling. Sharp and sudden, like someone behind me had just spat in the chip pan.

I knew what I would see before I saw it. But the sight still sent my head reeling. The girl in the tapestry was *moving*. Only her. Nothing else. Not the king, not the Fools, not any other figure, not even the flames, just her. Just her mouth, to be exact. Her mouth was opening and closing, a tiny black hole winking away in the middle of her sad, white face. I knew with dreadful certainty that she was screaming though I could hear no sound above the sound of the organ.

I somehow forced myself to take two steps closer to the picture. I bent towards the two-inch tall image of the naked girl. As I did so her eyes left off looking up to heaven and swung down towards *me*. At the same time her left arm then her right rose from the cauldron and settled on the rim; her whole body was moving now – writhing rather – yet her purpose was unmistakable: *she was trying to climb out*. But she kept slipping back because . . . (I stepped closer still, leaned forward, oh Jesus Christ Almighty, NO!) because she had no hands, because her arms finished at the wrist!

With my face less than a foot from the glass another sense came into play. Dreading the answer but somehow compelled to learn the worst, I reached out a trembling finger and touched the glass. Hot!

Hand on my shoulder. 'Don't touch, please.'

I gasped and spun round. It was the girlish-looking verger with the long hair and wispy beard. 'Sorry,' I mumbled.

His eyes narrowed. The organ stopped abruptly leaving a ringing silence. 'Are you all right?'

'Yes,' I said quickly. Too quickly. 'Yes, thank you.'

'The Cathedral is closed now. I'm afraid I must ask you to—'

'I'm attending Compline, sir,' I said.

The dark eyes stared a moment. 'All right, another,' he looked at his watch, 'twenty-five minutes, then you'd better start finding your seat.' He smiled with his lips, then turned and followed the other black figure now making towards the tall gates which shut off the nave. A bunch of big keys swung from a chain in his hand. I noticed his feet made almost no sound on the flagstones.

Last chance, I thought. Shit or bust. After throwing one fearful glance at the tapestry, I sprinted on tiptoe to the top of the Crypt steps, and started down.

12

I *will not* let this thing rattle me. There is an explanation for *everything*. Soon will be time for solving puzzles. Meanwhile, meanwhile I focus all my brainpower on the Matter:

What feet wore away these steps? Who polished out the two deep troughs on every tread? Monks? Pilgrims? Tourists? *Refuge seekers?* It's an interesting question, but it's the *wrong* question. The right question is not Who or What, but How and Why?

Empirical fact: *Nobody goes down the middle* – they never have. I observed that detail from the first step. Some folk would still have been shitting themselves, not me; I focus on what matters; I focus on the clues to what's really going on, under the surface, in the margins. There's no room for panic then. That's what I mean by control.

These steps are a thousand years old; the habit must be the same age near enough. Some *habit*!

Things have happened here; I feel them; by and by they'll come through. Already I know that a king of England came down here once to be whipped by monks. Which side did he tread? It wasn't the middle; there is a hump in the middle which nobody treads on; unless he was another like me – off the beaten track.

So I go down the middle, flipping my Dunlops to the centre to make sure I hit the crown of each hump – counting crowns. Kicking the habit, you might say. That's control too.

We're doing OK. And this is only the ante-room. Wait
till we get to the refuge proper. Wait till we get to the
Shell; then we'll see who's pulling the strings.

As for the thing we'd just witnessed up there . . .

Chemistry, said headvoice, **I remember, you said—**

Imbalance, that's it; illusion, brought on by electro-
chemical changes, brought on by stress, fatigue, false
accusation . . . And this place, of course, this *Matter* . . .
Let's face it, there's too many—

Candles?

Aye, candles. And crosses—

Too many Saints—

Too many altars—

Tombs—

Banners—

Mambas—

Ah, definitely! Too many creeping Mambas, you're right
there, old son.

Be all right when we get to the space.

The Shell, you mean. Oh aye. Be all right then.
Meanwhile . . .

A little adjustment?

That's it. You got it.

I sat on the bottom step – step number twenty-three –
withdrew my new half of Vat 69, unscrewed, swigged
twice, huffed and peered out beneath the stooping boughs
of stone and away beyond half-hidden altars where candles
flutter (though I feel no draught) into the gloomy caverns
beyond. To me the crypt had always felt like the rest of
the Cathedral but a hundred times stronger. The crypt
was emphatically *not* where I wanted to loiter.

Shadowland, I murmured.

**So it's dark. So what? I mean, what do you expect in
a crypt? This is the old part – no windows. Come on,
let's go. We don't want another 'imbalance', eh, mate?**

I was about to stand but stopped. Just a mo; who else
is down here?

Pause for listening. **I hear no one**. Standing up. Peering round corner to left. To right. **I see no one**.

Hang about then. I re-seated myself on the step.

Someone could have seen me come down. If I don't reappear . . . I need cover of some sort – a few tourists, a few worshippers, anything to get lost in.

That was what I told myself, but, as I waited on the step for my 'cover', the candlelight touched a memory. And other odours of the crypt – paraffin-wax, something tangy that might have been incense or something less holy, damp earth – these potencies took me back to a dark country lane. Smell of fungus. Pine needles. Black tree-trunks, tightly packed. Flickering between them as I walked the invisible track, light from a distant window. He'd tried to warn me about something, the doctor. What was it? If only I hadn't drunk all that whisky . . .

Leave it, mate. It'll come back. Soon as you stop—

Look. It's important, for Christ's sake!

I know it's important. But we've been sat here five minutes at least. What's the time?

I raised my watchless wrist. Shit! Haven't a clue, I said.

Half past, nearly, I bet. They'll be clearing out any second. There ain't going to be no more tourists tonight so—

Sssh. Hark. Oh yea? What's that then?

Sure enough, descending footsteps. A whole bunch, by the sound. Let's go, I muttered. I stowed the bottle quickly in my pouch, stood, and stepped out on to the soft-lit flagstones.

13

Moving out among the pools of light and shadow, I became aware of a presence. Behind me, to the left of where the steps come down, is a collection of Cathedral treasures behind thick armoured glass. I turned. Standing perfectly still in front of this was a dark, frocked figure. Behind it, the neon-lit displays formed a wall of light cleverly shaded so as not to project its rays more than a foot or two into the holy gloom. Against this confined brightness, the verger appeared as a black silhouette, faceless, motionless, unnerving.

I bobbed my head, smiled politely and approached the first display case.

I knew the man would not recognise my tracksuit as it bore no badge and was grey rather than the regulation navy with white piping. To be doubly safe, I thought up a sensible question about two silver maces I was pretending to look at. I could hear that the party behind me had almost reached the bottom of the steps. I moved slowly along the display, nodding again to the verger whose unsmiling profile I could now see. He was standing to attention like a palace guard. He ignored me. I drifted slowly away into the gloom, inspecting the carved capitals on the pillars as I went.

Manoeuvring a massive double pillar between me and the verger, I nipped through the Chapel of Our Lady, past an altar bearing a blue and gold virgin and child with

143

blue glass nightlight hanging above; past a white-faced woman kneel-sitting, head lowered, eyes closed; past a second pair of double pillars and so into the dim circle of the Eastern crypt.

It was empty, apart from a bank of chairs stacked three or four high, three or four deep. Masked from the praying woman by the second double pillar, I crawled into this thicket of wooden legs and rush seating and balled up to wait for lights out. Which was when it hit me.

No torch. Again!

I hadn't given a thought to the question of darkness and light. I could easily have borrowed someone's cycle lamp en route. It was a bad mistake. How long, I wondered, would it take me to find the tiny access door in the dark, by *feel* alone! In my memory it lay some distance to the left of the Eastern altar. I peered between the tangle of legs, trying to get a fix in my head for the darkness to come, but could not see the tiny oak door. I thought of the other times, the Bible raids, when Lawrence had been here to watch my back and me his. It was different on my own. In my mind it had seemed such a small thing, this passing through; I'd thought of the Crypt as no more than an anteroom or entrance hall to be crossed and forgotten. Now it seemed more like a test of some sort.

Suddenly my brain played a bad trick and brought up a memory – the memory of Confession and the Voice. (That's what I mean about the crypt being too strong, too full of bad habits, dodgy Matter.) For a moment my control just went; I forgot about the logic, why I was here, my scientific education; I wanted to quit, to up and run, anywhere, even home, so long as it was away from this place. The chair legs seemed a trap. I felt hunted, confined. My legs and arms began to thrash. Then I heard the voices. And the soft laughter!

I stopped moving, stopped breathing.

A girl's voice – Jesus! – but . . .

With an accent? A French accent?!

The tourists – they'd reached the Eastern Crypt. With a peculiar thrill I realised how their presence committed me to my course. What excuse could possibly permit me to appear smiling from beneath a pile of chairs? Besides which my refuge was so close now; beyond the door lay the Shell. I could clearly foresee the course of the next few minutes: the group would stand attentively while the guide did his spiel. Then there would be questions. Then more questions. Within five minutes a verger would come to marshal them away. The lights would go out. Those solid, black doors would close, their locks would be locked, their bolts slammed home. And I would be inside. In the dark. There would be no way out and the game would be on.

Problem: my lungs were already working too hard for a person lying still. Control is vital, I told myself. Ignore the Matter, concentrate on the clues.

The voices were clearer now. Peeping through the chair legs, I could see stockings and turnups and boots with little red heels, the leather scuffed and showing white plastic. An older man's voice, very pompous, was telling how the Cathedral had been completely closed and quarantined for a whole year after the murder.

We know why that was, said headvoice, **they thought it was polluted by the blood**.

Correct.

A woman's voice inquired, 'Why quarantine the Cathedral? I thought he was a saint.'

The guide didn't seem to hear the question. He spoke instead about the body being buried down here for a while, close to the Chapel of Our Lady, before being displayed in splendour in the Trinity Chapel upstairs where pilgrims by the thousand could come and see the wonderful gilded shrine, and the sick could be made whole just by pressing themselves into the special alcoves close to the body inside, and the monks could sell them all little bottles of dilute blood (which, by then, had become sacred again, one assumes) called *ampullae*.

Meanwhile, back in the South-East Transept, said headvoice, **right after the murder, before all that happened, the monks just mopped up that *bad* blood and stuck the corpse down here in the dark without even a proper funeral.**

Apart from the slice of skull the murderers chopped off. That was a holy relic. They put that in the Corona upstairs.

Not till the year was up, mate. Not till after the quarantine. Oh no.

Weird. I mean, how come *that* blood was supposed to be evil or malicious or whatever when the other blood – Jesus's blood – is supposed to *save* everyone, especially when taken by mouth once a week?

Exactly, mate. It doesn't add up. And why is the Virgin banished down here, eh? Why isn't she allowed up there with the others? Ask yourself that?

Unless . . . unless she was considered a bit dodgy too. Mark you, she was a *woman*. You can't help wondering, I mean, can you? About the blood, I mean. I felt a touch guilty thinking these things; it is just these sorts of questions that have lead to the rift between Pa and me, but I couldn't afford to stop now, it's all part of control. Lawrence told me he had read somewhere that menstrual blood was real bad medicine in the old days. You could blight a piece of land just by getting a girl with no knickers to run round it a few times when she was having her first period. Especially anticlockwise. Especially during a lunar eclipse. Especially if she was a virgin. (He said he was going to get Lucy to have a quick buzz round CJ's garden, on the off chance. But then he remembered she no longer qualified. He's a bugger, old Shag.) He says his granny

146

called her period the curse. Ma calls it the flux, but I think that's because she's mental, I mean as far as I know flux is for soldering stuff. The lads call it jam. I reckon that's more like it – cuts it down to size. Anyway, you can't help wondering, if there's a connection, I mean. With the blood, like.

Just then one of the French girls tried another question, but the big clock started donging the quarter from somewhere a long way off. On the second stroke, the verger appeared as predicted and whisked them all away. I honestly think some of those vergers are androids.

A moment later it went black. There were two big thumps followed by the rattle of iron keys.

14

An eye of blue-green light appeared, enmeshed like a glow-worm in a bramble bush. For a second this shook me badly, then, with a rush of relief, I realised that the bush was the finely carved latticework of the Virgin's altar screen, the glow-worm the everlasting flame in its blue dish. I weaved my way out through the thicket of chair legs, straightened my aching back and stretched my cramped limbs.

Out of the blackness a new crypt was developing around me, slowly – blue chairs, blue pillars, blue railings, blue tombs bearing blue stone saints, blue bishops, blue kings, all ghostlike under a forest of blue arches. I stole forwards, on tiptoe, rounded a pillar set half into the wall to the left of the altar, and there it was, dappled in faint blue light, a tiny oak door. My door.

I groped in my pouch for the key, and, with pounding heart, inserted it in the lock. The key had been used only once before in this door. On that occasion it had jammed badly and had to be forced round with great risk of breaking it – it being made of brass and not particularly strong. Since then, Lawrence had been to work on it. To my huge relief, it turned smoothly.

As I closed the door and locked it behind me, the darkness was absolute. The old feeling – the feeling of occupying *non-existence* – came on me as it always did but much amplified by the absence of Lawrence. For no obvious reason, my brain flashed up a picture of the keeper's gibbet I'd once stumbled on in a dark wood as a kid – eight frozen moles on a wire. I had touched their cold bodies. Fascinated. Velvet soft outside, frozen hard centres. They felt wrong. Deserted, somehow betrayed. Like this tight little spiral stairway. Empty. Patiently waiting . . .

I stood a moment, breath held, listening to the Cathedral, hearing far above me the wind and something rattling, something flapping in the attics, and the shushing of blood. I knew it was *my* blood but . . .

Don't be silly.

This tube I'm in . . .

What about it?

Bit like an artery, don't you think?

You know what I think? I think it's fucking cold. I think you were pretty stupid not to have dressed for the cold. I think you'd better stop thinking twerpish thoughts and *do* something about the sodding cold!

I was suddenly, shockingly aware that up to this point it had all been a bit of a game, that what Retreat meant to me was less a place to be alone in with my thoughts than somewhere free and new like an uninhabited island or forbidden planet or even the Garden of E; a place without rules, if you like, a place without programmes, timetables, laws. There was no pre-determined life schedule here, no one in charge – no Pa, no teachers, no habits, only the basic needs, like warmth, like sleep, like food. I wasn't hungry yet, but it wouldn't be long. I knew how to hunt, though. I patted the half loaf in my pouch. I'd brought the bait.

Odd how these last thoughts bucked me up. I suddenly felt alive, excited. Ready for action.

Come on then, said headvoice. **Let's go.**

Stretching out my hands, I felt smoothly curving stone in both directions. It was true, the Spidersuit and Y-fronts were inadequate; in a way I was worse off than a runaway in Cardboard City – I had no cardboard, not even an old paper to wrap myself in. How was I supposed to sleep up there? Hold on, I thought, the Bibles!

I knew roughly where the Bible store was – the question now was, Could I find that chamber without Lawrence? And in the dark? These were not attics like houses have, these were half the size of Blean Woods plus a warren of spirals and passages and access tunnels for those ancient masons to crawl up and down with their timber and limestone and buckets of mortar. Worse, the money had only just stretched to whisky and fags – not matches – so all I had for light was half a dozen green ones in a box I'd picked up at Georgy Porgy's.

For a shameful moment I considered going back and relieving the blue lady of her night-light, but I'm not a thief like Lawrence. I'm not superstitious either, but she had been my guide in a way. No point in asking for trouble, I thought. I wasn't afraid of the dark, after all.

Off cocks, on socks, said headvoice, copying Lawrence. Without further urging, I shot off up those cold stone steps on all fours like a rat up a rhododendron, as Lawrence would certainly have said.

But for my experience during the course of what Lawrence called our 'missionary period', I would certainly have been lost in this quarter. However, we had used this route for the last Bible raid, so I knew if I could remember the exit off the spiral – in the dark, which was different – I would come out on the Shelf. And the Bible Room would be close.

Even so, I seemed to have climbed a long way, and was beginning to think I'd missed the exit when my right hand went through into space. I stooped to peer along a low, narrow burrow. At the far end I could make out a dimly lit umbrella of stone ribs and plaster panels. Against this

151

ashy light, three of the pink-marble pillars which border the outer edge of the Shelf stood like young cherry trunks; I scrambled along the tunnel towards them.

The Shelf is a metre-wide ledge that runs above the quire aisle from the organ loft below the tower, to the high altar at the pointed end. The Shelf is right up where the roof meets the walls; there is no parapet and it's *high*. There's a story about a Master Builder falling off and what was left of him having to be carted back to France on a camp-bed, which was the best they could do for a stretcher in those days. Having seen it from here, I'd say he was lucky.

I emerged from the tunnel on hands and knees and turned left along the Shelf. The dust was so thick, after a couple of metres I rose cautiously to my feet. Before, when I'd been with Lawrence, we were in too much of a hurry to wonder about such things. Now I had time to think about the dust; why was there so much of it? What could it be made of? There was no doubt in my mind that here was more Matter, more evidence. Matter does not *have* to be organic in order to act on the thought processes; however, I had a strong suspicion that the bulk of the dust was in fact detritus from the once living – scurf, dandruff, that kind of thing – much like the stuff the invisible creatures live off between sheet and mattress. Organic Matter is normally the more potent.

Through a row of leaded windows behind me came the tangerine glow of the floodlights which nightly turn this Cathedral into a setting fit for monsters and princesses. I heard footsteps. Not daring to look, I squatted quickly, listening. This location was only borderline Shell, I felt tense, I still needed to watch things.

From far below came the glassy sound of people walking and whispering as if we might all be inside a tiled sewer. Dead on cue, a stream of piping notes crossed the vault from the opposite Shelf where the pipes of the organ are stacked. In my mind, I pictured the worshippers entering their dark oak pews, lit softly by the candles and red-shaded wall-lamps. I thought: Almost 6.30, then. Compline time. The audience assembles. The performance is about to begin.

Last whispers. Clearing of throats. Rustle of programmes.

The urge to blaspheme and yell filth into the hush arrived as expected but faintly and easily controllable. I put its weakness down to the distance and the fact that, up here, I was not confronted by the sea of awestruck faces.

The piping stopped. The people coughed as they stood; strange clashing echo. I was doubly committed now. Alien, outside the circle. If I were to be discovered, I could be a firebug for all they would know. What hope would there be of explaining?

A falsetto voice rose among the tiers of diminishing arches: '*O Lord open thou our lips.*'

All over my body the hair stood up, but, for some reason, I did not join the choir's response. To my cliff top, the words came scrambled by echoes; the sound was weird; hollow, machine-like voices; not so much holy – *unearthly*. I felt I was detaching from the system, floating free like a space walker with a broken tether.

Good, said headvoice, **that's why we came**.

I sat down in the inch-thick dust of the Shelf, leant back on the wall and wondered if the cleaning lady had done along here even once during the past eight hundred years.

Probably scared of falling off, said headvoice.

I tried for a holier thought. None came.

What the fuck. Get comfy. You can't move till chucking out time now.

I closed my eyes for a clue review.

★ ★ ★

The Shell is not designed for people. It isn't *designed* at all; like a cave in a mountain, it *happened*. You can imagine the world's greatest architect, just able to cope with the exterior construction of the noble edifice, and the stylisation of the interior, and all the time working at full stretch to the glory of God, or himself, or whatever. But the spaces in between – what I call the Shell – being too much of a problem, and not to be seen by anyone important, are left to chance and the rat-arsed brickies to sort.

To me it looks like it was created by giant spiders tripping on acid. There are networks of planks and walkways over pointed pits which are negatives of the roof below, iron-rung ladders thick with dust and rust and worm-eaten wooden ones and struts and poles and huge beams criss-crossing, and black holes and tunnels that just happened to form from the spaces between the pillars and walls and arches around them.

At the same time there is a kind of *alien-intelligence* feel about it. A mole (yes, one of those little buggers again) might feel this way if it came up inside, for example, an abandoned combine-harvester one moonless night. Doubtless it would start searching for meaning – mole-meaning, naturally – when all the time there was none. Every now and then, of course, Ms Mole would just happen to enter an oil duct or hydraulic pipe or something vaguely mole feeling and think, Yeehaw! Fucking cracked it! Riddle of mole Universe solved! Make way for the Theory of Everything! But really it's only another little attack of hope, as the mad Irishman said. The tough part is, the thing did have meaning, once, but that meaning wasn't *mole* meaning, it wasn't even human meaning if you look at it from an Abbo point of view, it was machine meaning, and that's like a different universe. Apart from which the thing is knackered. And when the machine stops, the only meaning left is – daa d'daa daaa – the Crusher. Wait till Ms Mole meets the Crusher (yuk, yuk, yuk), then we'll

154

see who's cracked what. Or who.

This, of course, was all far too in-tel-lec-tual for the oik in my head who could think of no more intelligent contribution to the philosophical debate than:

Bollocks!

Which coarse interruption, needless to say, I ignored.

The vergers (Lawrence calls them Mambas, they being black and legless like the wee snakes of the same name) occasionally pass through the Shell, but only on limited, 'human' routes – ladders, catwalks and so on. The rest is prime jungle, in the same way the space between motor-ways, under flyovers, inside big engines, boilers et cetera is jungle. It's not so much anti-human as non-human. That means it is habit free, of course. Habit-free locations are getting rarer all the time. Habit is the wrong word, of course. We just call things 'habits' so we can give them a tick and forget them. I won't forget them. Because I know what they *really* are. There's no word for it, naturally, because most people don't know it exists. I call it Matter – short for, Matter Over Mind. It's not supernatural; science will sort it out, eventually. But for now – just for the time being – it's dodgy. Like those steps in the crypt, you have to watch it. Take the runner bean.

People ask, Why do runner beans all – I mean, *all* – climb the same way up the pole, that is, anticlockwise. And why does the bathwater always turn clockwise down the plughole? Always, always, at least in this hemisphere. The know-it-alls say it's to do with the earth's spin. OK. But I can't feel it. I'm not aware that any of my habits are 'earth-spin' habits. They might be. But I'm not *aware* of it if they are. And take the little kids.

Ask any bunch of kids to come into a room and run about any way they want (the old Drama teacher at Lizzy's showed us this), they all end up going round in a circle. And that circle will always be turning the same way – *always* – and that's anticlockwise, or, as someone said,

155

Hearts to the centre. Some folks are hooked on 'mystery' – Lawrence is one of them. I've heard people say that it's all to do with our ancient ancestors, and pagan ritual, and 'winding up' spells and all that. They've even got names for the different directions, like Dersil is what they call the same direction as the Sun – that's supposed to make 'good' magic – and the other way is called Widdershins which is for 'bad' magic. Which is a load of metaphysical crapola, of course. Because what it really is is the old Matter again.

Anyway, enough of all that; the Shell is practically Matter-free. For that and other reasons, it suits me a whole lot better than the purpose-built right now.

Apart from the cold, I'm well equipped with the old Vat 69 – half-bottle, hip shape – twenty Capstan Full Strength and two twenties of Aspro for the lung-attacks. I'll soon be among the Bibles and everything will be rosy.

Lawrence told me the Bibles were bribes from guilt-struck muppies (medieval upwardly-mobile persons) trying to lubricate the hinges of the pearly gates for themselves when they should have been giving to the poor, ie penniless students and UB40s. So that meant the poor, ie him and me, were more or less duty bound to return these books to the public sector via his friend, the proprietor of the second-hand and antiques emporium known universally as Dirty Dick.

It seemed right to me that the residue now serve as my crib for the night. What more noble cause than Shelter for the homeless? Lawrence would applaud that – not that he gives a shit.

Something changed below. Peeping, I saw a man draped in purple and red following a Mamba holding a black mace with silver knob vertically in front of his face. They walked in step, eyes dead ahead.

At the big gold eagle, the Mamba peeled off and the man in purple opened the book. His words rang up through this stone chamber and I felt a lump in my throat and the goose bumps on my neck. Far below to my right, the green-draped altar on its square of red carpet, lit from somewhere up here. By chance the light-beam sliced through another glass dish – this time red – daubing the three-clawed feet of the cross in red light.

I thought how Pa would love this place with its banners and candles and crosses and statues of saints and soldiers. But the red light seemed a warning. I pulled back from the edge. It was a degree or two warmer here but I was still very cold so hugged my knees and closed my eyes and prepared to wait out the rest of the service, reviewing clues and generally keeping control.

15

I was only little when the misunderstanding happened. Auntie said I was too young to be under a shrink. Pa must have been desperate, but that is where he took me.

I don't remember much myself; I'm not one of those people who can recount every detail from the age of two – in fact I hardly remember anything much before I was six or seven years old. A lot of my early memories come from my Auntie. My first visit to the clinic is an example. Auntie came along in place of my mother who was not well at the time.

According to Auntie, Doctor Keylock was and, as far as I know, still is, consultant psychiatrist for the day unit of the child guidance clinic in Thannington. He was also the doctor who saw to Ma after her little spell inside, so he's kind of the family consultant too. Doctor Keylock is a grade A fart who'd believe anything he was told.

I answered his questions seriously for a while, but then got fed up and told him I was a Vulcan and so could not comment on feelings. He said, 'Uhuh, I see, old chap,' and made a note in his book. This is a good game, I thought. So next visit when he asked me the reason why I'd disgraced our family in church that calamitous Sunday two weeks after the accident, I'd told him it was because I had thought it was the devil up there in the pulpit, and, Vulcans being allergic to evil, I just had to shout out all the bad words I knew so that he'd go back to hell and

159

leave us alone; but that I understood now it was only the regular vicar and I was sorry for what I'd done.

Instead of telling me to quit the bullshit, Auntie says he congratulated me on my powers of self analysis and asked Pa's permission to do a paper on me for the *British Journal of Psychology*.

Of course, I know now that I probably thought it was Pa up there (which is more or less the same as saying I thought it was God), but I couldn't say that, could I? Not with him sitting there next to me.

For as long as I (or Auntie) can remember, Pa has had his own little shrine in the caravan which also serves as an office for the yard. But after the big show-up at St Peter's he decked out the shrine end – which had formerly been the sitting room and kitchenette – as a proper church, complete with altar and mini-pulpit, and we never went near St Peter's again. I myself was baptised in the caravan, well, just outside, to be accurate.

Looking back now, I believe that this boycotting of the parish church was only in part due to the disgrace of my outburst in church; there was also the row that Pa had with the vicar. This was to do with the ark and the Jonah stories among others. Pa being a fundamentalist, according to Auntie, he holds the Bible to be literally true. The Reverend McConnell made it very clear that he did not. There was a big row about this; but the final insult came when the vicar chose Lynda Seabut, the publican's daughter, to do the reading at the carol service instead of Pa. The family business was just then beginning to flourish, and I guess Pa saw this as a slight on his new standing in the village.

It was the crusher that gave Pa his breakthrough. Up to then he'd dealt in small scrap of all sorts but the crusher got him into cars. From cars he jumped to half a cargo ship, then, when the Navy moved out of the docks, he grabbed a big lump of that; in fact, he and Ffynch's carved up the biggest part between them. Now, according to Auntie, we must be one of the richest families in the area.

It has not always been so, far from it, and I suppose you could say that old habits die hard. But the truth is, unfortunately, Pa is a miser, though he calls it 'temperance'. 'The fruit of the spirit is temperance', Galatians ii 9 22, that has always been Pa's answer to Ma's requests for the little luxuries of life like Hoovers, fur slippers or weekends at Herne Bay.

In the past, my own biggest problems have been footwear and toilet paper. While my classmates at junior strutted and posed in the latest Adidas trainers, I went hobbling around in too-small plimsoles with their toes fixed together by a twist of copper wire. At home, the economy I hated above all others was the pages torn from the *Metal Bulletin* that were supposed to serve as toilet paper in the outside loo. (I wasn't allowed upstairs during the day.) This shiny paper was quite useless for the job. It moved stuff about, and that was all it did. My Y-fronts were in a permanent state. I spent my days worrying about a possible accident that might lead to the public disclosure of their condition. That had to be wrong for a millionaire's son; and that's what I was, near enough, Auntie says.

To be fair, Pa denied himself as much as the rest of us, even applying the principle to his religious life. For example, the altar in his caravan church is actually a small chest freezer lit by two second-hand radio valves – one either side of the Madonna – instead of the usual everlasting flame. Also he wanted the stained-glass-window look without wishing to incur the expense. Fortunately for him, the new stick-on lead strip had recently appeared in the big DIY stores. From this and artistic cut-outs of coloured celluloid, he made himself a pair of church windows: both lurid blue waterscapes with green hills in the background; one showed an ark-full of animals, the other, needless to say, Jonah being sucked in by the whale.

But strangely it was never the money I begrudged him as a young boy, it was always the crusher. It still is.

The Juggernaut FX 91 was then the most powerful car crusher money could buy. It is not the hard things like engines that test a crusher's abilities so much as the soft things like tyres and upholstery. Mostly these must be taken off first, but the Jug can cope if it wants. The Jug is dangerous.

No sooner was it installed than Pa must demonstrate its power to the family. The test piece was Lucky's solid rubber ball, a birthday gift to the dog from Auntie. There wasn't a sound from the jaws as they closed, just the soft hiss of the hydraulics. When they opened again, there it was – a perfect disc of blue rubber the size of a dustbin-lid and less than a sixteenth of an inch thick. I remember this striking me as rather unfair; not that Lucky ever got to play with the ball. The point is, nothing argues with the crusher. Being an impressionable lad of seven or eight, I naturally thought of my sister.

I owe a lot to the Jug; without it there would have been no escape for me for several years to come; even with the scholarship, private education still costs plenty. Not that Pa would have sent me here at all if it hadn't been for the accident and Ma's problem. So I've myself to thank as well.

In the midst of these thoughts, the organ struck up – all pipes full blast and up here that's thunderous – me nearly blasted off the Shelf.

Review over, I peeked down at the people carrying their overcoats and shopping, going home feeling good I felt sure. In the rear of the departing congregation, two Mambas appeared. I ducked. Unlike worshippers, Mambas are apt to look upwards. I felt safe in the shadows with the dust camouflaging my black hair, so after a moment I moved an eye slowly into the angle between pillar and edge. The Cathedral's shut-down routine I had

162

never before witnessed. It was my business to know everything now – if I was to keep my freedom, my asylum.

The altar candles, already extinguished, sent sooty coils
up through the spotlight beam, while the Mamba I now
recognised as the pretty one with shoulder-length hair and
small beard, the one who'd been guarding the stairs to the
Crypt, reached up with the snuffer and snuffed out a
seven-foot giant flickering on top of a gleaming gold stick.
I suddenly remembered the doctor's little black book and
wondered about the meaning of this monster.

The organ wheezed into silence and the last footsteps
echoed back from the darkness beyond the choirscreen. I
heard the clash of iron and knew the locking of gates had
begun. The tower clock told me the time was seven
o'clock. How long, I wondered, before the vergers left
too. Already the lights were clicking off one by one. It
struck me I'd soon be the only living being left in the
Cath, apart from the jackdaws and pigeons – and the
famous Cathedral Bug, of course (mustn't forget that little
charmer). I began to wonder if Lawrence was telling the
truth, if there really were bodies beneath those statues of
kings and bishops stretched out on their stone coffins.
Strange how in the olden days it was a must for the effigies
of the noble knights to have great swords between their
legs, hands pressed together above the hilts like they might
have been praying they'd be allowed to get stuck into
some black heathen the second they landed on the other
side.

Lawrence says there are bits of John the Baptist buried
under the high altar, as well as that chip off the Martyr's
skull already mentioned; relics, they're called. Good word
relic, I think it would suit the remains rather better than
Ghost – Ghost is a juvenile word to my mind – perhaps
a combination would be best: How do you do, Headmaster, may I introduce my sister's remains. Remains,
this is our headmaster, Canon Ramsbury; Headmaster, my

dead sister, Cymbeline Ghost-Relic.

Delighted.

Delighted.

I settled back in the dust to wait for the last lights to go out. The sounds of girlish laughter came faintly from somewhere opposite; I guessed it was the choir changing out of surplice and ruff. Soon they'd be back in the choir school for supper and prep, and I could get into the Shell proper.

The Bible Room I reckoned to be less than twenty yards along the Shelf from my present position, but I dared not crawl to it yet for fear of the dust cloud I would certainly stir up. My eyes felt hot and dry so I closed them again and waited.

Strange how any small change, like the turning off of the last light, will wake a person, even when that person has not yet recovered from a string of sleepless nights. But the sight which met my waking eyes might have been a Plutonian sunrise so strange was it. The vast belly of the Cathedral was in blackness now, and I was staring up at a ceiling spattered like a forest floor with tree-filtered light all in the gaudy blues, reds and greens of stained glass.

Sensing the lateness of the hour, and fearful the floodlights themselves might also be extinguished and me plunged into deeper darkness, I got up, turned left and groped along the Shelf towards my own little room-at-the-inn.

A series of small vaulted chambers connect along the wall edge of the Shelf. In reality these are accidental spaces, but the third or fourth along has been given a door. This is the space they use for the book store, the others being doorless and empty. When I came to the one with the door, I unlocked it and descended three steep steps into almost total blackness.

My groping hand soon came in contact with a pile of

smaller Bibles. So far Lawrence has disposed of less than a dozen such specimens, even these being not easy to smuggle out, but Dirty has promised to take all we can supply at the same price as soon as he's had time to establish a market. 'Somewhat of a specialist item', he called them, but that was to soften Lawrence up for a bulk price I suspect. It's surprising what the antique-junk-shops in a cathedral city can fence for their regulars; the Dean's china went a storm, even the Chaplain's old-fashioned bike fetched eight quid; boxing gloves, cricket pads and foils et cetera are the bread-and-butter lines for Lawrence. It's a matter of building trust as he says.

The chamber is about twelve feet square. At night, a small cloverleaf window high in the outer wall is the source of a faint orange glow reflecting off the arched ceiling above.

I decided to build in the middle where I was beginning to make out the dim shapes of the piles. My idea was to make a coffin-shaped nest by stacking the Bibles around me on the floor. First I would need a mattress of body-width Bibles of roughly equal thickness.

Most of the piles were waist high and separated from each other by a maze of narrow gangways – there was certainly no shortage of building material. I moved among the stacks like Gulliver in Bible-Manhattan, being careful not to topple any in case of a sharp-eared Mamba lurking below. Having found what I wanted, I laid five books in a row on the floor, then lay down to try them out. They were hard of course, but no worse than the beds in the dorm, so I started on the sides.

For this the Bibles could be any size provided the inside edges were flush and fitted closely together. I decided to allow just enough room inside for turning over, figuring too large an air space would be difficult to heat up. For the lid I found four of the largest books and carefully placed three of them edge to edge on top of the walls, resting the fourth temporarily on top of the third, which allowed me an eighteen-inch entrance. I felt good working on the Matter, bending it to my purpose. I could hardly wait to thread myself in, so inviting did the finished crib look, and was shortly sitting up in bed feeling like a man in a kayak.

I sat there a moment listening to the sigh of the wind and the something which flapped and the something else which rattled, then snuggled down inside. I thought about reaching out and closing the entrance with Bible number four, but decided to see if I would be warm enough without. Also, I thought, my lungs might decide to get claustrophobia or something. I was just dozing off when I felt an uncomfortable lump on my stomach. Bread and relics, I thought.

I quickly un-kayaked myself, reached into the pouch, put the waxed-paper packet containing maybe six thick-cut slices on the floor close at hand, then found a suitable Bible and laid the relics out on their own Bible-bed, with a certain care and respect, still safely in their polythene bag.

Until the break-in, I'd always kept the relics in my blue metal toolbox (another of Pa's money savers, the other boys all having varnished pine tuck boxes with their initials in large black letters on the lids), but after that the relics had to stay with me all the time. Which is how come they were in my jacket pocket during the Confession. Strange how one thing leads to another, I thought. If the intruder had been less careless and greedy with the Vegemite, I might not have noticed the break-in, the Ghost might not have been in my pocket and I probably wouldn't have been in this Cathedral now.

The memory was unwelcome. I did not want to think of the Chaplain or the other things that had driven me here. I was still afraid of the duck voice returning, despite my recent respite. So I snuggled down quickly and set about some serious control work. I focused hard on *real* things like where the best place would be to set up in the daytime, and what I would eat tomorrow. I had the bread, but my big weakness is meat – preferably red with a collar of good yellow fat – so that was another thing to be organised.

The sound I feared most remained absent, but my hearing was drawn far out into the giant body in whose small cell I lay. No sound entered the cloverleaf aperture, but the Cathedral itself creaked and sighed and ticked and rustled deep into the lightless dawn.

I lay listening for many hours, then, hearing the big clock strike three, I sat up irritably and groped over the edge for the bottle. I took a deep swig of the Vat 69, then used one of my matches to light a Capstan to calm my breathing which had become too fast and deep for comfort. I'm a great believer in natural remedies and only resort to Aspros if these natural medicines fail.

The match flame was enough for me to see that the polythene bag was undamaged and safely sealed with the white wire-and-plastic tie. She looked at peace on her Bible-bed, and when the flame died I snuggled down for the third time feeling hopeful that the whisky and nicotine would soon take me out of earshot so to speak. One thing, I felt I had been more than fair in my choice of venue; I had not shrunk from the challenge; there she was lying beside me in the darkness, isolated from all human contact, in a place fit for haunting if anywhere was (which I doubted, of course); the rest was up to her.

As I began to get warmer, I thought about a wank, but decided it was only out of habit and the frustration of not getting off straight away. Plus I hate mucky people and could see that being a problem even bearing in mind a couple of pages from the mattress might have done the trick; but I'm not that sort of a vandal, besides which I doubted if they'd be sufficiently absorbent and it seemed a pity to waste those ancient holy pages when I wasn't really in the mood.

Despite knowing better, and despite all my efforts at control, the thing that kept nagging me was, Would she start up? And what would she say if she did? Somehow I found I was lying there with my ears pricked in case a haunting happened without my being aware of it. After a further half hour or so, when I felt that the medicine had had long enough to make some impression, I began to get really ratty. I sat up again, popped four Aspros, washed them down with another good swig and eventually dozed off.

The pigeons woke me with their cooing just before seven by the big bonger. I was shagged but happy since the only kind of voice I'd heard in the night was that same tower clock chiming the hours and quarters. Lawrence would have said I'd been protected by Bible-power keeping the Ghost at bay like the garlic and the crucifixes in those moronic films he goes on about. But I reckoned I'd cracked it.

During my sleepless period I'd sorted out both major problems. In fact the solution to the meat problem would mean at least one less noise-polluter the next morning. I mean to convert all my bread into meat the same way.

With regard to the so-called Ghost-Voice, I'd decided to give her forty-eight hours from midnight to make absolutely certain there would be no question of cheating on my part. Furthermore, it was my intention that, crazy as it might seem, we would do this thing properly. By that I meant, *I*, for one, would swear on the Bible – and she would be given every opportunity to do likewise – that if she could not nail me – by which I meant not just *speak* again but actually *prove* that gross slander I *imagined* I heard during my bloody awful so-called Confession – if

168

she failed to do that before, let us say, midnight on Wednesday – then she'd lost the game. For ever. Full stop!

And bagsy no return.

16

I must have fallen fast asleep again for I woke to a blast
from the organ that had Bibles flying in all directions.
Jerking upright, I was blinded by a shaft of sunlight. The
dream I'd been having escaped, apart from the memory
of Lawrence's leering face, me tied to a bed, ankles and
wrists, and the single word (or it might just have been the
idea), *exorcism*.

There was also an ominous feeling in my gut I could
not think about because of the organ racket and the fact
that a straight line from my eye to the cloverleaf window
showed the sun to be already past its winter zenith. The
Mambas would have been on the slither for hours, this
space was no longer safe. Besides the insecurity, I fancied
somewhere a little less gloomy for the ceremony I had in
mind.

I quickly dismantled what remained of the Bible-bed,
restacked the Bibles, pocketed the relics and my other
belongings, plus a small, red suede Bible which seemed
perfect for the ceremony, and crawled up the steps to the
Shelf.

With the organ pipes bellowing cantatas less than a
hundred feet away across the choir vault, I crawled
through the smothering dust to the corner of the south-
west transept. There I came to another door into the Shell.
This was not locked and I was soon climbing a dim spiral
with the music no more than a tremble in the stone.

After a hundred steps or so I began to realise I'd hit the jackpot. Four fancy turrets crown Angel Steeple, the central tower of the Cathedral, but only one has a stairway leading up to it, the other three being dummies. With a thrill, I realised my day-time refuge might turn out to be the highest accessible point of the entire structure – the south-east turret of the tower. If I was right, it would be like having my own little castle in the air. I have to admit, at that moment, I felt specially blessed, or, at least, smiled on by fortune.

Climbing fast now, I passed another small door leading off, and, seconds later, an arrowslit window. The view from this confirmed my hopes; I was already on a level with the main roof ridge.

A dozen steps higher, the walls of the spiral changed abruptly from stone to narrow red bricks. Surprised, I looked up just in time to avoid banging my head on what appeared to be a rectangular lead drainpipe running diagonally across the stairwell. I crawled under this and, with barely enough light to see the steps, continued climbing.

Maybe a hundred steps later I came to a halt, confronted by a wall of rough, sawn planks barring the stairwell from edge to edge. I sat down on the step, winded and bitterly disappointed. The cracks between the planks showed day-light; it was obvious I was only a few steps short of my goal.

I peered at the barrier. The boards were sturdy, and, judging by the size of their heads, the nails, though rusty, had to be four-inchers at least. Stapled across the two central boards was a faded notice in a polythene bag. The paper looked old and stained but bore the Cathedral crest – a blue shield, quartered by a cross at the centre of which were the letters i and x. I stood. Moving close, I could read the faded type.

CONDEMNED – KEEP OUT, the capital letters pro-claimed. Then underneath:

> The South-East Turret and access is closed
> until further notice due to
> structural faults resulting from erosion
> by order of
> The Dean and Chapter.

Beneath was an unreadable signature, followed by the title: Clerk of Works, underlined.

It dawned on me then that I was looking not at a barrier but my own, secret door. I could not imagine who the notice was aimed at, but the point was, here was the strongest taboo imaginable for warding off even the most curious Mamba. If I could only break through.

For the second time in an hour, I was assaulted by feelings of special protection, special luck. It happens the elastic in the waistband of my tracksuit bottoms, not being of the youngest, is fatigued, in fact knackered. To keep the things up I must wear a belt. The buckle on the belt is wickedly sharp and has scraped my belly quite badly in the past. Now its vicious edge seemed heaven sent.

I had sadly underestimated the task.

Each plank had two nails at the top and two at the bottom. I would need to remove two planks. That meant shifting eight nails. By the time I had the first one free, my fingers were aching, the buckle was bent and the chinks of light between the boards were perceptibly duller. Shortly after withdrawing the second nail, I heard the distant tower clock strike the hour of two, confirming what I already knew; that I hadn't just dozed off this morning, I'd *died*.

As luck had it, the wood around the bottom pair of nails was soft and spongy. I had both out in minutes. I removed the board to give me more light. Through the gap I could see four more steps, and above these a glimpse of enchanted, fairy-tale turret. That was enough to set me gouging and levering, barely noticing the pain, like some maniac in a dungeon.

The minute the second board was free, I wanted to dive through and up the steps, but I made myself patiently straighten out the nails. I then partially replaced them and wriggled them backwards and forwards to ease the holes. When they were nice and free, I loosely re-attached the bottom of both boards to the frame, slid through the gap, then, by lining up the top pairs of nails one plank at a time, looping my belt round, tugged both planks and nails back into position.

From the outside, no one could possibly suspect the turret of having an occupant. Here, it seemed, was the perfect space; never designed for habitation therefore habit free; now to be inhabited, by me. In fact it seemed so very perfect I caught myself once more wondering if I might not be entering some fantastic grace-like state. As if in celebration, the tower clock struck three. I gazed around me in utter delight.

In a story told us in Classical Studies at Lizzys, I recalled Mother Earth suspends her new baby in the mouth of a cave so her husband can't find him and eat him, as he had his other male offspring, because the child would be neither *on* the earth nor *in* the sky, which meant he was *nowhere*. I too would be somewhere that didn't exist, somewhere neither on earth nor in the sky, but the space between the two – the non-existent space. And for that space to be '*condemned*' as well . . . My eyes were watering . . . It was almost too much.

I believe that I breathed a little thank you.

And that may have been my first bad mistake.

When my eyes cleared the parapet of the turret, I felt like a bird in a treetop. The three hundred and sixty degree view was broken only by eight slim buttresses. I looked up into a cylindrical space, much smaller than the one I stood in but, judging by the glimpses of daylight, similarly buttressed. Above that was a conical stone cap reaching its peak about fifteen feet above my head.

I looked about me so enraptured my eyes refused to blink and were soon streaming in the cold east wind. The aperture directly ahead showed a red roofscape and gloomy, winter-evening landscape beyond. Among the blue-grey hills to the west I began to identify places I knew: there was the black fringe of Lakevalley Wood and the road curving round towards Mapham (we'd done that a few times, Pa, me and Cymby on our visits to Ma in the mental home). Slightly right of this and further off I recognised Auntie's village by the top of its square-towered church just visible above a wooded hill line. Beyond that again, I could make out the parade-ground trees of the apple orchards, bare now but unmistakable.

The next opening right showed me the bypass sweeping off towards London, alive with silent machines racing under and over the old road at Hambledown.

I saw where the river emerged from under the High Street, divided and threaded its way between houses and car parks to join up again before the hump-backed bridge at Ducksford, where the school boathouse is.

Beyond the glowing mirrors of Westflete Lakes, I could just make out the dykes and flats which identify the near edges of the marshes. I strained my eyes to see if I might not be able to pick out the railway embankment and maybe even the house and yard, but twenty-odd miles was just too far to see on so gloomy an evening.

Ten degrees right: the ruler-straight line of the Roman road, and the hospital, and the clinic where Pa took me to see Doctor Valentine Keylock. There the barracks set among gorse-fields. There the golf course. There the main line to London, its polished rails catching the last dull glow from the west.

A window lit up. My attention shifted to a building inside the precinct walls. The Headmaster's brick mansion was the source of the light. For the first time I could see right down into his walled garden. As if sensing my eyes, Mrs Ramsbury drew cherry-red velvet across her French windows. As the Ramsbury standard lamp vanished from view, a window lit in the Bishop's flint palace, and two precinct streetlights – one beneath the crusty facade of Christ Church Gate and another beside the Cathedral Bookshop. The effect was of increased darkness rather than light.

I edged up to the parapet feeling like I imagined a parachutist might feel approaching the hatch for the very first time. Before leaning my head through the gap, I knelt down with both hands gripping the stone sill. I am not afraid of heights, but when I finally looked straight down the sight stopped the breath in my throat. The drop was unbroken. If security was number one, I had indeed cracked it. A quick calculation told me that, even if the tower was lying flat on the ground, it would take a sprinter ten seconds to race from the footings to the lightning rods with their little gold pennants; for a Mamba in skirts, spiralling up against gravity, you could make those seconds minutes, no sweat. That, coupled with the acoustics of stone tubes, put any danger of surprise attack out of the question – at least from within. Regarding the outside, that was even less assailable. The window openings were barely wide enough for my own narrow head and ears to pass through, no way normal shoulders and arses. So, even if a three-hundred-foot turntable ladder existed (and quite obviously it did not), even the skinniest and most determined fireman or police officer would be hard pressed to enter my castle in the air.

As I surveyed my kingdom, I wanted to howl with delight, but there were still *people* down there – bald heads and head scarves, flat-hats and boaters – I had to be sensible and realise that, at least for the time being, people were the enemy. That would change, of course, soon; soon I would be free to rejoin the human race, after I had put my house in order, after the ceremony, after my . . . let's see . . . Wednesday midnight, that will be seventy-nine hours in the wilderness.

I stood slowly, feeling I was on the brink of *everything*, right up on the trembling edge, physically and mentally – guts and head – the whole chemistry set. Something was about to happen, and *I* was the one *making* it happen.

I turned and crossed the yard and a half of flagstone to the opposite window. This opening faced north over the square roof of the tower. Between the dark turrets opposite I could see the naked tips of the Greencourt lime trees silhouetted against the evening sky, a little to the right a section of the green itself, the dining hall on its concrete pillars, the flint block of the tuck shop, the lighted windows of Sopworth's classroom, winking to blackness even as I looked. Further right, the unlit Deanery, the Dark Entry, the grey-green ridge of the choir roof, the ruined arches of the old Infirmary. A far-off bell tinkled and the ants in black uniform began to swarm.

Instinctively I drew back from the opening. The tower clock chimed the hour of four, end of afternoon session, not for me, my work was about to begin, but first I must check the castle walls; the notice had, after all, warned of erosion. I could not ignore that completely.

Between every stone of all eight pillars was a layer not of mortar but solder or lead. This impressed me; the joints themselves looked perfect though I had to concede a slight crumbling of the stone in the mid sections of the two west-facing pillars. However, even after tapping these quite firmly with my knuckles I could detect no movement and began to suspect another little ploy by the powers that be to consolidate their monopoly of the salvation industry – this being the closest point to heaven? Get your lucky key-to-the-kingdom here, folks; step right up for the Elixir of Everlasting Life, available only from Dean and Chapter, sole UK agents to Paradise plc. Look for the ix sign and beware all cheap imitations. If I happened to be one of the faithful (which I'm certainly not for the very good reason that one thing leads to another), I'd be well hacked off with the obstacles stacked round the Almighty by the very people you'd have thought would know better.

So there was me, lucky Jim Bishop, king of the castle and safer than houses, or so I believed. Without more ado, I sat on the floor and began to unpack my sister's remains.

Looking back, I can see that to me the ceremony was all just a game; the *word* from my early morning dream meant nothing . . . just so much air.

Whether it was lack of food or the altitude, the fresh clean air or none of these I can't say, but I do remember feeling a little light-headed, you might even say euphoric, as I tipped the relics from their polybag. I also remember saying the 'E' word in a short sentence – something flip like, 'Exorcise time for relics' – then immediately wanting to bite off my tongue. But nothing happened – of course not, why should it? – and I felt so perky, so in command, I was soon amusing myself loading up the ceremony with as much mumbo-jumbo as I could dredge up.

It wasn't until much later I realised that, ever since the dream, I had been harbouring the exorcism idea like a pregnant blowfly in my brain. Speaking the word out loud was like switching on the incubator. Just as God implies the Devil – who was it said that? the good doctor, who else – so exorcism must imply haunting. One thing leads to another. It's all Matter, Matter in another form, but Matter none the less – Symbolic Matter; just as deadly. The ceremony seemed no more to me than a silly hotch-potch of Shag, Dennis Wheatley, the court-room, Clive Barker, Pa, Confirmation classes, *Rosemary's Baby*, odds and sods of services in the Cath, any old thing I could think of. All just a bit of fun. All equally harmless. So I thought. Which only goes to show how deeply the habit infestation of the place had undermined my most sacred principles.

I must have been very confused at that point. Lack of sleep, or too much? I'm not sure. What I was totally blind to at the time was the fact that the idea, exorcism, was the grid into which everything else plugged and switched on. The idea of exorcism connected every crummy, disjointed, horror-comic idea to its neighbour and the whole parcel to me *via that word*. And the word . . . *became*.

Looking back, I also realise that I wanted more than anything to be *fair* to the Ghost. This was neither bravado nor brotherly love; I just didn't want any excuse for any person or thing ever to be able to accuse me of not giving her every possible chance to make whatever play she could. So I gave it, as they say, 'the bizz', occultwise.

I decided the corrrect way to proceed with the laying out would be to place the hands, the feet and the two eyeballs in as near as possible the positions they would have occupied were the deceased here in the flesh, so to speak, and reclining on some form of cross-shaped support. I'd barely finished placing the hands when I suddenly thought: Wait. That's too little. Since we *are* pretending, let us pretend *accurately*. If Cymbeline had, somehow or other, managed to 'survive' (or whatever they call it) after death, she would now be, let us see now . . . thirteen already!

That shook me.

I hotched my bum over to the square hole where the four steps come up from the barrier and began repositioning the relics. The eyes, of course, would still be horribly close together – my sister being the squinty little piggy she was – but Cymbeline had never been small for her age so the feet had to be, what . . . a yard away, at the least. I placed these carefully, side by side, still in their pink bootees (odd how the blades chopped them off so cleanly just above the boot-tops) and then placed the hands, palms up, one each side at estimated shoulder height, as though that imaginary cross were supporting her nicely.

I stood astride the absent knees to avail myself of the bird's eye view then stopped to position the blue and white orbs, trying my best to have them both pointing in roughly the same direction. Then I straightened with a satisfied grunt, little realising that, inside my head, the 'game' was generating its own meaning.

Looks a bit empty, said headvoice.

Empty? Where?

The middle needs something.

Like what?

Bit of writing. Drawing. Anything.

Got it! I'll write the word CYMBY. In big letters. Make a sort of wordychest shape – full stop for the belly-button, how about that?

What with?

Eh?

No felts, mate. No spray cans.

I scratched my head, then it came to me: Blood, that's what. It's *always* blood.

I looked at the quick on my first finger where I'd been chewing in the night.

You'll need some more work on that, said headvoice. **Could hurt, that could—**

But I was quite carried away – almost obsessive – by now. In one movement I took the ragged edge between my teeth, clenched and tugged away the hand.

Ah-shit!

For a second I was blinded by tears. When my vision cleared, I was pleased. My left palm cupped beneath the injured finger had already received two large drops and more blood was welling up from the left side of the nail.

180

I knelt, a knee each side of where her knees would be if she had knees, and began to write.

Less than halfway though the first Y, headvoice came up with a piece of pure Lawrence: **What about a pentangle? We'll need a pentangle. To protect us. You never know what might turn up in a place like this**.

Jesus, it's only a *game*. And this is a finger not a blood-bank, you know!

I carried on with the leg of the Y. To me the idea was ludicrous, but I had to agree that, since I'd embarked on the game, I ought at least to be consistent. According to Lawrence, the undead were wide open to possession by evil spirits.

How seamlessly my thoughts had drifted away from the *aesthetics* to the *function* of the ceremony. How blind I was. How naïve. The truth is, I was now being driven by the task at hand; my only concern was how to eke out the blood.

By taking a point at the centre of the south-facing window, drawing a line from there to the left-hand pillar of the west-facing window, thence to the right-hand pillar of the east-facing window and back to the starting point, a perfect equilateral triangle was produced. By the time I'd constructed another on top of the first, starting this time in the centre of the north-facing window, it was practically pitch dark outside. Below, in the city, the street lights had begun to light up street by street. I was suddenly aware of the cold.

It was then, as I stood hugging myself and huffing my fingers, that I realised what I had drawn was not a pentangle at all, but a hexangle! (If that means sixangle.) The hell with it! I said aloud.

Might be better, said headvoice, **more Hebrew**.

I nodded. There were, after all, six relics. And, certainly, the geometric shape now darkening the flagstones neatly enclosed the remains. Each foot, hand and eye seemed properly at peace inside its own little triangle, and the word CYMBY (CYM on the top line, BY centred beneath) made a fine feature – almost like a head stone – inside the central hexagon. There was a unity, a wholeness of design, apart from a short gap in one segment where the stairs came up – not enough to worry about, so I thought. The whole thing struck one as surprisingly *meaningful-looking*. It only remained to place the red suede Bible beneath the deceased's right hand and the swearing-off could commence.

My back ached. I'd earned a Capstan, I thought, and maybe even a wee nip, to warm me up.

The drink could be part of the ceremony, said head-voice. **What about words . . . chanting and that?**

I squatted in the lee of the parapet. Give us a chance, I said, irritably, lighting up.

17

I sat for a moment, quietly smoking, trying out various opening lines in my head. The one I liked best began: O Spirit of Cymbeline – But that was as far as it got before headvoice burst in:

Don't be so bloody wet. Give her rocks. Say, Listen to me, Pigshit. I never murdered no one. And if I did, as far as I'm concerned you don't even exist. So put up or shut up, for ever, right now. You got . . . hang on . . .

The tower clock had only just finished striking the hour of five. I did a quick calculation: three days, plus say seven hours for what was left of yesterday evening, that would make seventy-nine hours total, less twenty-eight for the length of time we'd been in up to now . . .

Near enough, near enough, said headvoice impatiently. **So just tell her straight, say: So you've got fifty-one hours left, you cow. End of message**.

Wonderful. That's it, is it? Nothing else? No attempt at psychic communication? No ritual, no summoning, no chanting, no compact? Just a load of verbal. Thanks, head. Now let me tell you something: this isn't about ultimatums and being dogmatic; there are people out there who *believe* in these things – bright people, Lawrence for one, maybe even the doctor, I'm not sure about that. I'm not saying I don't know where *I* stand. I do. But being open-minded is *not* the same as being *wet*, for Christ's sake. In fact open-minded's exactly what a sane person should be. It's *scientific*. This is the age of reason, you know. We do *not* want comebacks, right? – however ridiculous. So it's just not enough to be fair; we've got to be more than fair. And if that means being wet . . . we'll fucking be *wet*! I want this thing sorted. So I'm asking you, please, keep quiet and let me concentrate. *Please!* I'm trying to remember something, all right? So—

Remember what?

The video.

Video? Oh shit yea! *The Exorcist.* **Great idea. Try to remember that scene – the bedroom with the little –**

– girl. I know, but . . .

I remembered all right; the plunging bedstead, the kid retching and belching, the ropes of green ectoplasm erupting from her screaming mouth, the writhing, the sobbing, the hellish hooting, like an elephant farting Stravinsky, to use Lawrence's phrase. But . . . as to the *ceremony* . . . as to what the priest *actually said* . . . as to the *words* he used . . .

I began to breathe deeply the way Lucy had taught me, trying to empty my mind of all but the memory of that evening with Lawrence. I would need to approach the memory obliquely, I felt, via the surrounding circumstances, so as not to frighten away the central details.

It had been the evening after my night in the forest with Sopworth. Shag had suggested a pint at Georgy Porgy's, to help take my mind off the appointment next day. We would cut supper; he'd treat me to scampi and chips, he said. He was flush from a good deal with Dirty that same afternoon. He was happy to pay. So I let him.

Sitting in the corner of the function room. Peaceful. Too early for the lads from the Scotland Hills estate. Just the pair of us in the big dark room. Empty stage. Silent jukebox.

Lawrence tapping the bar with the edge of a fifty.

Barbara appearing, frowning, in a crumpled white teeshirt.
Her seeing him. He grinning . . .

'Two pints of Shepheard,' says Lawrence.

'Hello, darlin'. You're early,' says she, reaching up for
Lawrence's pewter pot.

'Couldn't wait to see you, gel,' says Lawrence, stretching across the bar to raise the hem of her already lifting
teeshirt.

'Oh, you!' says the blonde, without urgency. Barbara
never bothers with 'foundation' garments. She's proud of
her breasts.

With good reason, I thought, remembering the flash of
white flesh and brown aureole.

Never mind that, said headvoice. **The** *words*, **cock . . .
What about the** *words***? It's bloody freezing up here.
Why don't we get to the point . . . ?**

The point, yes . . .

Round table, wrought-iron legs, varnished wood, two
pints, one oblong black box. Under the transparent cover
of the box, a black photostat picture of a man in a hat
carrying a case, a black silhouette standing under a street
lamp, looking up at a house with lighted windows. Iron
railings. Bit of fog. And the words, THE EXORCIST, in
big white letters.

Me looking the question at Lawrence.

Lawrence laying a finger alongside his nose, closing one
eye, saying, 'Shifty copy. Uncensored. No questions, little
droogie. Right, right, right. Linger whilst I acquaint mine
hostess of our desires.'

Lawrence hunched over the corner of the bar, rough
head close to the blonde waves of Barbara. Murmurings.
Barbara nodding, switching the switch by the door to the
stairs. Lawrence turning to me. Beckoning. Me shaking
my head, feeling spare. Him coming over. Me saying how
I'm not into porn. Him explaining how the nearest it gets
to porn is when this kiddy lays there shoving a crucifix

185

up her fanny yelling 'Fuck me, Jesus' or something like that till she's all covered in blood then sticking her mum's face down there yelling 'Lick me, lick me.' And her mum's face getting all bloody too. Then me saying how I still wasn't bothered, and him hauling me up out of the seat. Marching me across the room.

'Come on, it'll do you good, kid. Take your mind off the other. And, you never know, you might learn something. Even you.'

Then the two of us climbing the stairs. Bare bulb on the landing. Smell of fish suppers. Budgie in a cage in the corner. Corduroy sofa, too soft. Barbara tugging together the curtains. Lights off. Screen on. Words coming up. Flickering pictures with three lines across, people moving fast and silent like a silent movie as Lawrence winds on. Big orange sun. Pictures of desert. Excavations. Winding on. A long way this time. A man with a tape recorder and a priest in civvies. Lawrence, now flat out on the sofa, head in Barbara's lap, pint on the floor at exactly arm's length, saying, 'This is the bit where he finds out the noises coming out of the kid's mouth is like language, only backwards, some of it's in foreign an' all, which proves it's demons, see, Jim? It's all based on fact, you know. This is how the old Jesuits do it. Kosher, this is mate. That Batty or whatever they call him done years of research. That's why they censored it. Hey-up. Nearly there. Wait till you see this bit, kid.'

All the time he's speaking, he's winding on. At last the lines vanish. A picture of an old priest in a forest of naked trees. He's reading a message. He looks ill.

Lawrence says, 'That's him. The exorcist.' Lawrence reaching up his pint. Drinking.

Suddenly it's the picture on the cover of the box. The exorcist arriving in his car. Getting out. The car pulling away. It's foggy under the streetlight. He stands black against the light from the bedroom window. Then he's inside the house telling this other priest, this young priest, to fetch things – holy water, regalia, some book . . .

What book? What's it called? It's no use just saying—

Roman something. I dunno . . . Yes I do; *Roman Ritual*. That's it; *Roman Ritual*.

Go on then.

I can't.

Can't? What do you mean, can't. Course you can. What's up with you?

What was 'up with me', and what I could not explain to that vulgar, insensitive bastard inside my head was the picture I was then remembering of the half-lit face of the girl lying on her vomit-stained pillow, her cheeks covered in oozing sores, lips split, nostrils flared and tilted like a little snout, and those eyes . . . those pale blue-green eyes . . . and . . . for pity's sake . . . she looked so like . . .

For fuck's sake, come on mate, what's next?

'SHUT UP!' Real words. A shriek.

Woosh – silence within, so complete and so fast I hadn't time to register surprise before the surprise vanished leaving *nothing* – not sleep, not death, not anything but a vague awareness of my head expanding at warp speed.

Something had changed, something that felt like a call had gone out. I experienced the first flicker of real fear. Fear? A wriggling under the skin at the base of my spine. I had to check my co-ordinates. *Now. At once.*

I was sitting upright in the central hexagon, legs crossed, hands together in front of my chest, facing due south . . . due south, where the eyes were just visible in the shadow cast by the parapet.

The video rolled in my head like a silent film in colour. The exorcist hesitating in the bedroom doorway, breath fogging in the cold room. (I feel myself shiver.) The young priest follows. Both hold red books. She glares at them with those eyes. Her arms are out like a cross. Her hands are tied to the bedposts which are padded. Her neck is bent up at right angles. Glaring. Wheezing. Growling, low, like a dog threatening.

'Oooo, I can't bear it!'

What the? It's Lawrence, of course. Taking the piss. Sticking his head up her shirt now. She laughing. She's laughing, but she's scared all right.

The old priest does the sign of the cross at the thing on the bed.

'Stick your cock up her arse,' it yells, something like that, in a horrible man's voice all belchy and deep.

'Silence,' says the old man. He turns on the lamp on the table by the bed. He unpacks his black pouch. Takes out the silver crucifix with Jesus on. Kisses it. Takes out a flat flask of clear water. Removes a small plug from the cork. Sprinkles his mate. Then her on the bed. She moans and wails. Both open their books. Both kneel. The camera zooms in. You can read the words! At the top of the page it says:

CHAPTER 41
Rite of Exorcism

The old priest begins to read. He says . . . He says, 'Our Father who art in heaven . . .'

Who art in heaven. Yes? What then?

She gobs on his glasses.

Gobs on his . . . ! Fuck me, boy! WHAT DOES HE SAY? That's the whole fucking point of this . . . this . . . *fucking charade!*

Her tongue comes out.

Great.

Like a big waggly snake. All black.

Amazing.

She says to the young priest . . . still in this . . . this voice . . . she says, 'Your mother sucks cocks in hell, Karras—'

I DON'T WANT TO KNOW WHAT *SHE* SAYS!

'—and drinks the slime,' or something like that.

God help us. You're bloody useless, do you *know* that?

She's snorting clouds of fog, like a mad bull or something.

You don't say.

—and the bed's crashing up and down and thunder's banging off and there's growling and howling and belching and that and she's jerking about tugging at the wrist ropes and moaning and bellowing and the lights are flashing and the ceiling splits wide open and when he lays his purple stole thing on her head all green stuff pours out of her mouth so the other one has to go out and wash it in the basin and then she starts laughing at the old one when he thought he'd won and . . . it's bedlam, I tell you.

Thank you, said headvoice, quite calmly, too calmly. **Thanks very much. But if you could possibly manage it, I would still like to hear the FUCKING *WORDS*. ALL RIGHT?**

I uncrossed my legs and massaged my numb ankles. The wind had freshened and was now hissing up the stairwell, flipping my long hair over my face. Cold. My blood had gone deep, and the cigarette? Shit! The cigarette had burnt itself out and was lying where it had fallen, across the inside of my thigh, its tip at the centre of a two inch circle of charred tracksuit. And there was no pain! Half a cigarette had burnt itself out on my leg, and I had felt *nothing*.

I backhanded the stub away like a poisonous spider. As I did so, my body leaned forward to the left. I watched my fingers pick up the relic-hand by its thumb – delicately, as though it might be booby trapped – aware, for the first time, of its perfect condition. There was no sign of decay in the tiny curled fingers nor even the severed wrist. Over my body the skin wriggled. I hesitated. Something was wrong.

189

Now what ? said headvoice.

I have to go first.

What—? began headvoice, but I was out of earshot, watching myself replacing the relic. I laid my left hand on the Bible and waited. Beats of nothing – bump-di bump-di bump-di bump – absolute zero, blank slate.

Behind my forehead, the glowing radio valve came into focus on an ocean of blackness, little glass tube with a point on top, silver plate, glowing coil . . . I dismissed it (took it by the left leg and threw it down the stairs – pop! gone) and the last of the static fell silent. My head was still. Like a cave on a dead world in a dead universe. I felt myself spreading outwards into the dark spaces in between. The hand at the end of my arm moved back to the Bible, laid itself gently on the red suede Bible. The mouth in my face spoke, hollow and wet like a mouth underwater:

I . . . James Bishop, swear by . . . swear by . . .

Swear by what? What do I swear by?

Silence.

A girl's voice, clear as a Walkman. A girl's voice heard as a *real* voice, not as a voiced thought. A girl's voice heard *outside* my head:

'*I will accept one finger, Bimbim. The one you wrote my name with will do nicely.*'

My eyes snapped open, flicked about the turret no longer dark but streaked, like the rest of the Cathedral visible through the windows, with gaudy tangerine light. I sat up with a jolt and stared at the relics. One eye was in shadow, the other lit orange like a hideous wink. Words burst out of me before I could think. 'God, Cymbeline!' I exclaimed. 'You'll give me a heart attack.'

It *was* her! No one but her ever used that ridiculous name; it wasn't a proper word even, just stupid baby drivel. Yet . . . the voice was *not* that of a small child.

My lungs had begun to heave and my eyes seemed

190

transfixed by that long-dead eye as if locked in a stare-out. Outside my body, the silence was waiting . . . *she* was waiting.

Say something, whispered headvoice.

'You've been quiet,' I stammered, trying hard not to blink or look away, 'I'd almost forgot . . . forgot you were . . .' I dried up, not wanting to speak the thought. From the inside, my voice sounded breathless, grovelling.

Beats of silence, then the sound of laughter. I shuddered so my teeth rattled like in a horror story.

'*But I* am *here, Bimbim. You asked for proof, this is it. So, do we have a bargain or not? My silence "for ever", your finger? You say I'm lying, that's fine; prove it and you win; that means I go away and never disturb you again.*'

'Prove it? How?'

'*Simple. I'll help you to go back, to relive the games in question – we'll call them "games", you'd prefer that, I know – then we'll just see who is telling the truth and who's lying, and that'll be that. The umpire's decision is—*'

'Umpire? That's you, I suppose.'

'*You really don't get it, do you, Bimbim? Think about cricket. Who is it points the finger?* (silence) *I can't say more – it's something a person must learn, James, before they can move on. Now then, I haven't got all night, so . . . are you taking the bet or do we carry on as we are – me stuck between worlds, you splitting down the middle? CJ was right, you know; this may sound unkind, but, madness is hell. It's up to you, Bimbim, you—*'

'Don't call me that.'

'*—choose. You've got until midnight the day after tomorrow – your suggestion, I accept. Unless you prefer to give in, of course – come clean, confess.*'

Cow, whispered headvoice.

'*I thought not. No. So, is it a deal then?*'

'I don't know . . .' I stammered, wondering as I spoke why I was playing her game so lamely, but, at the same time, somehow, unable to see the way out. Isolated bits of my brain began to flicker into life, fitfully, small bursts of reason which began to add up to half a theory: could this be what Dr K called an auditory hallucination? That had to be the answer, except I was talking, and the voice was *answering*. Hallucinations didn't hold conversations, did they?

'*Yes or no, James? Time has run out, you must decide now.*'

'Maybe,' I panted, 'but . . .'

'*No buts. And it has to be bitten, not cut. Biting is the old way. That's how it has to be here. So, big brother, none of your tricks or things could get nasty – quite hellish, in fact.*'

My brain began to buzz. How could I possibly believe what was happening only a few hundred feet above the city where the shops and cafés would now be emptying as they do on any normal Monday evening? Normal people would be making their way home now, thinking about football or food or the rail crash or the price of a pint, never dreaming that a real haunting was taking place in full view of everyone – not on Altair Four – on top of the floodlit tower of the Cathedral of ix where anyone could see. Except, of course, it ought to be pulsing with sickly green light . . . then maybe just one of them might look up and say to his missus, Eeee look, Ethel, t'Cathedral's got a green turret tonight. Call t'Ghost Busters quick, it could be our Jimbo having a haunting.

Fat chance. Real haunted turrets look like any other turrets – tangerine stone with a little gold flag on the top.

The silence was waiting.

Across the Cathedral, across the Greencourt, I knew that the last of the steaming mud-caked boys were pedalling home through the twilight or reddening their pink bodies in steaming baths talking about the tackles they'd made and the punches they'd thrown under the steaming scrum. A few metres below me the vergers were lighting candles for Evensong, the choristers wriggling into cassock and ruff, laughing, no doubt whispering about who loves who this week, as per. And here was I, worried sick how to defend myself against false accusations from something that couldn't possibly exist. Well I'd had enough. Why should I walk dumbly into her trap? I wouldn't. I'd stand up, and I'd stick my head out through the nearest opening, and, to the first passerby, I'd yell—

What? said headvoice. **What would you tell them, mate? 'Help, help – there's a ghostie up here and I'm frikened?' Fuck off.**

Look, you! I've had enough—

Keep it logical then. OK? Two things: if there *is* a voice – and I still say it could be you, but we'll ignore that for the moment – then one thing's for certain: it ain't no five-year-old; whoever belongs to that . . . that . . . whatever it is, is far too crafty.

So?

Think! How old was the monster when . . . when she died?

All right. So what? So time goes on on the other side. What else?

What else?! Shitting hell! I'm telling you; it's got confidence; it's got *style*. And it makes you sound like granny at the séance. Stop backpedalling, can't you, you gutless pratt? Dig in. I don't recognise you. You always took the initiative. It was always her who had to go snivelling and sneaking to the grown-ups, never you. So, come on: get it together one more time, but cool. Cool.

I nodded slowly, slowly shuffled my backside back to lean against the wall, then stared at the eyeball, unblinking. I took one deep breath. Held it. Swallowed. Twice. 'Fancy a little chat?' I suggested, 'Or a game of something?'

'*No more stalling, James. Deal or no deal – that's all I want to hear.*'

Silence – but for the wind, and something rattling, something flapping below. What could I say? Hadn't I come here to settle things once and for all. I had made certain moves . . . and this was the result. If I quit now, what would it prove? Nothing. I'd be back to square zero.

I said, 'Fair enough. You're on.'

'*Swear*,' said the voice.

'I swear,' said I. (Everything that could possibly be crossed, *was* crossed.)

'*What do you swear, Bimbim? Tell me.*'

'What? Well . . . that if I am . . .'

'*Guilty. Go on.*'

'I owe—'

'*All in one piece, now. Say "If I am guilty".*'

'All right! . . . If I am guilty . . .'

' "*Of murdering my sister." Go on.*'

'Of murdering my sister . . .'

'*Go on, say, "I swear that, if I am guilty of murdering my sister . . ." go on, go on.*'

My heart was pounding. I was amazed to find the anger rising . . . just like in the old days. 'All right! Cow! I swear. I swear that if I am guilty of murdering you – all right? – *if* I am, *IF* . . . I owe you a finger, all right!? Is that it?'

' "*Which I will bite off . . ."* '

Bitch! I hesitated.

' "*Which I will bite off . . ."* ' The voice was like flint now.

'Which I will bite off,' I gabbled.

' "*By Wednesday midnight. With my teeth." Go on, say it. Say it!*'

'All right, dammit! Which I will bite off with my teeth by Wednesday midnight.'

'*Good*,' said the voice, '*now swear.*'

I slapped my hand on the Bible.

'*Not on that, silly, we know what you think about that; on your life, Bimbim . . . on the big red muscle that keeps you alive.*'

With my left hand against my ribs, feeling the pump hard at work, I heard myself say:

'I swear.'

'*Good,*' said the Ghost. '*Now me. Now it's my turn. Thanks to you, I've got no life to swear on. So put my hand back on that Bible. Please.*'

I picked up the hand and held it for a moment in the tangerine light. For a breathstopping moment I considered hurling it and the other remains out into the tangerine night. But I knew that would only be like shutting your eyes when the gun goes off. On an impulse I moved the severed wrist to my nostrils; still hoping, I suppose, for some whiff of decay – anything to break the spell. There was nothing.

'*The Bible, if you please, James.*'

I obeyed.

In a strangely formal tone, almost as though addressing an unseen court, the voice said: '*In the event that my brother, James Bishop, is judged not guilty of my murder, either by intention alone or by act and intention together, then my voice shall be silent for ever and my flesh shall pass into dust. And this I swear.*'

Silence.

Not knowing what to think or say, I sat dumbly listening to the peristalsis and the sussing of my blood. After a moment the voice said: '*Fine. Just one more thing, then we play.*'

'Yeah. Sure. What do you fancy? Mums and dads, doctors and nurses?'

'*Don't be funny, James, it's killers and victims. You know that.*'

I stared at the eye, vaguely aware of cold saliva flooding my chin. I said, '*Fathers and daughters*, don't you mean?'

'*I meant what I said, James.*'

Once she'd been Playdo in my hands, now . . . This was it then. To my amazement the fear churning in my belly turned suddenly to blind fury. I literally spat the word, 'Cheat', into that unblinking eye, then yelled, 'Where is your *witness*!? Where is the *proof*!? Aha, that's got you, you cow.'

But the voice answered calmly, softly: '*Well, James, let's see now. There's you, for one. And there's me. And—*'

I laughed out loud. 'That's a fat lot of good,' I said, 'We *con-flict*, dear. That means, dear, we cancel each other right out. So—'

'*Oh, don't worry, Bimbim, things have changed. You and me, we work hand in glove, now. See things through one pair of eyes. In fact—*'

'One pair of eyes? Well, that's fine then.'

'*In fact, that's what I wanted to put straight. You see . . . How can I explain it so you'll understand . . . ? There's a couple of dark bits in the memory; smudged, you could say, like someone's tried to rub them out.*'

I felt my heart lurch as though it would burst through the cage and drench the turret in steaming blood. I had to shut her up. My ears must hear no more.

In that instant, headvoice hissed: **Go, Jimbo! Now. You can bring it on yourself, you know you can**.

I began to haul deep breaths, deliberately, faster and faster, straining for the self-induced symptoms of panic, symptoms I knew to be capable of inducing the picture shows.

Hurry, said headvoice, **go back, go back. Picture it – the sunshine, the garden, the blood** . . .

I felt myself stand on hollow legs, dizzy now. I put both hands out in front of me. I staggered two steps, wobbly but deliberate, *out of the hexagram* . . .

'*Wait!*' shrieked the Ghost in a tiny voice, '*I'm not ready! I haven't told you what—*' But the voice was fading, fading.

'*Cheat!*' squeaked the voice. By then it could have been the church mouse of the proverb.

Retarded as ever, said headvoice, **stupid little cow, the curtain's halfway up already.**

The Gateway

18

SCENE: *The Garden in Summer*
*A tall, ugly, c.1930 red brick house; sash windows, slate roof,
twin dormers, chocolate front door with full-length reeded glass
panel, anodised letter box. The rest is new, maroon paintwork,
the edges badly over-run on the glazing.*

*Flat marshland to either side. Behind the house, the railway
embankment stretches straight and level in both directions as
far as the eye can see, which is a long way.*

*The only other buildings visible are the multiple apexes of
a warehouse showing above the embankment, the pumping
house and eight vats of a sewage works half a mile west, and,
at least three miles beyond this, a small group of houses and
the square tower of a church.*

*A concrete road separates the open front garden from a field
of bright yellow rape. A flat concrete drive on the left of the
house leads to the rear. A strip of bare earth to the left of the
drive contains three black lumps of metal that might be car
engines, and part of a rusting harrow.*

*At the back of the house, a square lawn slopes down to a
vegetable plot. A fence cannibalised from old pallets divides
this from the scrapyard and a large, old-fashioned caravan
hand-painted in green and cream. The near, right-hand end-
window of the caravan is partially blinded by a crude leaded-
light depicting a pink figure with purple beard swimming into
the mouth of a big purple fish. Rising from the roof of the
caravan is an eight-foot Dexion cross guyed by a triple wire*

201

hawser. Both upright and cross-member are strung with orange light bulbs. Beyond the caravan, various sheds, a yellow crane and mountains of wrecked vehicles.

The grass of the lawn is green in a circle around a sprinkler (not turned on) and in a smaller patch around a longstanding leak in the hose; the rest is brown grass or bare, cracked earth. A pair of double sheets hang from opposite sides of a rotary drier at the centre. One of the sheets is worn to a hole, the other muslin-thin. From an open French window comes the drone of what might be 'Gardeners' Question Time'.

In the shade of the washing sits Cymbeline, straight brown hair elastic-banded into bunches. She is plump with ingrowing elbows. She wears only denim dungarees (one strap, unfastened, hangs loose) and pink bootees. The skin of her naked arms and shoulders is smooth, pink and, like the dungarees, dirty. She has water in her red teapot. Between her spraddled legs is a yellow gingham tea towel on which are laid two red cups and saucers, both containing water, and two plates with Smarties and hundreds-and-thousands on.

A thin, pale woman emerges from a side door with a basket of washing. Her hands and arms are streaked with maroon paint, a clot of maroon hair flops over one eye. She hangs the washing then kneels by the child and pretends to sip 'tea'. She makes sounds of relish: 'Mmmm, mmmm. Thank you, darling.'

From the front of the house comes the chug and clatter of a heavy petrol mower.

Today the breeze is from the west, and it stinks.

Enter: Me, grunting, carrying a large, overflowing grassbox.

I am helping my Pa with the outdoor work, as is right and proper. In September I move up to top class. Unfortunately I'll be stuck there for two years. As Miss Barraclough says, there's nowhere else to go for a star like me.

I smile at Ma and my sister as I totter towards the

202

compost heap beyond the garden shed. Cymbeline is too engrossed to notice, but Ma glances up and tells me, 'Cymby says she would like Bimbim to join her and Mummy in a nice cup of tea when he's finished his job.'

That's all she says, then goes back to their private party. I nod, but she's not looking.

Trudge, trudge, trudge. Puff, pant, phewy. Lift, grunt, tip. My fingers ache and I feel my face to be beetroot-red. I'm not complaining. Far from it. It's jobs like these that earn me my pocket money – forty pence weekly which goes straight in my savings account. When I'm ten, it goes up to fifty. Some of them at Marshside Junior get more than that already. For *nothing*. Spoilt brats, I say. Money doesn't grow on trees.

I lean into the compost box to grab a double armful of grass cuttings which I take to the courgette beyond the shed and carefully place around the stem. This is to stop the roots drying out; I have not been ordered to do this but am using my initiative. On the way back, I set down the grassbox, unplug the sprinkler and coil the hosepipe (which Pa, being always so busy, has obviously forgotten) in even circles around my hand and elbow, then go to the shed and lay it carefully over the two dowling pegs. I then collect the grassbox and jog back to the front of the house where Pa is waiting. I stand well back as the engine accelerates to cutting speed with a roar and a grind and a clatter of the blades. I love watching the grass fly into the box, and the beautifully cropped track the big machine leaves in its wake. And the smell . . . Pa is a genius with machines. He's the best. If he sees a worm or even a woodlouse, everything stops for the rescue.

The front is the shady side of our house; the grass here is long. Soon the box will be full again. I rest for a minute on our cardinal-red front step.

The Ransome Multimower 30inch Reel-cutter with seven horse Villiers engine is not new – of course it is not

– but it's *big*. Pa bought it at Faversham market where the man gave it away for ten pounds. There were minor problems with the belt and gears but, as Pa said, It's a great deal of engine for ten pounds, and Ma should not be afraid to use it. Especially since there's no electric cable to cut for the fifty-fourth time, he added, with a big wink so she'd know he was joking.

Ma is thin and she's not all that strong, but she did have a go, persevering even after it mowed down most of her prize herb bed. These things take practice, as Pa explained. It's only a matter of getting accustomed to the weight of tne clutch. You can't expect miracles.

But Pa is operating the machine himself today, it being Sunday and Ma having excused herself on account of the washing. I don't think Pa was too pleased, in view of his Sunday schedule, but he would never raise his voice to her, particularly on this day of all days.

He finishes at the front and brings the machine round to the back lawn where my sister is having her picnic. The old engine has bags of character, which makes it a little hard to start sometimes, so Pa has left it running while wheeling it through. Although the revs are low the blades are still turning so he has it tilted back on the iron roller. It makes very loud crunching, splitting noises on the concrete path.

At this point the outside phone bell goes.

Pa sets the Ransome down on the grass, runs to the caravan, which has its own telephone at the office end, and disappears inside. Although neither Mrs Chalmers, the light-bulb lady, nor old Frank who does tyres and drives the Recovery, work Sundays, Pa is always ready to collect vehicles himself at any time, night and day, week-ends included. This does not conflict with his religious principles because, as he says, he enjoys it. And if a person enjoys something, that's rest.

Sunday mornings, he records 'Morning Service' on

Radio Four, and, in the afternoon, he retires to the caravan to prepare the sermon. These activities, and Evensong itself, are top priority; at these times, Ma takes the calls indoors, which means I am in charge of Cymby and any cooking et cetera which might be in progress. Other than that, Pa's Sundays are spent on the garden, which is also 'rest', being his pride and joy. There are no flowers in our garden, but the vegetables are exceptional. Pa and Ma are both vegans. One of the courgettes has been allowed to grow into a marrow, ready for our own harvest festival. It's already as big as Pa's gumboot.

This summer has been bad for veg, apart from the courgette, which had special treatment. The hosepipe ban made it hard for Pa to water during the hours of daylight. The back lawn is so parched it barely needs cutting, but the Percy Thrower book does say that lawns must be cut at least weekly in summer, so that's what we do.

While Pa answers the phone, the Ransome chugs lumpily; the tickover being slow for such a large, single cylinder.

Although I am not a mechanic like Pa, the machine holds a strange attraction for me. It sets my imagination on fire. Miss Barraclough says I've a 'bizarre' imagination, which, according to Ma, means exceptional.

This morning Pa sharpened the blades. He has a special machine for this. It comes from the 1930s when they made things properly. My job was to spray the drive belts with belt gum whenever they started to slip. Sharpening the blades of an eighteen-inch cylinder is a four-hour job, so he really did need my help.

The blade sharpener has its own wooden shed. The machine is spragged to the walls to stop it from rocking, but it doesn't. What happens when you turn on the motor is the whole shed begins to vibrate. At first the belts slip round the flat pulleys – they're meant to – but as soon as I squirt the gum they grab and the shafts pick up speed real fast, and the spokes on the pulleys blur and disappear. Then comes the slapping sound of the belt-joining clips whipping round the iron pulleys, getting faster and faster as the whole machine gathers speed.

I watched Pa mark the first blade with yellow chalk, pull down his welder's mask, then winch up the grinding wheel till it just pinged against the right-hand end of the blades, throwing a couple of sparks. I had to stand back with my finger on the off button as he turned the handle which moves the grinding wheel along the blade. The operator must keep the blade in contact with the stone at just the right pressure with his fingers. This is to achieve a polishing action. Too much pressure, and you get a rough edge. After about an inch I was told to switch off while he checked the angle and depth of cut. Some blades are flat, but the Ransome has a slight feather down on the trailing edge. That is what makes it cut so cleanly.

He adjusted the angle slightly and notched up the vernier to increase contact. He then nodded to me, and dropped the visor.

Mainly the sparks fly down off the wheel, but some seem to cling to the circumference all round then fly up into the operator's face. With the mask down I could not see my father's expression. As I was watching the sparks bounce off the curved perspex, I suddenly remembered part of a nightmare I'd never remembered before. There were no details other than the knowledge of a fountain of sparks and my skin dissolving like hot margarine. Next thing Pa was lunging past me to switch off the machine. Up went the visor. His angry, red face said, 'Have you gone deaf, boy? Here, give me that.' And he snatched the can of belt spray out of my hand. 'Go and see if your mother wants you. You're nothing but a menace in here.'

I wasn't quite sure what I had done, or rather, *not* done, but whatever it was, I was thoroughly disgusted with myself. Father had lunch in the caravan. I seemed always to be letting him down one way or another. The afternoon job, grass boy, seemed to offer a wonderful chance to make amends, to show how responsible I could be when the opportunity arose . . . to show my initiative . . .

Now, whilst Pa is busy on the telephone, I keep my eye firmly on the coughing, vibrating mower. Partly I am mesmerised by its spinach-green tanks and cowling, its red pulleys, dogs and levers, its greasy leather belts, its twitching, glittering blades, stink of hot oil, petrol, exhaust . . . and partly I am praying for the chance that something – I've no idea what, but just something – may go *wrong* . . . so that I, Jimbo, the firstborn, may step into the breach and save the day.

The mower vibrates. Inch by barely perceptible inch it rotates on its axis . . . Imagine my joy when, slowly, slowly, all by itself, it begins to creep off down the slope . . .

At first I just follow.

I don't push it. I don't even *touch* it.

Ma is indoors now.

And Cymbeline – bless her heart – is down by the fence, still busy making tea for the workers.

I make no claim to supernatural powers, nor do I believe in guardian angels et cetera, but suddenly a vision of what is about to occur flashes vivid and uninvited, inside my forehead: the screams, the blood-covered sheets, Pa scurrying round the lawn snatching up the pink and white scraps, calling to his God then staring at the bloody morsels of his daughter as though they're a jigsaw with missing bits.

Gradually the huge machine gathers pace on the slope. If it were possible to yell for my Ma, that's what I'd be doing. Unfortunately my voice has seized up so that all I can do is throw my four stones at the iron handles. Dragging along behind, it is all I can manage to hang on.

The mower alters its fatal course not one half of half a

degree. Meanwhile my mouth keeps making the shape of screams, Ma! MAAA! but, as in nightmare, no sound emerges. I know then there is no one but me – only *I* can possibly stop the fountain of blood and minced flesh which my sister will become in those flashing, fluttering blades. My legs go to tubes of warm jelly. Someone give me strength, I pray. But Heavenly Father is out of earshot.

When he emerges from the caravan, Pa's reaction is not quite as imagined, and strikes me as rather odd. Staring around him at the butchery, he says, 'What a mess. What a mess. Come on, James, help Daddy clear up.' Then, noticing my quivering lip, he tuts and says, 'No grizzling, now. Accidents will happen.' This breaks me up.

'I tried to save her, I did, Pa,' I wail.

'I expect you did, James. You're a hero,' says he.

He has me fetch the plastic bucket from under the sink, then returns to the caravan with the bigger bits in the bucket saying he has some letters to write. He's really going to the chapel, I'm sure, but that is what he *says*. Ma has still not appeared, which leaves only me to deal with the scraps and slivers before the flies from the sewage works arrive.

All the Smarties have gone from the plates which now have small pink morsels on. One of the teacups has been chopped into little pieces but the other still has some water inside, which to me looks redder than it should.

Ma appears briefly at the French window, then disappears upstairs, running, holding her mouth with one hand. This upsets me even more. I know I must finish clearing up the lawn, but, before doing so, I decide to telephone Auntie to come over on her bike even though I know it will take her an hour to get here from Hambledown. The phone is high up on the wall. I can just reach to dial with one finger. After two tries, I succeed.

Auntie tells me not to panic; she'll come by taxi, and, has anyone phoned for an ambulance?

After saying goodbye to Auntie, I fetch the basket and stool from the utility and take the sheets in, thinking Ma will be even more upset if she sees her clean washing all splashed with red. I'm just finishing this, when Auntie arrives and takes charge.

She asks where Pa is. When I tell her, she says what a wonderful Christian Pa is, by which, I imagine, she means his calmness in adversity. She tells me the ambulance is on its way, then she fetches Ma downstairs and sits her by the Rayburn. She makes a cup of tea which Ma stares at, Ma is very white but not crying so I suppose that is something.

Auntie kindly offers me tea as well, but I'm beginning to feel iffy myself, so excuse myself, go outside, and quietly get on with the clearing up.

In the corner of the shed, I find the two short planks Pa uses for leaf collecting and set about scraping up the smaller pieces. Using my initiative again, thinking, there might not be much to be rescued here, but at least it's a spot of organic for Dad's favourite veg. I dig a hole with the hand trowel and pop them under the courgette – together with the hands, feet and eyes (which I'd already collected). I then take it on myself to swill off the blades and rollers so they won't put Pa off finishing the grass when he's done with the Virgin in there. Life goes on, as they say. After that, I sit on our front step and wait for the ambulance.

Dark. Sitting on the step. First thought: why is it dark? Second thought: why so cold? Third thought (weird – like coming out the flicks): I've been dreaming; this is the dormitory; must be late, there's no sign of the windows. Fourth thought: STEP? WHAT STEP? We don't have stone steps in the dormitory. Fifth thought: shit, this is the turret of the Cathedral; and it's dark because it's late and the floods have gone off.

At which point I turn and see that they haven't gone off at all, that I'm sitting on the fourth step, the bottom step, right up against the barrier.

I had no memory of descending the steps to the barrier.

I reached out and touched the rough, sawn surface. I shook my head, not liking this one bit.

Certainly, I'd had hallucinations before. Several times in fact, once on the tube train, twice on the ordinary trains, so it wasn't the pictures that upset me – Doc Keylock had explained all that years ago, it's all to do with the panting, what they call hyperventilation, causing a temporary malfunction in the brain – but I'd never had anything as vivid as the memory I'd just been through. And I'd certainly never sleepwalked before, if that was what I had done. Perhaps it wasn't. Perhaps I'd come down here *before* the . . . whatever . . . On the other hand . . .

On the other hand, what about that bald-headed cat? That bugger moved.

I heard myself swear out loud. I didn't know why, I just knew that the memory was unwelcome. Unwelcome or not, sitting in the darkness, head in hands, there came a picture of the somersaulting St Tom which rapidly turned into a circular blur like a white spinning-top with red stripes . . .

Could an animal do *that* and still be *unconscious*? I felt my head shaking from side to side. What was it the old boy had said? Some story about a raid, that was it, them finding ST with a stainless steel jig screwed to his pate, them sticking him in a sack, jig and all. Something about apes or monkeys too. I remembered him using the word malfunction, 'a surgically induced malfunction', that was it. And that would tie in with the markings and the holes . . .

Let's leave it, said headvoice. **I don't think it's a good idea right now . . . Like you say, you might have moved down here *before* the—**

Shut up a sec. Please. I . . .

A gut-churning premonition had hit me, the horrific conviction that the relics would have moved, just as I had moved. Or, worse still, vanished!

I stood, swayed, dropped my hands to the steps and crawled up.

The relics were exactly as I'd left them, inside the hexagram, nothing had changed. I let go a lungful of air, slumped back against the parapet and lit another Capstan. Deep drag, slow release – control. To speak or not to speak, that is the question.

What the hell? We won, didn't we?

Ssssh; why provoke? Besides which, you've missed the point as per usual: to speak is to admit existence.

To shit oneself is to admit existence.

Fair comment.

Feeling more than a little self conscious now that the adrenalin had ebbed away, I addressed the single, lit eye: 'OK, love?' I said. 'No need to tell you how sorry I am – goes without saying – but I wouldn't call that murder, would you? Unless you're accusing Pa. Is that what you meant by killers and victims? He was careless, true, but that's not murder, that's manslaughter, lovey. Anycase, you're not blaming old Pa . . . Are you . . . ? (silence) Are you, love? (silence) Eh, love? (silence) Cymby?'

No answer.

Outside the sounds of the city had dwindled to discrete vehicle sounds and a very soft hum. In the quiet of the turret, a flash of white light beyond the city, beyond the hills which surround the city on three sides.

The silence disturbed me – more than the voice.

I didn't know the forecast, but could see we were in for a storm. The floods had extinguished on the first stroke of the eleventh hour and I was sat watching the lightning fluttering like an electric city on the blink behind Gorsley Wood. It's pretty when it's silent.

211

Down below the watchman was finishing his round, slow voice echoing between the buttress:

'Eleven-o'clock-on-a-fine-night-and-all's-well.'

I had a little snigger; it had to be fully ten minutes since the last stroke of eleven, and the thunder had been murmuring dark warnings ever since. I'd a terrible urge to shout, Fuckall's well up this turret, mate! But then I thought, Where would we be without the night watchmen of the world, guys with the talent to ignore totally what's staring the rest of us in the eyeballs and tell us, in a good firm voice, preferably with a couple of well-chosen statistics how well it all is? When the ice-cap melts and radioactive codfish cruise the nave, the watchman will be there in waterwings, and we don't need ten guesses what the message will be.

What's the betting all was well the night the Vikings came?

Not a squeak from any Ghostvoice since the game.

I had to admit that, given my experiences of the evening, it remained a logical possibility that there might be some kind of entity out there skulking in some dark corner of the Cathedral, but somehow I thought not. I now had the distinct impression that headvoice had been right all the time, that it was in fact down to *me*, or rather the old 'guilty conscience' (which is well known to be capable of playing up without proper cause), playing tricks with my head. Now that I'd drawn the incident out from my unconscious, in much the same manner as Doctor Keylock or any of the so-called psychotherapists might have done, now that I'd faced it, admitted it to myself, thought it all through without holding back from any of the horror of what happened that sunny afternoon seven years ago, I could see that, whoever's fault the accident might have been, it certainly wasn't mine. So that should be the end of it, I thought, full stop.

If – and it was a megalithic if, but I supposed we should consider every possible option now we were at it – if, in some weird way the Ghost and her voice really *did* exist, then as soon as she'd got over her disappointment, she would have to admit she'd been defeated fair and square, and would just have to honour the deal and flit off back to heaven or wherever it was she lived now.

Whatever the truth of the matter might be, I felt more than justified in assuming that, by the same time tomorrow, I would be able to both see and smell – above all, *smell* – a real change in the relics. The turning to dust, and the eternal silence . . . I'd settle for that.

So, what now?

Good question. I promised to give it the fifty-one hours, so that's, let me see, forty-five left. And that's what I'll give it. Meanwhile.

I shook my head.

Meanwhile, folks, why not relax and enjoy the atmosphere: Jimbo alone in the tower. Darkness lurks without the paneless windows. And the storm approacheth.

You know something. It occurs to me, mate, this would make a neat scene for some kind of black-comedy gothic-horror viddy; just before the bit where the dismembered body – equals relics in this case – comes to life, and our hero gets—

Naar . . . not really . . . too far-fetched. It's been done, anyway.

I was cold, tired and hungry, but there seemed little point in going to bed until the storm had gone through. Thunder always got me buzzing. I certainly wouldn't sleep.

In the meantime, despite my reservations, I found myself reflecting on headvoice's idea: I had to admit, it might make a story. I decided to try out some opening ideas: *The storm has played grandma's footsteps with the terrified child* (that's me). *It has leaped the last few leagues in one bound* (great stuff), *and lands smack BANG on the*

213

Cathedral roof (or thereabouts). *Skull-cracking – flash-WALLOP, and not a lot between. Outside the black fabric rips from pole to pole showing glimpses of heaven bla, bla, bla . . .* Brilliant, eh, head?

Definitely. Hammer House out of Mary Shelley, said headvoice. **When all this is over, we'll go for it, eh? It's got to be better than scrap metal, or journalism.**

To the west, the intricate pinnacles of the clock-tower suddenly jumped black out of blinding light into the narrow stone frame where my forehead received the first raindrop big as a grape and cold. *Ace! You've done it again, oh Bearded Wonder. I am beside myself, fatally attracted to your photon display, lacking only a companion—*

'Kinell!' I exclaimed, leaping to my feet as lightning wrapped the turret, shaking the very stones (and putting a lid on the purple prose). 'Shit! there's a *conductor* on this thing, a green copper strip from gold flag to earth down the outside of one pillar.'

I remembered about acid rain, and what it had done to the noseless bishops in their crumbling niches, and the warning notices on this boarded-off turret: *Condemned . . . Keep Out . . . by Order of . . .*

'Christ Almighty!'

Three arched windows printed themselves in black and white on my retinas, the relics flared under a sizzling discharge between sky and turret. Suddenly I was jumping, yelling out as the flagstone beat my feet like a cudgel or stone cricket bat. Ozone buzz. I hugged my bursting shins, thinking, Ow, my fucking shins are *bursting*! Then thinking, *What if fresh relics should chance to get a million or so volts up them?* Jesus! anything could happen.

While trying to convince myself how ridiculous this thought was, the turret lit up like a flash-bulb and exploded, or seemed to. For a second I thought: I'm dead. My legs have split wide open and I'm paddling in warm liquid . . . sweet Jesus! my trainers are full of blood.

I felt through the Spidersuit for the gaping edges. There were no gaping edges, just warm, wet tracksuit legs, rapidly cooling: I'd peed myself.

The wind and rain arrived.

Let's get out of here. Now!

My ears were ringing. Rain firehoseing in one side and out the other. Nothing to stop it but me in between.

What I needed was medicine, real bad. And I needed my dry bed of Bibles.

I'd had the big three – fag, belt, Aspro – and was feeling much better inside the Bible-bunk. Lying there all comfy, I thought of the relics. I supposed that I ought to have brought the Ghost down too, but the priority had been to save myself from what seemed like imminent electrocution. I still couldn't hear properly, I realised, unless it was the walls being so thick they kept out even the sound of the storm; it was still going on out there; from time to time the cloverleaf aperture lit up steely blue. Strangely, this was a comfort.

I had wrung out the Spidersuit and Y-fronts and hung them over a Bible stack thinking how He would just have to lump a bare arse on His books for one night. Feeling the cold more than ever in my nakedness, I had, reluctantly, dismantled a poor looking cloth-bound work titled *A Victorian Psalter*, scrunched up the pages and stuffed them into the spaces around my body. After a few minutes, I began to feel quite snug. If I had a little light, I thought, I might be tempted to a bit of a read in bed. If I had a decent book.

The thought had barely come and gone, and I was in the act of reaching out to replace the whisky bottle, when a long burst of electric-blue light from the aperture showed me something that froze me in mid-reach. Flashing its gold title near the bottom of a huge pile of Bibles, was a foot-long, ivory-coloured spine. I knew at once I had seen its like recently. Almost immediately the location came to me: the glass-fronted bookcase in Doctor Sopworth's bedroom.

It was three o'clock by the tower clock when I finally forced my numb fingers to close the creaking covers of the *Thesaurus Exorcismorum*. By the flickering light of a hundred or more paper spills, and with no small straining of the eyes, I had read things to haunt the most sceptical, least imaginative mind, even on a summer's afternoon in good company. On this stormy winter's night, alone in the darkness of the Cathedral, I found myself falling prey to a host of disturbing thoughts. Soon I was pricking my ears at every hiss and rustle, every creak and sigh, every flap, scuttle and click.

The work was originally published in 1626, the flyleaf informed me. This 'modern' edition was printed in Venice in 1887. The bulk was in Latin, a language of which I had only the barest understanding from a single term spent in its study at Elizabeth Barton's. To make things more difficult still, it was printed in a typeface which I recognised – thanks to information received from one D. Dick – as Gothic Black Letter type. There were, however, abundant footnotes in English. Many of these were more than sufficient to set my thoughts racing. But of all I had read so far, nothing troubled me more than two notes I encountered towards the end of the seventh chapter. One on the subject of baptism, the other on something referred to as *stigma diabolicum*.

The first note seemed almost casual. It informed the reader: *Those possessed by Behemoth may devour only unbaptised children, having no power whatever over those properly* baptised by an anointed Vicar of Christ, inside a church or other consecrated place. [*Pollidori also informs us: 'Liability to possession arises from Original Sin not wholly effaced by*

*inadequate Baptism . . . and sometimes from other sins, great
or small.']*

I blinked at the last sentence as a disturbing memory
formed in my head. The Chaplain was asking me
something . . . or telling me: 'I take it you have been
baptised, James? Yes, yes, of course. Or you would not
be here. It's just that your father's letter . . . it seems
almost to suggest—' At which point the spill I was holding
burnt my fingers. I lit another from the ember, matches
being in short supply. A dozen spills later I came across
the *Stigma* note: Indicia *are signs which create a certain
presumption (proof). Menghi, however, asserts such presumption to be* semiplina *rather than plena (sufficient). An example
of such* indicia *would be the* Stigma (or Stigmata) Diabolicum – *bloodless, insensitive patches which may be discovered anywhere on the body of the possessed.*

I transferred the spill to my left hand, and reached into
the bunk with my right. I found the burn mark on my
thigh by its roughness to the touch . . . *not* by any pain
or discomfort. I heard myself let out a shuddering sigh.

Look, can we just *stop* this, said headvoice. **It's worse
than a medical dictionary, that is. Soon we'll have every
damned sign in the book. Just shut it. And let's get
some sleep.**

I agreed entirely. My only reservation was the assump-
tion that sleep would come. Concentrate on the Matter, I
thought, concentrate on the *ordinary*, start with the 'basic
needs', start with *food*. So far we have had precisely four
slices of bread all day. And there are only two slices left.
I think it's time to make that a priority. Tomorrow we
really do change the bread into meat. Low blood sugar
level, that could be half the problem.

Only as the cloverleaf began to appear as a grey shape
in the otherwise black wall did I at last fall into a dream-
wracked sleep.

19

In the morning, I slept through the pigeons, but around 8.30 a loud banging started down in the nave like they might have been building a scaffold or something. I sat up feeling strangely light-headed and carefree; maybe I'd not had much sleep, but at least I had beaten the organist, at least I'd been spared the Magnificat on an empty stomach. One should always think positive, as the good doctor said. I squinted around the bright walls and stacks.

The cloverleaf aperture shone down on the Bible Room like a brilliant blue sun, driving away the dark shadows, shrinking the inflated terrors of the night to their proper proportions. I stretched my bare arms. There was no such thing as possession; and even if there was, it would be those lumps of meat in the turret that were infested with demons, not *me*.

I leaped out of bed, scattering scrunched-up pages. After stuffing these back in the bunk-hole, I picked up the *Thesaurus* which was still lying open beside the bunk and re-stacked it underneath a big leather Bible. I had to concede it had made compelling reading, from an historical point of view, but I did not anticipate referring to its pages again, not in present circumstances. I did, however, check my thigh, just a brief glance. It now bore a long yellow blister, fag shaped and red round the edges, but there was still no pain, not even when I pressed it. This absence of feeling, I dismissed as damaged nerve endings.

What, after all, was cauterisation but the deliberate searing of nerve and capillary?

How different things seem with a little light on the subject, I mused. I noticed I was humming as I tidied my things; a little hymn; 'Green Hill Far Away,' as it happened.

Not everything was as I wished it, however. The Spider-suit was still sodden round the crotch. I felt dirty, hungry and cold; I'd a headache; I was running low on Aspros, and the Vat was nearly all gone. The most urgent requirement was food. Apart from that, as we watchmen say, all was as well as could be expected.

Then I noticed the Bible lying all on its own on the other side of the bunk; the Bible on which I had laid out the relics the night before last, Night Zero. To my surprise, its emptiness moved me, much as the empty high-chair at *our* family table once moved the young James Bishop. And the question I had been holding down with my domestic frenzy, my sorting and tidying, my focus on Matter, burst through: would the decay have set in?

My pulse was suddenly bumping hard. On a crazy impulse, I knelt by the bunk, hands together, eyes tight shut: 'Dear Heavenly Father, please . . .'

The prayer trailed off. I had not prayed for so long I didn't know what to say. I wanted to ask for help with the relics, and I wanted some moral support, but it felt wrong somehow, sort of like sneaking to an adult; an adult I didn't even believe in.

In the end I said, somewhat flippantly, I confess: 'Please ask Lawrence to come and find me . . . I need money . . . And an Eccles cake, if I may, Lord . . . Two, if he's got the dosh. Amen.

'Oh!'

The 'Oh!' was caused by a flash of insight; it seemed like an answer to the prayer I had *not* prayed, the prayer I had only *thought*. 'Got it!' I shouted aloud, then, remembering where I was, clapped my hand over my mouth.

What I'd suddenly recalled was a picture hanging over the altar in the caravan; this in turn had reminded me of one of the statues over the south porch of the Cathedral. Both were the same in one particular: both had one finger raised in what had always struck me as a rather rude gesture. The statue was probably some bishop, but the picture was supposed to be Jesus or God – a print of the Coventry tapestry, I now knew. I seemed to think that I'd seen scores of other holy pictures just like it; God with his fingers held funny and always with one pointing upwards. That had to be it! The *Umpire* – it had to be Heavenly Father! Who else? Fancy my not guessing at once that the Umpire She was on about was none other than the top man himself.

Well then, I thought, if I believed in such a being – which I had to confess I once did but no more – He (She or It) would certainly have to be on my side now, the game working out as it had. Perhaps, after all, a little prayer could do no harm – might even help, psychologically.

I closed my eyes, and once more put palms together. And I prayed; this time choosing my words with care and with deepest respect:

'If it seems fair to you, Lord, could your . . . humble servant, James Bishop, possibly be granted a small *sign* of some description . . . The relics . . . I mean . . . could they be . . . well, just a tiny bit . . . well, *rotty* this morning? Please. Thank you so very much, Lord. Amen.' That's it then, I thought, I'm not asking for miracles; just what's normal and natural: decay, moth and rust and all that.

I had to admit, I did feel good for a moment or two psychologically speaking, but when I stood up to finish tidying my room I began to feel rather ashamed, even though no one had been here to see me or hear me. Wasn't it a touch hypocritical to pray to a god one didn't believe in? Truthfully, I hadn't believed in Heavenly Father since my fourth Christmas Eve night, the night when Auntie trod on my brick-truck as she tried to sneak in with my present – a smart Apollo Candy with stabilisers, hand-painted maroon – Pa being out with the Recovery. Once woken by her fourteen stones hitting the deck with the play-bike on top, no amount of cotton wool beard or red dressing gown was going to convince a smart kid like me that those Australian curses and bandy legs stockinged in green wool belonged to Father Christmas.

More to the point, at that age, Auntie tells me, I saw no distinction between the two Fathers, both of whom lived in the sky. To me they were each the source of all-things-bright-and-beautiful, and therefore *identical*. The result being, this episode wiped out Father Christmas and Our Father in one flash of green wool. (This was shortly before the scene I made in church, so maybe the two were connected.)

But according to Aunt Mary, what upset me more than anything, including the Father Christmas thing, was the business with the rainbow. Apparently I practically lived in the Bedford for weeks after that. It also got me banned from our playschool, for life. In a way, Pa was responsible. How often had he told me a lie is always sinful and bad in itself. Always. I'd never, ever questioned his word. But after the Santa fiasco, I began to notice things. What happened was this.

One day Miss said to the group, Today we'll do finger-painting. You can all do a picture of a rainbow.

I've always been good at painting; I'd nearly finished my picture – which included the ark and a mountain – when Miss began telling us how rainbows were all an illusion caused by sunlight and raindrops.

Naturally, I was cross. I told her she was telling porkies because I knew for sure that God put it there as a sign he was never going to drown us all again or otherwise wreck the planet. And that people who told porkies went into the oven, and serve them right so she'd better watch out. Lying was a sin, I told her. It was probably too late to say sorry, but she'd better bluggy try!

Not surprisingly she got narky with this bumptious little turd giving her lectures in infant-theology and set about proving things with a prism. Apparently her lack of repentance only made me angrier. In the end I threw my yoghurt pot full of glue at her and said the 'f' word I'd learnt from Auntie. Her hair and spectacles were plastered in white treacle. When she took off the glasses I could see I'd overstepped. But the damage was done as far as my faith was concerned, which is probably why I went mad.

So anyway, that Christmas Eve night confirmed my worst fears, it was like a kind of 'royal flush' for the infant Jimbo: all three kings – Pa, Santa and the King of Kings – all down the pan together . . .

And to be honest, I don't believe *any of them* stands a chance of ever making a comeback with me. Not that there is anything to lose by keeping the door open, but really I believed it is every man for himself.

Which is why I must cover my traces, I thought, then go up and check the state of the relics. Naturally, I hoped for the best as regards the efficacy of my heart-felt prayer, but I had to be practical. And positive. Whatever the result turned out to be, I would need sustenance, (the Eccles cakes being something of a long shot), and that meant being prepared to risk leaving the Shell for a lightning raid into Pigeon Alley. It also meant speculating with the second to last slice of bread.

An hour and a half later found me flopped on the floor of the turret in a serious state – my vaunted practicality in utter disarray. I'd a lump on my head the size of a goose egg; I'd been through some kind of hell in the spaces;

and as for the relics . . . the change in them was *not* what I'd prayed for . . . it was not what I'd prayed for at all.

Crawling around the balcony en route to the spiral staircase, the sounds of banging and sawing and general hullabaloo from below had become too curious-making to resist. Peeping over the low parapet, I saw men in overalls building a platform or stage of some sort at the foot of the choir-screen steps. This fascinated me so much I failed to notice the Mamba slip out of the gate beneath me. Until he looked up.

It was Pretty Boy with the hair, again! I ducked so fast I wasn't sure whether he'd seen me or not, but it gave me a prickly feeling just to imagine it, so I scuttled for the door and legged it up the spiral stairway three steps at a time, just in case. As I ran, I remember thinking stupid thoughts like: How did he know I was up here looking down? Perhaps the guy has a heat sensor where his tonsure should be. Which shows how cool I was at first. I was totally confident I could lose any nancified verger on my chosen ground, provided I had a decent start, which was precisely what I was giving myself.

Now, I normally notice the point where the stone part of the spiral stairway becomes the brick lining, this time I missed it and WALLOP! I'm sitting on this step with my tongue bit nearly in half and the top of my head about flush with my shoulders.

When my eyes finished leaking, I looked up and of course it was the lead drainpipe.

I sat a moment cursing the junkie builders, then suddenly the thought came: Hang on, Jimbo, this could be good news (there's nothing like a crack on the nut with a lead pipe to wake a body up), this could mean we've got fresh water piped to the back door whenever it rains, and sucks to the waterboard.

I gingerly fingered the rapidly rising egg . . . no blood . . . it almost seemed worth it. Then I heard the footsteps . . . coming up fast . . . an echoing, slapping sound making me think of a great bird or bat flapping up from the bottom of a well . . .

Get out of here quick, said headvoice. But I'd already started up the spiral. **Not that way, idiot! It's a dead end, isn't it. We'll have to go down**.

The speed of the Mamba's ascent shook me. I turned and plunged downwards, hoping my footfalls would be masked by his, making plans as I went.

I knew that this spiral joined the crypt to the turret via the south-east corner of the tower. I figured I might have rather less than ten seconds to beat the ascending Mamba to the balcony, from there I'd take the door which leads to the vast western attics and unexplored spaces beyond. Enough time. Just.

I practically fell through the door to the balcony, shut it after me, turned left, scrambled the twenty or so feet to the door in the south-west corner and plunged through, closing this too.

I stood in the darkness, panting. I could just hear the footsteps; they seemed a little slower, and . . . I held my breath . . . yes, they were fading. He'd passed the balcony and continued on up. For a second I relaxed but another thought struck: Had I refixed the boards behind me when I'd fled the turret during the storm? If I hadn't . . . If he entered the turret . . . What would he find? The memory of lightning flaring between the cracks in the boards and me pushing home the four-inch nails with numb fingers arrived simultaneous with the patter of descending footsteps . . .

The Mamba was coming back!

I searched the darkness. From the tiny amount of light leaking around the door behind me, I could just make out the boards of the platform I stood on, and the first few feet of three narrow walkways emerging from the gloom, one cutting sharply away to my right, another straight ahead and a third branching left off this a few yards along.

I shuffled forward as fast as I dared along the central walkway, figuring this to be less likely to lead me towards a choice-limiting edge. After only three or four paces, a loud crash came from behind me. It sounded as though the door from the spiral staircase had been flung open.

I took off at speed with the flimsy boards flexing and bouncing at each stride. I prayed there would be no sudden turns. From the deadness of sound, I judged I was in the main roof-space. As I ran, I weighed the odds. Although there were four possible exits from the balcony, and three different walkways for my pursuer to choose from, I could not take chances. But even if he chose lucky and came straight for the exit I had taken, I reckoned I could make at least twenty yards before he would open the door behind me. By which time I would be off the 'purpose built', heading for the spaces . . .

He'd never find me in the spaces.

After twenty paces, I threw myself flat, rolled to the edge and over.

The drop was not great. I landed on all fours, stayed on all fours, then scampered off into the blackness. The ground felt as I imagined a first world war battlefield might feel – all pits and trenches – but dry. I'd made maybe ten yards when the door crashed open, and some grey edges appeared in the darkness before me.

The opening yards of the passage – if we should call such an accidental meeting of two surfaces a 'passage' – gave no clue to the horror it held in its depths. But in any case, my former cockiness had evaporated. Somehow my pursuer had guessed correctly at every turn. Now, with the torch beam sectioning the darkness above and behind me, I gratefully entered the dark cleft and began to pick my way over the lumps of rubble and mortar beneath my feet.

My shoulders brushed both walls at once, so I twisted

slightly to cut out the sound. After maybe ten or twelve yards, the right-hand wall gave way to a right-angled turn which felt of a similar width to the one I was in. Another chance, I thought, another opportunity for the Mamba to choose wrongly. I would not calculate this time, this time I would try to select my route in a random way. So far he'd read me too well. Maybe logic was the problem.

I turned to look back at the softly gleaming, parallel surfaces converging towards an oblong of dimly lit structures, an oblong much taller and narrower than any doorway. And as I looked back, into that zone of lesser darkness there silently drifted a dense moving shadow. A light source wavered slowly back and forth. The light could only be from a torch – obviously – but there was something oddly fragmented about it. And the shadowy shape was also wrong . . . something about the shoulders . . . too bulky and hunched, almost like those of an American footballer but more upwardly curving.

What the hell was he wearing?

Dead centre of the oblong, it stopped.

Silence.

The light extinguished. The dark shape was still visible against a background of dimly lit beams. It seemed bigger. Suddenly it shortened to half height, less.

'Shit,' I whispered. 'He's leaving the walkway. He's coming this way!' How did he know? I'd hardly made a sound.

Using the corner to steady myself, I slowly and silently turned about and moved to my right, into the blackness of the side alley.

Once round the corner, I moved forward as fast as I dared, though the going was very uneven. Ahead was pure blackness; I tried closing my eyes; it made not the slightest difference. Suddenly, from behind, I heard the crunch of rubble. I stopped to listen, holding my breath. The sound ceased.

Silence, but for the hiss of blood in my ears and the thud of my heart. Why did the man not shout for me to stop, to give myself up? Why this silent pursuit? It was not natural.

No voice came.

I hurried forward again, trying to tiptoe with little success . . .

It was then that I felt the first cobweb – one sticky tendril, unbelievably strong, across my right eye and the bridge of my nose.

I jerked back, tingling with fear, feeling it peel off like a strand of elastoplast.

Behind me the sound again of moving rubble; from the change in sound quality, I guessed he had already entered the passage. This was immediately confirmed by a sound similar to that which my own shoulders had made on first entering the narrow space. But there was a difference. The sound I heard now was lighter and hollower and . . . somehow familiar . . . Jesus Christ – *Wings!* – the dry, hollow rustle of quill against stone.

I tried to deny it, but it was too late, the thought was there.

Twin terrors combine in the instant with nightmare logic: *feathers and cobwebs, cobwebs and feathers* . . . and now . . . *words* . . . words burned into the blackness . . . white words, black words . . . seen, yet not seen . . . silent, yet heard . . . words I had read in the Book and forgotten but now *knew* again . . . *word for word*:

Satan is the ape of God. It gives him great pleasure to incarnate himself in the shape of man as Christ himself did.

Suddenly, and with terrible certainty, I knew that what was behind me was no ordinary verger. Verger it may have seemed once, down there in the sunlit nave . . . but

228

up in the spaces . . . with no one to witness . . . it no longer needed that shape. From the very first, I had sensed something *wrong* about the long-haired Mamba . . . for one thing a man should not be that beautiful. Now I *knew* what it was I had then only *felt* . . . I knew what the creature would look like without its disguise . . . I had seen it before, many times, as a child. In the cellar. At home. In the Roombed also . . . Soon it would reach the place where I had turned to the right. It would make no mistake. It would follow me here . . .

I had to go on. There was no other choice possible.

I sucked a huge breath, ducked low, praying I might yet slip through beneath the bulk of the web which I knew must be draped across the passage in front of me. But when I moved forward, my face was instantly smothered in cobweb so thick and heavy it seemed like damp, clinging rag.

With a gasp, I swiped at my face and neck and plunged forward, shuddering, flailing my arms wildly in front, feeling the drapes of web building on me, dragging me down.

From behind came a dry, hollow rustle . . . close now . . . and the stench of the poultry house . . .

When the eight legs marched across my forehead I was already beyond shock. The soft, cool abdomen drew one sticky line from temple to ear . . .

I might have been the butterfly I'd watched enmeshed on the hanging geranium in Auntie's backyard. She should never have fluttered the way she did. Never provoke. After the bite, the lingering poisonous kiss, she could not move . . .

A small corner of my brain ached to send the message: Hand rise up and smash the soft, repulsive body away . . . but . . .

He inside me . . . the Father inside me . . . forbade it.

So what could I do? Without blood in my legs or the tips of my fingers . . .

229

. . . I went down.

SCENE: *The Attic – Summer*

The roof space is very hot. A bare bulb illuminates the scene. Empty black plastic sacks are scattered about, together with piles of crumpled brown paper. To one side stands a part roll of fibreglass insulation. Beside this a man in blue overalls, wearing a cheap aluminium facemask, is cutting off the strip he has just laid between the joists. He wears pink rubber gloves, their tops stretched over the overalls' cuffs. With his right hand he works a large pair of red-handled scissors. Less than half the area has been completed.

I am seven years old. Ma is still away. I miss her, but must be brave. And helpful. Today, my job is operating the big industrial vacuum cleaner, to clear all the crap between the rafters and joists while Pa deals with the cutting and fitting. I have been allowed to take off my shirt and am working in just shorts and plimsoles.

I know that I am not meant to vac up the spiders, just their cobwebs. But when I can see he's not looking, I do so. Because they scare me. Even the little ones. There are quite a few spiders in our attic . . .

'I'm going down for another,' shouts Pa over the howl of the cleaner. 'Make sure you do properly under the eaves.'

I turn and nod as he disappears backwards through the hatch. I am glad that the rolls are too big for me to handle. I hate the way the fibres prickle your skin; you can't see them, but you can't seem to brush them away either.

I step off my chipboard kneeler on to a joist in order to slide the three-foot square board up near the eaves in the corner. And that's when I see it. The biggest blackest spider I have ever seen in my life. It seems to be looking straight at me, its knuckled legs poised, tense, waiting I know for one false move from me to trigger it into an electrifying spring . . . straight at me. Straight at me where I kneel unbalanced, precariously lodged between joist and board.

Moving like a boy in treacle, I rotate on the axis of my right knee and pick up the yard and a half of large bore nozzle between hands slick with sweat. I swing round slowly, slowly, and slowly level it to aim at the spider, slowly push it forward against the pull of the concertina pipe behind. The four-foot-long nozzle is heavy for me and hard to hold level, but I do not take my eyes off the spider. Not for one instant.

The creature is square on to me, spread across four inches of brick chimney breast. As the nozzle gradually closes in, its shadow, thrown by the bare bulb behind me, creeps across the chimney towards the spider. I am no longer breathing. Nor do I notice the sound of the vacuum cleaner. Nor the creaking of the loft ladder . . .

The nozzle is still four or five inches short of target when the spider vanishes with a quick shushhh and a sickening thud from the body of the cleaner.

'I am watching you, James,' says Father. I jump so hard I nearly fall off the board. 'And I'm afraid you are going to have to pay for that sinful act. Downstairs, please.'

I gather up my shirt in silence and start down the ladder.

'All the way, James. I'm sorry, precious boy, but you simply must learn.'

If I had known what he intended, I believe I would have run. But he smiled with his lips, as usual, giving no clue to change. I thought I was just to be shut in the cellar, as usual, the light turned off, as usual, the better to think out my wickedness, the better to pray for forgiveness.

No light comes into our cellar. Even when hunched on the top step, no chink can be seen leaking around the doorframe, because it is perfectly insulated with foam plastic strip.

231

Although I put my hands together every night – with Ma, when she's home, otherwise on my own – I have not *prayed* since the rainbow incident. (I may have gone through the verbal motions once or twice, but that's all.) I do not pray down here. What I do, when I'm sent down here, is sums and tables.

Today it is counting, adding and subtracting in base seven . . . until I hear the scraping sound . . . that stops me. In all the times I've been down here, I have never heard that sound before.

There then comes a sound that seems to me like a brick or tile being moved. A sudden spear of light strikes across the distempered roof timbers. The source is at the top of the right-hand wall, the outside wall. The ceiling joists sit on the top of this wall. Between them are gaps about a foot wide and six inches deep. One gap suddenly shows daylight.

Something moves in the depths of the gap. The light reduces. The nozzle of the big cleaner appears, it keeps coming until it falls on to the furniture and other junk piled against the wall. The light around it blinks and disappears. Silence.

I still don't get it; I suppose because, to me, vacuum cleaners are all about *sucking*.

'Can you hear me, James?'

It's him. Just the other side of the door. What's going on, I think, he never speaks to me down here?

'Yes, Pa.'

'I have checked in the bag, and you're lucky this time. Fortunately he's still alive. And so are the others, James . . . you really are a wicked child, aren't you? I cannot imagine what possesses you. When I switch on, I want you to go down the steps, sit down quietly on the floor by the end of the nozzle . . . and I want you to apologise. Is that clear?

'And we'll just have to hope they forgive you, that's all . . .'

Silence.

'Are you there, James?'

'Yes.'

'Yes, what?'

'Yes, Pa.'

'They all look extremely angry to me, James, and hurt. Hurt and angry. So you'll just have to hope they calm down. You'll just have to hope that they're a great deal *kinder* and more charitable than you are, James. You'll just have to pray they forgive you. You are not coming up unless and until they do, I'm afraid. That would not be fair or right.

'I'll be listening, James. I shall be able to hear everything perfectly through the tube. So make sure you do as I tell you. Exactly as I tell you, James, clear?'

'Yes. Pa.'

'You may start your apologising as soon as I switch off the machine. Is that clear? Then we'll see what they say . . .' (Silence. While I contemplate screaming for mercy.) 'Is that clear, James?'

'Yes.'

Silence. I guess he has gone to switch on. I guess the machine blows as well as sucks. I am numb with dread. I am literally shaking. And I'm crying like a fucking girl, but silently. Silently.

Beyond the wall, the vacuum cleaner howls into life. A wind fills the darkness. I am struck by small objects and my nostrils fill with the stink of rot. Down below, two points of red light appear, one at a time like a wink in reverse. I hear the stirring of wings. I feel myself falling, painlessly jolting down the steps.

20

I stood a moment, staring at the empty floor of the turret. Then a wave of feebleness swamped me and dumped my body on the top step. The barrier had been in perfect order when I arrived – boards secure, nailheads flush – so through I'd come, tugging it all closed behind me. But the second my eyes cleared floor level I saw that the relics had gone!

There was the hexagram, a bit washed out, but no mistaking it. And there were the two, four, six dark patches where the feet, hands and eyes had been and the water had yet to dry out . . . But where were the things themselves?! Where were the relics?

I lit up with trembling fingers. Long drag. Fight for control. First question: Me. Am *I* all right?

Of course you are. We've had a bit of a scare, that's—
Bit of a scare! Christ . . . !

I fingered the lump on my head where I'd struck the drainpipe. I felt like a clubbed seal, but that wasn't what worried me.

I'm in bloody trouble, you bastard. You *know* it. What's going to happen to me now?

Ssh – take it easy, take it easy – 'control', remember? OK, so you swallowed a spider—
Not just a spider, you bastard—

All right. All right. You think it was *the* spider, and you think you might have—

235

Not *might have*, DID, damn you. I felt the bastard go down! I felt it wriggling, fuck it! Why don't you—

Look, calm down . . . And think. You were in a panic. Right? You took a bad fall – twenty feet, maybe – almost vertical. Right? It's hardly surprising if the old imagination started—

Imagination?! All right, how come I still feel it, in here? (I prodded my solar plexus.) It's the one all right. The size of it, Jesus Christ! When I came to . . . ughh, fuck . . . mouth wide open . . . laid on me back . . . choking . . . swallowing . . . (Blank slate. Memory censored. Silence. Apart from the wind. And something flapping, something rattling below and far off.) And what about that other *thing*? Don't tell me I *imagined* that too. It followed me! I saw it, for Christ's sake! You know what it is. Same as I do. And you know where it went. It changed shape again. You know it did, you bastard, don't *pretend* . . . Jesus, I'm bloody terrified. *Terrified*. And all you can do is—

I took another long drag at the Capstan, and inspected my trembling hand. *Control* . . . I had to regain it. And *keep* it. That was the whole object of my being in this place. I didn't *want* to be here; it's a trial.

Concentrate on the Matter. Start with the objects at hand – rather, the objects *not* at hand – that's the way . . . that's control. Focus on first causes . . .

Last drag, a long, long draw, fizzing the baccy, burning my tongue, making me dizzy, ahhh. Right; fags out. Now, *concentrate*.

My first idea was that Mambas had found the relics. But then I thought, Why would they replace the barrier exactly as I had left it? Unless . . . Unless they wanted to spring a trap, of course . . . In which case . . . why weren't they here, waiting?

My second idea was jackdaws; the barrier had almost certainly not been opened; the tower was unscalable from without; who or whatever took the relics must therefore have *flown* in. It would certainly be possible for a jackdaw to get in through any of the eight window openings, but then I thought, No. Jackdaws are supposed to be great collectors, but even a jackdaw could not fly off with the hands, feet and eyeballs of a four year old crammed into its beak all at once. Either it would have to have made six separate trips, which was mad, or else there would have to have been six jackdaws. Which was just as mad. Where were the feathers? The droppings? Surely at least one would have been caught short at some point during the operation. And anyway, why would the Cathedral jackdaws suddenly break the habit of centuries and come to the south side when their haunt had always been on the north?

Fingering the lump, I began to scrape the theoretical barrel-bottom; I had prayed for the whiff of putrefaction hadn't I? Yes. All the same . . . I could hardly imagine the relics rotting away to *nothing* . . . all in the course of a single night. I even managed a small snigger at that one. It didn't last long. With jackdaws and Mambas both out of the frame, I found myself considering the bizarre idea that the *storm* had something to do with the disappearance of my dead sister's remains.

I should say at once I was not harbouring any weirdo Lawrentian notion that the lightning had zapped the little cow back to life the moment I left the turret; for one thing there was the matter of missing parts. No, when it comes to resurrections, I believe in the defibrillator and that's about it; which means I have less trouble with Frankenstein than I do with say, Lazarus, to cite one of Pa's favourite yarns. (I'm pretty certain I never believed that one, I mean the guy had been dead a week, for Pete's sake. In that climate he'd have been well past his sell-by date.) But in any case, it seems to me that resuscitation is a mechanical problem, to do with parts and labour rather than séances or last suppers. That's all.

With regard to the relics, I was prepared at least to consider the possibility that there could have been some sort of *automatic* response in the nerves and muscle fibres triggered by the lightning. The walls and floor of the turret had been awash with storm water, after all. And water being a conductor, the charge might just possibly have bridged the gap by this means. (We'd learned in science about Galvin and his electrically operated frogs' legs; if they could do it, why not relics?)

I felt the control returning. My relief grew rapidly as I warmed to the theory. I began to feel I was really homing in on the answer: involuntary spasms had sent those lifeless appendages hopping about the turret like bingo balls on a current of air . . . until their trajectories just happened to coincide with not-wall, not-floor, not-ceiling (which I quickly worked out was better than a one in three shot every hop). That had to be it! Their departure was pure chance, devoid of all sinister significance, non-sentient; no supernatural explanation required. In all probability they were now far apart, lying – sweet Jesus – wherever they happened to fall!

Holy Shit!

The thought sent me dashing to the window slits. If I had guessed correctly they would be out there somewhere, lodged in a gutter or on the flat roof of the tower. Or – God forbid – down on the pavement waiting for a party of schoolgirls to tread on them!

But, although it was still early for tourists, the relics were in none of those places. After an exhausting hour – having dared the open roof to dredge the lead guttering behind the parapet – I was forced to abandon both search and hypothesis. Not only were the hands and feet not in any of the places I had thought possible, but I had come to realise that the hypothesis was quite inadequate to explain missing eyeballs, these being hopelessly ill equipped for hopping, volts or no volts.

Looking back I realise that, if there ever was a moment when I might have quit, admitted defeat and abandoned the Cathedral to throw myself on the mercy of school, home or child guidance clinic, this was that moment. But to me, then, that seemed the road to insanity . . . or worse. There were just too many unanswered questions now, too many battles to be fought and riddles to be solved. I still felt I could do it. But, at that precise moment, that climax of black confusion and fear, I desperately needed a refuge. And time to think things out and assemble some positive strategy.

Obviously I could not relax and take stock in the turret after what had happened, so I worked my way back to the Bible Room, closed the door quietly and lay down in the bunk.

I remained motionless for a while, practising the muscle relaxation techniques I had learned in drama, sending round my mental supervisor to check that every part was free from tension, at the same time, striving to calm myself mentally, to empty my mind by focusing on the One, then dismissing that also. But the thought refused to depart that my refuge, this whole vast Cathedral, stone, paper, metal, cloth, wood, everything had gone wrong, sick, contagious; it had turned against me; even the Bibles were against me; I seemed to feel their angry pulse on my back – bump, bump, bump, bump . . . Things weren't getting *better* in here, they were getting *worse*; what had happened in the passage; I daren't even think about that. I had blocked those thoughts. I'd clawed my way back up the mountain of rubble like a demented animal, and returned to the turret on automatic pilot. But where could I run to now?

Nowhere, said headvoice. **Pull yourself together. Do something constructive**.

Such as?

We haven't eaten for . . .

(A burst of hysterical laughter from me) Haven't we? I have!

. . . thirty-six hours. I suppose it would be naïve to suggest we might just be hungry.

Yes. It would. Can't you see when a person's upset.

Let's hunt relic then. We need *action* . . . positive action.

On an empty stomach?

OK, let's eat then? But for God's sake, do *something*. Let's get the meat.

(If only Lawrence was here, I thought, he'd cut through the crap. What would Lawrence do, in this situation?)

'We'll get the meat,' I said.

21

There's a narrow space between the north wall of the Cathedral and the Chapter House where the sun never shines. Here the pigeons roost and nest in holes in the wall where stones are missing. The walls are black and slimy with lichen and pigeon shit. It smells of worms and leaf-mould. Because it takes the run-off from both eaves, it's never, ever dry. The only light comes from a metre-wide strip of sky fifty feet above, and the little that falls through the arch at the end. We call it Pigeon Alley. It's another alien space.

An iron ladder descends this accidental chasm from the nave roof, but it stops a good fifteen feet above the moss-feather-and-shit-covered earth. The only way to reach the bottom rung is to jump from the roof of a wooden hut the builders occasionally use for storing things. It was lucky I knew this.

If I wasn't an animal-lover there would have been no problem, but when it comes to catching pigeons I draw the line at the fish-hook method on humanitarian grounds. How anyone could thread bits of bread on hooks then snag the poor buggers in the crop and just reel them in I'll never understand. You won't catch me behaving like that. But it was this anti-cruelty attitude of mine that almost cost me my liberty.

As with so many worldly matters, it was Lawrence who had introduced me to the gravel and grain method of humane culling, but only the theory of it; I'd never yet tried it in the field. From the shadows of the chasm I had already spotted the beige and white pigeon goose-stepping around on the grass just outside Pigeon Alley, apparently pecking at sweet f.a.

Hungry, I thought, like me.

I inched my way along the wall towards the narrow opening. I could see no tourists or other strollers so quickly cast out a handful of breadcrumbs. She jumped a bit at the unexpected prezzy, but Cathedral pigeons are raised on bread and pretty soon my bird was tucking in, which is when I followed up – a bit harder – with a handful of precinct gravel. It wasn't hard enough though. My supper flapped off round the corner in a storm of feathers with the blood coming out of the side of its beak. I'm off round the corner after it like Wally the cat; then I pounce.

There I am on the neatly mown grass that says Keep Off Grass with the pigeon pinned under my armpit trying to bend its neck double and it smacking me in the face with one wing, when all of a sudden there's this: 'Oi!' Then again, 'Oi!'

A man in a raincoat is running towards me. From nowhere a Mamba appears and I'm up and running with the bleeding pigeon up my jumper playing the bongos on my chest. As I run I'm computing the Mamba's speed in that heavy black frock against my chances of making it up the north transept steps before he rounds the corner. The answer is a raspberry, so it's over the shed, drop down the back, breath held, pulse racing.

I hear leather soles smacking the flagstones rapidly, they stop, then heavier, rubber footfalls, then voices. I'm cursing because the pigeon chooses this moment for an escape bid up the neck of my Spidersuit, plus I can tell they know I must be close but can't quite imagine the transshed escape route I've taken. As the neck of the pigeon clears the neck of the suit, I grab it, double it back and pinch the bend as hard as I can – remembering you have to be cruel to be kind – scratching my own neck quite badly in the process. The wings go berserk and the whole thing is beginning to make me feel rotten, then they stop and I figure I've done it. There's blood on my hands, mine or hers I don't know.

After what seemed an age, Rubber Feet moved off towards what they call the Lavatory Tower (not what it sounds like), Leather Feet must have figured I'd gone inside the Cath because he pattered off up the steps, which of course meant the end of all hopes of returning to my refuge via the Crypt. All was quiet inside my Spidertop which I'd tucked under my belt. The pigeon lay soft and warm on my belly, and I stood listening while my metabolism returned to something like normal.

The north side of the Cathedral is not the public, tourist side, but faces the school. Fortunately the Chapter House intervenes and is so tall it not only screens the full height of the iron ladder but also one of the half dozen hatches dotted around the parapet which lead directly into the roof-space. Less fortunately, that particular hatchway gives access to the loft of the northeast transept, the place I call the Wild Wood. I could get back to base via that loft . . . but the thought of it made my scalp wriggle.

The Wild Wood is one gigantic nest. The entire loft is a matted tangle of sticks and twigs brought in by the jackdaws over God knows how many centuries; in parts it is many metres deep. It's the kind of place best avoided after dark; it makes me think of poor Moley, and Ratty's warning, and that's why I call it the Wild Wood. I tell you it's . . . weird doesn't begin to describe it. And the sun already down.

The worst of it is, the Wild Wood is alive with the most hideous of micro-monsters; by which I mean the so-called Cathedral Bug – though 'bug' is too cosy a name for that black abortion – Satan's Crab suits it better. Anyway, the Wild Wood is seething with them, and in its endless darkness the beasties multiply; they've no enemies to control them, and they've been at it for centuries! (If ever I get the DTs I know what I'll see and it'll be Cathedral Bugs and more Cathedral Bugs all the way down to the bottom.)

I've actually seen them only once – Lawrence and I wandered in there one morning, the torch beam just happened to fall on a clutch of them sitting tight on the wall, right by my ear. They were waiting to pounce, I know it; that's how they live; they hang about in the dark, watching (such a creature will see in the dark, never fear) and listening and feeling for the minuscule rise in temperature and small vibrations which signal a passing vascular system, then they hop on board and they . . . *suck*. Yes. And that is exactly how they look – like things that jump out of the dark and land without a body feeling them and burrow into living flesh, flesh they have numbed with preliminary injections, and . . . *suck*.

According to Lawrence, they drink nothing but jackdaw and pigeon blood – he also told me they were brought here by Crusaders returned from the Holy Land, which sounds about right – but I don't buy the other: blood is blood, I reckon. They may only be alien ticks, but their shells are so hard they are almost indestructible, and they can survive for years without a meal of any sort . . .

They revolt me.

The striking of the half hour alerted me to the incoming tide of darkness. At any moment the floodlights could come on, then even this ladder would be too risky. I climbed on to the shed roof and gathered myself for the jump. I used what mind control I could muster to blot out the thought of what lay ahead – at least I'd have food to eat – after the gauntlet was run.

I steadied, and jumped.

The iron was ice-cold. I climbed fast for fear my fingers

might freeze to the rungs. Within seconds, I'd rolled over the parapet, scrambled along the lead gutter to the hatch, drawn the bolt and entered – all without giving my head time to jam the works.

Wall of darkness and . . . *stink*.

The Wild Wood has a different smell to Pigeon Alley, more like the chicken transporters that make you gasp when you can't get the car windows up fast enough – a cocktail of scurf, shit and butcher's shop. I tried breathing through the sleeves of my tracksuit. Useless.

Other than the light seeping through the hatchway behind me, the only thing visible was twin columns of dim stripes from a pair of narrow slatted windows in the end wall. No direct rays could enter, and I knew that, as soon as I closed the hatch, I'd be travelling blind.

But I couldn't give in; one monster is much like another – once you falter, you're done.

As my eyes accustomed to the gloom they began to make out details close by. I was standing on a catwalk three boards wide. To my left was a rough wooden handrail, below, to right and left, I could now make out the grey slopes of two of the conical pits formed by the vault of the transept beneath – the floor under the catwalk was really a negative ceiling – but, apart from a yard or two near the edge, it was completely submerged in nest, as was the catwalk itself a few steps further in. The handrail was visible for a yard or two more, so I figured the catwalk might still be passable; beyond that I could see nothing.

What about the Bu—, began headvoice.

Shut it! I hissed. I closed the hatch, gripped the rail and shuffled forward into the Wild Wood.

22

I moved fast, hoping to catch the creatures napping, or, at least, cause them to miss. But soon after the point where the catwalk turns left along the centre line, I found myself high-stepping through deep, brittle nest. A moment later even the handrail was covered by the mat of twig and fibre. I was forced to a standstill, gagging on the charnal stench of the place, suddenly aware of aeons of jackdaw mortality.

Don't stop! wailed headvoice, **they'll get us**.

Fuck this! I snarl, but just as I'm turning about this *itch* comes . . .

Oh! Oh! I cry, grabbing myself. Then comes this scrabbling round my belly-button and I'm walloping myself as hard as I can. God help me – my belly's alive! Jabbing me back, *exactly as the infant Cymbeline once did with her puny fists!* My legs buckle and I fall off the catwalk shouting, 'Stop it! I didn't mean it! I didn't mean it!' As if I was the infant and she the elder! Then down I go, over the edge and into the pointy pit overflowing with Lord-knows-how-many fathoms of stinking nest . . . and Lord-knows-how-many Crabs of the Prince of Darkness.

The more I wail and thrash the deeper I go, just like in any swamp or quicksand. In seconds I'm over my head in stinking nest, my feet still not touching the bottom. Then these hideous scrawking, banshee noises break out of my belly . . .

Ahh! I hear myself scream in the treble, and, Ahhh! and Ahhh! again.

My belly is writhing and wriggling! Christ! Is it about to rupture and spew forth a real-live *Alien* in a fountain of blood and shit!? Ahhhooo! No no noooo, please, pleeeease . . .

Going down . . .

I grab at my belly again, and feel . . .

. . . a small claw . . .

BLOODYHELL!!

'My turn to go first.'

'What?! No. Hang on, I—'

'You started last time; that's fair.'

'But you *lost*! And I was *innocent*! I proved it. So you shut it. Shut it! That was the *deal*. You swore on the—'

'Sorry; you cheated.'

'I never! I—'

'Sorry, James, I insist.'

'Insist?'

'Insist, yes. Going down.'

'Not me!' I cry, and I reach out and, lo and behold, I touch wood and I know that it's one of the posts which hold up the catwalk. So I lock my arm round it and . . .

'No choice, James. Feel your body, feel that crimson muscle inside your chest, and those frothy pink bellows of yours, pumping away. The doctor calls it a panic attack, I call it a trip down memory lane for big bro. The real memory lane, this time.'

'I'll fight you, you cow.'

'Think about the Bugs, James, it'll take your mind off things. Did you know they always head for the warmest, softest parts of a person, parts like a boy's teddy-tail, for instance. Just ask yourself, whereabouts on your body is the skin most like plucked pigeon. I'll give you a clue, it's round, and there's two.'

248

'Ahhh! Ahhhh!!'

'You've got it, big bro, that's where they like to burrow best, and next to pigeon blood, the thing they like most is a nice drop of fresh semen.'

'Ahhhooooeeeeaye!'

'That's why we call them Satan's Crabs, on this side. Going down . . . That's the style . . . relax . . . let yourself go . . . the anaesthetists are really first rate . . . you won't feel a thing down bel. . . .

'Oooooooo!'

SCENE: *The Garden – Sunday Afternoon, Summer*
I step out on to the patio carrying the tray with porcelain mugs by Boots the Chemists. The mugs are three-quarters filled with tea and there is no mark on the white melamine, not a single brown ring, not a drop of spilled milk, not a grain of sugar. The sun flashes like an Apache signal off the two rocking circles. I halt at the edge of our lawn which is the colour of dry prairie.

It is wrong to slop and make messes that others have to clear up behind one. My muscles tense to stop the rocking pools of light, circles within circles, dazzling. (Something flaps, something else rattles in my brain. The end of my teddy-tail is tickling like mad, but it is not-nice for boys to scratch down below. Besides I might slop.) The circles grow steady. A moment more. To be certain. Good.

I proceed.

'Oh, thank you, my darling, that's lovely. Pop it on the table, there's a pet.'

This is my lovely Ma speaking to me in her love voice. But I will not look up from the tray until I have it safely landed on the white plastic table. Then I'll look up with a smile, and breathe freely. It pleases me that she called me my darling and not my little prodigy as she once did; this is the best sign yet that I am winning her back.

Her forehead shines whitely above the dark glasses; she

249

has not been well but the resting home has allowed her to visit us for the afternoon.

There is no deck chair for me so I sit on the lawn at Ma's feet and draw some barley water up the straw, gently so as not to disturb Pa who is reading. The morning breeze has died completely and my prickly grey shirt attaches to my spine. (Good; it'll take my mind off the other itch.) In a moment I will massage her poor feet which have swollen due to inactivity and the hot weather.

From beyond the palletwood fence comes the sound of Lucky dragging his chain over the concrete. Back and forth, back and forth; continuously on the move.

Without appearing over the newspaper, Pa says irritably, 'What's the matter with that animal? Didn't you water it this morning, James?'

I am acutely conscious that I have been a source of aggravation to Pa recently over my stupid allergy to vegetables; it cannot be pleasant to see the products one has slaved over summer and winter being regurgitated on to the dinner plate of one's elder child. However, it is one of my duties to supply the guard dog with water and to clear up his doings each morning before school. He is never allowed off the chain, so can't help the mess and smell he makes, but it is one of my least favourite duties. I never neglect it, however, and am hurt by the suggestion. So I do not hear it.

This causes him to fold down the top half of the newspaper, to see if I have set off, and to lose his place.

Things have not been quite the same between the two of us since the business with the vacuum cleaner in the cellar. I feel his glare now, but let my own eyes wander past the fence to the yellow lattice of the heavy lifting gear and the big iron disc of the magnet hanging down, and the motorcar-mountain that has built up over the holiday season.

'James!'

250

I manufacture a little start. 'Sorry?' I say politely, pleased to observe that the fly on the rim of his mug is taking refreshment now. 'Sorry, did you—'

Ma intercedes: 'Would you mind, dear? When you're ready.' She withdraws the blue-veined foot I am soothing and smiles sadly down. 'Poor Lucky, it must be baking in the yard.'

Ma tries her hardest to divide herself fairly between my own and Pa's needs, but sometimes she must find it difficult, and it hurts her that, as yet, she can only be with us for these brief visits, and always seems tired. However, I prefer to do things about the house out of the goodness of my heart rather than on request and consider making a little tut noise with the tip of my tongue behind my top teeth. But this would now seem directed against the invalid so I hold back, thinking, in two years I will be at the comprehensive and only five years after that – providing I pass the scholarship exam, which I easily should – I'll be at boarding school, and then I'll be *free*, free to scratch and do whatever I like. Furthermore there will be other scholarship boys beside myself, and hopefully my intelligence will provoke less spite than it does at Marshside Junior.

In the middle of this quiet preview of my academic future, Ma does something – only a small thing, but it breaks an unwritten law of the household – and that's what started me off . . .

It was my own fault really, for not remembering the date, September 15th; it's hardly surprising she was acting strange . . .

The accident had brought about certain changes in our house. Almost immediately, things began to disappear. The day after the ambulance took Ma away, the rotary drier vanished; on the Sunday it had been loaded with sheets (I had taken them down myself, I couldn't forget that) and by Monday night it was gone. Some households take them in when not in use, I know that, but we never did, ours stayed there all the time like a yellow and blue tree. So this struck me as odd.

Pa began taking our family wash over to Hambledown every Saturday evening in pillowcases. On Sunday mornings Auntie would bring it back clean, cook lunch – which always included the one vegetable I can stomach, ie beans-in-a-tin because they're not disgusting green – and afterwards she and I would play the test match while Pa worked on his sermon.

The next thing to disappear without mention was the Ransome. Now that *did* surprise me, knowing how highly Pa rated it, as a machine. It was this disappearance that really roused my suspicion, and started me searching for some kind of pattern to make sense of these changes.

For a while I was stumped, I confess. The Ransome was replaced by a small Black and Decker in orange plastic, (secondhand, naturally) – hardly a classic of the engineer's craft. The whining motor couldn't cope with the long grass by the fence, and it melted the extension cable when Pa forgot to unwind it fully from its blue plastic drum. After that, it too was turned in for a Qualcast with loppy handles and collapsible wheels.

But it wasn't until a fortnight after the accident, when I took it upon myself to see to the downstairs – particularly the kitchen which was in a state – ready for Auntie's visit next day, that the riddle was solved.

Pa being occupied with his sermon, I grabbed the chance to empty the teapot which, for economy reasons, is only done once per week, there being, according to Pa, 'A power of goodness in well-mashed leaves.' (I suspect it's his way of getting some vegetables down me considering the number of soft, plump leaves that end up in the bottom of my cup when the pot gets to be half full of the things. I knew Auntie wasn't that keen, either.) The point

I'm coming to is this: on that particular day, I had reason to open the lid of the dustbin. Imagine my shock when, just as I'd begun thumping the bottom of the big brown pot, I chanced to look inside the bin and there, half buried in rubbish, was Cymbeline's red plastic teapot.

Everything fell into place: clothes drier, grass cutter, teapot – what did they have in common? The answer is, all three had featured in the accident. All three had now been secretly disposed of. The reason was obvious: the accident was not to be spoken of; the accident was not to be *thought* of; the accident *never was*. Period.

At that moment I realised for the first time that not a single word had been uttered on the subject since the accident happened. Not by *anyone*. Including Auntie. Until that moment this had seemed perfectly natural to me; I never imagined it to be something contrived, something worked at in secret, something which even had Pa acting against his most sacred principle: Waste not, want not. True, I'd had trouble with nightmares the two nights following the accident, but the medicine which Doctor Keylock brought sorted that out, and afterwards I never gave it a thought. I now realised that there must have been other little gaps and vacancies about the house but, between the tablets and the total absence of any careless talk, I had wiped the whole unfortunate episode right out of my head . . .

Now this . . .

A single, thoughtless action from poor, dear Ma . . . and it all comes tumbling down . . .

'Have a Smarty, dear. You've earned it.'

I stare at Ma, dumbstruck. My scalp wriggles and writhes. *Smarties!* Gentle Jesus – even the *word* is forbidden . . . and here she is showing the *objects themselves!*

An awful thought comes. My brain grabs it: What's the

253

date? I start counting from Wednesday which I know because it was the first day of term. When I get to fifteen, I *stop* . . .

Her birthday cake always shone with Smarties. It *had* to, even the first. A Smarty number in the middle and a double row round the edge. Today would have been the sixth.

I could picture it clearly, a big number 6 made of all the colours in the tube. My sister would have eaten the lot, by herself. But, there was more to Smarty-power than that.

It was Smarties that made the coloured hand prints on the wall; with Smarty 'buns' she would charm all the grown-ups, and with Smarty 'prezzies' they would encourage her performances and tricks; with Smarties she would entertain her invisible friends; Smarties bribed her to bed, to bath, to the toilet. Smarties *were* Cymbeline; Cymbeline *was* Smarties.

On Mother's hand lie all the colours in the range: brown, lilac, red, yellow, green, pink, orange. As I stare down with racing heart, the hand seems to shrink, and grow plump. Its paleness turns pink and smooth . . .

'No,' I croak.

I feel dizzy, shut my eyes, squeeze. Behind my forehead . . . fresh dug earth bulges, breaks open. I see a mushroom . . . that *isn't* a mushroom. . . It is part of the dream, the nightmares that came before, the one that would not let go. . .

Please, I moan in my head.

Above the dark lenses, Ma's eyebrows rise quivering. 'Are you all right, dear?' she asks. The moan must have escaped. Not trusting my voice, I nod. But I know her eyes stare on, worried, alert, reading me. She's a psychic my Ma (maybe they all are), I know I must cover up quickly.

'I mean, no thank you,' I manage in almost a normal voice. But inside my head is a warning: She's rising like Lazarus! Hurry. Go quickly.

254

I'm aching to run, but make myself sit for a second while she watches me through the black circles. Control. Good. I blow up my fringe, and yawn, and slowly stand up.

'I'll go get him some more water then, OK?' I say.

Ma stretches her lips and lowers her head back on to the headrest. 'Thank you, darling,' she says.

I rise and move quietly away. Heart pounding. I draw a can of water from the outside tap, and make my way towards Lucky's tethering place.

The animal is asleep on the turd-laden concrete, his chin resting in a pool of saliva, black-brown lips splayed on either side. I hardly notice the stink of drying dog piss. I reach over the palletwood fence and pour water from the long spout into his half-empty ice cream tub, then straighten and stare at the huge, inert body, my mind searching for an excuse to proceed beyond the shed.

Not a bird, not an insect, not a zephyr relieves that hot, heavy silence. I am panting.

'He's OK for water,' I call softly over my shoulder.

I feel cold though the sweat runs down my back. I glance behind me. Both parents seem asleep.

'I fancy a spot of weeding,' I call, in case they are awake and pretending. I set down the watering can and start for the vegetable plot. I collect the long-handled trowel as I pass the shed. The sun presses down, and the toad in my belly gurgles. For some reason I am panting, my heart is pounding, my fingers tingle, and my legs . . . my legs are like cool jelly . . .

Only I know what lies beneath the courgette plant, whose yellow trumpets are so curiously attractive to blue-bottles. As I tread the grass path between the two plots, I hear again, in my head, the roar of the great machine, the chattering blades; feel its handles in my palms . . . I killed her! I killed her!

Rubbish. It was an *accident*, says a voice inside my head. You meant to steer it away. You were too little,

that's all, not strong enough.

A cloud of flies rises buzzing and zooming, several striking my face and hair.

This new voice persists: **The bits and bobs will be down there all right, happily rotting away. There's no funny mushroom. And there's no Ghosty. But you go ahead; see for yourself, then perhaps you'll be satisfied, Doubting Jim.**

In a daze, I set to with the trowel. The thick rasping stems draw white grazes with little beads of blood on my tender young arms. I pause to roll down my shirt sleeves and button the cuffs. For the first time I notice the great hairy leaves have five fingers.

The topmost foliage is taller than me and the growth is so dense I cannot be seen from the lawn as I dig into the muddy trench which forms an oasis round the stem.

Ignoring my presence, some of the flies have returned to their unnatural feast. Suddenly from among the lichen and lank chickweed drawn up by the gloom of the canopy, comes the first flash of pink.

I turn the hand with the trowel's tip, feeling faint. A thousand-legged worm crawls out of the severed wrist. It moves with surprising speed. My stomach clenches and my lungs pump. A little mud clings to the infant hand but otherwise it is perfect. No sign of nibblings, no shrivelling, no darkening of the flesh. *In twelve long hot summer weeks, putrefaction has not touched these remains.*

I feel tears of frustration starting: Little cheat, I moan. And dig on.

23

To extract the bike means shifting a sack of dried dog food, a pile of gardening tools and a dozen old floorboards saved from the extension, 'just in case'.

The maroon paint is old and scratched now, and the once shining rims quite chromeless. Though far too small for me, the bike had been saved to be passed on to Cymbeline; somehow it had been overlooked in the purge. I thank Heavenly Father, for it is the only escape I can think of.

Both of the playbike's tyres are soft, but, Pa being Pa, the pump is still attached, fixed on with masking tape to make sure.

After the pumping, I feel hot and dizzy. I sit on the wooden floor for a moment to gather my strength, also to decide exactly where I should take the relics to dispose of them. Somewhere far away, I'm thinking. (Perhaps out of nightmare-range?) A place they can never be disturbed . . . Where no one would ever dig . . .

Got it!

I stand up.

The river!

The river is perfect. Ten minute ride. Good long throw and it will all be over. Finished.

I feel calmer already.

I find an old plastic carrier bag, tip out the few bits of string and wire it contains and replace them with a handful of rusty bolts from the biscuit tin. I weigh the bag in my hand and think of it plummeting into the swirling, beige water of the estuary. (Perhaps I smile. Perhaps not.) The six relics go in, and, after carefully expelling all air, I fasten the neck with string and push it into the white saddlebag.

With wildly beating heart, before opening the shed door I rehearse the lie I am about to tell him – just like in drama – including the correct tone of voice: 'Just going for a quick bike ride, Pa. Five mins, OK? Want anything from the shop?' That's it. Let's keep this casual.

With the bike's front tyre, I push open the shed door, wheel the bike through . . .

And that's when I hear it:

'Bad Bimbim! Me telling.'

I stare at the saddlebag, open mouthed, feeling my legs drain of blood. Trembling. Into my head rushes a total insanity – no thought processes occur – the voice comes . . . and it's there – complete: this is the voice of dead Cymbeline, who is five years old – sorry, *six* now.

My head shakes violently: *'No!'*

My legs will barely hold me. Aware that I have barked the word out loud, I glance towards the lawn. No movement there. I lay the bike down on the grass, turn back to the shed, slowly push open the door . . . peer inside . . . without entering. The shed is quite empty!

I stare again at the saddlebag, feeling sick. My stomach is gurgling again. What am I to do? What am I to do?

A green bonfire is smouldering down by the heap. The smoke drifts to me . . . and a little attack of hope.

'No!' says the voice. *'Bimbim bad. Cymby be wiv Bimbim. In Roombed.'*

I feel dizzy now, close to passing out, I feel. What can I do?

I pick up the bike and return it to the shed. I open the saddlebag, take out the polythene carrier bag and tuck it, cool and heavy, down the front of my shirt. I return to

the lawn, make an excuse to go to my room where I lock
the relics away in my blue metal toolbox . . .

And that's where they have stayed, quite quietly
until . . .

Ever had a tick in your knob end? Head buried, nothing
to see but the brown velvet belly full of blood, all soft
and bloated like a spider's abdomen. Don't laugh: it could
be *you*!

I knew I'd been dreaming again (or whatever we call it)
because, when I came out of it, the wooden post – that
old pile I'd clung to like a drowning man – was nowhere!
I was still submerged in stinking, suffocating nest, but –
and here's the rub-a-dub-dub – I was at least three pits
further out.

How I ever found my way back is a miracle, but, eventually, I touched wood again and, somehow, managed to
haul myself up and over. When I finally arrived back
at the Bible Room, headvoice was giving me unmerciful
stick:

—what *she*? *She* doesn't exist, for fuck's sake!

My head ached. I felt sick. Look, I groaned, it's something to do with the spiral . . . can't you see? No, you
can't, can you? You *never* see anything. All right, I'll try
to spell it out: the beginning was the dream – don't ask,
I don't know, I only know that's where the word came
from – I mean exorcism – that word. That word – that
idea – started the rot. It was an *admission*, a crack, a thin-
ended wedge. Things come in pairs. You can't have just
one, you have to have both . . . Shit! I remember now . . .
Old Sopworth, he said it: 'If you want God, you've got
to have Satan. If you want Angels, you've got to have
Devils. If you want to understand Theology, you'd better
take a gander at the Demonology too . . . That's what he
said.

So what?

So what?! I'll tell you so what, you thicko, exorcisms, that's what. If you want *exorcisms* – *and that is* what we both wanted, you may just possibly remember – if you want all the comforts of that gem of ecclesiastical mumbo jumbo, you'd better get ready for the opposite an' all . . . You'd better be prepared for the hauntings, because hauntings is what you'll bloody well get. They're a set, see? Hauntings and exorcisms; you can't buy them singly.

You see what we've bloody well done? Between the two of us clever bastards, we've opened the bloody door, that's what! And now, now it's as if there's a spiral stairway built out of pure bloody fear. It leads straight up from hell to that turret. I made it! Me, with my *fear*. To *fear* something is to *believe* in it – there's no fear without belief. You're *scared* of something, you've *got to believe* in it . . . that's another little pair for you . . . That's what I'm trying to tell you. It's a vicious spiral: she feeds *it*, I feed *her*—

So? It's not real. So what does it—

– and it's getting bloody worse every time . . . *I'm moving . . . in the games, I'm actually moving* . . . I must have moved, what . . . ? twenty feet under that filth. I could easily have – Christ!

What now?

Sopworth's cat, ST, St Tom!

It's a freak. What about it?

Shut up. I'm thinking . . . It's coming back . . . Yes . . .

When he finished his pee, Doctor Sopworth shut the door and drew an old army blanket across. He then shuffled around the room cupping his hand around the chimneys and blowing out one lamp after another. With only the fire's glow and the light from the lamp on the table remaining, he stretched out on the sofa, the tumbler between his hands bobbing gently on his domed belly. He closed his moist, red-rimmed eyes and, in a voice soft and careful, told me the story of St Tom.

'There is a research station, not light years from here, James, where the professors and gifted students of the department of behavioural sciences torture apes and other animals for the benefit, they tell us, of all mankind.

'Until recently, Tom was helping with their inquiries – on a strictly *in*voluntary basis, you understand . . .?'

The red eyes popped open, turned to me. I nodded, totally relaxed, slightly dizzy. His eyes lingered, reading mine. Apparently satisfied, he went on:

'Sources close to these clever men – in distance, that is to say, not philosophy – last week informed our coterie of the cruel nature of these . . . in-vest-igations, the effects of which you have yourself witnessed this very evening.' His eyes indicated the room above where all was now silent, the sounds of hunting having subsided.

'The prize these men seek is indeed remarkable. In brief, it is Superman; Creator-man, more accurately. Creator-man will simply create his own universe around him, precisely as he wishes it to be. Furthermore, his body will respond to this self-made reality precisely as it would to what we now regard as "*the*" universe.'

Again, the doctor's red eyes sought mine. This time he certainly saw blank incomprehension mixed with a liberal dollop of incredulity. In a voice now noticeably slurred he went on:

'Perhaps it would help if I were to relate all this to what is known among the micro-electronic geniuses as "virtual reality". You've no doubt heard of these helmets which can feed a man's senses a crudely simulated universe – a cartoon universe – with which he can interact physically; he rotates, it rotates; he hears a sound, he turns towards it, the source is where it should be, so on and so forth. They use the idea for designing the interiors of buildings and so on; essentially it's a toy in its current form, but it

261

gives you the idea. Hmm? And it seems to have given these madmen the idea of producing a biological version, capable of creating a world *indistinguishable – indistinguishable*, I ask you, ye Gods! – from reality.

'In other words, James, they believe that Creator-man is with us now, inside every human skull. Tomas was simply the latest in a line of cats drafted to the realisation of this insane ambition. Cats are nothing, you see? They're expendable; like test-tubes; you bust one, you buy another; or *steal* it; or *receive* it. They like cats especially, it seems, because cats are apparently good strong dreamers. But . . .' The doctor rose slowly to his feet. 'I happen to *like* cats too, I and my pals . . .' He was rummaging under the cushions of the armchair next to mine; leafing through magazines, one after another, and discarding them. 'Excuse me,' he said. I stood up. 'There's an article here somewhere. Where the devil? Ah. This is it: Can Faith *Make* Mountains? Reads like a joke, Jim, but it's not. Oh no. Not to the cats. Not to us either. I've marked the relevant passages. Read 'em. See what you think.'

I picked up a folded-back magazine and began to read a passage pointed up in lime highlighter.

Early results of the DSR (Dream State Reactivity) – the so-called, Night Jerk – research suggest the remarkable possibility that the inhibiting function of the DSD (Dream Suppression Device), sometimes referred to as the 'Gateway', may indeed be chemically overridden for periods as great as .073 of a second when the brain is in Dream Mode; this state being identifiable by the usual REM (Rapid Eye Movement) sleep and related EEG brain rhythms. So called slow-wave, or 'deep' sleep terminates, and the subject is 'virtually' awake. The distinction between this state and the state of normal dreaming being that movement and other physical responses take place.

It has now been established that in cases where the Gateway has been totally excised, this condition may be extended indefinitely. The Gateway itself is situated deep in the brain stem. Improvements in the difficult techniques involved in its excision are one of the laboratory's most notable triumphs.

All the more reason, therefore, to deplore the proposed reduction in Government funding outlined by the minister on—

There the yellow highlighter stopped. I looked up, shaking my head, wondering as much about the English teacher's two personae as the article, not knowing what to think about either. Or say.

Sopworth smiled, extended the bottle and poured me another half inch. 'There's more, of course,' he said. 'It goes on to explain how the geneticists and the neurochemists – neurotransmitters and all that – are in on the act . . .' His red eyes searched mine once more, then turned away to stare at the solitary lamp. 'I don't know how you feel, but to me it's not progress, to me it's an obscenity – successful or not! Christ!' The old man sat up with a jerk, slopping scotch over his hands which I noticed were shaking. 'He can't even hunt, the poor bastard . . .' He looked back at me. I could see he was close to tears. 'They're not feeding them, you see, Jim; they want to see if dream mice will keep them alive . . .' He slugged back a mouthful. 'It's *insane* . . . it's bloody . . . Christ, I could. . .'

The doctor drew a shuddering breath. 'Sorry,' he said. 'Trouble is, the poor brute won't eat. He's starving but he just doesn't seem to *know* it. It's terrible. They've wrecked his brain, the swines. Sorry. Sorry. Not your problem.' He swallowed thickly and stood up wobbling slightly. 'It's just . . . you remind me of Michael. I shouldn't have . . . Sorry. Please . . . just forget what I said. Can you manage that, Jim?'

I nodded.

'I'm just a senile old Luddite, I suppose. But . . . Tom . . . he's never been a mouser in his life, I don't imagine. He's a *domestic* pussy. We did that to him; we humans. Now he's dependent. And those loonies expect him to—' He cut himself off with a hard slap to the bald head. 'Sorry. At it again.' He smiled, staggered a little. 'You'll be all right on here,' he said, patting the sofa. 'I'll fetch you a blanket. We'll leave the fire in. It's frosty outside now.'

'Who's Michael?' I asked.

'My grandson. He's dead now. Meningitis.'

When he returned with the blankets I must have been asleep. I never felt him cover me, or tuck me up . . .

Sometime during the night, I was woken by my cold feet, a warm weight on my chest and the loudest purr I had ever heard. My neck ached from being forced up by the arm of the settee. The lamp on the table was out. By the fire's steady glow, I could see the shaved and scarred head of ST. The cat was neatly folded on the centre of my chest, its smiling face bare inches from mine. When I moved, it settled in the hollow made by my drawn-up knees. I fell asleep to its slow rattle and wheeze. In the morning, ST was still there. Still purring . . .

The memory fades into spiralling fear. I'm left with one thought: Creator-man.

What's it to do with us? Nothing. We're not a cat. And if we were, we—

Who's responsible for this lot? Who's in charge here? Oh, Christ Jesus, what am I to do?

Stop it, will you! Feel your heart rate – that's danger-ous – cut it out. Now! We need *sleep*.

What about . . . you know . . . down there?

Down there?

Scrotum.

That? Ridiculous. A wind-up. It's obvious . . . Look, if you're worried, we'll . . .

Not now. Not now . . . Later.

I picked up the bottle beside me and took another long swig. Until the medicine started to work (come on, medicine!) I could only lie there staring, burning more pages to hold back the dark, because every time I closed my eyes I saw the same thing: the dark shadow of a manlike creature with shoulders curving up in two great arcs on either side of its head . . .

I looked around the Bible Room, and again thought of Lawrence. I remembered that first time we had come here. How I had despised his brutishness then, and how I longed for his toughness, his uncomplicated, animal certainty now. If only he were here, I thought, how different things would be . . .

At that precise moment, I heard a sound from beyond the door . . . footsteps, outside, on the balcony, softly treading the dusty Shelf. I held my breath. Were they approaching or going away?

Talk of the devil . . .

Fumblingly, shaking with excitement, I struggled to pull up my tracksuit trousers, half praying, half whispering: Wait, Lawrence. Don't go. Don't go, *please*. I'm here . . . I quickly trod out the flickering twists of paper, and scrambled across to the door. I opened it cautiously, only a crack, just in case it might not be my friend – though I could think of no one else who would be here at this time of night. I was amazed it had taken him so long. What was more, I would tell him so, in no uncertain terms . . .

I knelt on the top step and poked my head through, near the bottom of the gap . . .

There *was* someone there . . . a figure in grey, half lit by the floodlight entering through one of the leaded glass windows at the far end of the Shelf . . . Lawrence! Thank God! Lawrence's tracksuit was grey, like mine . . .

It *is* Lawrence! Let's call him.

Sssh! Hold on. I'm not sure. It looks . . . a bit dark . . . a bit big. Which way is it facing?

Don't know. Wait. It's turning, I think . . .

My God! Those shoulders . . . Get back. Get back.

I pushed the door to slowly, silently, crept back down the steps, into the corner and bunched up small. Silence. Seconds grew to minutes. The clock struck some half hour. Nothing. Not a sound. The clock struck eleven chimes.

There's no one there. If there was anyone . . . they've gone. But I don't think—

Trick of the light, you mean?

Yeah . . . Yeah . . . a trick of the light . . .

Plus the worry.

Plus the worry. That's it. That'll be the—

It wasn't . . . It wasn't *Her*, was it? It wasn't—

Don't be stupid . . . How could it be—

I dunno. It's crazy . . . I've just got this crazy idea that . . . that somehow She's out there . . . maybe . . . maybe in another form, another shape . . . I dunno, fuck it. I just can't stop myself thinking She's out there . . . stalking around in the dark . . . hunting . . . for *me*.

That's . . . that's just daft. That's potty. I mean, that's really, really potty, you know?

I know, I know. I just . . .

Come on. Light another taper. Let's have some light in here. We've got to face things. It's not facing things, that's the cause of it all. Let's take a butcher's at those bugs. I mean . . . what are they? I mean, really! They're nothing. Right? They're just little bugs.

I felt for the matches. Head was right. Things had to be faced.

I lit the taper, twisted another dozen pages, lit one more

and pushed the waistband of my trousers down to my knees.

Stop panicking, can't you—

Panicking?! Look, you know they can give you brain diseases, don't you. There's people in Canada gone nutty from tick bites. They reckon we've got it in England an' all. In the New Forest . . .

This isn't the New Forest. Just pull the bastards down, will you. And let's see.

In the light of the fly leaf, the end of my penis looked like a peeled pomegranate. There had to be more than a dozen black bulges hiding under the foreskin. I felt the blood rush to my centre – legs, fingertips, head all emptying at once in a rush—

No! You can't get out of it that way!

I quickly stuck my head between my knees, remembering . . . remembering. Sometime, someone said, don't pull the body off or the head'll stay in and go septic. Spray them with something. Alcohol? Was that it? What if it made them go deeper? Jesus Christ! No. A cig! That was it. Burn them out – *roast* the buggers! It's the only way.

I took out my next to, next to, last but one Capstan, and lit it with trembling hands. I took a deep, deep breath . . . peeled back the hood, and . . . rapid eye movement . . .

Out wriggled . . .

Tumbled . . .

A dozen fragments of broken nest!

My clothes, hair, ears, trainers had all been full of broken bits of twig . . . What was the matter with me? Why hadn't I guessed? There were no bugs anywhere else on my body; what on earth had made me think . . . ?

Well . . . I'll be . . . She really got you going there, Jimbo? What a wind-up! Jesus. The cow! Almost another panic-attack there, eh, son? Touch more, and

267

you'd have been off on episode three . . .

You're handing it to her on a plate, you know that?
It's all in the mind, man. For fuck's sake get a grip. I
mean, really: Satan's Crabs! And an *Alien*. . . !? That
turns out to be a half-dead pigeon. Holy shit! what a
dork.

Thanks.

Don't mention it.

By the way, what was it you said? 'She really got me
going . . .' et cetera; you did say, '*She*', didn't you? I did
hear correctly, I take it.

Figure of speech. That's all. I didn't mean—

That's OK, I just wondered.

Up yours!

The pigeon had still not passed on when the last fly leaf
sputtered out an hour or more later. The big bonger
chimed midnight as I put the finishing touches to our
Bible beds (hers has a closing lid, of course). I'd decided
to leave the '*coo' de grass* until the morning when I would
feel more up to it. The trouble with pigeons is the neck;
it's like old celery; you double it up and squeeze like
buggery but it still won't snap. Really, I was too shagged
to bother, but also I had an idea she would pass on
peacefully in the night without any more help from me.
I love animals myself but everyone's got to eat and there's
only a crust in the Sunblest bag now.

I closed my eyes to shut out the glow from the cloverleaf
window and tried for sleep. I had stopped seeing the
nightmare shape when I shut my eyes but every so often
the pigeon stirred just enough to keep me awake. Then
my stomach began to play up, gurgling and rumbling.
The one thought I could not tolerate kept bubbling to the
surface: had I really *swallowed* it?

All my efforts at control failed to keep this horror at
bay. I imagined it inside me; still alive! I even thought I

felt it moving about. A more hideous thought still came. Supposing it wasn't a spider at all . . . supposing it was a big tick. . . ? Jesus Christ, what would it do in there . . .?

There were six Aspros left in the strip. I popped the lot and tried my hardest to meditate. Hopeless. I decided to focus on the Matter. Lying rigid in the dark, I had caught a whiff of myself – a dreadful pong, horribly nesty. This made me aware of how badly I'd done with the domestic arrangements. Above all I needed water for washing, and drinking, of course.

On the subject of personal hygiene and 'standards' in general, I had noticed that I was beginning to *swear* rather too much in my own thoughts. Admittedly no one could hear, but that was hardly the point, *I* could. Things like that can easily turn into thin-ended wedges. Swearing is a sign of weakness. 'Let your yeah be yeah', as they say. These are my walls, as Hamm says in the play.

The clock struck one. The pigeon settled down. But sleep would not come. I decided to focus on the Matter again; the cooking facilities; it looked like it would have to be a barby of some sort, with paper logs made out of Bible pages twisted up and tied into knots – not the lovely picture pages, they remind me too much of Ma and Pa's bedroom – perhaps a few letters to the Corinthians; nice and dry. I did not think He would mind this, especially if I made the whole thing into a sort of combined barby stroke burnt sacrifice. I realised I'd be doing the eating so it wouldn't exactly be going up to heaven in a cloud of smoke, but as CJ says, it's the thought . . .

At that moment I heard a small scratching sound. I knew at once it was the pigeon again. I reached for the matches, and lit a spill.

She looked like a goner piled into the corner, one claw poking out, eye a milky slit, panting like a cat in a car. I wanted to help her. On impulse, I knelt down (the second time in twenty-four hours), hands together, eyes closed . . . and waited for inspiration.

It came at once in the form of none other than the mighty Lord's Prayer; but it wasn't until I got to the line about daily bread that I saw the light – I hadn't given her any! Or daily water either.

I could not help thinking that something beside mere chance was at work here, showing me the way. But for that prayer, I might never have thought of nourishment (not for *her*, anyhow). I knew there was only the one slice left, but I've never been the sort deliberately to starve an animal to death, so in it went. Crumbs and all. (I hardly expected her to eat it.) No sooner had I completed this act of, shall we say, mercy, than a wonderful feeling of peace and calm came over me.

And I slept.

24

I awoke to total darkness and something crawling into the bunk hole beside me.

Terror. Me rigid.

I had been dreaming of Cymbeline riding piggyback on my shoulders. Becoming a monster with terrible claws. Strangling me. Tearing my throat out, so I cannot even scream. Her drinking from the fountain of my jugular. Slurping her lips. Purring . . .

Whatever was on my shoulder now . . . was covered in hair; I felt its coarse hairs prickle my neck . . . Smell of wet earth . . .

My belly writhed. Bitter gall in my mouth. A cold lump rising from my stomach. Soon I must vomit.

I felt the thing on my shoulder dig claws into my flesh . . . it began to growl . . .

The lump of vomit reached my throat . . . back of my tongue. I felt myself convulse violently, twist to the side, spew . . .

The creature moved from its place on my shoulder . . . *deeper* into the bunk, stirring the balls of screwed-up paper against my thigh.

With a cry, I leaped from the bunk, scattering Bibles.

A hideous howl from the bunk.

I felt the hairs stand on my head; my legs were fast emptying.

I searched the pouch furiously for matches. Struck one,

breaking the match which fizzed out on the floor. Swore. Struck a second. Cupped the small flame with a trembling hand. Cast about for a taper. Found one on the floor. Squatted to light it. Saw the vomit, yellow and translucent on my training shoe lying beside the bunk. Saw the huge black spider close by; standing; glistening; staring straight at me. Saw the wreckage of the bunk. Saw the creature emerging . . .

I heard laughter . . . horrible laughter . . . *my* laughter. The *creature* . . .

(Who is in *charge* here? Who's in control?)

. . . The *creature* now crawling slowly from my bed of Bibles was . . .

. . . none other than . . .

Tomas, the cat.

I had barely time to recognise the shaven and scarred head emerging from the heap of Bibles and screwed-up paper, when a quick movement caught the corner of my eye. The spider was scuttling towards the door.

Before I could react in any way, ST was on it, both paws. In the mouth. One shake of the head. Gone! Gobbled up! Dead or alive.

I stopped laughing and sat on the floor, back to the wall, legs out straight. The spill in my hand was beginning to sputter, but I noticed that the cloverleaf aperture was now glowing pinkly. I dropped the stub on the floor, still sputtering.

Headvoice was screaming: **Where did that *thing*, that Godawful *object*, come from?!**

I shuddered violently, thankful I was already on the floor.

ST came to me and rubbed against my side, purring his rattling, wheezing purr.

I touched his back, wanting to comfort him, wanting his company, yet not wanting to touch the ugly shaven head. Under my hand I felt the knobs of his spine. The

272

spill went out. The room was suffused with soft, pink light.

'I thought you were off food,' I said. 'I thought you weren't eating, old Tom.'

He stepped on to my lap and began to tread my crotch, purring loudly. I put up with the small pricking claws. People with cats live longer, I'd been told. (Nothing about cats who eat spiders.)

I ran my hand gently down the bumpy back. Awake, like this, the animal seemed perfectly normal, not at all like the crazed, somersaulting creature I had seen at the cottage.

I felt my pulse slowly returning to normal. St Tomas was filthy, I now noticed, caked with mud, his fur barely recognisable as white. He had to have travelled the better part of five miles cross country and another two from the edge of town in order to reach the Cathedral. I remembered Sopworth saying how the cat had no sense of territory, how he'd only just caught it the first time it escaped, racing north along the A2.

'Why here, puss?' I murmured. I felt my eyes prickle. 'I'm very, very grateful, but . . .' A deep memory stirred. Still stroking the scurfy back, I said, 'If you wish to live and thrive . . . Do you know this, ST? If not, you'd better listen . . . If you wish to live, and thrive, let the *spider* run alive.'

At that moment there came a faint scratching from the box I'd built in the corner last evening for the pigeon. Surely the thing was not *still* hanging on.

ST's ears twitched. He stood and strolled over to the box. He sat down and pushed at the lid with one filthy paw.

I rose and followed him. 'No,' I said, 'You can't have that one. Sorry. That's mine.'

I picked him up gently, just to move him back so that I could look into the box . . . And he bit me. Hard, through the heel of my thumb.

I swore and dropped him, clutching my bleeding hand.

The door was ajar. In a flash, he was through it and gone.

I was left gaping.

I felt empty suddenly, and terribly disappointed. And scared again, like I'd felt when I'd woken before. That must have been in the middle of the night. I'd heard scratchings, that was it. Rats! I'd thought. Then I'd lain rigid, like the man under the pendulum, not knowing whether it was dawn or midnight. Then the bonger had struck the hour and it was only *three* bongs, and my feet were numb with cold, the Bibles had been kicked askew. Another dream, I'd thought, and tried to remember, but remembered the pigeon instead: it wasn't rats, it was her again, winding me up. Why wasn't she dead? Then – horror beyond all bearing – imagining *Her* in every shadow of the chamber. The thought coming back that somehow the Ghost had managed to add *movement* to her other impossible trick: the voice trick . . .

I must have fallen asleep again then . . . I think so, yes . . . I think that's when I had the first nightmare . . . I don't really know . . . My screams woke me. For seconds the dream-picture remained – a spiral stairway, a worm with a thousand legs moving in waves, climbing fast. Then that other dream, the piggyback monster . . .

I shut out the memory, but my stomach was rumbling again. It was definitely hunger this time – not unnaturally – this was, after all, day three, and so far I'd eaten precisely half a cut loaf.

I picked up the empty bread wrapper. Made a funnel of the waxed paper, and tipped it into my wide-open mouth. Nothing.

I stooped and lifted the Bible lid a couple of inches at one side.

One black, twinkling eye. Alive then. Quite perky, in fact.

I raised the lid further. Half the crust eaten, the other half shat on.

Shit! No breakfast for me, then.

This is hopeless, said headvoice.

So? I said, sitting on a stack, head in hands. What do you suggest?

If you want to know . . . I suggest we try learning from our mistakes—

What does that mean?

Try thinking back to last night, for a start.

Meaning?

Meaning we cut the knee jerks and start using our *brains*. Think about it. Think where we are. This place. This is a *Cathedral,* right? A *holy* place, right . . .?

Get on with it.

I'm not saying I believe this, and I'm not saying I don't, but . . .

Oh, for Christ's sake—

But . . . *if*, as they say, this is all in the mind, ie it is all down to your guilty conscience – excuse the expression – why not do something about it? Eh? I mean *why not*? Either way, a good deed never hurt anyone, did it? Mmm? You know the sort of thing I mean: 'For as much as ye do it unto one of these my children—'

What conscience? Cut the riddles. I'm not in the—

– Or creatures great and *small*, for example. Small, sick *creatures*. Or *wounded* creatures . . .

Look, do we *have* to have the parables? Why can't you—

Do as you would be done by, old son. Think of others.

Like? Oh! *Got* you . . . I think.

Virtue is its own reward, mate—

Ah haaa. I'm beginning to—

Get the Umpire on our side, eh? Then—

The umpire . . . right.

We can do anything. Right?

Right.

Sky's the limit. Right?

Right.

Get some good karma around us. Set an example. I mean, who's the man of the family, right? Who's the eldest?

Eld–*er*.

You are, right?

Right.

OK, let's go, team. Operation Nightingale.

Good scene, head.

I have discovered two new rooms in the tower; the lower, immediately above the fan ceiling, has bell ropes dangling and is obviously still in use, whilst the upper is bare, dusty boards apart from a giant treadmill in the centre which might once have been used for hauling up stone but is clearly redundant now. I have moved the patient in there to be closer to the turret, the better for me to nurse her. The door – which I had to unlock – is only a few steps down-spiral from the turret, so I shall be visiting often.

She seemed to have taken a turn for the worse, her eyes had gone dull and slitty again with a third kind of lid coming half across. No way could a person *eat* something like that – not that I had any intention of killing and consuming the poor creature, now that my eyes had been opened. However humble, I now saw that the pigeon was one of God's creatures. As a human being I had to respect that. Certainly we had been given dominion over them, but that didn't mean we had to go cramming their little corpses down our necks like there's no tomorrow when soya beans and wheat mountains rise up from Mother Earth like a sign saying: Meat is Murder.

Holding her gently in my hands and feeling her warmth and the trembling lightness of her, I was genuinely moved to tears and am not ashamed to admit it. You have sinned,

Jimbo, I told myself out loud, but it is never too late to repent.

It is hard to describe the feeling I had as I persuaded her scaly old feet on to my finger and gave her a dose of my very own medicine. She immediately sneezed and perked up, and her eyes opened wide. I was really choked up for a moment.

Then she went and spoiled everything by behaving as if pissed, lurching backwards and forwards till she ended up hanging upside down from my finger, gripping so tightly she almost drew blood. When I prised her off and tried to stand her on the floor she kept rocking back and sitting on her tail, then falling over sideways and lying there like a stuffed parrot. I admit love deserted me for a moment, but I pretty soon realised that this was not her fault. I mean, neither of us had eaten since the early hours, and drinking on an empty stomach is dodgy.

Also, half a capful might have been rather a lot, weight for weight.

She dropped off to sleep, I believe, and may have snored in her own quiet way through the two little holes in the top of her beak.

I had rebuilt her box in the bottom of the treadmill. I now sat by her bedside and worked out ratios. As far as I could tell she'd drunk a litre and a half, allowing for spillage, so her behaviour was understandable. Although she was asleep, I whispered, I forgive you, and made a mental note to be more professional in the future.

I was so hungry now I could hardly think. I kept asking, is this fair? Nobody answered. Not that I really expected them to; I could hardly expect the Umpire to side with me so soon. All in good time . . . Meantime:

Food.

We cannot live by bread alone, but it helps. Indeed, for me the need was becoming more and more urgent. My famished brain kept throwing up the same line, and I had not the strength to control it, even though I knew it was wrong: *Cymbeline Ghost-relic has returned from the Other Side.*

I felt certain that nothing would cut out this mad idea until I found those missing relics, *and* the un-supernatural explanation I knew, in my heart, existed. At the same time I just had to find something to eat, for me and the patient. Also a receptacle for catching rainwater.

Action stations, said headvoice. **Only people with soft heads stick them in the sand and wait to be kicked up the arse by little cheats and liars.**

25

After hours of fruitless searching, wandering through the attics and passages of the Shell, I drifted into a dim chamber filled with piles of what seemed junk somewhere above the north quire isle. Giddy, weak, no longer interested in the inedible, and with even my fear of meeting again with the Mamba overridden by ravenous hunger, I stumbled over a heap of damaged hassocks towards a door marked in red letters, FIRE DOOR – KEEP CLOSED. I listened briefly, jerked the bar up, entered, blundered down a flight of wooden steps into a second, cupboard-lined room, and . . . Stopped dead, eyes locked on what seemed a miracle (in comparison to which the loaves and fishes seemed small beer). There, resting against the foot-pedal, under a scratched and battered grand piano, was a paper bag bursting, overflowing, with Glacé Mints.

Could it possibly be mere *chance*, I asked myself, that this manna from God knew where just happened to be my absolute favourites *bar none*? Or was there an *Umpire* after all? Was this a sign, a reward for my good deeds of the morning, a promise of better things to come? There looked to be over a pound of the delicious, translucent sweets – the bag was bursting, spilling over so that a dozen or more lay scattered on the dusty floor, gleaming like diamonds through the wrappers.

Normally a sucker, I sat under the piano and chewed ravenously, ripping the cellophane off the next and the next as I did so. Crunch, splinter, gulp – three, four, five at once. Within seconds, I felt the power returning. 'Thanks,' I spluttered to no one in particular, then concentrated hard on eating. After a minute, with a quarter or so inside me, I began to slow down, to look around.

The room was cluttered with hymn books and psalters and shelves stacked with boxes with handwritten labels such as Magnificat, Stanford, Nunc Dim and Jesu Joy. Three long, wooden stalls occupied the centre where I guessed the choir stood during practice.

I climbed to my feet, stuffing the bag of mints into my pouch. The blue paint of the practice stalls was scarred with initials and hearts and anarchist signs among others. It occurred to me such deceptive 'little angels' would not be above nicking the odd relic if they happened to come across it. I was wandering between the stalls, searching, though with little hope to be honest, when a bright object caught my eye: hanging from a music stand, beside the piano, was a three-inch knitted choirboy in pink and purple with white knitted ruff. The face, with its black bead eyes and singing mouth – a vertical red line, one stitch tall – although knitted, was peculiarly alive looking; its expression somehow innocent *and* wicked at once. It made me think of Cymbeline.

I moved to the leaded window, looked out. Ruined arches, black branches, grass island the size of a football pitch but round, a police car with blue and red stripe parked outside the bursar's flint-fronted office. (Someone in trouble?) Black and grey figures streaming out of the dining room . . . *Benedicat nobis* . . . Boiled cabbage – almost taste it through the dusty diamonds of glass.

Strength returning. Strong enough to deal with options? How long can a person go on mint-flavoured sugar? Long as it takes. Is that an option? Are there *options*?

Sure. Wednesday midnight the wager is up.

That's it, is it? We can go then, can we? I'd love to think so.

What do you mean, 'think so'? We're going. Full stop.
You don't imagine we can simply walk out of here, do you? – win or lose, up stakes and toddle off back to the world of boiled cabbage and beds with sheets? That's not an option, that's a delusion.

Lose? Who said anything about *lose*. We're not going to let that little bitch—

Sssssh. What's that?

Treble voices. Ascending from below. Coming quickly. The choir! Get out of here, fast.

I ran on tiptoe for the steps. Something made me snatch the woolly choirboy from its metal gallows (even at that moment I noticed its surprising weight). Up I skipped, through the fire door, into the low, dark junk room above. The fire door had a fierce pneumatic return. It took all my strength and nerve to control the final inch of its closing. Boys pouring into the room below, laughing, chattering, me seeing them through the crack. At last the door seated against the jamb. I was free to inspect my hiding place.

To judge by the piles of broken stone, chunks of gargoyle, carved oak, black-brown and shot with wormholes, the upper chamber must once have been a workshop but was now a dump for unwanted Cathedral tat. The only source of illumination was a low arched window which had leaded lights and a sill barely twelve inches above floor level. I knelt and wiped a diamond pane with my sleeve. The window gave on to a small lead roof beyond whose parapet I could see the topmost branches of the elm tree, the ornate brick chimneys of my own House – School House.

After a moment, my eye was caught by something lying in the gutter at the base of the parapet, then almost immediately by two similar objects at the opposite end. I cleaned another pane with my cuff. Among a mass of bloody feathers lay what appeared to be the remains of two, or it might have been three, freshly killed pigeons.

I looked back at the first. That was definitely one pigeon, though its head was missing. For a second I considered whether I might not be able to make a meal from the remains, but, not only was the edge off my appetite, there was something repulsive about the thought of eating carrion, however fresh it looked.

Babble of voices below – a man's voice calling for quiet.

I settled on the floor between two small statues. Both lay face down and, at first glance, appeared to be Virgins sculpted from some dull, black stone, but, when turned, revealed skulls under their hoods, rib cages, skeletal shins and feet peeping out from their gowns. I pushed them away with a shudder, but when I looked up I saw, lying on a shelf opposite, an infant or Cupid carved in black marble. It was obviously made to stand up with its foot on something which at first I could not make out for all the dust and dirt but eventually realised was a *skull*.

Cymbeline would love to do that to you, said headvoice.

Really, I said, popping in a Glacé Mint. I placed the knitted choirboy on the floor beneath the heel of my trainer. Like this, you mean?

I was trying to be cool, but the statues were not funny to me. They were weird; unlike the other contents of the room, none was broken. I could not understand why they had been banished to this dusty attic. Until this thought: hadn't Sopworth mentioned objects like these? In Shakespeare's day, didn't he tell about people wearing skull rings and brooches to remind them of death. *Memento mori*, wasn't that the phrase? Perhaps objects like these had been fashionable in churches once upon a time, but no longer, hence the attic. Or perhaps, in the old days, people were even *more* scared of death than we are, so tried to appear friendly towards it, as a woman might try to appear friendly to a rapist in the hope—

Bollocks. You talk some right—

Sssh. Something happening below: Tap, tap, tap. 'Ready? In the key of G then – la, la, la, laaaa.'

Outside the window, light fading fast. This could take a while. When it's over I'll go on down. Plenty of time. Eyes closing. Sweet and sour memory:

Me and Lucy walking the sun-dry common. Should have been Lawrence, not me. Lawrence couldn't make it. 'Entertain her,' he said. I didn't twig. Until later.

[Treble voices – rising sweetly: *Gloriaaa*]

Lucy in black sleeveless polo neck – so smooth and tight it makes me dizzy. Hawthorn pollen on the breeze. Hand in hand, my head composing witty excuses to lay hands on those ball-aching boobs – break the ice, break the *duck*. Too late; she brushes herself down, roughly, I feel, making them jiggle. Making me release her hand and walk with my hand in my pocket. Benny, her mongrel, foraging ahead. Here, Benny. Fetch, Benny.

Fine dark hair on her lip, fine black hair on her fore-arms. Smooth brown shoulders. Smooth brown legs. Five foot tall in flatties and something else . . .

[*Gloria Gloria In excelcis de-ee-o*]

Lucy sees it first: forty pounds of barrel-chested, pink-eyed albino bull terrier, charging down on Benny, bandy legs flying – white rhino in a hurry in a collar with two rows of studs. 'Don't like the look of that.'

'Nor me,' says Lucy.

No owner in sight. Benny's time has come, I think, searching for a stick all the same.

[*Gloria*]

Like a rhino close up, it skids to a halt, grrrr, grrrr,

yellow and black teeth. Next thing, damn me, out comes four inches of crimson willie.

'Holy shit!' says Lucy, 'He's got his lipstick out!'

Now, Benny is a dog, plain and simple, and what Benny is into is rabbits and balls, balls and rabbits. Nothing much else. But it soon becomes clear that rhino is keen on other things. What rhino likes is fucking and killing, killing and fucking; he isn't at all fussy which end he fucks, so long as he gets to fuck. And fuck hard.

Very sensibly, Benny stands perfectly still while the psychopath reaches up on tiptoe and attempts to screw his earhole.

[Gloria Gloria]

'Archie! You bugga,' calls an aristocratic voice.

Looking up I see an ageing female, flowered hem in one hand, Panama held on head with the other, racing towards us. 'Sorry. Sorry. He's an absolute bugga,' she pants, grabbing towards Archie's collar, but not getting close.

'Mine's a boy,' says Lucy, staring with obvious distaste at the fucking Archie.

'Matters naught to this bugga, I'm afraid,' grunts Panama. 'Dogs, bitches, fur coats, small boys, gerbils . . . I could kill him. He's not mine, he's my husband's.'

Meanwhile Archie negotiates round to make hot pelvic thrusts in the rough area of Benny's tail, pink eyes rolling in passion, or hate.

Lucy says to Panama, matter of factly: 'You can make a dog stop that by sticking your finger up its bottom.' I glance across. Her face is quite serious.

Panama shoots her a quizzical glance, moves round to a position directly behind Archie's plunging rear and, saying, 'You can do it like this an' all, dear,' delivers her chunky brogue with astonishing force into Archie's tight scrotum. Yelp!

'Reminds me of Lawrence,' says Lucy, as Panama and Archie (now walking, it seems to me, more bandy-legged than before) retreat down the track. 'The male animal at its worst. Not like you, Jimmy. You're different, you know that?'

Should I be pleased? I wonder. She takes my hand. We walk on. After a hundred yards, I ask, 'Different? What way?'

'You're nice. The nice boys don't normally talk to me.' She smiles almost shyly.

I say, 'I'm not a nice boy, actually.'

She laughs more. 'Say it again.'

'Say what?'

'Actually,' says she, exaggerating the poshness I had not realised was in the word.

Only to cover my embarrassment, I say something really stupid. I say, 'Actually, I'd rather care to feel you up, blue eyes.'

She stops and looks at me. There's real hurt in her eyes. Then she says, 'Sorry,' takes away her hand and walks on slowly.

I don't mean what I say next either, it's just I'm furious with myself, but it comes anyway: 'I suppose a fuck would be out of the question?'

She doesn't answer but keeps walking, me standing like a zombie watching the action. Without turning, she shouts back, 'Sorry, Jimmy.'

I see that her shoulders are shaking. Laughing or crying? I don't even know the answer to that!

I kick at a flint, hard, missing and catching my other ankle. I sit in the grass at the side of the track, rubbing the skinned ankle.

Suddenly there are two brown feet. I look up. She's staring down at me, smiling, woman to child. I say, 'Why

285

not, Lucy? Why Lawrence? Why not me?'

She says, 'Lawrence is an animal.' She sits beside me in the grass, not looking at me, picking cloverleaves between her feet. 'If we did, you know, you couldn't handle it, Jimbo. We wouldn't be able to, to talk like we do. It would change things . . . the mind things. That would all . . . it's not that I . . . quite the opposite . . . it's just . . .'

'What about *him*?'

'I don't *care* about *him*.'

'Lawrence said I was to entertain you.'

She flashed me a look. 'Bastard!' she said, standing up. 'Bastard! I hate his fucking guts.' Her voice sounding hard now. 'Did he tell you—'

'No. He never told me nothing,' I blurted.

'I bet!' she said. Then she laughed, then she stooped and took my hand. 'Right,' she said, towing me into the tall bracken. 'Animal!'

Her breath smelled of wild garlic. It wasn't garlic though.

When I kissed the dark mole, she laughed again and held the back of my head, tight so I couldn't breathe. But I would not pull away.

[*In excelcis de-ee-ooo*!]

Cold. And the chamber seemed darker beyond the elapsed time. Soon it would be night again, the question still unanswered. I felt my pulse quicken.

Don't get heavy, said headvoice. **Look on the funny side; I mean, supposing, just for a sec, we pretend that, somehow or other, the little cow had actually managed to come to life. I mean, what would she *look* like? Eh? Eh? Imagine it. No body.**

I began to snigger. An image had come of her standing before me, just hands, feet, eyes and dress – knickers round her ankles – nothing to keep them up, not even ankles, to be accurate, well maybe half an inch, no more . . . but the image changed. Snap! Just like that. The laugh cut dead. Now there were bones – full set, ribs, pelvis, clavicles the lot – draped in bloody shreds of denim. And, beneath her heel . . . the head of Jimbo, bloody and bawling!

I rubbed my eyes hard. Stars danced. I blinked. I swore. The picture vanished. But She was close; I *felt* her.

You must keep *control*.

I felt my jaws clench, teeth grind together. My pulse was beginning to gallop. *Control*. Must keep *control*.

Reasoning would be useless. Who could reason with *that*? She was the sort that keeps coming, that never knows when they're licked . . . the mad cockerel I once hit with my toy cricket bat – it was an accident, of course it was, but I had to *keep* hitting it and hitting it until it was nothing but a bloody pulp on splintered sticks. Then even as I was grinding its neck into the gravel it was trying to peck my heel. Even with its beak all splintered to fuck.

I shuddered at the memory. I would need to do more than just *win* this game, I would need to annihilate her like the cockerel; more, I would need to *break* her completely.

My eyes returned to the statue of the infant with its foot on the skull. Suddenly I seemed to know why, to understood the reason for my presence in this small, forgotten chamber with its images of death. Two worlds were coming together in this place, the Creator-man world – the world I *make* – and the world that *is*. And nothing I could do would hold them apart. . .

Shifting my foot. Absently bearing down on my heel. Shit! A jet of warm liquid catches me full in the teeth. I wipe with the back of my hand . . . look at this! – crimson smear – blood! I spit. The woollen choirboy under my heel! I stare in horror at its bloody mouth, that vertical stitch of red wool now dribbling crimson. Get away! My leg lashes. The doll shoots across the floor, into a pile of carved stone, leaving a dark streak in the dust.

Lungs pumping. Fingers tingling. Legs emptying fast.

Scrubbing my mouth with my sleeve, I feel the Cathedral lurch beneath me, tilt towards a new trajectory. Eyes shut. Shocking brightness under the lids. A pool of light, expanding circles, merging, dragging me down. In the centre a dark oblong grows, distant figure radiating shadows like a child-drawn sunset. Here comes the light of the world . . .

Ma? What are you doing here?

She does not wear the dark glasses now. I see her face clearly, the care lines and pouches have gone, it is the face of a young woman. Her expression is stern.

Though her lips do not move, I seem to hear words: I am to go back – to sort out this nonsense, once and for all.

That's not fair! I'm not ready. No, Ma! Please!

'They're waiting to begin, Jimbo . . . to begin at the beginning, dear.'

Before *She* arrives? Before the *Monster* arrives, you mean?

'Now, now. Big three year olds don't call names.'

The figure recedes, the circle dims, the piano plays softly so far away . . .

The Monster

26

SCENE: *My Blue Bedroom – Evening Sunshine*
Pa is standing on my blue nursery stool. He is taller than the light bulb. I am standing beside the stool, helping. We are working as a team, putting up the mobile. It is not an easy job.

'Right. Again, James. And try not to drop it this time, please. Is this the place?' He points to a spot on the ceiling.

I nod, pointing to the same spot. (He has already decided.)

'Agreed,' he says.

I do not like the mobile, but it is a present from my new sister so I pretend. My new sister is a disgusting colour and very ugly. It's no wonder she cries all the time. Myself, I have never been happier. Everyone is being extra nice to me and, best of all, Pa is taking me to the yard tomorrow. I am Pa's best boy. I aim to stay that way. I do not like the dark.

'Pass it up then, James.'

I stretch up with the bundle of sticks, thread and cardboard fairies (or angels or whatever they're supposed to be).

Before Ma left me to collect my new sister from Maternity I would not have been able to execute this upward stretch unaided, now I hold the pose perfectly, without touching the chair back. I am sorry Ma has missed this, she would have been proud of me. Pa is too busy with the drawing pins to notice.

Pa stoops with a big grunt, emphasising the effort we are both putting in. (This is part of the game.) As he takes the mobile from me he says, 'That's my best boy,' and I feel my legs do a little dance. Ah, the joy.

He thanks me: 'Ta.' He presses home the pin and steps down.

For the briefest second I wonder why my Thomas the Tank Engine mobile has been taken down, but assume it is to be re-positioned to make room for the present.

Pa throws the clips and drops the side of my blue cot.

'Now then, James, plastic mattress.' He holds out his hand without looking. 'Baby won't be a nice *clean* person like you.'

Baby? What does he mean?

Pa turns to look at me. 'Mattress, James.'

My legs have stopped dancing. They feel empty.

'There, on the landing. Pink for a girl.'

My legs are wobbling, they could dump me on the lino. The sun has gone in. This room is MY room. This bed is MY bed! It must be a joke. I laugh, but he does not laugh with me.

'New babies wet the bed, James. They can't help it. You'll be in the big bed now. In my old office. Won't that be nice.'

Pa's face melts and the colours of the room run together. Whatever I have done must have been really, really bad. But, so help me . . . I have done *nothing*! I have not woken them at dawn with my racket, I have not drawn on the wall in felt-tip, I have not hugged Wally the cat round the neck, I have not spat out my liver and spinach, put worms in the watering can, cacked my pants, made brown finger paintings on the wall . . . So what *have* I done!? My cheeks burn.

'Go toilet,' say I, stumbling to the door.

Shocked, half-blinded by tears, I blunder along the passage towards the bathroom. At this point there is no particular plan in my mind, I just know my head will explode unless I immediately kick, bite or scream. And Pa will not have such behaviour in our house. Which means . . . the darkness, and serve me right.

I reach up and bolt the door, which I am not to, but cannot control it for once. On top of the cistern I spy the new vinyl doll they have – for who knows what weird reason – bought me. I grab it. My sharp teeth sink themselves into its nose. Arrgh! Arrgh! ARRGH!

The lavatory seat is up, maroon bowl stained white, unflushed paper, a dark sinker lurking like a sub in the U-bend. 'Baby barf NOW,' I say aloud, ramming the doll in head first. I swing from the handle till the water dragon roars.

As the bowl fills, I think of Ma. Back home for one day – *one* day – and already she's *smaller*. She wants the Monster out of her room, of course she does, but to give it *MY* room!? And what next? My high chair? My pedal car? My, my *umbrella*!?

With the long-handled brush, I jab down hard between those squashy pink legs – again, again, again – till the vinyl head squeaks round the bend.

'What's going on in there? Come on, James, unlock this door.'

It's amazing how much better I feel. I answer with surprised reasonableness, 'Barf le bubba.'

Pa's response comes in the flat voice I know, and fear, 'Talk properly, James. Open the door. Now, please.'

Don't give way, whispers the voice of temptation, you're in charge in here.

I give the pink botty a thorough good scrub, putting in plenty of elbow grease. White shreds cling to the bristles as I churn the water in frenzy. And serve it right. I am too busy to answer.

'It isn't baby's bathtime yet,' continues Pa, speaking very calmly now, 'You do Cymbydoll while Mummy does Cymbeline; that's after tea.'

The door knob rattles.

'Now! James.' His other voice, the voice he uses before something happens to teach me a lesson: 'Come along please, you're getting overexcited.'

There is a silence while he seems to be listening. I stand still. 'And it's tea-time,' says he.

Silence. I am hungry having been too upset for my morning egg because of a difficulty with the soldiers which Pa refused to do anything about, then heartlessly reproduced the very same egg for my lunch. I have to say, if he wanted to make me mad, he was one hundred per cent successful. But I keep it all in; it's far more exciting. If you holler and scream it all gets used up. And then they just smile at each other and look away and talk about the weather et cetera.

I am about to suggest maybe the new baby would like to return to Maternity or wherever, when a new voice comes through the door. Pa talking like this reminds me of the witch in the *Snow White* video: 'Cymbeline's bought you strawberries and ice cream for tea,' it says.

Warning voice: 'James. Open this door. Now, please.' Pause. Witch voice: 'You like ice cream, don't you?'

Next to steak, ice cream is what I like best. So I open.

It is typical of my childishness to suppose Pa meant that I should have ice cream – *today*. But, naturally, disobedient boys do not get treats. Oh, dear me, no. So in my new bedroom (which used to be Pa's office until he gave it up, just for me, and moved into the caravan), we work out a prayer together, to help me not to be led into temptation again. God willing, Pa says, I may get to have a double helping tomorrow. I want to ask about my sin, but Pa is already through to the Lord, praying hard on my behalf. To interrupt at such a time would be selfish

and babyish – which I had only just promised Heavenly
Father not to be. This being Ma's first day back, I am
excused the dark, which I so richly deserve . . .

Black diagonals crisscross. Black branches moving over
night sky, clouds lit from below. Dark building. And . . .
me, come to at the junk room window, kneeling, elbows
on the sill, neck wet, chin slick . . . Blood? Taste . . .
No, not blood, saliva.

Silence. The silence seemed . . . wrong.

Fear in my belly. Weakness. Panic attack? All over
now. But why? Something frightened you . . . ? Try to
remember . . .

A sound is missing. The choir! The choir has gone. Bits
of the jigsaw. Think hard. Something else. Swimming up
slowly – a mouth, my mouth, and it's red. Blood! Blood-
spitting choirboy-doll! Got it. Where is it now? Gone.
What happened next? Circles of light. Circles of bright
light . . . and . . . a woman. Not *any* woman, a special
woman. Who?

I cannot re-mem-ber . . . !

Two windows in the roof. One lit up suddenly. I placed
my eye to the diamond pane . . . the pane *I* had cleaned
with my sleeve . . . how long ago . . . ?

A girl appeared in a black sloppy jumper, getting the
last from a bottle of Squeezy, her hair up all round with
wisps like a Victorian, like (almost remembering, grabbing
squirts it away) my Ma . . . (now I see her) before she
went (now I don't) . . . away.

Hopeless.

The girl was bright, every detail clear in the bright
rectangle in the black slab of the roof. She was singing a
love song, you could tell by the eyebrows.

'Times have changed,' the Canon said. 'We have girls
in the sixth form, mm?'

'And some of them do a turn,' said Lawrence. 'Smell

my fingers,' he said. So I did.

'Been to the chippy?' I asked. His laugh is horrible. Why did he laugh? I still don't know why he laughed.

The girl at the window had finished washing up now. Was rinsing her hands.

I rested my head on the glass, and up went a pigeon. Roosting on the ledge outside, I hadn't seen it. One *live* pigeon, sitting on the wall . . . up she went between the dark cliffs, clap clap clap clap . . .

What about *my* pigeon? My pigeon can't fly, poor thing. And it can't feed itself.

And it can't eat Glacé Mints.

So dark. Evensong had to have started down there. No more relic hunting for today. How to get back to *her*, that was the question. And food. Food for the invalid . . .

The window catch was rusty but opened. This could be an alternative route back to the turret, I thought, a route to bypass the quire. But someone might see me out there . . .

The girl pulled back, leaving an empty frame.

Without real commitment, I straddled the sill, climbed out into the freezing night air.

The small roof slopes gently away to a curving, foot-high parapet. Grass and moss sprout along the grey-green ribs making the lead slippery. In the grey gloom, the white and beige feathers looked surprisingly bright. I avoided looking at the headless pigeon in the gutter.

Focus on the Matter. And on the action to come.

Eight feet beyond the parapet, across a black chasm, a buttress with iron ladder attached. The ladder has hoops every yard of its length, to stop a person falling, I guessed. The top of the ladder hooks over the main parapet twenty feet above. The closest iron hoop is five or six feet from the edge. Not a big jump. But the earth below is ten times further. That makes it *big*.

I lifted one foot to the top of the parapet. My legs began shaking. The other foot refused absolutely to leave the ground. Even just to practise. I stepped back. Retreated. I might find a plank in the junk room, or some rope or cable to make a life-line.

Back inside I felt sick and my stomach gurgled, starting me off on a worry about the absence of toilet facilities. The problem seemed not to be urgent, but counting back, it had been three whole days . . . or was it only two? I had lost track a bit . . . Anyway, it seemed sensible to at least find some paper in readiness. After a search along the cluttered shelves of the now almost blacked-out room, I found a pile of dusty leaflets, the front pages of which read: The Order For Evensong. In capital letters at the bottom are the words, PLEASE DO NOT TAKE AWAY.

I shoved twenty or so into the pouch. They are smooth and stiff but will serve if I scrunch them up before use. I thought about the gutter outside, surely less obnoxious, less sacrilegious than in here. But more risky. I began to approach the window. Then stopped.

What was this sudden obsession with the ethics of defecation? I didn't even want to go!? Suddenly I was aware that all my actions since the attack had been aimless distractions – action for the sake of action.

Memory flash: Two stags on TV. Crashing antlers. In mid-battle they break for a bit of a graze. After chewing the cud for a minute or two, they continue the fight.

You're no different. Playing for time. Anything to avoid what's going on. There's been another game, and you *know* it. That doll – that knitted gobshite – when that thing spat at you, you weren't anywhere near the window, you were over by the statues, on the other side of the room. You've been on the move again, haven't you. Haven't you? I don't *like* it.

I scrutinised the Spidertop. Blood spots on my sleeve. More on my chest. I prised off a scab and gave it the tongue test. Blood? Could be. It's not certain.

It's a thin-ended wedge. Cut it out.

Christalmighty I'm trying as hard as I can! Don't you understand, for the first time in my life *I'm afraid* of her . . . That bloody doll . . . it's her instrument . . . I feel like . . . I feel like She's *touched* me through that; She's been dead seven years, now She's *touched* me. Without my say! I feel . . . dirty . . . It's . . . horrible . . .

OK, look . . . I'm not hassling, but . . . well . . . this isn't working out, is it? I mean, why don't we call a truce, eh? Say you're not well. Well, you're *not*. I mean, look at you. You've tried to do what the man said, tried to face up to things, the things that we all know trigger you off. That's why you're here. Well, you've tried, and it didn't work out. Nothing to be ashamed of. It's asking too much. He should *know* that. Practise control, he said, steady breathing. That's a laugh. Look what's happened! You're right in the shit. Worse than before. Far worse! I mean, what's going *on*? I don't understand any more. Why blood? Where'd that *come* from? Jesus Christ!

The blood's no problem. That's easy; shock tactics. Association of ideas. She's using psychological warfare. Nothing weird about that. I'm supposed to think I'm *blighted, cursed* – you know, witchcraft – that shit again. I don't buy it. Never have, never will.

Oh, you don't, eh? How come you keep saying *She*, then? How come it's always *She's* doing this to me, *She's* doing that? You *say* it's all crap, but you're starting to *believe* in it. You told *me* off before, now *you're* at it. You and Pa are like one of a kind, if you ask me – he believes in miracles, you believe in magic. What's the difference? They're both supernatural. You talk about thin-ended wedges . . . What do you call *that*? You've actually got yourself believing your dead sister has risen from the dead and is running loose in this

Cathedral, hunting you down like an animal. Next thing you'll be telling me the little cow's summoned up the 'forces of Evil'. We've had Satan's Crabs and Dolly-of-Dracula, let's bung in Frankenstein and the Werewolf. What the fuck?

Hm, I said, sitting down on a split rexine tuffet. You could even be right, head, the little cheat almost had me believing in blood-spitting puppets. What's happening to me? It's a *woolly doll* for Pete's sake – knit one, purl one – I saw it. How could I be so . . . ?

I suppose that's what She wants . . . She wants to confuse me, undermine my confidence so I begin to doubt my own sanity. Well that just shows how little She knows me.

There you go – *She, She, She*. You've got to stop—

It's a *metaphor*, dammit. It doesn't mean . . . It's a tool, a focus, that's all. Forget about 'truces', I'm not quitting, no way! So shut up. I'm thinking . . . It was you said we had to face things. Fair enough. When I'm good and ready, when I'm fed and rested and calm and peaceful, I'm going to just let my mind go right on back into the past, and I'm going to remember *everything* there is to remember about my childhood. And hers. Nothing's going to be hidden, no skeletons in the cupboard, no dark secrets, everything out in the open where I can deal with it. But first . . . first I must deal with this stupid funk I've got myself in. I have to face the Matter as well, you know, and in this case that means that fucking doll or manikin or whatever we call it. When I find it . . . I'm going to unravel the little prick's knickers, and I'm going to expose its little rubber bladder, or whatever it is those obnoxious bloody choirboys filled with joke-shop blood, then I'm going to fill it up with piss and hang it back on that music stand.

And, when I've dealt with the doll, I'm going to collect some nice wafer biscuits I just happen to have remembered the location of. And after that, I'm going home to my turret, my Castle-in-the-Air. On the way, I'll call in at the Wheel Room, to feed my poor invalid, then . . . You know what I'm going to do? I'm going to bed. To *sleep*. Because, tomorrow . . . tomorrow, head, you and me are *leaving*. How come we're leaving? I'll tell you: we're leaving because the little cheat's time will be up at midnight, son, that's why. 'So, if you're out there spying on me, read my lips, little cheat: big brother is not going screwy, young lady, and your thin-ended wedges stop right here!'

I immediately set to work unpiling the pile of broken gargoyles. The lumps are heavy but I drove myself till my arms cried out and the sweat ran down my back. But suddenly, just as I grabbed up the half-eroded head of a carved-stone monkey, I found my finger caught so fast between its gritty teeth that a gasp broke from me. Frantically I tugged my finger free, dropping the head, crushing my plimsoled foot. Something pink and purple flitted with a scream (that might have been mine) across my other foot and away. I heard panting like a hunted stag. It was *me*!

She's done it again! I feel the flagstones lurch beneath my feet . . . invisible stage-hands bring on the kitchen table set for tea.

300

27

SCENE: *The Dining-Room – Eight Months Later*
*Pa stands at the head of the table. On his left, head bowed,
eyes hidden by her fringe, sits Ma. She smells sweetly of Nivea
and stale milk. Beside her my sister bounces in what was once
my high chair, pumping puffs of ammonia out round the edges
of her Pampers.*

*It is high-tea; time for another feeding frenzy. But first,
grace.*

*Pa's eyes close above the tips of his fingers then pop back
open, catching me out. I lower my head. He speaks:*

'For what we are about to receive . . .'

Peeping again, I watch the monster gorging itself while
the family prays. Once more I sense the evil in our midst.
When will Pa *do* her? *When?* Is he blind?

'. . . the Lord make us truly thankful.'

Amen, say we three, and the Monster? The Monster
delivers forearm smashes – one, two, three to the liquid-
ised liver and spinach, spattering Ma's face and pink cardigan. Its black devil eyes fix me. I quickly look away.
Meanwhile, sweet, innocent Ma absently cuts my fish fingers though I have been self sufficient in the cutting of
food since before my fourth birthday. I fear she is no
longer with us, everything is up to me and Pa now. Maybe
today the Monster will go too far, maybe today Pa's eyes
will be opened. I pray so. I pray so.

The Monster scowls and a green tongue emerges that is

altogether too long and snakelike; green slurry flows down its chin into the plastic bibdish. Not for an instant do its eyes leave mine. I cannot bear to look. I turn aside and bite off food for which I have no appetite. As I chew and chew without swallowing, the Monster's slobbering and sucky-grunting falls silent making me look up in alarm.

The feeding has stopped. The mouth is stretched in what would be a howl but for the fact that no air is passing. In or out. Its oozing fist is jabbing spasmodically in my direction. Spite-rays flicker in the black boreholes of its eyes.

Ma leans across with a tissue and wipes away the green drool. 'There there, wassa matter den? Wassa matter? Poor baby. Ohhhh, ohhh.' She waves a silver spoonful, coaxingly. But the Monster's eyes are locked on to mine. I begin to feel the force of its will. In her innocence, Ma keeps waving the silver spoon. If only I weren't so tired . . .

Now it is a fact that this creature so recently come among us – gross, obscene and incapable of manipulating cutlery as it is – has nevertheless succeeded in getting itself equipped, just like big brother, with its own plastic spoon. This spoon it *must* have, though it cannot use a spoon for spooning but only brutishly wave one while mashing fistfuls of food – the feeding is done by Ma. (No more than a childish charade you may think. You'd be wrong.)

Suddenly – still without drawing breath – the Monster lashes out, backhanding the silver spoon and contents away across the room.

Ma glances towards the head of the table. Pa's face is stern. Ma pretends amusement. She turns to the Monster: 'Ooops,' she laughs, 'there now, we've dropped it. Never mind. Never mind. Mummy pick it up.'

Still no breath. The Monster's colour deepens. Ma begins anxiously patting its back. Pa's left eye quivers.

I feel myself grow pale. Unlike Ma, I know what it wants: not *a* spoon but *my* spoon – in fact precisely that spoon belonging to the tea set which became a part of me last Christmas. My spoon is red; the Monster's spoon is yellow. Now it wants my red spoon but the Monster's passion is as boundless as it is evil. What the Monster really wants, its ultimate objective, is to take for itself everything that is mine – I mean *everything*. Yesterday a high chair, today a spoon, tomorrow it could be the clothes off my back. If the Monster's lust for what is mine ended there, with mere material possessions, I could stand it. But it goes further. Much further.

Objects can be replaced, conceivably. Not so *personhood*. Not so that unique *me-ness* that makes James Bishop James Bishop. It is this personhood which is the Monster's ultimate objective. Though I lack words to describe such devilry, I will try.

What a person *does*, that person *is*, yet whatever *I* do, the Monster does the same, and *more*. Take laughing: I have only to titter and, in seconds, the Monster also is rocking with pretend laughter. Any fool can see it's not genuine laughter – being grossly exaggerated, and ridiculously forced – but, always, she wins the attention of my parents, regardless.

I'm aware that, on its own, this example sounds petty, but there's more. Take the splashing: the Monster and I must share a bath now. (I hate this, but what can I *do*?) Whenever I splash, the Monster splashes. Always right *at me*, till I'm half drowned and choking with suds in my eyes. But if *I* dare to retaliate . . . if even so much as a minute flick of water lands on the Monster's piggy-pink face . . . I'm branded 'spiteful' or 'vicious' . . . 'She's only a baby,' is the cry. 'She doesn't understand. You're old enough to know better now, James.'

Then there's kissing: I kiss anyone, doesn't matter who, could be the milkman, who stinks, or the cat, and, you've guessed it, every time, the Monster starts reaching up with its podgy arms and its lips all crimped into a wet sucky snout. 'Oh, isn't she lovely,' everyone coos. So's poo, think I, but what can I do? And if I cry . . .

If I cry, the Monster cries – more piteously, longer, louder – not because it is sad, of course not, never out of sorrow or pity, no, merely because Jimbo has cried and thereby been noticed, for his *self*.

These scraps of attention the Monster would take from me to the last smile, the last nod, the last little pat on the head. As the Monster waxes, so Jimbo wanes; total eclipse is a whisker away.

This stealing of the *self* is impossible to counter. What can I do when there exists no *object*, no stolen thing at which to point and say, She's taken my this or that? Imagine my Ma's response to: 'She's taken my best smile,' or, 'Give me back my hug round the legs.' Vile and contemptuous as it is, mimicry is not a crime, though it should be, the worst.

And all the time I watch for some sign of awareness in P and M. None appears. Only once was I innocent enough to voice my fears, bringing down wounding charges on my head. They actually called me the green-eyed monster. Monster! Me! Anyway, I learn quickly; it showed me that I'm on my own – my dear parents, bless them, are simply too pure and innocent to see what is so obvious to me.

I grip my spoon tight and lower my head to my meal. Across the table, the spinach-jam breaks with a sob and a gasp. I wait for the bellow. It comes:

'WAAAAAAAAAAAAAAAAAA!'

'Oh, poppet. Oh, dare dare dare dare dare. Never mind.'

The Monster writhes on the horns of a dilemma: to breathe or bellow. As she silently squirms, I would swear her purpling head is expanding; dumbly, her eyes seem to bugle the pressure within.

A vision comes: ruptured pate, boiling humours venting from the fontanelle. I pray the dilemma will not be resolved. Anything seems possible: silent asphyxiation, loud bang . . . I know this is wishful thinking . . .

But, wait! Can it be? I really believe . . . Yes! At last, *at last* he has seen. Hallelujah, and the heavens be praised . . .

He is giving it *the look*. He is dabbing his lips with the napkin. He is rising . . .

Ma is trying to apologise for it with her eyes as she sucks khaki splodges from the sleeve of her cardigan. But . . . he is not moved . . .

The Monster, meanwhile, is oblivious. With a flailing of arms it drags in a huge breath; it roars, then sucks, then roars again. And again. And again. And again, the din rising steadily towards some unimaginable climax. At last – miracle of primordial communication – a *word* emerges: 'Doon!' wails the Monster. Ma flashes Pa an amazed look; Pa's frown merely deepens as the Monster hurls itself up, over the tray of the high chair to belly flop on the table in a wreckage of china and dream topping. There it lies, pounding and kicking in blind fury, bare inches short of its target – my spoon!

I scramble down from the table, back away, the red spoon gripped tight in my hand.

Ma gathers the Monster to her. 'Oh bless her, she wants Jimmy's lil red spoon, the lil treasure.' She threads the Monster back into the high chair where it stiffens, collapses forward, stiffens again, slides down to the crutch-stop and lies there half under the tray, flailing its arms and legs like a crab on its back . . . and *howling* – howling like the hell-sent creature it is.

Inside I am delirious, but then comes the bombshell: Ma turns to me and, shouting over the screams, says: 'Let baby have your spoon, dear, there's a good boy.'

I'm astonished, devastated; truly, she is lost to me now.

Forcing back the tears, I reverse into my bolt hole – the narrow gap between the cooker and the washboiler. The Monster continues to scream as if it would blast me from the cosmos. Then, quite suddenly, it stops screaming and begins to sob piteously – bottom lip out like a septic sausage – wracked by spasms, downcast, pathetic, feigning abject defeat. Fear, rage and awe contend in me – such talent for deception in one so young!

From my crevice between the two machines I can just see Pa's face. His mouth is a trap. Oh, joy, oh mercy, he is not deceived. Praise be. He nods slowly, sits down. He speaks:

'The Old Adam, Mother.'

Ma flicks him a look, twists her hair. 'She only wanted—' she begins, but Pa cuts across her:

'Original sin; it must be expelled. "The first or second Sunday next after the birth," that's what the prayer book says. Our daughter is months overdue.'

'Yes, dear, I—'

'Tomorrow. I promise. Come hell or high water.'

There is panic in Ma's dark-ringed eyes. She grips Pa's wrist: 'You've been busy, Edward. No one can—'

'There can be no excuses, Mother, not when a Christian soul is in jeopardy. Priorities, my dear, priorities. I have left this too long already, that's plain.'

'Why not have a professional this time, dear? Why not—'

The silence is deafening. Pa is white marble, left eye working like a semaphore lamp. 'Pro-*fessional*, Elizabeth?' His voice is low, dangerous. (For a mad second I fear Ma could end in the Dark.) 'After his insulting behaviour towards me?'

Ma looks at him. Smacks her forehead as if remembering the obvious. Manufactures a smile. Takes his hand in her two hands and squeezes. 'Of course not, dear. Of course not. I forgot, that's all. But, Edward—'

Suspiciously: 'I'm glad. Very glad.'

'—It's just that Cymbeline is . . .'

'Go on, Elizabeth? Our daughter is what?'

'It's nothing, Edward. I'm sure you'll take care . . . It's just that . . . She's been a bit snuffly . . . It's her teeth . . . And the weather's so cold now.'

'Tomorrow, Elizabeth.'

Quietly: 'All right, Edward.'

The door closes behind him. My mother stands, gathers up her sobbing offspring and, smiling sadly, approaches the entrance to my retreat. Although she is outwardly blind to the truth, I believe that, at some deep level of her psyche, she knows it is far too late for the expulsion of Original Sin. Even the full immersion, even pure rainwater from the caravan roof, cannot prevail when the Devil has such a hold. But her mother's instinct will never permit her to admit such a thing to herself.

I return her smile with such reassurance as I can muster. She looks so thin and tired my heart aches for her. Damn my sister to hell. I think the creature is beyond the power of holy water, however administered, except possibly by sack and breezeblock.

In response to my smile, Ma asks would I give up the spoon, to humour the baby. Miserably I point out that Cymbeline has not behaved well.

Ma nods, looks pleadingly and tells me in her love-voice: 'She's only a tiny baby, Jimbo. She doesn't understand.'

Yes. And baby monsters grow, Mother, I think. But she reaches into my bolt hole and the red spoon is being coaxed firmly from my fist.

I will store the incident with the others; this one feels like the straw my back had been waiting for.

Today it is raining. Again. I think it's been raining all night which is hardly April showers.

Pa has given special permission for the godparents and

307

me to stand inside at the Jonah window, while he does the immersion outside. The top light is open to enable us to hear him so we can join in with the responses, but the rain is beating so hard on the roof, we keep coming in raggedly and late. And Pa keeps glaring.

Mrs Chalmers is standing beside me, tutting and shifting from foot to foot – she has varicose veins, and does not like standing, which is why she always sits down to sort the bulbs. Next to her is Michelle, her daughter, who helps with the bulbs in school holidays. Michelle is second godmother – Auntie having refused point blank. Standing close behind me is old Frank who is deaf and keeps shouting 'Amen' for no reason (except maybe the threat of redundancy). It makes me jump every time.

Kind Mrs Chalmers holds the prayer book high, as if for Frank – who can't read – to see it.

Being short, I am forced to watch through the greenhill on the window, so the picture outside is not only wriggly with rain, but green. Standing beside the water tank, on top of the caravan's portable step, Pa looks as tall as a Zulu in his red stole (brown, for me) with the black umbrella held over his head at full stretch by Ma who is standing behind in the mud and wet with a white towel draped over her arm and her hair flat and all dark with water.

Pa has just pulled up the sleeves of his jacket and taken the Monster from Ma. I feel pressure on my back as Frank leans forward and pushes me against the window with his paunch. My chest feels suddenly empty, in spite of the pressure.

Pa raises the naked, wriggling, wailing Monster. It immediately stops wriggling, and falls silent.

Cymbeline Bishop looks suddenly small and, though green to me, white.

Pa is speaking, face raised, eyes shut. I hear the words 'sanctify', 'mystical', 'washing away sin'.

'Amen!' bellows Frank.

Pa turns and shouts, 'Name this child.'

Mrs Chalmers lashes back with her heel, simultaneously shouting, 'Cymbeline Margaret Bishop,' while Frank shouts, 'Ouch,' and Michelle mumbles something inaudible.

'Cymbeline Margaret, I baptise thee,' says Father, dipping his shoulders, the Monster vanishing into the galvanised tank, 'in the name of—'

Comes a terrible vision: the closing of green waters; a hollow voice ringing through the iron; dark shadows looming.

'—and of—'

A cry in my throat which, like the water, closes over.

'—and of the Holy Ghost. Amen.'

I feel I must rush out and stop him. Without thinking, I brace my hands on the window and push back hard, but Frank is very big, very soft, and seems not to feel me.

Too late now. Luckily. For it is only now that reason returns to me: she's putting it on, you know she can do it. A monster's a monster, naked or clothed. Look at poor Ma. Pa knows what he's doing, he always does. Always.

'—the communion of Saints, the resurrection of the flesh, and the life after death—'

When the Monster resurfaces, it looks a lot darker. Pa draws the cross, then they all come inside.

28

I came to jammed into the corner of the work room, squatting, fists clenched, staring up at a ribbon of orange light across the ceiling and a stack of timber beside me. I didn't know where I was, only that I wanted to leave. Also I'd been crying.

As I slowly unbunched my fists my blurred vision settled on the pile of broken gargoyles. I remembered the monkey's head. The bite – my hand was throbbing – that was the *cat* surely . . . wasn't it? Yes. The monkey too? My foot hurt. I had dropped the monkey's head on my foot. Crushed my toes. Then what? Then . . . nothing. Nothing? Wait. What thoughts are these:

Two kingdoms come together in the place . . . nothing can keep them apart . . . black birds roosting in the turret . . . sing Come and play come and play some body up here want play with you . . .

I am no longer in control. A pattern is forming – a strategy, *her* strategy – her acting, me reacting like a frog's hind leg!

I fingered the masterkey in my pouch, brought it out, stuck the ring end into my mouth, clenched on to the shaft and massaged its smooth, hard surface with my tongue. I turned it and inserted the blade end, felt its planes and spaces with my tongue's tip; the edges were perfect – perfect Lawrentian craftsmanship. There was power in such Matter – great power. I thought of its maker;

Lawrence the animal; Lawrence the mastercraftsman; such an amalgam, so potent; take away the magic of hand and eye – no replica of the key; take away the brute – no key to replicate, for only a brute could have done to Holy Harding what Lawrence did to Holy Harding – Holy Harding, school monitor, altar boy, server in the Cathedral of ix . . .

Shag found out about the wet-dreams. Somehow, I don't know how, he got his great maulers on a letter from Harding's mum saying how she was sending her son a dozen washable condoms to help with 'the problem'. Also, apparently, Matron had been overheard making some indelicate comment to one of the cleaners about the state of Harding's sheets. Lawrence made the connection – Lawrence would.

On the way to assembly he made his approach.

'Wonder if you could spare a moment?' he said politely.

'Hm? What is it?' said Harding. School monitors are distinguished in many ways, the most obvious being the vermilion gown; they may also grow a moustache. Harding's was long, thin, dark and greasy. When Lawrence spoke to him, the tall, white-faced youth did not look to see who was addressing him but strode on, chin high.

'I'm having a spot of bother with my periwinkle,' said Lawrence in a cultured voice I'd no idea was in his repertoire.

'Really?' said Harding, still not looking. 'What bother is that?'

'The fucker keeps shooting its load,' said Lawrence, quite loudly. Four boys in front turned round and grinned.

Harding stopped dead, and turned to Lawrence. He was whiter than white, totally colourless, maybe a touch green round the mouth.

'It's right embarrassing. The sheets an' all,' said Lawrence, smiling openly up.

312

But Harding was rallying his faculties fast; I was certain Lawrence had gone too far this time. I wandered on a yard or two, pretending to look elsewhere.

Harding was *looking* at him now all right, voice shaking as he fought for control: 'Firstly . . . Lawrence, isn't it? Yes, it is. Firstly, Lawrence, you do not use *language* when addressing a school monitor – remember that, will you. Secondly, Lawrence, I fail to see what your . . . *problem* has to do with me.' With that, he turned and strode on, speaking as he did so without looking up, 'So if you would kindly—'

Lawrence cut in, shouting after him, 'I wondered if I might borrow one of your washable johnnies, mate? That's—'

Harding was back. 'Shut up!' he hissed. 'You little— Yes. Yes. Come to my study. After assembly. Now, for goodness' sake—'

'Only kidding,' said Shag, with a big, horrible grin. 'You know what I'm after. I asked you last week, mate.'

A worldliness came into Harding's face. He nodded slowly at Shag. 'The key,' he said, reaching into his trouser pocket. 'I'll have it back before supper. Understood? Without fail, understood?' The monitor's hand reappeared, palmed something to Lawrence.

Lawrence was nodding, smiling happily. Still keeping my distance, I watched, fascinated. 'Providing I'm through, mate. See what I can do for yer. No promises, mind.'

'Tch,' said the monitor. He whirled and strode away.

Lawrence shrugged and shambled. after, feet splayed, arse under, hands in pockets, grinning like a dirty monkey . . .

The Cathedral was silent now, Evensong long done, I felt sure, candles snuffed, faithful departed, gates locked, doors bolted, empty – this quiet, it *had* to be. I was glad.

I'd had more than enough of this place and its unnatural Matter; now, perhaps, I could withdraw in safety.

The ladder was out of the question now, what with the floodlights. In any case, with the church deserted it would be quite safe I felt certain – provided there were no more nasty shocks, I'd have to take a chance on that – to descend.

I'd go down through the choir practice room and St Andrew's chapel beneath it, make a quick call at the sacristy (where Holy Harding does his serving), then cross the quire to the south side, where, with the help of the Talisman of Shag, I would enter the spiral stair at ground level, and so – relicless but, hopefully, bearing precious manna for the invalid – to the Sanatorium (formerly known as the Wheel Room) and, after that, bed. And tomorrow? Tomorrow, at the first stroke of midnight . . . adieu.

To celebrate, I popped in a mint.

I rose and groped my way towards the fire door.

No more surprises, please, whispered headvoice.

Apart from the sacristy – that won't take a sec – we're stopping for *nothing*, not even a dump, I said.

Could it have been to make up for Cymbeline's cheating that the Umpire permitted me to find the sacristy so easily? Maybe so. (Though it was in fact close by the high altar steps, so perhaps a little logic came into it too.) The chamber had priestly vestments draped on dummies like olden days tailors might have used, and I identified it at once by the basin and marble slab in the corner. From somewhere above, fillets of amber light fell aslant a small oak door armed with iron bosses and the usual Chubb lock. I looked up; high in the rough hewn wall, a narrow arched window with bars. The place was a fortress. Holy of holys.

The oak door yielded at once to the key. Out of the gloom of that stone vault things glowed and twinkled with their own wondrous light. There was the silver paten shining in the dark like an oval moon, and there a jewelled chalice (making Father's communion goblet seem like something got with filling-station coupons). From a wall-niche, a pair of crystal decanters glittered like splinters of ice, and beneath them the object of my search, the pyx itself.

The simple cylinder seemed like gold polished to shine like silver. (Father uses a tartan McVitie's shortbread tin.) I raised the lid. At first I thought it empty then noticed a knob in the centre of what appeared to be the bottom, but was not. I pulled the knob and out came a circular weight covered in purple velvet. Beneath this lay sixty to a hundred communion wafers, each no bigger than a ten pence piece, each with four small Xs crossed by vertical letter Ps embossed on the surface. They were thin and tasted of very little but would certainly keep the pigeon going, for now.

My heart began to flutter as I lowered the heavy pyx into my pouch. I also borrowed a small silver bowl for collecting water from the drainpipe. Feeling a little like I imagined a tomb-robber might feel, but knowing that my motives were of the very best, I relocked both doors and left without a backward glance. (My intention was to leave both bowl and pyx with a little note of thanks on vacating the premises.)

The thought of the pigeon sitting alone in its Bible-nest inside the big wheel, with black shadows all around and no one to talk to, set me scurrying off like the returning hunter. Even though I had not found the relics, I felt amazingly good inside. If the Ghost did exist (by no means proven) then her cheating strategy had backfired; I had gained bread, of sorts, for me and my ward, and She, by her terrorist activities, had lost the moral high-ground. And that's what the whole thing's about.

The Pin

29

At night, no light penetrates the interior except through
stained glass. The floodlight rays fall up, not down, daubing the high canopy with jungle colour. At man height
the quire aisle is dark with thick arteries of shadow con-
necting every feature to its neighbour – steps, sepulchres,
arches, screens all laced together and to the towering pillars by these black branches from which thick clots of
blue and red hang like deadly, tempting fruit. All one
cavity, one forbidden grove.

Tilting back my head, I saw shrouds and regimental
colours hanging like winter leaves when the flesh is gone
and only a gauze of capillaries remains, scab of red,
mothwing of gold.

And me turning about like a drowning fish in a mesh
of shadows drawing round.

Down the steps, beyond the quire screen, the empty
nave a whale's throat yawning darkness with dim glows
and mysterious sparks like phosphorus in dark water that
is very deep. The smell of wax. The smell of dry cave.
Forbidden. Secret. Kingdom more alien than the attic
wilderness above – history's interface with death.

Cut the shit and get out of here, said headvoice.

I felt the weight of the pyx in my pouch. No urging
needed – I had a mission.

To reach the south transept and access door meant passing from the north quire aisle across the quire with its

brass eagle and dark mahogany stalls and out the other side. I moved to the iron gate in front of me. Locked. I worked my way along the haphazard-looking perimeter fence formed from the tombs of kings and bishops; all one piece, all stitched together by a web of carved stone and iron railings. The single entrance gate bears a lock from the age of dungeons.

Nasty feeling creeping up. Not for the first time was I confronted by the limitations of the mighty Talisman of Shag; neither the giant oak doors of the western entrance, nor the south porch, nor any of the transept doorways yield to it. All exits from the Cathedral are guarded by massive iron locks, all reinforced by systems of bolts and rods and bars, none of which can be sprung from within; a fact which had surprised, but not alarmed me, until now. Now my heart performed a little jig, impromptu. I sensed a shift in the cavity. A sound? I stood listening. High above something flapped in a draughty attic.

The tower clock chimed a quarter, three notes rising, signifying nothing but the passage of time. Quarter to or past sometime, what did it matter?

Biting off fingers matters, said headvoice.

No answer from me – if there was an Umpire, he would know what was in my heart – instead I gave myself orders, pumping myself up with little pecks of the head: Concentrate. Take no chances. Stop for nothing. Bring home the bacon.

Home? Was that how I thought of it now – the Bible Room and the Wheel Room, the stairs and turret? Home. Yes. She'd be there, waiting, in her own way praying I'd make it back OK. Without *me*, no bread; without bread, no pigeon.

A new thought came to drive me: what if she should die *before* I got home, give up the ghost and pass on, alone in the dark? That got me moving east fast, searching hard now for access to the quire.

Along the aisle, half running. Within a dozen yards, I came to a set of iron gates closing off the steps east of the high altar. The whole eastern end was sealed off. Christ! What if she should *get better* before I got home – all on her own, without any saving by me? I turned back, running hard now. Another iron gate, completing the quire-screen barricade, closing off the steps to the nave.

Trapped. About turn. Search the barrier.

A glimpse of statue pulled me up short.

Stretched out on a stone slab, under a crusted canopy, lay – to judge by the mitre and colourful vestments and the pairs of angels at feet and head – a bishop. The upper part of his tomb had been made part of the perimeter by a grill of fine arches behind. There was no way into the quire climbing over his lordship, but *under* . . . ?

I dropped to the floor, hopeful I had found a gap in the defences, and stopped dead. Waxy flesh – cage of ribs – naked – male – *corpse!* Ah! shit! You little bitch! Hoppity hop heart beats, dizzy, fingers a-tingle . . . Wait, wait, wait. Corpse? Even in that jungly light I see something doesn't add up: can a corpse have half a nose and two fingers busted off at the first joint? This is no meat and bone corpse, this is another statue, another *memento mori* if my suspicions are correct. His grace will have had the tomb made in advance, to remind him of things to come. Above, he's represented in all his earthly splendour; below, this emaciated body, wearing nothing but a kind of nappy, representing his (and all men's) fate. I sniggered with relief.

Three wide arches support the slab front and back; I could easily scramble through. There was nothing to stop me. Nothing but the thought of rolling over the awful figure within. Treading on graves has never bothered me, but this seemed different.

We're stopping for *nothing*, remember? said headvoice. **Not even a dump, you said. You're asking for trouble,**

mate. Get going, for Christ's sake.

I was full stretch on top of his grace when the eyelids rolled up and showed me two white lights. A pair of waving ginger hairs appeared in the corner of a mouth the colour of old putty. The mouth opened a crack and out slid a worm with a thousand legs, foul breath, and four words: '*James Bishop murders babies.*' The big muscle jerked. I had time to feel bony legs clamp under my buttocks, then down I went without even a scream. (My body is learning.)

SCENE: *The Dining Room – some days later. Saturday – that is, washday*
Ma is clearing lunch, and the Monster (who had proved as immune to holy caravan water as predicted), is sprawled on the rug stinking the place out as always. The wash boiler is on in the kitchen so you cannot see through the French window for steam. Auntie is seated in the armchair behind the Monster who must be constipated because she is even more red-faced and cross-eyed than usual.

As it happens it rained after lunch so the test match with Auntie was cancelled. I was miserable at the time, but later I realised Heavenly Father was looking after me because if Aunt Mary had said play, we'd have gone out, and I'd have missed the breakthrough. This is how it came about.

'Everything all right out there?' calls Ma through the hatch.

Auntie doesn't answer. So I look up from the jigsaw I had for my birthday.

To my amazement, Auntie's eyes are squinting, her lips are a tight line, her face is bright red and her cheeks are out like balloons. For a second I think she must have gone mad, then she makes a really loud rude-noise with her lips, winks at me, points at the Monster and laughs. Auntie's laugh is like a man's laugh – deep and loud.

Ma's head comes through the hatch and says, 'Mary!

322

Little pigs have big ears,' which is code for Jimbo is listening. This only serves to alert me of course, though my brain has already caught on.

Since the advent of the Monster, 'going potties' has become a miserable, solitary business. More often than not Ma starts me off only to leave me stranded above the waterdragon with my backside wedged into the Young Person's Patent Toilet Seat Adaptor (another trophy won from the WI jumble by Pa). My achievements in this department now pass unnoticed. Grunt, splash, wipe and it's over; no praise, no hug, no kiss, nothing. The Monster has them all.

Watching Auntie's performance, the Plan comes in a flash, fully formed: since the Monster wants to be me, I will become the Monster. I will take the game to her, plus interest. Love and attention being the rewards of infantile behaviour, it only amazes me that I did not think of the idea sooner. I will become a little child again, incompetent, inarticulate, dirty, greedy, self-centred.

My heart races with excitement so that I cannot concentrate on my Light of the World jigsaw showing Jesus standing outside the vine-covered door, lantern in hand. I can't wait to begin, but where? Suddenly it comes to me: I want to 'go' *now* quite badly. But I won't. I'll hold back. Accumulating. Cross-legged. Waiting for the moment. Purposeful. Determined. Totally in control.

By bedtime I still have not been. By morning I'm a timebomb.

Ruined. Undone. Sent to the Roombed without any tea.

Here I lie in this vast, unpopulated bed (so big it fills Father's ex-office wall to wall, hence Roombed), knowing that beneath me the Monster squats on *my* mother's lap, draining her love balloons to inflate its once wrinkled body drum tight. Now it is my beautiful Ma who has the wrinkles! I am close to despair as I think of her – her hollow eyes haunt me whenever I drift towards sleep – being slowly sucked dry by that *thing* in Pampers. I *know* the truth – Heavenly Father sent me a message, last night, like little Samuel only not just a voice, a vision, a terrible, terrible dream that would not go away . . .

I dreamt that my mother was calling me from the bottom of a deep, deep well. Her voice was tiny like a doll's voice. She wanted me to help her. I stood on the round wall and wound the handle as fast as I could, but when the bucket was still just out of reach, the rope kept slipping so I could not reach the bucket. And the Monster was sat in the bucket, filling the bucket with its bloated pink body, its great bulging legs hanging over the edge. And my Ma . . . my Ma was sat on its lap all tiny like a shrivelled-up doll. And the Monster was pinching Ma's bosoms with its hideous clawed fingers so that blood squirted out. I wound and wound but the bucket slowly descended, Ma calling my name in a voice getting smaller and smaller. And I could see her quite clearly, all the way to the bottom, which was not full of water but blood . . .

So I *do* know what's going on, you see. But I am afraid to tell. Same as Samuel was afraid to tell Eli. What else can you expect? Everything I do or say is turned against me.

I begin to sob silently. Over and over the events of the day I go, vainly searching for where I went wrong . . .

I started first thing by refusing to dress myself. At breakfast I completely wrecked my egg while clumsily trying to open it – egg all over, nice and sticky – and could not cut a single soldier without upsetting the plate. Throughout the day my talk was all ber bers and doo doos, and I hardly was able to understand a word spoken to me. Despite the discomfort, I crawled everywhere, even in the yard. I dribbled, I wet my pants, even banged my head on the furniture, and bawled . . . bawled almost non-stop. My performance was unstinting. I drove myself on in the certainty that I held the 'trump' card behind me, quite literally. By tea-time I was aware of walking strangely, and dared not run for the little beeps my botty made. At table there were some small, preliminary escapes, nothing much; I was determined to save everything for the climax.

When Pa came in from the yard, he sniffed the air with a puzzled frown. 'What's for tea, Mother?' he asked. Ma told him, pilchards on toast. He shook his head, grunted, placed his oil-grained hands on the back of the carver, lowered his head, then, having given us all one look from under his tufted brows, closed his eyes.

Apart from the Monster, we all did the same – even Auntie. I closed my eyes tight for once and placed my palms together. Silence.

Standby.

I am ready.

Fire one.

I relaxed those muscles I had been clenching. What emerged was acoustic only, but startling. Even I jumped.

Pa's eyes were two round circles. Even the Monster stopped troffling.

Silence.

Auntie made a strange moaning noise behind her hands.

Fire two: the business. I felt it erupting beneath me. The stench was appalling.

Auntie, unfortunately, had to leave the table, a handkerchief to her face.

This was by far the best bigjob I had ever achieved. I was uplifted. I flashed the Monster a look of triumph and waited for the attention to begin. The scent of victory was in my nostrils, not to mention that other, more earthy aroma.

No one could possibly ignore my efforts here tonight.

The Monster blinked, for the first time in its life it looked shaken. Ma was out of her seat. My arms were up in triumph. But what's this?

My wrists were gripped, my body swung up and away.

I glimpsed Auntie sitting on the bottom stair as I flew past above her head. Her mouth was covered, the tears running down, she was crying, I think, howling actually: 'Oh crikey, oh crikey, oh crikey . . .'

No time to ask.

Upstairs, I was stripped quite brutally. Bathed and bedded in ghastly silence.

'But—' I stammered, as the light went out.

Ma answered through the door. It was her hate voice: 'Boys who behave like dirty babies go to bed at babies' bedtime!' I heard her stomp downstairs, stop, shout back: 'And don't forget your prayers. Ask God to forgive you – *He* might.'

I could only conclude she was now so weak that not just her body, her mind also had come totally under the Monster's control. I prayed for us all in the family prayer:

God bless Mummy, Daddy, all our family, those
throughout the world;
Keep all Evil from our home,
And by the great mercy defend us
From all the perils and dangers of this night, amen

But I did not hold out that much hope . . .

Six miserable hours have passed now. I've heard them all come merrily to bed, as if there were no misery in the world. Too upset for sleep, I am forced to lie listening to the sounds. And imagining. And hating. Hating as I have never hated.

Ma is almost gone in her mind now. I know that, were it not for Pa, she would not only feed it in her own bed, but have the thing sleeping there with them, in the same room as them, all night, just in case it should wake wanting more. Luckily for her, he won't have it. He is still our best hope; our *only* hope. If it wakes him in the night, he gets angry, I've heard him, not the actual words, just the voice low and terrible. So that most times she wakes first and creeps back and forth in the dark. I know because I have heard her. One night I peeped through the keyhole, this time the light on the landing had been left on, there was poor Ma in her nightie, pale as a ghost, staggering, literally staggering, along the wall with her black-ringed eyes almost shut moaning, 'All right, I'm coming, I'm coming.' And the Monster commanding her with a series of little short, bad-tempered grunts. I honestly believe she feeds herself to it whenever it demands. I fear she is beyond my help, now. But why does he not *do* something?

Some might call it jealousy I suppose, but it was once *my* joy to lie between Ma and Pa and listen to the stories of Noah and Jonah which Pa read to me out of the True Book. Now I have half a page of Winnie the Pooh, if I'm lucky, and don't get the jokes at all. Call it what you will, it hurts.

It's feeding on poor, dear Ma again. It never stops. Through the thin partition I hear the greedy sucking and smacking of lips. I am weeping in my pillow. There is no sound from me. No one knows but me.

I suddenly hear Ma cry out: 'Ouch!' A short silence – my breath is held, my ears are picking up every creak and rustle – then: 'Ouch! OUCH! You little monster! You're not supposed to *bite* Mummy.'

Monster?! Did she say, Monster? For a moment I think I am dreaming. Then I hear Pa laugh. His wife, my mother, is being eaten alive in his own bed, and he laughs!

Ma shouts again, this time I know it's no dream.

'Oi! You hurt Mummy, you brute,' says she. 'It's Monday tomorrow, dustbin-day, sunshine. One more like that and you're out with the rubbish.' Then to Pa, 'And you can stop grinning. Look here at these tooth-marks.'

'Well, my dear,' says the voice of my father, 'if you will persist in breast feeding an eight-month-old infant, with three great big teeth—'

'Oh, Edward. That's a little unfair. It was you said how

327

it was wrong to waste what the Good Lord provides us for nothing, only to throw away hard-earned cash at the Superstore buying second best. That was what you *said*, dear, I remember dis—'

'You know, the trouble with you, dear—'

'I know, dear; no sense of proportion—'

Together, they complete the family motto: 'Moderation in all things, that's the golden rule.'

'Shall I ask your sister to pop in and get some, on her way over here, next weekend, Edward?'

'We'll see how it goes, my dear. We'll see how it goes.'

The sucking continues.

After a moment, another sharp cry from Ma. 'OW! That really does hurt! I'm warning you, babikins, I meant what I said, you know.'

To me it is like a miracle. How many times have I told Ma, send the baby back, only to be laughed at and pinched on the cheek? I had thought her a goner; now this – from the victim's own lips. And the answer so simple: what is not wanted . . . *goes in the bin*.

I scarcely dare breathe for fear of missing what I yearn to hear. Then, from the darkness, I hear it, this time louder, more hurt: 'HEY! You little – That does it! Don't say you weren't warned.'

It is enough. I know what to do. I'll creep down later and borrow a couple of items from Auntie's handbag and then I'll be set. The rest is up to fate . . . fate and the Eastlea Rural District Council.

It is that time of year when dawn and dustmen arrive together. Well before both, my alert mind has me up and about my mother's business.

The cot side rattles as I lower it. I stop breathing. Waiting. Listening. They must not be woken. It is to be a *surprise*.

My big worry is that the Monster will come wide awake

and ruin things with its gross demands. To guard against this I have filled the Bopeep Baby Soother with honey mixed with brandy from Auntie's flask and half a Disprin, just to make sure. Although the dummy used to belong to me – still does, by rights – I slip it into the sucking mouth: small sacrifice.

Then, though it threatens to break my back, I drag the Monster's reeking nappied arse along the vinolay to the stairhead. From there I twist and lower, twist and lower, one bump at a time, me standing on the step behind, it between my knees; my arms under its, hands clasped round its chest. Bumpety, bump and it's off to the dump, I hum inside my head.

Getting its feet into the black binliner is difficult but I manage by laying it down on its stomach and pretending to play this little piggy with its toes till it goes into its silly reverse-crawl routine. Twisting the wire tie is hard too, but the binning itself is something which would certainly have earned me a Rainbow Award at play-school.

I begin by trying to lift it in, which is hopeless but, in the process, the bin falls over. I drag out another, half-full binbag which is already in there, cutting my thumb on a jutting piece of glass. It hurts quite badly, but I do not cry. I suck the blood up, then I roll in the wrapped-up monster all the way to the bottom, squash the half-full binbag back on top, tilt the bin back to its upright position, next to the bin with ordinary rubbish in, and replace the lid. I stand listening for a moment – crying could ruin everything – but there's only the rhythmic suck-suck, suck-suck, suck-suck as it breathes and sucks on the medicine. The wet concrete is cold on my bare feet. I run to the house, creep back up to the Roombed, and take up position at the window.

I keep sucking the blood from my thumb, so as not to spoil things by messing the sheet.

Pa and Ma are both snoring as I watch the yellow

dustcart reverse up our track. It is raining and the men wear woolly hats, collars up, necks down. A man in a smart orange coat hangs from the back by an arm and one leg while two others, one each side, walk, twisted sideways, waving and shouting directions. They arrive at our drive where the bins stand side by side. The lorry stops.

Our man wears a cheerful yellow hat. He shoulders the bin on the left, the bin with no Monster inside, and pitches the contents in between gleaming pistons. The lorry stands digesting, rocking gently from side to side. The hanger-on stirs the rubbish briefly with his stick. I hear him say, 'No treasure here, George.' Hiss go the pistons and down comes the slab of steel.

'Never is here, Den,' says George, then he throws off the lid of the Monster's bin and heaves it up on his shoulder.

The events taking place on the concrete track are not subject to change; they recur every Monday morning, summer and winter, rain or shine. I know this, but my breath still comes quickly, and the net curtains flutter rhythmically as my whole body marches in step with the thing inside my chest.

The man in the yellow hat flexes and snaps his knees and the bin with the Monster in ejects its load. The binbag arcs towards the garbage-filled trough. The engine roars, the pistons hiss, expand.

I feel that a flaw in Heavenly Father's plan is about to be rectified by immutable powers. I barely hold back a hurrah, but cannot stop myself from doing a backwards roll during which everything seems to go into slomo and clarify like a TV closeup: my backward roll begins, the picture outside the window slowly slips downward. I detect something happening to the profile of the flying binbag; at the top of its arc the shape bulges in its upper surface, a small clenched fist bursts through, punching the dark. The hanger-on shouts, 'Oi!' lunges forward . . .

The picture flicks down like a faulty framehold, vanishes beneath the rising sill. I listen, breath held. The engine roars on, quite long enough, I'm sure. Bye bye bubba! I yell into my pillow. The tears are of joy now.

I snuggle down thinking, how much better if I wait until the Teasmade goes off before announcing my big surprise, but, believe it or not, I fall straight into a deep, dreamless sleep. What wakes me is my head being slapped, and the screaming.

30

'You devil! You murdering toad!' It's my mother, screaming, at *me*: 'Ohhh, ohhh. I can't bear it! I hate you! I
HATE you!' Slaps and hard punches rain down. More
words I can't take in. A glimpse of her face – hardly recognisable. Being dragged from the bed, along the landing,
me sobbing and screaming too. She suddenly gone,
because . . . I'm falling downstairs, crashing, rolling. Col-
liding with Pa. Going down. Hitting the hall floor in a
bundle with Pa. 'It's all right. It's all right, Pet,' he calls
– not to me – but she's gone. I hear shrieking and moaning
upstairs. He picks us both up. 'Why, James, *why*!? What
in God's name possessed you?' he demands, face close to
mine, pinching my shoulders, tilting me back so I can't
look down.

'It's a monster,' I blubber. 'She said so. I—'

'What? That's absolute nonsense, James. Go to your
room and wait there till I—'

But I'm already running – not to the Roombed – out of
the back door towards Bedfordshire.

'Come back here! Come back here, you—'

I keep running. Nothing my father says can enter my
brain for the words already in there screaming: Murdering
toad. HATE you! HATE you!

Half blind with tears, I fly past Lucky who growls, everyone HATES me. In the distance I hear Pa call, 'All right,
Elizabeth. It's all right, I'm coming. I'm coming, Mother.'

★　★　★

It is several hours and nearly dark before anyone comes to find me. Then Pa arrives. I am sitting in the cab crying the tears of the hopelessly misunderstood. He opens the door. 'Go away!' I shout, and I punch out but miss. He lifts me out without speaking, takes my hand and leads me, snivelling and sobbing, back towards the caravan. 'I wish' – sob, snuffle – 'I was dead,' I blubber. He does not reply.

As we approach the van door, the photocell triggers and the orange bulbs light up the cross on the roof. It seems like a signal to me. I brace myself mentally.

Inside the chapel, the only light comes from the two glowing valves screwed to the wall one each side of the picture of God with his finger pointing up. The statue of the Virgin stands on the altar in front of this; her face is in shadow. Pa sits me on the wooden bench he has built facing the altar, and himself sits down next to me. His arm goes round my shoulders. I feel myself shudder; I have come to learn that such touchings normally precede a trip to the Dark. He speaks:

'All right. All right. You can stop all the crying now, precious boy; there's only me to hear it. And, in any case, there's nothing to cry about now. What has happened is nothing short of a miracle; Heavenly Father has heard our prayers; He has watched over our family, and everything is all right.' He looks at me. I glance at his eyes and read disgust. The reason, I realise, is my nose is bubbling, and it's all down my mouth and chin. I give it all a big swipe with my arm, but my chest won't stop jerking, making more bubbles come. He fishes a piece of torn sheet from his pocket and scrubs my face, hard.

'Stop it, now, James. It's all over. God guided the dustmen to rescue our little girl. She's upstairs with Mummy, right now. I mean it. You'll see her. In a minute. Later on. That'll *do*, I said. Hush now. You'll see her, I mean it. Later on. All right?'

The question, for some reason, sets me off blubbering again. 'She HATES me!' I howl, and I throw myself down on the floor.

'Now that is *enough*, James.' He grips my arms and dumps me back on the pew. 'Sit up properly. That is *not* how we behave in here. Mummy didn't mean those things. She was upset. Naturally, she was. We've had a good talk now. I reminded her about the things she said last night – the things you apparently overheard, so you say – and she now realises she was quite wrong to say those things, even if they were supposed to be some kind of joke . . . and . . . she is sorry for saying them because she now understands that those careless words of hers were what basically caused the misunderstanding.' I felt his eyes, but didn't look up. 'It *was* a misunderstanding, wasn't it, James? Hmm?' I don't answer.

'Your sister is not a monster – of course not – and Mummy had no intention whatever that she should be put in the dustbin. That would be silly. That was a joke – a bad one, she knows that now – because little Cymby *accidentally* nipped Mummy's bosoms – *accidentally*, with those new teeth of hers. That's all . . . that's all. So now you can stop crying, boy, can't you.' He handed me the square of now sodden sheet. 'Go on, blow hard. Go on. And again. That's better.'

I have begun to sense that, despite the touching and the 'precious boy', I may not be headed for the Dark where the soft, fat spiders watch and wait. My sobbing begins to subside. I decide to press my advantage.

'See Mummy?' I say, then add, a little late perhaps, 'see Cymby?'

'I'm afraid Mummy's under sed— She's had a big Aspirin to help her relax. You see . . . Mummy *blames herself* for what happened. Never mind. The doctor has been. Mummy may have to go away for a . . . a little rest, James . . . with Cymby. We'll manage, all right, you and

I. My sister is coming, for a few days, at least. You like Aunt Mary, don't you? Yes. Hold on – that could be the ambulance now. I'll be back in a minute. Wait there.'

As he stands, I say, 'When I die, will He put me in the oven?'

'Oven?' He turns in the doorway. 'Oh, the *oven*. No . . . not if you *really* did do it for Mummy, of course . . .' He steps back into the caravan, staring hard at me. He squats down in front of me, face level with mine: 'There is only one person who knows the answer to that, precious boy. There is only one person who knows what was in your heart of hearts, James. And that person is *you*.' He tilts his head and gazes into my face as if searching for the answer. After a pause, he says, 'Why don't you have a little talk with Heavenly Father while you're waiting for me? Kneel here, by the altar. That's where He lives. You can talk to Him. Tell Him everything, just like you do down below. Tell Heavenly Father what was in your heart of hearts. Be sure it's the truth, mind. He is the Judge of Mankind, remember, and remember . . . *he already knows*.'

What upset me was hearing the door locked. Why? Why couldn't I see them, and tell them sorry? It was almost dark outside now, and the tiny chapel was full of shadows. My nose was running again, and my thumb was throbbing where I'd cut it on the piece of glass in the bin. I looked at the altar; in the orange glow of the valves, I suddenly saw the vision, the nightmare of the well-shaft – there was the huge seated figure, and, apparently, sitting on its lap, the dark shrivelled form of the Virgin. I shrank back against the wooden seatback. I knew that the altar was only an old chest freezer with a sheet thrown over the top . . . but . . . there *could* be something inside it.

Did He really know? And if He did, *what* did He know? What *was* in my heart of hearts?

At that moment I heard a commotion outside. I sped

336

to the Jonah window and pressed my forehead to the greenhill. I could see green sleet falling straight down on a big green ambulance backed up our drive. The rear doors were open, steps down. As I watched, Ma came out of the house between two men in green coats, Pa following. The men were lifting her elbows. Her slippers were trying to walk, flapping an inch above the green slush. She was carrying Cymbeline wrapped in a green towel. I waved, but they lifted her straight into the ambulance and laid her down. One man stayed with her, the other climbed out, shut the doors, walked round to the cab. It drove off without any siren or light.

Pa went back inside. I sat on the pew sucking my sore thumb, staring at the glowing valves, waiting for my father and the hard questions I knew – whatever he *said* – were coming.

And that's where I came to: sitting on a pew in the choirstalls of this dark and deserted Cathedral, sucking my poorly thumb . . . Sucking my . . . Oh, for Christ's sake . . . my thumb has a deep cut. How did *that* happen?

You've been dreaming.

Dreaming? What do you—? Wait. Oh, no . . . I *remember*: there was a . . . a dustbin. I was putting something in . . . something *alive*! There was glass – broken glass – I got cut . . . but . . .

Come on. We'd better go.

It was a *dream* – a *dream* – so how come . . . ?

Move, will you. She's waiting. Stop asking questions. Just GO.

Escaping from the quire was no easier than getting into it. In the end I was forced to climb the choirscreen with its curtained box seats, up over the castellated organ loft, like some human fly, and down the other side using the encrustations and statuettes as toeholds. And all the time my cut thumb reminded me of what I must forget to stay

337

sane; all the time sick with worry about what's happening to *me* so I have to keep ordering myself: Think about the invalid. Think about the *mission*. That's your Good Deed. That's how to keep things all square with the Umpire.

For a moment I felt better, then my face chanced to come alongside the face of a three-foot-high king in a crown – I'd been pushing down hard on the bishop's-corpse memory, now he reared up again . . . And I froze.

Don't stop! squealed headvoice.

Instant thaw. I let go. Fell to the nave steps and ran.

Jesus! You never learn, do you? We don't stop for nothing. *Nothing!* All right? The mission. Think of the mission, nothing else.

I didn't answer. I was already entering the south-west transept. The access door was somewhere in that square. Of this I was certain since, but for a short, horizontal passage running behind a row of blind windows, the main spiral leads directly, in two long verticals, from crypt to turret. There was nowhere else the door could be.

After a brief search, I found it tucked into a corner, guarded by the pikes and pennants of the Twenty-First Lancers. The key worked perfectly. As I opened the door, a white streak flashed past my ankles and vanished around the first turn of the spiral. I cried out in shock, then gaped at the empty stairs disappearing into blackness. An image of a skinny white body and a *head with wings* was printed on my retinas. As I began to recover, the thought came: What's skinny, and white?

Answer: ST, the cat.

Good. Now, a head with *wings*?

I shook my head, my pulse still racing from the shock.

What has wings, and gets into cats' mouths?

I sniggered. Course. Then another thought came. But—

I know – 'He's a *domestic* pussy', he's not supposed to be a killer. Well it seems he's learnt. Remember the junk store window – the gutter? Who do you reckon did that little massacre?

I felt myself nod. I thought of the spider, then blanked out the thought. I took a deep breath and stepped forward. Soon I was groping my way up the tight, black corkscrew, mole-mode. As I climbed, I tried to remember if I had shut the Wheel Room door. I thought so. I *hoped* so. After no more than two dozen steps, a terrible dizziness had me flopped down in the darkness. The cause had to be lack of food, the mints I'd had earlier had obviously worn off, but, soft-hearted fool that I am, I was trying to wait so that me and the invalid could sit and break bread together. That's how I pictured us. That's what I wanted.

I stuck my head down between my knees. After a minute or two I felt well enough to resume the climb, all the time now focusing my imagination on her waiting, sad but hopeful, in the Wheel Room, in her box made of Bibles.

In the entire three hundred feet of stairway there are only three windows. Each pane has eight pairs of tiny glass oblongs set in lead, each so dirty as to be practically useless. I'd passed the first some way back, the second I knew came just before the horizontal passage. I set off again, counting steps this time.

Sixty-three, and there it was: a dull orange glow. I scrubbed a square with my cuff and peered out. I could make out the Headmaster's fancy brick chimneys, three shaped like corkscrews, three with brick diamond patterns, also the black branches of the elm tree shining wetly in the light of a precinct lamp-post. It was the view from my turret, but lower.

'Good. Master's coming, sweetheart, grub's on its way,' I whispered. I took hold of the hand-rope, and the glimmer of light was soon a memory.

Climbing quite slowly in total blackness, I eventually reached what I now think of as 'the landing' (though it's quite unlike the landing of my real home, which has a sash window one side and a row of pale blue banisters the other; this one is barely shoulder width, and blind both sides). Two minutes and one window later, I was turning the key in the Wheel Room door. My heart was beating fast, partly with anxiety, more with excitement and anticipation.

When the door swung open, I could see nothing but bars of light, curving together like a luminous zebra skin high above. The source could only be the south-facing windows, but there wasn't a glimmer in that direction; the light seemed to have slid through without touching the stone shutters. The effect was weird, making me dizzy again. I wanted to light a match, but knew there were only four matches left now, and that I must wait until I reached the Bible-box where I could first make a handful of paper spills to keep the flame going.

There are ropes, buckets and other building materials scattered about the floor of the Wheel Room. I dared not move until my eyes had made more sense of the place.

While waiting I tried to imagine what she might have been thinking. For certain she would be hungry, like me. In my mind's eye, I imagined her nestling warm and soft in the palms of my hands, trustingly accepting morsels of moistened wafer from between my lips, maybe cooing a little – not to say thank you, I'm not daft enough to think that – because she would be so happy. By the flickering light of tapers, burning merrily on an upturned bucket or something, I would watch her sick eyelids retract and her eyes grow black and glittery like before . . .

Standing motionless, a yard inside the room, I began to pick up a strange hissing noise. It came and went in waves. I was mystified, and alarmed, then I suddenly twigged it was rain. Outside there was a storm going on, the rain was being driven in furious gusts against the stone slats. I became aware of eddies of cold air. In the brief lulls, my ears strained to catch the sound of the pigeon's soft, wheezy breathing. Impossible; the wind was too strong now, and fast growing stronger.

After a minute, maybe more, an arc of the wheel appeared dimly from the darkness, high to my right. I watched it grow at each end, slowly, like a negative developing in the reflected light of the zebra. I felt myself stagger, and quickly looked down. From the curvature of the arc, I had already begun to estimate the position of the hub. Soon it would be safe to move.

It screwed me up thinking how the invalid's hopes must have soared at the sound of my entry, and how she must now be falling into deeper and deeper misery because of the silence and the nothing happening. Enough, I thought. I began to shuffle forward, hands stretched out in front.

I somehow avoided all of the obstacles and my fingers soon touched one of the wooden spokes. I groped for its neighbour, found it, ducked through the gap and up on to the curved deck of the treadmill.

I remembered the Bible-box being about a yard in from the edge. I squatted, swept the dusty boards with my hands, felt a thick leather spine, found the lid, opened the top cover and tore out several pages.

With a dozen spills to hand, I reached for the matches in my pouch.

31

The pigeon's behaviour being quite intolerable, refusing the food and generally playing up, it had to be disciplined and, unfortunately, passed on. That, needless to say, was not my intention, but these things happen. We have to remember that pigeons are vermin.

What to do with the remains, though? What would be correct, in the circumstances?

To kill something and then not eat it is wicked, but, to be frank, the pigeon was a bit of a wreck *before* it met me. In its present condition, it wasn't worth eating. I half suspected it might be diseased, and cereals are safer when all's said and done.

I dismantled the Bible-box, hid the Bibles under the wheel, peed on the embers and exited. Halfway though locking the door behind me another thought came: Shouldn't I have buried the remains, or, better still, burnt them? Vermin or not, she *was* one of God's creatures.

Hang about, mate. Less than twenty-four hours ago we were all for eating it. If you don't fancy it, fine. But why waste time burning the thing? I've never heard nothing so daft. I mean, think about the maggots. Don't they have rights? Come on, will you. You're driving me potty with the soul searching.

I completed the locking, murmured, 'Rest in peace,' crossed myself and turned to the stairs. I wasn't entirely comfortable with the decision, but figured the Wheel

Room – along with every other room in the building –
was on hallowed ground and, in that sense, part of one
big tomb.

Right, let's go, said headvoice.

I felt my head peck.

Next stop – the drainpipe.

Peck.

**It's not forced to keep raining all night, mate. Without
water we're knackered. So let's move it.**

Peck.

Without water, no life.

Peck. Peck.

Climbing again. In the dark again, thinking. That's what
the dark is for: thinking. Thinking about what you've
been up to in the daylight.

In the dark of the spiral I was thinking about the pigeon.
Thinking how patient I'd been, how I'd bent over backwards to show her what to do with the wafers . . . Those
wafers were dry, mind, like eating lumps of chalk – which
is why I let her get away with it for so long – but after
I'd moistened them for her, in my own mouth . . . after
I'd wasted bloody ages coo-cooing and stroking bits of
soggy wafer against the side of her beak, trying my hardest
to persuade her . . . And her just turning away all sulky
like that . . . treating *me* like shit, like I didn't even exist
or something . . . Christ! I think I was *entitled* to be mad.
Bloody right . . . !

Maybe I was a bit rough, though. After. Maybe I
shouldn't have shoved so many down her throat at one
go. Maybe I did hold her a bit tight, after . . . FUCK IT!
NOW I'VE BLOODY UPSET MYSELF. WHY DID
SHE HAVE TO DO THAT? SHE KNEW HOW I
FELT, NOW SHE'S FUCKING DIED . . . !

COW!

Still climbing. In the dark. Counting in tens. Counting

to calm myself . . . twenty . . . thirty . . .

Crying now. In the dark. Trudging up to my empty bed. Crying for myself, for lost innocence. Aching to love her. If she'd only given me a sign . . . one sign, that's all . . . met me halfway . . . quarter even . . . even a millionth. To turn away like that . . . to close her eyes and turn her head. What could I do? What could *anyone* do? Fuck all. There's no answer to that. None. That's why it's such a lousy, stinking trick. I feel bloody awful.

Concentrate on the action; keep counting; fifty, fifty-one . . .

Headvoice chimes in – nothing meaningful – a hobbyhorse: **Tears mean nothing, man. We get hurt; we cry. We get scared; we sweat. Drink a pint, piss a pint. Nine-tenths water, that's us. Bit of carbon, bit of phosphorus, bit of sulphur, bit of iron – odds and sods. Nothing much in a person. We've been put on this planet to pollute water. That is our purpose, our *raison d'être*. It's all part of the divine fucking plan.**

You're just an atheist. Don't talk to me, please.

Seventy . . .

Bing, bong, bing – quarter to something; at least I knew *that*.

Eighty . . . ninety . . .

If God is love, he's got a funny way of showing it, that's all.

Hundred . . . hundred and ten . . .

Newsflash from the *Thesaurus* – footnote (vii), white on black like the new computers in Business Studies – verbatim, weird: 'Diabolical Possession – the two ways: i, With God's permission, the *maleficium* (demon) enters of his own will. The symptoms of this may be any or all of the following – swollen limbs; immobility; cedar coloration of the visage; pains (various) in limbs; sensations of the heart being squashed or pricked or as if gnawed by a dog; [shitting hell!] orifice of stomach constricted; the vomiting

345

of *food* or *signa maleficii* such as balls of hair, needles, knives, wood, glass, caterpillars, spiders, feathers . . . [*Spiders*! Fuck! I interrupt this newsflash to collapse on the step. I shut my eyes tight. The display of white letters continues regardless:] '. . . egg shells, buttons and so on. These may emerge through any of the seven bodily orifices. Other symptoms include convulsions, opisthotonos [*opis-what?*], tympanitis, indecent movements and difficulty in swallowing—'

'STOP!' (I'm remembering the Drama Studio – the writhing, the screaming, the lashing limbs, *Tamsyn's pelvic thrusting*, me bringing up . . . what was it? – a *hairball*?!) 'STOP, I COMMAND YOU. I REFUSE TO THINK YOU.'

The screen flickers, the letters vanish.

Phew . . . Nasty, said headvoice, **You were quite right to switch off. Ignore it. This is the twentieth century not the Dark fucking Ages. It's got nothing to do with—**

All right, don't go on. I'm trying to forget it, all right!

Sure. Sorry.

Silence.

I stand up, take a step up, feeling shaky, another step . . .

That's the second time. Why does it keep doing—

Look! Shut up, will you! How the fuck do I know.

Sorry. Sorry.

Climbing steadily. Counting. Concentrating on the steps, the rough old rope in my left hand, the ache in my calves . . .

What's a Signa maliwhatsname?

BLOODYHELL! Work it out, can't you. Signa, signal; mal – French for bad; fac, factory – makes things. So that's: signal-of-bad-makes-things, now you know as much as me so SHUT THE FUCK UP! RIGHT?

Sure. Sorry. It's just I was—

Shut—

up. I'm counting.
Yep.

Trudging up the vertical helix. Not like before; going
home, but it's not *home* now, because the house is *empty*
– no *dependent*. Life goes on. The show must—
Alarming thought: How much whisky had I saved?
Enough to last till . . . when? Till WHEN?! The DEAD-
LINE! WHEN'S THE BLOODY DEADLINE?!

**Whoa. Steady boy. Don't panic; work it out. We came
in . . . let's see, Sunday wasn't it . . . ? That was it,
yes, Sunday – Confession day. So what happened
Sunday night? Nothing. Monday? Monday was the exorcism. And she spoke – or you *thought* she did – you
brought that on yourself, you nutter. Never mind.
Monday night – the storm . . .**

SHIT!
Pardon me?
Today's Wednesday, then?
What about it?
Christalmighty!
What?

I thought it was Tuesday. But it's not. It's Wednesday!
That means it's TONIGHT! Midnight Wednesday, that's
the deadline! That was the deal; that's what I swore on
the Bible, remember? I either had to prove I was innocent
by Wednesday midnight or I would have to confess –
which costs me one fucking finger, remember? Bitten, not
cut, or else . . .

I could feel my heart hammering inside my chest,
lumpy, dangerous.

. . . Or else . . .

**Bollocks. Why should *you* prove things? *She* hasn't
proved anything. She can't. For the simple reason, *She*
doesn't exist, mate. Look, you've given it a fair crack;
you've done the rounds – done all you can, done your**

347

bit. And where is She? Eh? Where *is* she? Not a squeak since yesterday evening. And why? Because it's all in your nut, son. That's why. Think about it.

Well, yes. In a way, I suppose that's correct. There hasn't been a lot, not really. Apart from the choirboy thing, and the monkey – hey, what about that monkey – and the bish—?

Imagination. Pure wind-up. Look at it this way: did anything actually *happen*? I mean, did you break any bones, jump off the roof, burst into flame? OK, you moved a bit. So what? People do. When they sleepwalk. Nothing supernatural about that. I tell you, it's all in the mind, mate.

I stopped climbing, stood still in the pitch dark. It's funny, I don't even remember any dreams – or games, or whatever we're calling them – apart from that first one, the one with the mower . . . But . . . well, I just wondered . . . Last time . . . I seemed to think . . . it's barmy, I know, but when I came round, I felt sure I'd *cut myself*, on some broken glass . . . something like that. You don't think . . . this cut on my thumb . . . I mean, remember the cat . . . That was really—

Look. No one – *no one* – can say James Bishop hasn't given the ghost of his dead sister – if there ever was such a thing, which there wasn't – every chance to come through. I mean, loads of people hear voices, right? Joan of Arc, that kiddy in the Bible, Carl Jung, Evelyn Waugh, the retired schoolmaster, a whole bunch of housewives – you read the article, it's just not that uncommon. It means nothing. Look, if She can't raise a genuine haunting in this house of horrors, where the fuck can She? Eh? Anyway, time's run out for the ghoulies and ghosties brigade, and there ain't going to be no injury time. First stroke of midnight, we're off, boy. Right? Had her chance, muffed it. That's it. *Finito*.

Fair enough, I suppose.

For some reason Lawrence entered my thoughts –

maybe it was the way headvoice was talking, or the thought of an ending to all this – anyway, I realised, with some surprise, that I actually missed him. I was genuinely looking forward to seeing his pouchy face again, and telling him my adventures. Lawrence would be impressed.

I tried to imagine how the teachers would react to my return. What would Piggy say? And the Canon? And Sopworth? And Pa? Especially Pa. Would he go ape, or would he play the Counsellor-and-Understanding-Pal Pa. I never knew with him. I certainly hoped not; that always made me want to roast myself over a slow fire. But really I thought it would be neither of these. I could see myself put into 'care', as they say – most likely back under the wing of Doctor Keylock's 'special' day unit. In fact, I'd prefer that. At least you got a laugh; as far as I knew *he* still believed that *I* still believed that I was a Vulcan.

Get your arse into gear then, said headvoice. **I'm thirsty**.

Sure thing. Let's go. Oh. By the way; what time is it?

Haven't a clue. Quarter to something, just turned.

Quarter to what? Eight? Nine?

Something like that.

I began to climb again. After a moment I said, You know something? I reckon you're right. Thinking about that king statue back there – the one on the choirscreen, how it nearly got me going, but didn't – I reckon that proves it, you know. I reckon it's been me all along; doing it to myself, just like you said.

Right, pal.

If I hadn't got a grip of myself back there, I reckon it would have been just the same as the other times; I'd have been off in a dream or hallucination or whatever. As it was, I stayed cool, got busy, controlled the old breathing, thought about something else . . . and the panic went away. Just like that. There's an explanation for everything, isn't there?

Sure as hell is, pal.

I climbed in silence for a while, another thought hovering in the dark. Then out it popped: Jimbo's First Theory of the Conservation of Relic Matter. You know what? I said, I've been thinking. About those relics. The way they never decomposed. I don't know what you'll think about this . . .

Go on, professor.

I know it sounds weird, but, well . . . Do you reckon it might have been something to do with the Weedol?

Weedol. Yeah, sure.

No, seriously. Pa practically drowned the soil under the courgettes in that stuff, you know. I bet he used three or four gallons over the course of the summer. I mean, that stuff kills just about anything, seems to me, maybe microbes included. They'd have got a good dose.

Hmm. I see what you mean. Could be, I suppose. I must say, I hadn't—

And me keeping the relics sealed up tight in a polythene bag like that . . . that could have kept the vapour in. I reckon that's it, you know; I reckon there was nothing magic about it – nothing *supernatural*, at all. They didn't go rotten . . . because they were *pickled*. What do you reckon? Possible?

Could be, I suppose.

I *know* it. I can *feel* it. I'm positive that's the answer. And you know something else? I reckon it was only those . . . bits not behaving like they should have behaved that set me off imagining things in the first place. Yeah?

Well I reckon you could be right, old son.

So, now they're out in the fresh air – somewhere, wherever, doesn't matter where – those little old meat molecules have got to be behaving just like any other meat molecules. By which I mean rotting. She's probably rotting off this very minute. Must be. Thank Christ for that. Jeez, the relief . . . Talk about a load off my mind; it's better than a good crap, that is. Well . . . that's it, then: I'm with you, boy – on the stroke of midnight, we're gone. Hold on . . .

My right hand had just told me we'd reached the point where the spiral lining changes from stone to small bricks. That meant the lead pipe was close.

There's one little snag, said headvoice, mildly, as if the thought had come up for the first time.

I know. I know. It's driving me mad: How the hell did the relics move *themselves* out of that turret?

Spot on, old son. How the hell *did* they? Still, like you say: There's an explanation for *everything*. Never mind now; here's the pipe.

Boring a hole with the corner of the key took ages. The draught didn't help; cold fingers hurt. I kept twisting and twisting, trying not to listen to the wheezing and sighing from the attics and turret which made me think of 'Jack and the Beanstalk' when the giant is asleep (he hopes) and snoring, and Jack's about to nick the goose. I knew it was only the wind, of course, but, remember, it was dark, and I could see absolutely *nothing*; not even whether my eyes were open or shut. Apart from which, it's some hell of a storm that could make the stone step tremble under my backside.

Suddenly the sweat broke all over my body. If the water hadn't come at that moment – I don't know – I think I might even have jacked it in there and then and legged it. Then I remembered the Cathedral doors don't open from inside. More important, I knew that to give in now could mean the end of sanity. She would enter my world at will, day or night, my mind would never again be my own. And that, as the Chaplain said, would be hell.

An ice-cold trickle down my arm got me cracking. I took the key away and held my palm under the spot. Nothing. I stroked the underside of the gutter. There was water clinging to it, running downslope, straight out through the gap in the wall where the pipe went through. I untied the lace of one trainer, pulled it out and tied it round below the hole. I positioned the silver bowl. There came a sound like a man peeing in a tin bucket. I pulled the hood of the Spidersuit over my head, sat on the step and waited for the bowl to fill.

The water was wonderful, not just cleansing my mouth of sugar and mint, but somehow recharging my spirit. I left the bowl filling, thinking I might need more before midnight; if not, it would certainly give the Mambas something to wonder about after I'd gone. It had been a long day. I felt that I'd earned a rest, and maybe a wee drinkie to warm me up. In a couple of hours maybe, three at the most, midnight would chime, and then I'd say farewell to this pantomime castle, for ever. As to the future . . . at least I'd have got the *past* off my back.

Feeling good now, mentally and physically, I climbed the few remaining steps to the balcony level and the door that opens on to the Shelf. The floodlights were still pouring their tangerine light through the row of diamond-paned windows on my right. By the light of this, I picked my way carefully through the dust so as to avoid kicking too much up into the air, and came, after twenty paces or so, to the short flight of steps leading down to the Bible Room door. One step down I stopped.

Something was heaped against the door at the bottom of the steps, a dim, dark huddle flecked with white, like snow on a tramp's coat, I thought. The skin on my scalp began to wriggle. But the shape was not quite large enough to be human. Again I thought of *Her*, and froze rigid.

Don't be daft, said headvoice, **look at the shape; it's just a heap of something. And how could it be Her? –** Jesus – I thought we'd agreed—

All right. All right.

Strike a match, if you like.

I've only got four.

352

Well let's take a closer look then.

Sitting on the bottom step, I counted up to twenty separate corpses before giving up. There must have been fifty to a hundred all told. Most had no heads, some were half plucked showing white pimply chests, others had missing legs and wings, but none – as far as I could see in that shadowy well at the foot of the steps – showed any sign of having been eaten. Headvoice spoke first – whispered, actually – breathed, rather:

Well, I'll be . . . fucked. His Satanic Majesty, Tomas the Gaderine Cat, is now well and truly among the pigeons . . .

What exactly do you mean by that? I demanded.

Obvious, isn't it: it's gone into Tomas . . . you sicked it up, poor old Tom swallowed it. Now he's a serial killer or—

CHRIST! I need that sort of talk like a kick in the crutch.

Sorry. Didn't mean it.

Oh, what the hell, I was thinking it anyway.

No, really . . . I really didn't—

Shall we go in, then? I could do with a drink.

Let's go in.

The force required to push open the Bible Room door, and the rush of escaping air should have warned me. They didn't. Not till the wind ripped the door from my hand and slammed it against the wall; then, not till I was choking in the dust storm which the Bible Room became in the draught from the cloverleaf window, and, even then, not till I'd managed to light a big taper outside and gone back in with it roaring in my hand with the orange sparks weaving and zooming all round the blazing pages. Then it did, vaguely, but I chose to ignore it.

Inside, with the door shut, the wind died at once. But

the air was saturated with dust, so that I couldn't see my own arm, only the flame and the dancing atoms.

I felt something very bad was about to happen, but didn't suss what it was. Then, without warning, the whole chamber blazed bright tangerine – like a whiteout, I imagine, but coloured. I felt like my skin was shrinking then immediately expanding – a split second, no more – then pop! and the air was as clear as a frosty night. The wind had gone completely and the flame rose vertically – impossibly steady, and vertical – from the burning taper in my hand.

Silence.

I looked around the room, slowly, knowing there was something terribly wrong, unable to think what it was. In the flickering half-light everything seemed as it should be. The Bible-bed looked tidy enough with my belongings – my bottle, my Aspros, my cigs – all lined up alongside. Nothing out of place, nothing disturbed. So what was that orange light all about? And why had the moths begun flapping in my chest?

At that moment, the tower clock started its chime – first the fancy prelude, then the low booming notes of the hour. Still looking about me, I counted the notes, out loud, so as to be certain: one, two, three – the big iron dogs ground slowly round up there in the clock tower while the nasty feeling grew and grew in my guts – on the seventh stroke *realisation* struck. My legs emptied fast, I staggered, dizzy again: it was the tidiness itself, the order, the made bed, my things all in a neat little pile – *that* was what was wrong. I'd left it this morning in a hell of a state, and even if I hadn't been in a state, I would *never* have made up the bed because I'd have dismantled it as usual and re-stacked the Bibles as I always did in case of a snooping Mamba. Now here it was, all made up and ready to climb into! Like the three bears story but turned on its head.

I stood and stared while the strokes boomed on. I'd lost count, but when, seconds later, the floodlights' glow vanished from the cloverleaf window, I *knew* what the time was. A tickling started at the base of my spine.

32

Pain in my fingers made me drop the stub of taper. Instantly, the world shrank to a small patch of stone between my feet. I grabbed the nearest Bible. As the flames popped and fluttered, I ripped out a fistful of pages, twisted them, squatted, held them to the rustling embers, and whispered a prayer. Slowly the corners browned and curled then, without sound, the flame was climbing the fanned edges towards the twist. At which point, I glimpsed the movement. In the margin, beyond the terminator, something had moved.

My head came up fast, wrenching a muscle in my neck.

I could now make out gold letters on the spines of the six Bibles that formed the head of the bunk. By chance all the Bibles in the bunk-wall facing me were spine out and dark. Something *had* moved – a pale blur where the mouth of the bunk would be.

I froze, half squatting, thighs trembling, not daring to blink, breath held.

Nothing – perhaps just a shadow, set in motion by the wavering light. Yet, in the air, there was *something* – not smell, feeling – a seething energy. I want to call it a breath of fresh *death*. She was here. I knew. What I had so far only heard, I was about to *see*.

But even as I stood gaping at the bunk, a quick movement caught my eye from the direction of the cloverleaf aperture. Flapping of wings. My head swung towards it.

There, in the aperture, a hideous round head palely gleaming, hissing like a snake between black beating wings, green eyes fixed on *me* . . .

Get away. Get away, I moaned without sound. I know who you are . . . You're the thing that chased me – you change shapes, you are the—

Two voices, one shrieking, one yowling burst from the creature . . . I realised my fingers were tingling and I could no longer feel my legs. I hauled air, fighting to hold on . . .

The noise of the beasts became words, words I knew well, words that turned my bones to water: *Come and play come and play somebody up here want play with you.*

With a flurry and shriek, the wings detached from the head which pulled back and vanished. I dropped to my haunches as the jackdaw flew straight at me then circled the chamber three times before crashing down in the corner behind the piled books. I slowly straightened, my eyes fixed on the mouth of the bunk where the first frizzy strands had now appeared.

I quietly urinated.

A head and naked shoulders rising, slowly, like in a dream (a dream? if only I could gallop out of here on that old mare), she sat up straight inside the bunk, her back towards me. My body sprang to attention, literally shocked. The pyx jumped out of my pouch, spun to the flags, scattering wafers. When she turned, there were no eyes in her white face; the sunken lids leaked rivers of syrupy plasma, or tears – over cheeks, neck, shoulders.

A pile of Bibles slumped to the floor behind me; I stumbled and fell backwards on top, scrambled up, backed away till the hard wall stopped me.

She waved a handless stump. It too was wetly seeping – not blood – clear liquid. White ribbons of tendon hung down. Two bone ends protruded, the shorter horribly splintered, the longer a perfect blue-white polished knuckle-joint. Her body was the colour of candles but for the shadows which appeared green, her hair long and kinked, the bridge of her blunt nose peppered with freckles making her face seem whiter than the rest of her body as though the freckles had used up the last of her colour. Her breasts were no bigger than some of the boys' round here, the nipples indistinct and pale.

Her mouth opened. I saw small, even teeth set in gums the color of putty, a marzipan tongue moving to form a word. The word was all just breath but I heard it; I heard it quite clearly and my whole body began to shake. '*Bimbim.*'

I stood trembling, my hands pressed to the wall, gaping as she laid her forearms on the sides of the bunk. Awkwardly, she levered herself to a kneeling position. The Y of her crotch was visible now, the auburn hair, like the hair on her head, almost black against her waxy flesh. The smoothness of her body making the wounds a thousand times more hideous.

She shifted her weight as if to stand, whereon, imagining her shattered ankles, my legs collapsed under me and I found myself squatting, elbows on knees, peering out through a cage of fingers. Her mouth opened again. I held my breath and waited. This time the word she hissed was: '*Cheat.*'

I was trembling and my head was shaking mechanically from side to side.

The wind started suddenly, as if a sound effect had been switched on. For a second I thought someone – a Mamba maybe – had opened the door and the storm had returned through the cloverleaf window. But then I saw her heavy, crinkled hair rise up and out to the sides like a spun mophead. My guts gave a twist. Impossibly, this wind was blowing up from the hollow of the Bible-bed, now more fiercely than before. The cover of the edgemost book flew

359

back, and, as if moved by invisible hands, the dry pages commenced to rattle back and forth in a blur of gold and white and bright colour.

Her hair was now streaming straight up from her head. Suddenly I realised I'd seen her like this before, that she was the dancing figure from my long ago dream in the Upper Study, the figure that grew from the flames then danced among them. Every detail confirmed this – the rippling flesh beneath the chin, the tears blowing back up their runs to lodge in minute droplets among the dark hairs of her eyebrows, twinkling like diamond dust . . .

Bloodless lips quivering now, drawing back at one corner. Smiling?

The wind moved everything. With a cat-like yowl the lid of the bunk heaved, then one Bible, then another, then a third lifted clear, hovered, slipped sideways, thudded to the floor. More Bibles flapped on top of their piles like injured gulls, while others – the heavier, brass-hinged monsters – rocked back and forth. Wind screamed round the pale figure; it hissed in her upstreaming hair; it lifted her arms – up, down, up, down, each time higher than the time before – like featherless wings, it seemed to me – like a mutilated angel failing to fly. And yes, she was smiling. And that smile set my scalp wriggling and writhing over my skull.

Between my fingers I peeked in horror as the pale body rose into the air. Slowly, slowly, it rotated backwards, like a human spaceship controlled by small jets. It came to a stop, impossibly at ease, apparently born up by the howling blast, half turned towards me, the hacked and splintered ankles lightly crossed above the stumps – a hideous parody of the painting in Sopworth's bathroom. And there she hung – strands of copper hair whipping her mouth and neck – a yard above the bunk.

My head had stopped shaking.

All this happened in a fraction of the time it takes to

tell. I saw every detail, though I tried to see none. I ached to scream, but nothing came; to run, but my legs refused to function; to faint, even slide down into some unknown game, but my body would not let go.

Then the flaring taper burned me for the second time. I dropped it and the wind took it and dashed it out against the wall in a shower of red sparks.

Blackness.

I leapt to my feet and ran.

One pile of Bibles, then another went down. I heard the pyx (or its lid) clatter off into a corner; then I was stumbling up the steps on all fours.

The darkness of the Shelf was absolute; I thought of the chasm a yard to my right, but not even this slowed me down.

I hit the spiral access door hard with outstretched hands, wrenched it open, slammed it after me and flung myself down the steps.

Blind, half jumping, half falling, I hurtled down with the curved wall crashing against my right shoulder and my left foot jarring and wrenching against the narrow wedges of stones. I knew that to lose my footing completely would be the end of me – death by a hundred stone cudgels – and yet I must run. And all the time the darkness perfected a head-picture of dead Cymbeline which no amount of blinking could remove.

So down I went. Down the tunnel of darkness. Down and down and down and down and down . . .

What stopped me I can't say – for certain I wasn't counting steps. One moment I was racing down with no thought in my head but flight, the next I could think of nothing but the madness of a staircase which *grows*! I did not know how many steps I'd descended, I just knew it was more – many more – than the number that should exist between the turret and the landing. Long before this point, the stairway should have been broken by five metres of horizontal passage. It had not been. And that was impossible.

I sat down on the step, in the darkness. Quite simply, I did not know what else to do. I wanted to lie down, close my eyes like the snow-bound explorer, give myself up to the blackness. Sleep.

Three rising notes caught me napping. They seemed then not merely the tower clock giving information about time but evidence from the camp of sanity, a little attack of hope, last spasm of the rational organ.

Somehow, I must have become confused. I'd had a shock; after believing it finished, I'd been hit with something a whole order of magnitude weirder. There was one thing left to do now and that was to get out, to leave the Cathedral, and the sooner the better. And the way out . . . was down. I would keep my eyes peeled for the window, and, shortly after that, I would arrive on the landing. Of course I would. I recommenced the descent. Counting, this time.

Long before step number one hundred I knew something was wrong. But I refused to give up earlier because that was the number I'd decided was the limit or deadline, and these little rules were all I had left to control. The counting had made me feel better for a while – counting and measuring, the scientific method – but, as the total mounted and the window still failed to appear, I became gripped by a rising sense of dread. As far as I could see I was now down to three possibilities: I had miscounted by a factor of at least ten, or the window had been bricked up in the last half hour, or – sweet Jesus save me – I had been *creating* new stone steps, a new spiral staircase like a spider with a concrete-mixer where its arse should be. I could see no other option. In logic, none existed. If the spiral had remained as it had been when I came up I would by now have passed both windows and landing. In fact I would be at the bottom of the stairway – that is to say, at the door of the crypt itself.

And if it was all an illusion . . . how was I to break out of it? What difference, if any, exists between reality and inescapable illusion? Another question – equally logical, equally insane: what happens to the creation when the creator has gone? Is anything left behind? Or does it reabsorb into nothingness as a ship's wake returns to the ocean?

A hideous image came out of the blackness; my own, nightmare-screaming head, shaven, bristling with steel clamps and laser knives. Behind my head, in mask and gown, the eyeless surgeon preparing to fire. *Somehow She had found a way to interfere with my brain.*

An idea came, a test for truth, brilliantly simple: I would fling myself backwards up the steps as far as I could – without thinking about it first, so that She wouldn't be able to change the rules or cheat in any way – then, if I still felt steps, they would have to be real. If not . . . If there weren't any steps . . .

Without thinking (almost), I did it. And felt . . .

Stone steps. Solid. Cold. *Real.*

But how could I be certain the thought hadn't leaked?

I felt dizzy and my head ached. I sat down. The test for truth was a bucket of shit – if anything it made things worse. If She was watching She'd be pissing Herself. Christ! How could She accuse *me* of cheating? It was *Her* who was the cheat. She was breaking the laws of the universe – The Law of Conservation of Mass – matter can neither be created nor destroyed. Cow!

One thing about it, She was short of the wherewithal to chase after me, wasn't She? I'd seen that with my own eyes. And I still had some things of Hers, and when I found them, I'd make a big bonfire of Bibles and I'd light it – even though it would be the last match it'd be worth it – and I'd bloody burn them. No question. It's no use trying to be nice to terrorists, which is what She'd become.

Having made this decision, I felt a little better. And at least She had not followed me down here. I began to think of a fourth possibility to explain the absence of the horizontal passage and window: maybe, just possibly, in my initial panic I had raced past the first window, through the landing and on past even the second window, without knowing I had done so. Might not that first, blind rush have been very much longer than I believed? A person in the grip of panic is often unaware of the realities. The question then would be . . . where was the transept doorway? Since my last stop I had not let go of the hand-rope; hand-ropes did not continue across doorways! To miss it would have been . . . impossible (that word again), unless . . . unless I had passed below that landmark too in my initial panic. I shook my head. Surely I couldn't have climbed down nearly four hundred steps, believing it less than a hundred? Besides, if that had been the case, why had I still not reached the basement, *ninety-eight steps further down*? I *knew* there were only forty-six steps down from the nave to the crypt . . . I remembered counting them that first evening.

These thoughts give the impression of a rational mind working calmly towards a logical conclusion; in fact they came piecemeal through a haze of nauseating fear. However I juggled the numbers, the answer came out the same: the spiral staircase now ran deeper than the foundations of the crypt. Much deeper. And that was . . .

Impossible.

There was nothing below the crypt . . .

Was there?

And . . .

Something I'd forgotten. Forgotten completely: the drainpipe! No one could miss the drainpipe. The drainpipe would have cut me in half!

* * *

The old freezing horror of a mind locking up. Panic. Pan Nic. Pandemonium. Pan Daemon.

Bastard! Get back!

Help me. I can't hold it.

Action. *Do* something.

What?!

Find a reference. A base. Anything.

The crypt. The crypt is the foundation.

Find it. Fast.

On hollow legs, I rise, start down for the third time, this time counting *out loud*: hundred 'n one, hundred 'n two, hundred 'n three . . .

It was somewhere between a hundred and fifty and two hundred that the other voice started. At first it was barely audible and I could pretend it was only my imagination, or a trick of the wind, or a weird acoustic of the spiral. Then it grew louder. For a while I counted stubbornly along with it, but the other continued to count in a tormenting, singsong voice, sometimes saying the same number I was saying, sometimes a different number, until I became hopelessly muddled. When I stopped, it stopped. I felt that old playground feeling – fear and fury seesawing together. I stood in the darkness, not turning. (Don't let them know that they've got to you, boy. Pa's advice.)

'OK,' I said. 'You want my finger? You can have it. Just as soon as I get to the crypt, OK?' (Needless to say, behind my back, the finger in question was crossed with its neighbour.) 'No shit. It is a deal or not?'

I waited.

No answer.

My own words echoed mockingly in my head – *You want the finger? You can have it*. Did I say that!? What was I thinking of?

Beyond feeling foolish, I called out: 'Cymbeline? Are you there?'

No answer.

I waited.

Aware of a whining, grovelling note in my voice, unable to control it, I called again: 'Cymbeline? Cymbeline?'

I waited.

No answer.

I sat in the darkness. I've no idea how long. A long time. After a while I must have licked my lips. The taste of salt told me I'd been crying. I touched my lips with the index finger of my right hand – not deliberately, not *intending* anything as far as I know – my mouth just opened on its own, as if for bad medicine, and the finger went inside, feeling what it was like to get ready to be bitten off, I suppose. When the finger touched the back of my tongue it made me retch. Before my teeth could even begin to explore the knuckle joint I was heaving from stomach to throat.

I took out the finger. The thing was impossible. I heard myself moan and say:

'It's impossible. *Impossible*. That's not fair.'

And I was crying.

I stood. I stepped down. Mechanically, one step, then another, and another, dumping my legs from step to step, not bothering to count any more.

A narrow vertical of blue-green light appeared, blurred by tears. I ignored it. A dozen steps further down I was on flat stone, touching a half-open door with my fingertips. The door had the feel of oak. I stood still, listening, not knowing what to do.

No sound came from beyond the door, just a faint smell on the updraught of the turret, a smell that made no sense – scorched vegetation, weeds of some sort – not grass, but something familiar.

By the feel of the door, and the colour and dimness of the light, I realised I was finally, and despite everything, at the door of the crypt. I had only to walk through that half-open door . . .

I had expected to feel joy and relief but instead there was only more fear. It seemed to me that, in the end, I had reached the crypt far too easily. It stank of trap. I hadn't forgotten the 'deal' I'd offered, but now I knew I could not pay up, even if I wanted to.

Meat-eaters get out of gin-traps by biting off the bit that's caught. But this felt more like a net than a trap. Nothing gets out of the net.

A number of minutes passed before I could make myself push on the door. When I did so, it opened. Head width. And creaking, naturally.

When I pushed again, harder than the first time, the door pushed back. My head was through. I only had time to take in the shapes of heavy pillars, a low, arched ceiling and . . . something behind the door – *a man's head* – before the gap began to close. Firmly. A man's voice spoke, flat, efficient:

'You're too early,' it said. 'There's a query. Concerning some gaps in your record. Small inconsistencies, nothing much. Go back up. First door you come to. Quickly please, everything's ready and waiting.'

The door shut in my face. A key turned. And I was in darkness again. It was crazy: a real live human speaks to me and it seems more ghostly than the ghost-voice I've been hearing . . . or imagining. There was a man in there, for fuck's sake, an adult, just beyond the door, he could help me . . .

I stood, hovering, fist raised, ready to beat on the door. But somehow I could not beat on the door. My fist refused orders. It was . . . impossible. After a moment I turned and slowly remounted the steps.

Another narrow band of light appeared, this time white and horizontal. As I climbed towards it, the light descended to the level of my feet. Another door. The light shining through a gap beneath it. Illuminating a strip of stone step.

There'd be no fumbling or hesitating this time. This

time I was going through, hard and fast, no matter what. Who or whatever I found in there – they could have me.

I felt for the handle, braced myself to withstand the impact, hesitated, dropped to my knees, lowered my cheek to the stone, attempted to peer under the door. The light was blinding.

I stood up, stroked the wood surface, felt vertical planks, a cross stanchion, iron hinge, moved across, found a twisted iron ring, drew a big breath, wrenched it round, locked out my knee, threw my shoulder forward, hard . . .

The door burst open.

Dazzling white light.

What I saw – when I could see – was a young boy, his back towards me. He wore khaki shorts, wellington boots and a white, short-sleeved shirt back to front and open down the back but for the top button which was fastened behind his neck. Tied loosely around his neck was a yellow J cloth. He was leaning over a bench covered in green rexine. Someone was lying on the bench but, from my position in the doorway, I could see only small, bare legs from the knee down.

Smell of dead nettles.

'Bedfordshire,' I breathed.

I moved forward. The boy stepped into the margin, and was gone. To the figure on the bench I whispered, 'Lie still and you won't feel a thing.'

Angel with Horns

33

The picnic was Pa's idea. The family, he said, would be reunited in the beautiful grounds of the resting home, at least for the afternoon, maybe more. I was very excited; I had not seen my mother one single time during the three years, two months and twelve days since she went away. And that's pretty hard for a seven year old. But today would be wonderful, today the sun would shine, the birds would sing and everyone would laugh again. That's how I pictured it.

(There was a picnic later on, but it wasn't quite like that.)

We'd parked round the back where the big iron fire-escapes and the dustbins on wheels are. Pa had gone in to collect Ma and Cymby leaving me and Lucky sitting in the transit with our cardboard box full of vegan pasties and stuff. It was hot in the van so I sneaked a half inch of the Appletise. After ten minutes he was out again with my sister under his arm, and no sign of Ma. Striding across the tarmac in his blue Sunday suit, he looked cross. His mouth was working. I kept quiet and listened while he re-ran both ends of the conversation he'd just had.

It turns out the doctors and nurses at the resting home all belong to one family, the Cretins, and that they had decided Ma was not ready for picnicking because she had caught a delusion and needed more rest. Frankly, I was amazed she'd let Cymbeline out of her sight, considering the row she'd kicked up when they tried to separate the two of them the day of the misunderstanding. But Pa explained how one of the Cretins had given Ma sleeping medicine less than an hour before we arrived, and that she was asleep. Our taking Cymby home with us was some sort of a test, they said; if Ma passed this one she might be allowed home for Sunday visits quite soon.

So we took the picnic and Cymbeline home.

By this time, of course, Pa and me had had the little talk and special ceremony which had changed my whole attitude towards my sister. To me she was no longer the Monster but a kid with problems who needed help. Sitting between us on the bench seat, she looked prettier than I remembered, and more petite than ever. I mentioned the latter to Pa who said that hospital grub wasn't very special and that she'd fill out when she got stuck into some good, fresh veg again. I thought about Ma shrinking even more then, and it made me sad. But then I remembered that this would be my first opportunity to show the new me in action, my first real chance to start making up for the terrible mistake I had made.

I decided there and then that I would take my sister to Bedfordshire, all on my own, for a special coming-home treat. We would picnic in the old ambulance, just the two of us together, while Pa checked his recording of 'Morning Service' and prepared his sermon for the evening. And after, she and I would play the game.

The journey home was quiet, Pa being in one of his thoughtful moods. This was the first time I'd been allowed to visit; every Sunday since the misunderstanding when I asked if I could visit too he had told me the same thing: 'Patience is a virtue, James. When Mother is ready, she will see you. Doctor knows best.'

As the transit crunched down the drive between rows of dusty evergreen oaks, I was busy making plans. There was a second reason I was keen to go ahead with the picnic, and that was to do with a particular problem of poor Cymby's – a problem I knew I was uniquely qualified to help with. We could play the game and cure the problem at the same time. It was perfect.

By the time we reached the big iron gates I had every detail worked out in my head. I squeezed her shoulders. 'Cheer up,' I said. 'Soon be home. And I've a surprise for you.' She started to ask; but I raised a restraining hand. 'No. Don't ask,' I said firmly. 'You'll have to wait and see.'

She nodded and blinked her long lashes. I thought, maybe she really had changed in there. I noticed that Pa was smiling at the windscreen. I began to practise my inwards whistling, which is what I do when *I'm* looking forward to something.

Nettles and docks grow side by side, like God and the Devil (guess which is which).

34

Bedfordshire the ambulance has a flaky-chrome grille which reminds me of sharks' gills. It's magic. The body must have been white all over once upon a time but now there are brown stains under the headlights and green ones where the gutters flow down each side of the windscreen. Above the windscreen, in the middle, is a sausage-shaped window with a notice saying Ambulance, in black letters; the perspex is yellow and mouldy now but you can still read it. The tyres are near perfect, being flat only at the bottom even after all this time.

Inside the cab is the nerve centre where we paramedics do our life-saving work. You have to know what you are doing in that cab. For a start there are dozens of switches with names like Saloon Heater, Double Flasher and Intercom; in the middle of the dash, there's a big silver box with six chrome switches in a row called Simms; those are the high-tech switches; no one but the driver is allowed to touch those.

Between the green seats is a lever which makes a noise like a football rattle when you pull it up. Above the windscreen the green lining has a zip opening so you can get to the bulbs which light up the Ambulance sign from inside. Both bulbs are there but they really need changing, I expect. Behind the driver's seat is a sliding glass panel you can see through. The windows of the saloon are one-way, of course, so from outside all you see is your own face.

The best thing of all is the two-way radio which has both switches and knobs. The flexilead has lost its talking bit but I still use it to call up the hospital and tell them my ETA, what doctors to put on standby, the state of the patient, what apparatus to assemble, et cetera. I can't always hear the answer, especially when the one-two-five goes past, but I always acknowledge their efforts with a big Ten-four.

On the afternoon of the picnic the sky was white, matching the heat, except at the centre where it burnt a person's eye to look. But this didn't bother me; I was properly dressed for the expedition; I'd no shirt on – that was being saved for later – just khaki shorts and wellington boots. I'd packed everything we needed – even remembering anaesthetic – into a good, strong Sainsbury bag, and was sat in the Roombed, with Cymby beside me on the bed, listening. As soon as I heard the organ music coming up from the lounge, off we tiptoed, hand in hand, down the stairs, out through the kitchen, and across the back lawn.

The yard proper starts at the palletwood fence. My sister had no shoes on and the concrete was hot enough to fry sausages so, when we reached the gate, I put down the bag and hoisted her on to my shoulders. I'm not big but I'm wiry and strong for a seven year old. Lucky was back on his chain now and sheltering under the low loader so I had to make a detour round the back of the caravan. I think he must have been asleep. Anyway, he didn't bark at us, which was a relief.

The Bedfordshire trail begins with a tight squeeze between a stack of grey filing cabinets without drawers, and an upright gas freezer. Once through, you are into the Labyrinth – my name for the narrow alleys between the dexion racks which hold the really good stuff like batteries that work, and tail-lights and hub caps et cetera. From there you turn right along the corrugated fence, past the iron bed-frames, under a big yellow combine and out on to the cinders where the Crusher is.

Between the Crusher and Bedfordshire-the-place lie the Leaning Mountains. They are not real mountains but heaps of cars and vans and lorries all twisted and squashed and torn, and piled so high they block out the sun even at midday on a day like this. I call them Mountains because of their height and the fact that you can climb them and might fall off like a real mountaineer.

Some of the wrecks tickle me. Like there's one here now – an XR3-I, metallic, five door – with the steering-wheel poking up through the sun-roof like the driver was really into fresh air. But there's a serious side to them too. I always come down here after a new delivery to take a look. Sometimes I can look at a wreck and straightaway picture in my head exactly what happened – whether it skidded or spun or rolled, how many times it went over, how many cars were involved et cetera. Those are the ones I call Specials; they don't come every day, so when they do I make the most of it.

The outside of a Special is one thing, the inside's another. To get the full picture of what happened inside, I have to climb. The new arrivals are normally at the top, so I have to climb high. It's the most exciting thing I have ever done in my life or am ever likely to do. I imagine a mountain-lion hunter or bear hunter would feel how I do when I'm on the trail of a Special. Usually I can't even see the target once I've set off. I have to memorise the landmarks – the vans and cars en route, so that way it is very like tracking an animal. Then there are the dangers of the terrain: the chasms that appear beneath one, down into the darkness, bottomless pits, and the treacherous footholds – wrecks not properly balanced which groan and sway when you tread on them; but I always get through in the end.

Sometimes the trail ends in disappointment; some

Specials I can't get into at all because they're so squashed. But usually I manage to find a way in through the windscreen or boot, even if the doors and side windows are still intact and jammed. Getting into a Special is like the kill – either you get in (hit the vital spot), or you don't. There are no half measures. If you do, that's great, she's yours. If not, there's always another coming along, tomorrow or the next day or the next.

The great majority of my medical work is based around this accident research of mine. Once inside a Special it's quite easy to picture the heads going through the windscreens or being swiped off altogether, the fire and the blood and the screaming. A world of fascinating evidence opens up; there are stains, loose hairs, bits and pieces in the door pockets and wedged down between the seat cushions, broken toys, sweet wrappers, condoms (used and unused), shopping lists, letters – all tell a tale, and the variety is amazing. Within half an hour I can tell whether it was a man or woman driver, the approximate age, whether there were kids or grandparents in the back, any pets on board and so on and so forth.

When it's all as clear as can be in my head, I climb down. I go straight to the ambulance, contact base and tell them that X-Ray Delta Foxtrot 120 Juliet is on her way with whatever it is in the back. Then I switch on Simms numbers one and six, which is blue flashing light and siren respectively, then it's nee-naw, nee-naw and off we roar at emergency speed with the cars all pulling in to let us through, ignoring traffic lights, keep left signs, the lot. Like I say, it's magic.

Today was different, of course. Today I had brought a real-live patient along with me. Today, I was not plain Jim Bishop, ambulance driver, but Mister James Bishop, FRCS, fully equipped and ready to go. I would perform the operation with my own, long and wonderfully sensitive fingers. No charge would be made for my work – charity is its own reward.

I could feel the heat of the cinders coming through the soles of my wellingtons and was glad when we reached the shadow of the mountains, despite the smell of hot oil and diesel. As we threaded our way between the wings and bumpers, I began to practise my inwards whistling. 'Green Hill Far Away', was the tune. I'd just heard it on the wireless.

Bedfordshire the place lies between the Leaning Mountains and the embankment. It was once a rubbish tip. When it got full, the men came with tipper-trucks and bulldozers and spread dirt on top. Pa bought it last year. He admitted he would not need it for a while, and, in fact, it still contains only three items – the ambulance, a binder and a battery-hen transporter full of galvanised cages, but it was an investment, he said. Auntie called him a jackal, but Pa wasn't having it. There'll always be cars, he said. And there'll always be idiots. And in case you don't know, Mary, idiot is a Greek word meaning a private person, someone who has no interest in his fellow man, the killer with a Cosworth and a car phone where his ear should be. They're the motorway mercenaries – no morals, no mercy. Why bleed for shit?

For a religious person, he's really no-nonsense, my Pa.

We emerged from the Leaning Mountains into the fierce glare of the afternoon sun. I could hardly believe that, back in the spring, Auntie and me had played cricket down here; now the docks were too big, and the earth had cracks that would swallow a tennis ball. Or a baby rabbit.

The Sainsbury bag felt heavy.

Yes, the docks were taller than me now, their leaves like old green leather with red veins. As we weaved through, they shook and flowering tops like bunches of rusty iron filings rained seeds, hundreds and thousands of seeds, down on to us; they stuck to my neck and shoulders where her legs were making me sweat, and my arms and my forehead and my tummy. My sister was hot too, I could smell her.

About in the middle of the dock forest, the Sainsbury bag seemed to double its weight. It cut into my hand. Also I wished that I'd worn my white hat, like my sister. But on was the only way to go.

I smelled the nettles before I saw them . . .

And . . .

The big burning ball swung over . . .

The white sky swung over . . .

Darkness descended . . .

And cold . . .

Cold wind sighing . . .

Dead nettles . . .

dead . . .

nettles . . .

cold . . .

Darkness . . .

Something rattles, something flaps . . .

When I came to I was lying face down in the dirt with her sat beside me. Staring. Not crying. I was glad about that. This was supposed to be a treat.

I sat up thinking I'd better have a drink.

We both drank.

She looked frightened. Like she might have been worried about me. I said:

'Could've been worse, kid.' Then I laughed to give her the right idea and said, 'Could've been the nettles, eh?'

I felt a bit better then. I picked us up and off we went, her holding my hand now.

In a dozen strides we were out of the docks.

Bedfordshire is protected on the far side by the embankment and a fence made of railway sleepers soaked in a mixture of used engine oil and Dark Oak Woodcare by

Cuprinol. On top of the fence is a double spiral of razor-wire. This palisade was built to keep out the rough element from Moorend. Now Moorend has been developed into a margarine warehouse it's no longer needed. But I like the fortress-feel it gives. In the summer, the other three sides are guarded by nettles.

The nettle patch is normally terrible – a week before I could only just see the white roof of Bedfordshire from the edge of the circle, but something had happened. Now I could see the top half of the windows and the whole of the wing-mirror on this side. What had happened, of course, was the drought.

The nettles were almost black, and covered in small white flies. Although they were thin and shrunken and the leaves looked crispy like it had been raining Weedol or something, they still smelled peppery and dangerous to me. I hesitated; the wellingtons might not give enough protection. There was, of course, a well-worn track to the cab, but today we were heading for the saloon, which meant beating a path to the back door. I sat Cymby down to wait while I went for a stick from the elder bush.

The surgery was hot despite the roof vents and rear door being open, and the smell of crushed nettles was everywhere. From above the embankment the sun poured through the two side windows undiminished by the reflecting glass, so the two of us sat on the operating table, which luckily is on the opposite side, with the picnic between us: two pasties, two bananas, one fork to squash Cymby's banana, one small spoon to feed her with, two red plastic plates, two plain digestives, half bottle of Appletise, half bottle of Bacardi from the dining-room cupboard, one red plastic beaker for me, and Cymby's own, calibrated bottle with teat attached, all laid out neatly on top of the flattened Sainsbury bag. The medical equipment – stethoscope, needle and thread, bandaids,

Superglue 3, mask and operating gown I temporarily stowed in the locker. The only medical item I kept out was the Bacardi (which was really the anaesthetic) that, I figured, would be best administered mixed with two parts Appletise.

Cymbeline flatly refused to eat anything – pasty, banana, digestive – all were refused. I tried pretend eating, making slurping, lip-smacking noises over her spoonful of squashy muck; I tried the aeroplane trick which Ma used to do where you zoom the food around the place like its a stunt plane then when she smiles you fly it straight into her cakehole; I even tried half eating the pasty for her then spitting it back on to the spoon – like the mummy birds do. Nothing worked; her lips remained stubbornly sealed.

I felt myself becoming quite annoyed. Selfish little madam, I thought, after all the trouble I've gone to. Then I gave a great gasp of alarm: I'd just remembered, in the nick of time, that it's strictly NBM, which means, nil by mouth, for at least twelve hours before any op involving general anaesthetic. What an idiot. And how lucky she'd lost her appetite. And how close I had come to possible tragedy. Surgeons have been struck off for less.

She seemed thirsty now – which was a blessing – and took the anaesthetic without fuss. In fact, when I tried to take the bottle away from her, not wanting to overdo it, she hung on and kept glugging it down. 'Oi,' I said, 'How about leaving a drop for Mister Bishop?'

Really I was pleased, of course. I had thought it possible she might decide to play up; not every sick person appreciates help when it's offered. But the way she was swigging the anaesthetic put paid to that concern. She was lying back now, flat on the operating table, eyes closed, holding the bottle herself while I squeezed it.

As the bottle emptied, I felt for her pulse with the first three fingers of my free hand. I could see she was almost gone; the anaesthetic had begun to flow back out of her mouth. I didn't want her to choke, so I prised it out of her grasp and set it down. Then I smacked her forearm, sharply, three times, to make sure she wasn't asleep yet. First we had to have Consultation – things had to be done correctly.

I put on my white surgeon's gown – in view of the heat, not bothering with all the buttons down the back – hung the stethoscope round my neck, tied the mask loosely round my neck ready to pull up when sterile conditions were required, and bent over the patient.

The light dimmed.

Sudden chill.

I spun to look at the open door. I shivered. No one there.

Small cloud, I thought. Maybe a storm brewing. That could ease things.

The light brightened.

'Now then, Miss Bishop,' I said. 'What seems to be the trouble?'

No answer.

The anaesthetic seemed faster acting than anticipated. I sat the patient up and gave her a firm, but harmless, shake. Immediately the operating table, the front of my gown, my shorts and my feet were soaking wet. Her eyes were open but she was fast asleep. And she'd wet herself.

Of course I was not annoyed; doctors never, ever get annoyed, because they know that the patient cannot help his or her condition. I just nodded, 'Hmm, hmm; I see; just as we thought.' Then I laid her back down and her eyes closed again.

I looked at my Timex Electron with digital second display, it read 4:57.34. I made a note of this on the pad I had brought. On the line below I wrote: Patient under. Exploratory commencing.

Just in case, I bent low and whispered:

'Lie still and you won't feel a thing.'

The first time Pa tied Teddy-tail up with string I cried and begged to be undone and, when he refused, screamed the roof off half the night. I was too young then to appreciate what Pa said about it often being necessary for a grown-up person to be cruel in order to be kind. I see all that now, but, at the time, it did seem quite heartless.

I had started the filthy bedwetting habit about a year after the misunderstanding. It was another of my selfish ploys for gaining attention, so I had to be cured. He cleverly tied my wrists to the bedframe, to prevent me from meddling with the knot. Me being only a stupid infant, of course, I thought I would fill up with wee-wee and burst, like King Herod. I also believed that the end would drop off; I had learned a little bit about tourniquets in the playground at Marshside from one of the boys who went to Beavers; enough to know that a tourniquet must be released every so often or things can go bad . . . And mine wasn't being.

Long before dawn it stopped throbbing, all feeling went, and I just *knew* it had gone. I was too terrified to keep crying then, and ashamed. Ashamed that my Pa would come in in the morning and find that the bit that made me like him had gone for good. In fact it was still there – they're tougher than they look teddy-tails – but that's what I thought.

To my mind, that was a straightforward case of bad communication. (I could see no reason why Cymbeline should suffer as I had. Which is why, before commencing the op, I had carefully briefed her whilst the anaesthetic had time to get started.)

It was after the Teasmade as usual before Pa came in and untied me. It hurt soon enough then all right; it was agony. I was so relieved not to have lost it, I remember, I burst out laughing and crying and just couldn't stop. Then we both knelt at the foot of the bed and prayed that the special devil which had got into this particular part of my anatomy, making it wet my bed, would take warning and leave us alone from there on.

It certainly worked that day; I couldn't do wee-wees at all until tea-time. But the nights were a little different.

This little devil or demon . . . it did not exactly leave me, but what it did was come into my dreams. It was always the same one – like a goat with horns and wings and a violin sticking up between its legs, which it played wildly so that sparks flew up from the top in a great fountain. Most times it didn't wake me up, but, from that point on, I was able to get out of bed and go along the corridor to the toilet, even when still fast asleep. Except just one time when he – that is Pa – was already in there himself so I could not open the door and I could not stop in time.

When he came out he must have stepped on the wet bit of carpet with his bare feet because he did a little jump and said, 'Honestly.'

This obviously meant the cellar, and serve me right.

Naturally I am aware that girls are not the same as boys in that department. Girls' parts are just an opening. As Pa explained to Auntie at tea one day, it is through that opening that the Devil gets into this world. (She said he was 'warped'; I looked the word up, but don't really get it.) Clearly that wasn't my chief concern anyway, but, either way, the op would take care of everything. Mister Bishop was well prepared.

Now the patient lay on the operating table, her frock and knickers neatly folded beneath her head, resting after the op. Maybe not just resting, maybe still out, I wasn't sure. It might be as well if she was, I thought.

Plenty of bed-rest, that's what the prescription said: bed-rest and hot, salt baths. And not too much liquid for a couple of days.

A passenger train clattered past along the top of the

embankment, making the earth shake and the ambulance with it. Most of the carriages were empty, but, here and there – faces: a face reading, two faces in conversation, a face looking down into Bedfordshire, a curious male face, a face with pouchy eyes and not much on top. Even so, everything is private in the surgery. Everything is decent, the glass being strictly one-way.

The train rumbled off and a rumble of thunder came in its place. I glanced at my watch – it read 5:54.37, which meant the whole operation had been completed inside one hour. Excellent work.

I was sitting on the floor beside the bench, leaning back against the cabinet door. Suddenly I felt tired and hungry. I ate an apple, thinking what to do next. A cool breeze entered – moving the door an inch or two on its squeaky hinges – and with it came the smell of baked nettles. Pa would be in the caravan now, in his private chapel, playing back the service or preaching to his imaginary congregation (Old Frank and Mrs Chalmers have been refusing to attend recently, in view of the wage dispute, I believe). Time to make a move.

If I put a spurt on I could easily have her bathed and in bed before the end of Vespers. That would save an awful lot of questions.

I have to report a disaster. I am in the cellar again. He has turned off the light because I'm supposed to be having 'a little think'. But I'm too scared for thinking. I've also been crying because it is so unfair.

The hot water had seemed to make her sleepy again, so that she couldn't stand up on her own, which is why I had her laid across my lap to towel her dry. I'd barely started when I heard the stairs creaking. I suppose I might have pushed her tummy a bit hard, to stop her from jumping up and maybe falling, but I never *meant* to hurt her, that's for sure. Anyway, apparently I must have, by accident, because she started blubbing. Of course, when Pa came in and saw the tears he immediately assumed I'd been spiteful to her. You can easily see how he'd make a mistake like that – her being so little and innocent-looking with her big blue eyes and bunches – but I was so hurt at the time, what with trying so hard to do right, I couldn't seem to say anything in my own defence, but started to bawl myself. Which I know makes me look ugly and stupid. I just couldn't stop.

Then he spotted my handiwork.

The Superglue didn't show particularly, being mainly internal, but the bandaid was still half attached with one end poking out between her legs like an accusing finger.

Pa stared at it, his thick eyebrows almost meeting in the middle.

'Why did you do that?' he asked with a frown.

'Don't know,' I said.

His hand rested on my shoulder. He must have felt me shudder; I couldn't help it; it was less than a fortnight since the vacuum cleaner spewed its dreadful, angry contents into the Dark; I had survived that time, but . . . could I hope to be so lucky again?

'In that case, precious boy, we'd better trot off down below and have a little thinkies until we *do* know. Hmmm?'

I did *try* to explain but it was all far too late, and too muddled of course. As I descended I remembered Pa's warning. I wasn't too sure what 'thrive' meant, but the 'live' part was clear enough. And that meant, no killing. Strictly.

I've been down here a while now. The strange thing is I've just seen the lights – a row of glimmering, blue stars – winking at me from the blackness. It's mad, because I know there's no light down here, but I've tried blinking and rubbing my eyes and turning right round in a circle, and it's still there when I look. I've never dared move from the steps before. But I have to investigate this – creatures or not – something is calling me; it's like a promise, like the Pillar-of-fire-by-night which guided His chosen people out of the bad men's land; it's my *sign*, and it's calling me to the Promised Land, the land where *I* am in charge of what happens to me . . .

'Wait a tick. I'm coming.'

35

Our cellar is crammed to its low, whitewashed rafters with junk. The stuff at the back could never be dug out in a month of Sundays. So why does he keep it?

I haven't told anyone yet, not even Auntie. They wouldn't believe me if I did. But I know the answer: there'll always be room for more in our cellar; our cellar *eats* stuff. And he feeds it, deliberately. I don't mean the metal – the bunches of keys, the fireguard, the push chair, paint tins, shoe lasts, stair rods, aluminium pots et cetera – all that just turns to powder, brown, green or white. I'm not talking about that. I'm talking about the other stuff, the stuff that once grew. That stuff is pure cellar-food.

The soft stuff goes quickest – the cardboard cartons and clothing – then it's newspapers tied up with string and books and soft furnishings, mattresses, armchairs et cetera. But everything goes in the end – tables, chairs, hallstands, chests – dead or alive, it makes no difference; they once ate two trays of seed potatoes, and most of the wooden trays as well, in less than a fortnight. Last week a bird got down here, God knows how. It might have been a thrush. When I saw it it was covered in thick grey cobweb. Next time he sent me down, only two days later, it was a skeleton. They'd even carried off the feathers, or eaten them. Two days after that there was only the skull. Today, nothing.

They've started on the ceiling too, it's riddled with holes and there's sawdust everywhere – up among the flakes of whitewash caught in the webs near the light bulb, along the stairs where the brick wall joins the panelling, all down the steps – little cones of powdered wood where they've bitten off more than they can chew. They'll have the whole house in the end, basement to attic, I know it.

Whenever I'm put down here I sit on the last wooden step, with my feet on the concrete step below; that way I know where I am. Once all the steps were wood, but the bottom two got eaten and, sometime last year, Pa replaced them with concrete blocks. For the rest of the cellar, I've always kept well clear of that, especially after lights out. But this time was different. This time, just before it went black, I noticed three items at the front of the stack which were definitely not there last time: my old blue cot, the blue highchair and the playpen with its three rows of bright coloured beads on a wire.

Why? I thought. Why has he thrown those things down here when my sister still needs them? Unless . . . he didn't *expect* her to come home, *really*. In which case, now she is back, why hasn't he collected them? I mean, what's she supposed to sleep in tonight for a start? It has to be well past her bedtime . . . she's already been bathed, by me. It's not easy keeping track of time down here, but it must be a couple of hours at least since he switched off the light . . .

Unless . . . (nasty thoughts creeping up, I don't want to think them, but . . .)

Is *she* to sleep with *him* now? Is *that* why they don't need this cot?

And (please, not this thought, not this thought) is it really that Ma is *never* coming home? Does my Ma still *exist* even? Or is that a story too? Like Father Christmas, like the Rainbow . . . ? Is the Monster really a *Monster* after all? – Heavenly Father, help me if you will – and did He really know it all the time? How blind I must be! How *stupid!* *My Ma has finally been consumed away to nothing?! They're in this together!*

I began to whimper. But quietly. So as not to disturb.

The cellar creatures have always been my reason for not leaving the steps after lights out; even before the Angry Ones came and the one I have christened in my head the Black Prince. I've seen things moving about down there among the nibbled plywood and mouldy oak even with the light still on; big things with velvet bodies and quick legs, shiny blue-black things that scrape and click as they go. And once, further in, I saw a pair of red glowing eyes. They were still there when the light went out – I counted to seven before they vanished, one at a time, like a wink. I know just how Moley must have felt; they didn't believe *him* either, but he was right, wasn't he? Those spiteful wedge-shaped faces and slitty, slanty eyes – he wasn't *imagining* them, there really were creatures in that wood, but nobody ever did believe him, not even his best friend, Ratty. Same as here. Exactly. They nearly got him too, and I'm not telling stories.

The other thing is this: all the time the light stays on the stuff that once grew – the tree stuff – is a perfectly normal pile of old furniture et cetera. But the minute he switches the switch, it changes. Slowly and bit by bit. I *hear* it. Clear as anything. Ticking and creaking as it turns into the Wildwood. All the legs and the arms and the spokes of all the chairs, and the tables and the tea-chests and old floorboards – they all melt together in a big steaming heap, like the big steaming heap at the end of our garden, then they grow things – roots, branches, bushes, brambles, trunks, leaves, creepers, toadstools, the lot, till the whole forest is there in our cellar. I can smell it – mould, moss, mud, everything. It takes less than a minute. When it's finished the creatures come out of their holes –

not just the spiders, the others, the ones with hundreds of legs and the ones that suck blood – then they *really* begin to move. Nothing is as it appears down here. Everything changes shape.

I thought nothing on earth could persuade me to go down those concrete steps. But my blue Lights were calling. When I finished turning round on the spot and found them still there I remembered how the Children of Israel were led out of Egypt by the Pillar of Fire by Night. I may even have breathed a little prayer of thanks; anyway, down I went, bold as brass. Why wouldn't I? It was the Light of the World. All the fear and dread had gone. I just said, Wait a tick, I'm coming . . .

And I went . . .

One, two steps down. One, two, three paces forward on the flat, hard-packed earth. My two hands waving in front touched . . . what . . . ? Wooden beads, a thin metal rod, another rod, more beads. The playpen!

And that, of course, could mean only *one* thing: tonight, for the first time ever, the stack had not transformed itself into the Wildwood. The reason was obvious; the Light of the World had stopped it.

My eyes pricked and the tears poured down, but not with misery this time, oh no, this time I was crying with the joy overflowing from my heart. I began to climb over the old nursery furniture and up among the chair legs. Whilst I could see even one small glimmer of my blue Light, I was safe from the seething creatures below.

There came a moment, a heartstopping moment when my Light vanished completely behind a wickerwork sofa which my hand went through as I bore down on it. I had only just started to recover from the shock of this, and located my guiding Light again, when both my legs went crashing through the back of what might have been a wardrobe lying face down in the middle of the stack; its door must have opened from the inside as I fell, letting

392

me pass straight through so that I found myself upside down deep inside the stack, wedged between what felt like a tin bath and a pile of wet sacking, with the suffocating stink of mould in my nostrils, and I could not see the Light – not even a glimmer – and I dared not scream but lay perfectly still, biting my lips together, snorting breath through my nose until something soft and cool as a chilled plum touched the back of my hand. And I felt my whole body go rigid in its position as if I had already been bitten like the butterfly on Auntie's geranium.

The spider rested awhile on the back of my hand, its body pulsing gently. I could feel two of its legs on my wrist, the other six I could not feel at all. Under my hand was what felt like a carpet rolled inside out. If the other legs were still on this, its span had to be . . .

What *spider* was ever this big?

A third leg settled gently on my fourth finger, just above the nail, one of the front legs lifted and tapped my forearm a little higher up.

'Look, I'm sorry, Black Prince,' I whispered. 'I didn't mean it. It was an accident. The pipe was too heavy. It slipped. I'll never do it again. Please . . . please don't climb any higher.'

The tapping foot settled and its neighbour moved two inches forward, simultaneously a fourth foot then a fifth, sixth, seventh, eighth settled on my fingers . . .

My pulse beats ran together like a vibration and my shirt and shorts were soaked with my ice-cold sweat. The idea that entered my head then was not a *plan*, it came straight from my guts: if it moved any higher I would fling up my arm as hard as I could, whatever lay above me, and then I would dive forward and up towards my blue Light. Only the blue Light could save me now and oh how I wanted to Live and Thrive . . .

The other front leg lifted.

I drew a deep breath, held it and sent my whole

consciousness into my right arm. If my arm obeyed me, I could yet be lucky again . . . If it merely twitched . . . What did the big garden spider do to Miss Butterfly when she made that mistake? She should never have fluttered like that . . . he fixed her for good. They don't kill things, Auntie said, not straight away. They bite them with something so the creature can't move, then they wrap them up in very strong cobweb and hang them in the larder until they are hungry . . .

The second leg landed, high up my arm . . .

I erupted like the Incredible Hulk, dived, crashed forward, rolled, dived again, sound of breaking sticks, jab in the back, aware of tearing my skin but no pain . . . and there it was again, the Light. And I could see now that it was not a row of separate twinkling lights at all, but a continuous narrow strip of pale blue.

The top of the stack had shrunk down from the ceiling until – several metres before I reached the door, (don't ask how I knew it was a door) – I fell over what felt like a fireguard and found myself standing on what felt like dry earth.

I dashed forward, careless of injury, reached out, and immediately felt a twisted iron ring. I glanced down at the blue Light illuminating my black, elastic-sided plimsoles; my wonderful blue Light.

'All right, Light,' I whispered, 'I'm coming.' Then, without further hesitation, I yanked the ring round, and pushed.

I did not actually see the dark shape that scuttled through the crack before me.

36

For a giddy moment I believed myself in the caravan – not the office end, the chapel end – that I had passed out (or something) in the cellar and that Pa (or someone) had carried me to the chapel while still unconscious – that the *thing* that had touched me, the Light and the door were just part of a dream. It's not hard to see why.

In front of me was an altar. Just for an instant, it looked to me like Pa's altar – low light, altarcloth, cross, statue – but in fact was quite different. For one thing, the light was the wrong colour, being blue-green, not orange, and it came not from two radio valves but a beautiful blue glass dish suspended from three gold chains which contained no candle but only a living flame. Also the feeling produced by this light was not hot and suffocating like that in the caravan chapel, but cool and mysterious like I imagine the view from a whale's eye might be.

Another similarity was the Virgin at the centre of the altar. But this Virgin was made of some metal that gleamed dull green-gold; she wore a crown instead of a plain, blue hood, and sat on a narrow throne with baby Jesus between her knees. Pa's Virgin was quite different; Pa's Virgin stood upright with her head slightly tilted, and where it was chipped you could see it was made of chalk painted bright blue. Also this one didn't have lipstick.

But these were all details. The real difference lay in the size of the place . . . there seemed no boundaries ahead or to either side . . .

Behind me the oak door swung closed with an echoing click, making me start and look round. For an instant I considered the option of retreat. I quickly dismissed it. This was where my Light had led me. Besides, I thought, better a mysterious place than a through-and-through nasty one. I turned back to face the blue-lit space. Only one thing made me hesitate before moving away from the door. I leaned forward, shielding my eyes with one hand.

Despite its dimness the hanging light was the source of *all* light. Perhaps for that reason it was difficult to see beyond it. But I had to. Before I could begin to explore the wonders of this moonlit forest of stone I needed to assure myself there was nothing to spoil its magical peace – nothing hidden in the gloom that might reach me with a sudden dash, or drop on my back from the ceiling. The stone floor seemed clear. I looked up.

I drifted out among the petrified trunks, slowly revolving, gaping up at the low arched ceiling, amazed that a space of this size existed beneath an ordinary house like ours. Also, up to that moment, I'd believed that our cellar had only *one* room. Now here was another – if room it was – so huge its boundaries were lost in shadow.

Pausing beneath the Light I felt a sudden chill and remembered I was still in my medical clothes still damp' with the sweat of terror. A small sound made me turn . . .

Five yards behind me, a huge double pillar . . . had something flicked around it to the back, like a squirrel round a tree trunk? I shuddered. The pillar was right at the edge of vision . . . It seemed to me strangely misshapen . . .

She was standing perfectly still, staring straight at me, her body half hidden by the pillar. Without making a sound, she stepped out and forward. I could see she was tall and slim in a black dress that reached to the floor. She had shoulder-length hair which gleamed softly in the faint blue-green light. To me she looked exactly as an angel should look, young and beautiful with a fine soft beard like the Light of the World. Only one thing was lacking: no wings.

I stood still.

She came towards me quickly.

Her feet made no sound. I considered running, but there was no time. And where would I run to? The cellar? Hopeless; she'd catch me in the stack; in any case, there was no escape from the cellar itself, Pa always bolted the door on the outside. I watched her approach, trembling for some reason, maybe the cold.

She spoke as she came, wagging one finger. 'No, no, no. You have not yet finished.'

The voice surprised me. It was not the voice of a woman. As she drew close I could see that the hair on her chin and top lip was fine and silky. She was very lovely. But for the skirts and long hair I'd have called her a he.

She gripped my elbow and steered me firmly along beside her. As we went, she stopped to speak in my face: 'There is one last detail to be clarified, James. Not the misunderstanding – we find no difficulty there – our problem lies only in that episode you refer to as "the accident".'

I gasped.

The dark figure stopped and squatted in front of me, looking up into my eyes as if talking to a silly infant. 'I take it that we *are* still referring to this episode as "the accident", James? We have not changed our mind?' She stood slowly, still holding my gaze with her green-blue eyes. 'No. I was sure we had not.'

I stared at her. How did she know about the accident? Inside my head I began to rehearse a statement: It *was* an accident. It was not my fault.

Out loud, I asked: 'Are you the Ump—'

The finger went up and wagged in front of my face. Her eyes held mine. 'I ask the questions, James.' She took my hand firmly and drew me on again.

We arrived at a door in the wall. 'Through here, James.'

I hesitated; I hadn't been concentrating much on direction, it looked like the door from our cellar, apart from the addition of a small square of polythene-covered paper on which were the words, NO ADMITTANCE. FOR THE USE OF FUTURE AND PASTPERFECT PERSONNEL ONLY, typed in block capitals. I looked up at her face. 'Is this the way out?' I asked.

She squeezed my shoulder, 'This is the way forward. I'll leave the door ajar. I might pop in later. Goodbye, James.'

With this, she twisted the handle, opened the door, ushered me firmly, gently into the sunshine.

The sound of an engine.

The smell of cut grass, exhaust . . .

Now I'm watching the toes of my black, elastic-sided plimsoles skipping across the grass, trying to get a grip on the grass but slipping all the time because of me being on tiptoe, because I can only just reach the handles of the Ransome, because I'm little. At the same time I'm watching Cymbeline's back getting closer and closer – she must have gone deaf now as well as being dumb – dumbo Cymbeline, Cymby-the-dummy, why don't you move? Why do you sit there just pouring cold water from the red plastic teapot into *my* red plastic cups! You *must* be able to hear this engine, it makes enough noise after all. Maybe I'll shout you a warning . . . maybe . . . in a minute . . .

Then again, maybe I won't. Who's going to hear me, after all? Ma's in the washroom, Pa's in the caravan . . . That only leaves you, and you're dumb.

The sunlight reflects from the white sheets billowing, turning on the rotary drier, round and round they go, Persil white. Sunlight dances on the bright shining blades as they spin, red and silver, lovely, and the fountain of grass . . . beautiful . . . beautiful sunlight, beautiful grass . . . fountain of grass falling like rain on her mouse-coloured hair . . .

Whoops! What's that? Something has jammed the blades.

Let's have a look. Ah. Dear me, a small severed foot has jammed the blades. Never mind; apart from that, everything is just as it *should* be: the white sheets are shining with fresh red blood, the whole of my front is slick and shiny, bare arms, grey shirt, khaki shorts, hands, hair, lips. Scraps of smoking meat, splinters of bone all over the grass. The base of the drier now has its own eye, with strings attached. Here a hand. There a foot. Where's the other eye? In the birdbath. Oh dear. It's a Birdseye. That's awful.

Hey up, the engine is straining, clanking and clonking as the drive belt slips round the locked-up pulley. Look smart now. Pull the clutch in. Here comes Pa. And he doesn't look happy.

Neither should you.

Here he comes, white faced, running like hell. It's the cellar again, I can tell. And serve me right

but it's worth it. This time, it really is. The Monster is dead.

Darkness.

The prisoner spins in the horizontal. (Or, the blackness spins and the prisoner stays still. It's the same.)

Time passes.

Other sensations come . . .

He feels his hair is caked with dry vomit which also clogs his nostrils, forcing him to gulp air through his dry, caked mouth. Arms by his sides, feet together, he tumbles full length across rough boards. (Or, rough boards roll beneath him.) Over and over and over he goes. Out in the dark a torch, or candle or moon, flashes like a lighthouse geared to his revolutions.

The thought comes that he's been at the whisky and forgotten the details. It seems to fit the circumstances. Apart from the boards bumping past – their spinning seems independent of him, and indifferent to him . . .

Later, his ears gather in a deep rumble, the slap of bare

feet, soft panting. This does *not* fit his theory. He must think again. He sniffs. Behind the vomit he smells burnt paper. And urine.

His stomach convulses. He tastes bitter juice. He must stop the spinning so sticks out an arm, which works in so far as the rolling stops but the boards beneath continue to slide past, their coarse grain dragging the garments across his back, trying to spin him on down. He braces his arm harder, moaning at the energy it costs to stop the spin. The Light is now constant though oscillating vertically. It resolves into the rear view of a young girl, naked, glowing with her own flesh-coloured radiance, yet casting little beyond herself. She is running away from him up a steep slope of planks without growing further off or higher up. From time to time wooden beams arc through the glow at either side and vanish behind him.

He retches on nothing in his stomach. His elbow picks up a huge splinter causing his arm to retract as if electrocuted. Again his body submits to the spin of the treadmill. Iron and timber rumble.

The light dims.

This is hell, he assumes. And it serves him right . . .

The prisoner stops spinning but the blackness begins to whirl about him, absorbing his lost momentum into a cyclone of darkness . . .

The first monster appears from behind his right shoulder. All around is darkness, being void. Though its hundred or so legs do not move, the creature writhes and bobs its scaly neck and lashes its whiptail as it circles him on the black wave of the invisible merry-go-round. He knows it for the mount of the torturer. (But for the beak he would say it was a dragon.)

Exactly ninety degrees after the dragonbird comes a grey shape that at first sight appears to have three heads but quickly reveals itself to be an upright goat with wings curving up from its shoulders before folding together down

its back. It has great curling horns and sagging breasts.
Thrusting up between its breasts and under its chin a violin
furiously saws, throwing not sounds but showers of sparks
over the prisoner's naked body which he cannot extinguish
for his hands are crossed and fused to his chest as if the
flesh had partly melted then solidified, like two pork chops
back to back on a grill. His legs too are fused together. He
cannot move, not even wriggle like any poor worm under
a blowlamp.

The goat now bows a huge erection where the fiddle was
and the sparks gush up in a blazing fountain then hop over
his body like white-hot hailstones. He gapes in horror at
his blistering, smoking flesh, howling silently for someone
to tell him what he must say. The air is filled with sizzle
and spit and the smell of Sunday ovens, hot and sour.
There is no pain, just the terror of non-existence. If he
could only roll over he might put himself out. He tries very
hard . . .

A figure draped from top to toe in royal blue rounds the
dark headland. The prisoner knows it to be a young woman
though its back is to him. On her shoulder sits a badly
stuffed pigeon or dove. Please help me. Please help me,
sobs the prisoner. The figure turns slowly, her red lips
smile sadly, then she opens her silky blue gown to show
him all she has, which is bones. She speaks:

'You are dreaming,' she says. 'You may wake if you
choose – take a chance if you wish. It could be better than
this . . .

'. . . or worse.'

'Anything's better than this,' I reply.

True, my feet are burning; true, I hear a sound like tropical
rain or burst pipes or overflowing gutters; true, my mouth
is clagged up with some sort of powder, my nostrils stopped
so I can hardly breathe. And yet . . . I *know* that I'm glad
to be here, I am actually *glad* to be here . . . hurting.

401

But there's something I have to remember: it was the skeleton-woman – her words of permission, permission to *choose* – which freed me from that hideous place, not these crude, bullying sensations. It seems to me important to remember that. She released me – in spite of the nightmare in the garden. I was *not dragged* back, kicking and screaming, by some squalid reality . . .

Dreams! God! They make you laugh, don't they? I mean, where do they get their ideas from?

Never mind that, said headvoice, **here comes the damage report: You are lying face down in dust, top half on the Shelf, bottom half on the steps leading up from the Bible Room. Your feet are indeed on fire, at least, the soles of your shoes are. I think it's about time we—**

Hey. Would you look at that ceiling? Fabulous. That light! It's like liquid gold shimmering on the vault up there. Reminds me of something . . . bonfire night, on the heath, firelight flickering on the underside of the evergreen oak trees. All the family together, and happy, so happy . . . just the three of us. No Cymbeline.

But it's pouring out there. Strange how the rain hasn't spoilt the bonfire. I feel kind of peaceful just lying here, roasting . . . beautiful firelight, beautiful – Jesuschrist-almighty – fire! I'M ON FIRE!

And the splashing – that's not *rain* – it's the sprinklers! the sprinkers pissing it down everywhere!

Except here.

Why not here? And what is that smell? Roast chicken?

The pigeons. They're cooking down there.

I twist my neck round. Through the doorway, not much more than a metre behind and below, I see that the Bible Room is bright orange without detail, like a furnace with the door open. As I look, a huge orange timber sags into the holocaust sending up a fountain of orange sparks, and a scorching blast towards me. Smell of burnt feathers. And rubber. I think: my trainers are on fire, take a look.

402

I try to twist my body but there's something badly wrong with my arm. The heat is terrible. I manage to wriggle forward, dragging my legs up and over the top step. I can see now my trainers are trailing molten rubber which is burning smokily. I draw them up as far as I can, meaning to smother them somehow, but only succeed in setting fire to the thick dust of the Shelf which pops into flame, rapidly spreading round my right side like flaming brandy round a Christmas pudding. I lunge away automatically . . . and scream out loud. A knife of white . . . what in God's name? Bone! My very own skeleton has breached the flesh above my elbow . . . through the Spidertop too . . . startling, white on dark grey . . . I can hardly believe . . . Heavenly Father, help me! Please!

Wetness. In my sleeve. Blood. *My* blood!

Now I'm wet all over . . . soaked in panic juice . . . things swimming about in front of my eyes . . . row of pink pillars, diamond panes reflecting firelight . . . pretty . . . Christmassy . . . Here we go . . . weeee . . . I'm on the slide, baby, going over the edge, weeeee . . . dark, darker, darkest . . .

Not now, idiot! Get your head down, quick!

I duck my head quickly, blood flows back making my ears sing: not now, quite correct, now's not the time . . .

I try to sit up.

A voice shouts: 'Who's there?'

But my sleeve is alight and I'm setting fire to more Shelf-dust even as I struggle to drag myself clear of the flames.

'Is somebody up there!? Hallooo!' calls the voice.

Lights coming on – in bunches and batteries – spots, floods, wall lights – nave, quire, everywhere, lights.

A different voice . . . sounds angry, dangerous: 'We know you're up there. It's no good trying to hide. The police are on their way. You can't get away. So show yourself please. Come along, please . . .'

* * *

403

Dear Auntie,

my problem is this: firstly a burning river of dust is advancing on me at a speed of approximately one foot per second faster than I can crawl away from it; secondly I could faint at any moment, turn into a small pile of ash and that would be that; thirdly, if I should manage not to faint, I might try to go a little faster except if I do that I'll stir the dust up into a cloud; fourthly, I have now remembered why I was so afraid of the sparks round the taper in the Bible Room – back . . . whenever – namely that, at a certain critical density, a mixture of organic dust and air will *explode* when ignited, even by a single spark; fifthly, the right arm of my Spidersuit is on fire but I can't beat it out with my left arm because that's broken and there's a hole in it which hurts like a bastard. I've good reason to believe it's a compound fracture of the humerus – and that's not funny. Otherwise, Auntie, I'm fine – well, except that the dream says I murdered my sister, and there's a pack of dogs down there who no doubt think I'm a Muslimfunde-fuckingmentalistSatanistpyromaniac or even a footballsup-porter. What shall I do? Your loving nephew.

Go! says headvoice, **Or we're fucked. Savvy? Fucked. C'mon! the dust is only along the Shelf – *it ends at the spiral*. FUCKING SHIFT IT!**

The spiral . . . my only hope. There should even be a bowl of water to dowse myself . . .

P.S. Question: can our hero make it to the spiral before the flames make him? It'll be close. He'll have to risk the dust cloud. No choice.

Whimpering softly, I begin to scrabble, half crawling, half running like a wounded ape, along the Shelf, the dust rising in great billows around me.

The funny thing is, it's not so much the fire that drives me . . . it's the other place . . . no way am I going back to that treadmill!

37

The access-door slams behind me, cutting dead all sounds – the shouting, the water, the fire. I fall back against it. The latch clicks down like a hammer on an empty chamber.

My sleeve is smouldering orange in the dark, burning me now. I lunge across to the wall to scrub it out, whimpering like a baby, but the material continues to smoulder – a constellation of expanding orange circles – as one patch dims, another blooms brighter. 'Come on. Come on!' Frenzied scrubbing. It's more than fabric burning now, I can smell me burning. She's doing this to me. She's *telling* me, like a horror story – a nightmare I'm forced to live out, even now when I'm wide awake, burning . . .

'Stop it! STOP IT!' I yell.

The words bounce back off the stone.

Panting. In the dark.

I *know* that a terrible explosion is about to take place. How do I know this? I hear it in my mind's ear as surely as if I'd just finished reading it in the last pages of the story. I also know it will seal my fate. There is no question about this. So, do I flee *up*, or do I flee *down*? Either way, the flames are coming.

We went down last time, and look where it got us.

Yes, but up's a dead end, so—

This waste of good brain time is cut off by a bright picture in the blackness; the door – its outline, individual boards, keyholes, knotholes – all sketched in brilliant lines of light. A split second later it has changed to a green after-image, and the sound of the blast begins – a terrible sound, like no other I've heard – the start is a whisper, but I know what is coming.

I ball up against the wall. Whisper turns to scream and between the two the stone stairway trembles as though a diesel express is passing. Blast, like a piston, belts the oak door off its hinges and jams it across the stairwell below me. Flames roar . . .

The illusion of choice is gone.

Me, the smoke and the flames race each other up the stairs – me gibbering with pain at each step, the flames popping and hissing in the smoke-filled tube. Small mercy: the blast (or the updraught or my own blood and sweat) has almost extinguished my burning sleeve, but my other arm is one bolt of black agony. Also, with flames licking my back I know I could re-ignite at any moment like the running fireballs in the war films.

Just in time I remember the drainpipe and duck, but I'm too late for the water bowl which crumples underfoot, then clanks down the steps to be smelted. For a moment the flames fall behind, but the smoke and the heat are terrible so that I know I must be inside the turret within seconds, literally, or turn to smoked meat right here.

A gap in the handrope tells me I'm passing the Wheel Room. A billow of smoke drives me on cursing, hauling breath like an asthmatic. A dozen more steps and I'm at the barrier. I claw at the boards. My lungs pump for air which only chokes me. On the brink of collapse, I find an edge, wrench back the two middle planks, enter, close them behind me as best I can and, coughing and gasping so the stars dance, crawl up the five steps to the turret. There I collapse against the parapet, my bleeding arm hung like a rag arm beside me.

The night air stabs my lungs – ice cold, clean. Rest now, in my refuge, my church in the clouds.

But what does the authoress intend? A calm passage, touch of comic relief? Or must it be tragedy, tragedy all the way?

In less time than it takes to hawk and gob – the tale continues – I *know* that the smoke has begun to leak through. And that is *before* I can smell it, taste it, feel it stinging my eyes. The flames will be close – of course they will, it is only logical – this is no longer just a spiral staircase, this is a three-hundred-foot chimney with an exceptional draught. And I am stuck on top like the poor crow who thought the owner was away for good.

Seems He's back. Seems He's lit the boiler an' all.

How did I make a mistake like this? Where was I before? Somewhere cool . . . somewhere blue . . . What sent me up here?

'**Satan is an Angel, one of the Sons of God—**'

Who said that?!

'**He is the accuser in God's court, deputed to the task of punishing the unrighteous. His evil is not evil. He is the Angel who can do no wrong. He is the Angel with Horns.' Who said it?**

Jesus! I don't know. *Who said it?*

Job said it. The good doctor said it. After he warned us about CJ.

Fuck. So he did. So he did. Hey . . . The beautiful person . . . the Mamba . . . You're not suggesting . . . No, that's crazy . . . I didn't see any horns.

It's a metaphor, pillock.

No. It's insane. I'll never believe in that stuff. Never ever. *She* is the instrument of my downfall. Her. The cow. And nothing can stop her now.

I've been a fool. I underestimated her all along. She was clever. As clever as me. I never would admit that. Think how cunningly she used to twist things so it always seemed *my* fault. 'Bimbim break it. Bimbim take it. Bimbim hit

Cymby on the head. Waaa, waaa!' That was always her speciality: shifting the blame to big brother. She hasn't changed. Take this fire. Only *I* know that if she hadn't appeared out of the Bible-bed like that I would never have lit those holy pages. But would *they* believe me? That pack down there? 'The reason I lit up, sir, was because the Ghost of my mowed-up sister flew out of my bed and frightened the crap out of me.' 'Oh, that's OK, sonny. We'd all have done the same.' I think not.

Too late to change the story now, though. Fires must burn, wounds must bleed and characters like me . . . characters must do what they're told; that's the rules.

Fuck the rules! This character's not burning. And he's not begging either!

I strike the match – the *last* match in the box. There, sure enough, snaking through the gaps in the boards – coils of yellow-grey smoke. Worse; the wavering matchlight shows that, outside, the turret is wrapped in a billowing blanket of smoke. The Cathedral is become pyre, just as the writing foretold. Where to run to now? There's nowhere left.

Except down.

Down? You mean down to the *Wheel Room?* Would James Bishop do *that?* I ask myself . . .

Let me try to make this clear: when I asked myself that question, I had assumed that, in spite of all the traumas, it would still be my headvoice – that embarrassing animal which is nevertheless part of my own brain – that would answer. Well . . . it wasn't. She had taken over that function, it seemed – that part of the game was lost – She was *inside me* now, answering *my* thoughts in *Her* way. I don't say the thing I call 'me' or 'I' was finished – far from it – I still had control of my body, and the *important* side of my brain – the *feeling* side, the side that intuitively senses what's *really* going on, the side that distinguishes right from wrong, amongst other things. She had the computing side, that's all, the logic circuits and the bit that stands high up and watches itself.

The hell with that, She can have it, I thought, what good has it ever done me?

I can't quite decide, says the voice of the Ghost from somewhere between my ears. *Try a rehearsal. Go back, take a run at it, see how it feels to you, OK? Right, go.*

My lips and tongue begin to move. (Things are a little bit worse than I thought.) Words wriggle out of my mouth like wilful, living creatures, like maggots of meaning deserting the host. Here's what they say:

'He strikes the last match, and there, sure enough, snaking through the gaps in the boards, coils of yellow-grey smoke—'

The words stop. There's a brief hesitation, a spluttering, dribbling stammer as I struggle to stem the flow by slapping my good hand over my mouth, pinching my lips together between first and second fingers. The hand comes away *against my orders*. I slap it back, but this time only succeed in scratching my cheek and jabbing myself in the eye. Fairies dance in the blackness. My mouth bulges; more words burst out:

'—vering matchlight shows that, outside, the turret is wrapped in a billowing blanket of smoke. The Cathedral is become funeral pyre . . . For the prisoner there's nowhere to run . . .
  Except down. Except down . . . to the Wheel Room. Except back down to the Wheel Room and the treadmill and the ovens and (splutter) . . . and . . .'

The rage mounts inside me; I feel myself gaining some slight control; some of the words begin to obey *me*:

'and . . . and that filthy . . . that goat-thing . . . that disgusting, perverted . . . *thing* . . . that *thing* that shoots bloody fireballs from its prick . . .'

So? What's the decision? Does he go down, or not?

'Never! He'd never go back to that hideous nightmare. He'd kill himself first; chuck himself off the top of the tower.'

All right then. Suppose we agree; he's not quite ready for that. There's one last item on the agenda – the 'Little attack of hope', as the Irishman said. Maybe he'll change his mind after that. But first, we schmaltz it up a bit, right. Try this, says the voice, and my mouth spits more words into the darkness:

'The prisoner looks at the last flame of his life and sees that already it is dying, the matchstick already three parts black and twisted. It seems *right* to him then – an image of supreme poetic beauty, a masterstroke of the writer's art – that he should see in the humble splinter of wood his own blackened, twisted body and, at long last, finally accept . . .

'Oh, *what*!?' I yell, ' "masterstroke of the writer's art!? Image of poetic . . ." what a bucket of CRAP! Accepts it, does he? We'll see about that!'

All this is bluster and bluff and I know it, but playing for time is the only game left. Without moving my injured arm, I transfer the carbonised head of the still-burning match to my other hand. 'A little longer, light,' I beg. 'Just one last flicker before the dark . . .' The flame climbs hungrily to the top of the tiny splinter, darkening first the angles, then the planes, finally extracting a last blue puff from the severed grain. And in that dying gasp of light, close by the hand which holds the blackened matchstick, I glimpse it – a faint, wine-coloured stain on the flagstone, a V-shaped mark, broken but undeniably there. I recognise it at once, and my heart thumps in my chest: it is part of the *magic hexangle* I painted long ago. It kept Her at bay then . . . If only it were whole . . . might it not . . . ?

The flame in my fingers sputters out. Blackness. A deep, ominous rumble below and outside to my right. A bitter smile twitches my lips. You were in control then, I tell myself. Now look . . .

My arm is throbbing in time with my head, my left hand now glued to the flagstone by congealing blood; I am trapped by fire, and possibly . . . possibly losing my mind . . .

Suddenly I just want an end. Any end, it doesn't matter, so long as it isn't the flames . . . I do not want to burn. Not *burn*. To be alive, watching one's own living flesh dissolving into smoke . . . and ash . . . and dripping . . . To just soak away into the earth. To be blown off by the wind, to become . . . *nothing* in your own sight! Anything . . . *anything* . . . but that.

Is it the fire whispering to me? Or is it Her again? Her voice again, fainter than ever, but deeper inside me and far, far more potent . . .

The record has been corrected now. The prisoner knows he must pay up or . . .

Like a man in a trance I place the first finger of my right hand between my incisors, being careful this time to fold it at the first joint so as not to make myself gag and retch. (There, it is possible after all.) With a juddering sob I begin to close these teeth together, feeling for the joint of the knuckle. Sweat breaks over my body. The pain is astonishing; only a crazed thing could go through with it. My brain screams: Pass out! Why not pass out?

The choice is yours, prisoner. Descend, if you wish. Invite me in, if you wish. I have only to enter through your feeble barrier of wood, show myself to you like before . . . and down we will go, together. And there will be no more fighting, and there will be no more quarrelling, no more seeing things differently . . . ever again.

411

'Never,' I whimper. I begin to twist and wriggle the joint, feel the flesh tearing hot and stinging like salt in a gash, feel the joint open a fraction, the start of its dislocation, like wrenching the leg off an undercooked turkey. If I am to bite off my finger . . . if that is the price of freedom, I yell at myself, then let's get the bastard done! I tighten the muscles of my jaws till they tremble and judder. Blood roars in my ears. My voice shrieks through the bones of my jaw. 'It won't go! It won't go! Please, God, let it go!' I belch hot vomit . . . but it's only a dribble of bread. Or blood? Is it blood? *My* blood?

My blood! The first hexangle was drawn in blood . . . I might yet repair it, even now with the tendons of my finger still partly attached, the nerves not yet severed . . . ? If only . . . If only I had *light*.

There comes the sound of howling, screeching, racing engines. And the shouts of *men*.

The turret is ablaze with Light. Though filtered through the smoke which billows outside the narrow windows, the glare is almost blinding to my wide open irises. It seems a sign . . .

Not of Hell . . .

Something else. Abruptly the howling ceases.

Without stopping to wonder, I pull the finger from my mouth. Black blood wells from deep crevices above and below the knuckle. Fountain pen? Where did that thought come from? Never mind. Get cracking. I place the bloody finger at the apex of the southernmost triangle and drag it across the rough flagstones. In the wavering, golden light I can clearly see all six angles close to the parapet where the weather has barely touched them. I only need join them together, that's all . . . I work fast, ignoring the pain.

Behind me, down the steps, I hear a scraping of fingernails against the rough boards. She means to come through to me, to take me back down! Hurry.

The blood flows freely so that I am able to paint as fast

412

as I can drag the finger along each line . . . Five lines are already done . . . only one remains to complete. But surely the boards cannot hold. Heavenly Father, please help me, I moan . . .

A shadow falls over my work. I look up. And my mouth falls open.

A dark figure looms across the luminous clouds outside, shuttering the light from the three south-facing arches. Its massive shoulders are outlined in light; beams of light radiate into the smoke which surrounds it. Its head is encircled by a dazzling circle of yellow-gold.

'Jesus,' I breathe. 'It's the Light of the World.'

'Come with me,' says the figure at the window. And its voice is deep and full of tenderness.

Slowly, I rise from my knees. 'Willingly, my Lord,' I stammer. 'Oh, willingly.'

I take one trembling step towards the window . . .

And stop . . .

My cheeks bulge. My lips burst open. And the traitorous words spew forth:

'But . . . the prisoner dare not leave the magical wall he has drawn round himself. He has been shown the wickedness that dwelt in his mind – the evil intention no words can erase. Now he knows that he must pay for that wickedness. And *in full* – half payments won't do. And so, with deep regret, he answers in a voice loud and clear: MY LORD, I CANNOT GO WITH YOU.'

'Eh? You what? Look here, don't muck me about, lad. This lot could go any second. This turret ain't safe. Come along now, give us your hand. Your hand, lad. Come on, we ain't got much time.'

A golden gauntlet enters the aperture and gropes towards me.

413

'Can't,' I wail, 'She'll get me.'

'That's enough, lad,' says the voice, brusquely. 'Come on, son. Let's be going.'

The hand almost touches me. I draw in my extremities, like a spider that's netted a stagbeetle by mistake. Behind me, the sound of scraping becomes louder and more insistent. I turn to look, but there's nothing to see. Not yet, but surely . . . Turning back to the windows I see a lick of flame pass over the figure. It speaks rapidly now:

'Give me your hand. Now, please. Look, don't be a . . . Come on, lad. It's bloody warm out here.'

'No,' I bawl, 'I can't leave the hexangle. Go away. Go away!'

'Look, if these windows wasn't so narrow . . .' The statement is punctuated by grunts. The arm waves and one shoulder forces its way through the opening. More grunting: 'It's no use, you'll have to climb out here. On to the platform. Nothing to be scared of; like going down in a lift, it is. Come on, give us your hand, sonny, please. Toot sweet, or we're both going to friggin' well roast.'

I don't answer. This person is certainly an imposter. I can tell by the language.

'Come here!' shouts the figure, 'NOW! you little . . . MOVE!'

Aha, I think, just as I thought. 'Get stuffed!' I shout back.

'All right! That does it! Wait there. I'll fetch Dad.'

It does not surprise me at this point to observe that this figure departs in a downwards – rather than upwards – direction. Horns or no horns, he never really fooled me – not after I'd recovered from the initial shock – and as far as I am concerned he never existed. I can't deny being curious to see what She conjures up next, though I'm reasonably confident the 'Father' will be no less phoney than the Son.

A change of sound makes me turn. The smoke has

stopped coming through the barrier; between the boards I now see slits of bright golden light. Is it the flames, or is it . . . *Her*? Is it the Ghost now lit up and ready to enter?!

It *is* Her! I know it. The Ghost becomes fire. Dear God, She meant it. I have not paid up. She has come to burn me alive!

'No wait,' I wail, 'I'll do it. I'll try. Please . . . don't burn me, not yet!'

Once more, I fold the half-severed finger, the first finger of my right hand. Once more insert it, draw back my tongue, search out the lacerated joint with my cutting teeth. My whole body is trembling. As I haul a great breath, I have time to wonder why I've not fainted a dozen times before now. Strangely, I've never felt more alive, more awake.

Breath complete. Hold it . . .

Head? Is that you? You've come back!

Sssh. Control.

I seem to hear the baying of the pack and the horns and the shouts of men . . .

Summon the power – all blood, all will to the biting muscles of the jaw . . .

I am ready . . .

BITE
TWIST
BITE AGAIN
AGAIN
AGAIN
Now . . . WRENCH!

I am lying on my side, my cheek to the flagstone. The walls of the turret are focused. The flagstone is wet, sticky. The finger is still in my mouth, still curled, I can feel it. My right arm is somewhere else, stretched out on the flagstone behind me. It does not hurt me either; my jaws open; it tumbles on to the stone. I swivel my eyes towards the steps and the barrier . . . I stare at the barrier and begin to sob silently . . . *The Ghost is still there, but now blazing brighter than ever.*

Too late! After all I have been through; the hour has struck. *And I am too late . . .*

A shadow falls across the floor of the turret in front of my eyes. With a moan I rise to my right elbow. A new silhouette is at the window, this one also has a large, haloed head, but its body is narrower than the giant just departed. A second figure hovers, further back to the left. An engine starts up. And a rushing, hissing sound.

The nearer figure speaks. When I hear the voice my heart stutters.

'Are you there, James? I can't see you.'

'Pa,' I breathe.

38

I try to answer with all my might, but only animal grunts come out. A beam of light hits me full in the face, blinding me. I hear my father gasp, 'Good God, James!' The light goes out. My father's voice says, 'Yes. I think it's him.' Another voice, deeper, says, 'Quick as you can, sir.' My father's voice sounds strangely muffled, but somehow I *know* it *is* Pa and not another of Her creatures; only he would call me James, as if I'm the bloody chauffeur.

The weird hissing is louder now. It seems to come from the second figure whose outline I can just make out through the window on Pa's right. There may be a third shadow, further back on the other side. I can't be sure. The smoke is thickening all the time, and orange now. Now there are bright orange sparks flying up away to my left.

My father is speaking again. Somehow he really *is* up here, hovering outside the window of the south-west turret of the tower, more than two hundred and fifty feet above the sleeping city, talking to me like I might have been too long in the bathroom or something. Because of the rumble and hiss and the engine noise below I hear only part of what he says, but the style is unmistakably Pa:

'. . . you're up to? The fireman says you refuse to come out, James . . . this all about?'

Fireman? I think. *Fireman?* I feel myself giggle. Oh, shit! How stupid! So it was neither crown of glory *nor* hellfire; it was a poxy fireman's helmet. They must have searchlights down there . . . yellow helmet, bright light behind . . . say no more. And the hissing noise? A hose of course. There's an explanation for everything, as someone once said. Suddenly I want to laugh and cry at the same time. But what Pa says next sobers me:

'Your Ma is fearfully upset, James. So, please . . . this selfishness, and . . . out at once.'

I want to say, Help me, Pa, help me, but it comes out something like Uhrrmpuh, umpa.

My father's tone changes to what Auntie calls his Ovaltine voice – the one he uses to soothe Ma and negotiate deals on the telephone:

'. . . doesn't understand, Jimmy, [he *never* calls me that!] neither of us does. So please . . . out now . . . good fellow.'

This voice triggers a memory, so clear I can smell it: Ma towing home a pongy little girl from the gypsy camp for Cymbeline's sixth birthday party. The problem – apart from her being a grotbag and complete stranger – was that this was at least a year *after* the accident. How do you explain to a snotty little gyppo, who you know is only in it for the jelly and sausage roll, that the birthday girl is absent having been chopped up by a motor mower and that the nice lady who invited her round is not quite right in the head? And all this without upsetting the lady, who is a child herself in a way? Answer: with the power of words and your soft, sweet voice, that's how. Same as when Ma decided she had to breast-feed Lucky in the park. Same as when she tucked into a large tub of ice cream straight off the supermarket shelf. Same as when . . . never mind – Pa coped.

And he's speaking to *me* in that voice now; soothing me, calming me down: If I've made a mistake, he explains, I have only to *own up* and everything will be all right. He quotes a whole bunch of stuff from the Bible then says, 'How about it, Jimmy? You and me and the One Who Forgives – no one else. Not the clinic. Not the school.

None of them. It's none of their business. Come, boy, give me your hand. "I am the Way . . . I am the light of the World," remember?'

I hear his words and think: If only I could believe that, Pa. Once you really were that bearded Lord to me. But when the night came, you turned out the light. How can I explain to you that somehow the Ghost of your daughter broke into my mind and twisted things round so that my effort to save her from the mower – the heroic deed you praised so highly – was made to look like murder! How can I find words to tell you that me and the Monster are *still* squabbling – that she's *still* sticking it all on me . . . *seven years after her death*?

What I needed was a *witness*, Pa, not a father-confessor or a handsome white god with a lantern. But you're too late now. Poor Pa, you don't understand: if I so much as set one toe outside these magic walls, these walls I have drawn with my blood . . . the Fire Monster will clatter in on her splintered ankles and whisk me off down the winding stairway to *hell*, burning me all the way down.

The hopelessness overwhelms me. Tears pour down my face. Through the blur I see three tongues of flame lick my Pa in quick succession, consuming the smoke for an instant and showing a glimpse of the grey, glass-fronted hood he wears. Both of us could die here, I think. I want to ask the question now, before it's too late: Why no funeral, Dad? Why didn't we bury my sister, Dad? Why was nothing ever *said*? Why was nothing ever *done* to mark her end – not even a DIY job in the caravan? You left it all to me, Dad – the clearing up – that, surely, was wrong. Can't you see what it did to me – this extraordinary omission? This lack of any ending?

These things I want to ask, but my father's gloved hand comes through the aperture, and the moment is past. 'Here, son,' he says, 'at least put these on.' A bundle drops by me. His voice sounds dead. I have never heard this tone

419

before. Maybe he doesn't understand; it's not that I *won't* answer, I *can't* . . .

'Say something, Jimmy . . . Please . . . Just something. Don't shut me out. I'm your dad. I . . . I love you.'

He *loves* me? The words barely make sense to me. *My father* loves? He loves me? ME? *My father loves me?!*

Everything hits me at once – the groping hand, the voice, something about the slope of the shoulders – he's suffering! Out there, he really is bleeding . . . for *me*! Perhaps it is true; perhaps he does love me . . . in his own way! My lips are trembling, I'm blubbering so hard I dare not even try to speak. Then all at once I don't care any more. It all seems wonderfully simple . . . blubbering or not, my father loves me. He *loves* me . . . and maybe . . . maybe that means . . . maybe that means, I can say . . . things . . . tell him . . . things. *At last* . . .

'I MURDERED MY SISTER,' I wail. 'I MOWED HER TO PIECES. ON PURPOSE. SHE SAYS SO.'

The dark shape of my father appears to stiffen. Silence, but for the rumble of the fire, shouting voices far below, the hiss and thud of water on the roof.

When his voice comes again it is low and muffled: 'That's . . . not possible, James,' he says. 'That's—' Drums roll in the attics below; the rest is inaudible.

'Can't hear you, Pa,' I cry.

No answer.

'Pa, I can't hear you!'

I'm bawling again, trying not to make a noise with it so my mouth stops working.

The deep voice shouts: 'The lead, sir, it's melting. It's on the move. You'll have to hurry, sir.'

My Pa is speaking up again: 'I said . . . it's IMPOSS-IBLE, James.' He shouts the word, seeming to blame some-one (me, I guess), then his voice drops again. 'I've wanted to explain,' he mumbles. '. . . tell you . . . and years . . . opportunity . . . Your little sister, God bless her . . .

passed on, four . . . five years before . . . business with the mower . . .'

What is he saying? Something inside tells me: listen hard, Jimbo, this is your one chance to scrape up some meaning . . . the meaning of life is being revealed, and it's going off like a fart on the storm.

Forgetting the danger, I move towards the window. 'Could you repeat that?' I ask politely. (Inside I'm roaring.) My father's hand whips out and grips my wrist – my *left* wrist. A bolt of pain shoots up my neck, my mouth springs open, but I choke off the scream. He has never talked like this before; I will do nothing that might stop him now; not if he pulls my arm in two.

He chews out more precious words, every so often jerking my arm for emphasis. Not a whimper escapes me, though I'm swooning with pain as the bones click and grind . . .

'. . . misunderstanding, that's all. There was no *evil* in you. Ours is a God-fearing house. Always has been, apart from your aunt – she's lost, I can't help that. I baptised you myself – full immersion. How could there be evil in a four-year-old believer? How could they blame you? They couldn't. It was never your fault. It was the dustmen. I'll never forgive them. Never!' (The jerk is so fierce here, I bite a piece out of my lip. It hangs, a big flap.) 'They ought to have checked. It's part of their job to check the refuse. They *never, ever check* the refuse, those men. Never!' (He's shouting now. The second figure turns, then turns away. I hear distant sirens howling towards us.) 'Totally and utterly unprofessional. Callous louts, that's all they are . . . ignorant, reckless louts and . . . and . . . and . . . *criminals*!' (This time I *do* let slip a moan, dribbling blood down my chin. But Pa is in full flow. And the sirens are here now. Two more engines by the sounds.) 'They're all the same,' shouts Pa, 'Scum of the earth. I wrote to the Council. Waste of time. The swines closed ranks like they—'

Sudden roar. A cascade of orange sparks flies up. Flames

421

rise after, lashing and billowing, crimson spinnakers in a gale, too many to count now. There *is* a third figure further back. I see it. All three are briefly engulfed in flames. The second figure moves towards Father. He bellows: 'Roof's gone. East transept. Couple of minutes . . . We'll have to pull out. Have to. Sorry, sir . . . if this one goes . . . That's *it*.'

Pa nods. When he speaks again his voice is filled with desperate urgency: 'It's the truth I'm telling you, boy—'

I hardly hear what comes next, my mind is in such turmoil. Could it really be that what I believed to be an imagination game all these years, wasn't a *game* at all? That it really had happened?! That I'd actually thrown my baby sister in the dustbin when I wasn't even old enough for proper school?! It seemed utterly beyond belief. But even if it were not . . . even if it really did happen . . . She had been *rescued* . . . Baby Cymbeline was snatched from the jaws of the crusher by one of Pa's ignorant louts; of course she was. One of the dustman rescued her. In my *game* he did . . . Pa can't have it *both* ways; either the game was true – all of it – or *none* of it was. And either way, she lived.

My father's voice breaks through the spiralling thoughts: '. . . me, Jimmy, I . . . I *beg* you. I'll explain everything . . . *everything*, I promise. The minute we have you safe. But we must leave this place, now, or it may be too—'

Out of nowhere come three thoughts, crash, bang, wallop: the first is enough to blank out all incoming messages. Lawrence said it: The longest turntable ladder in the country is one hundred and fifty feet fully extended. That makes it approximately one hundred feet SHORT of this turret! The second follows from the first: fire burns – but *that* fire isn't burning *them*! Question: What has wings and can fly and doesn't mind flames? I'll give myself a clue: it plays the fiddle too . . . Bloody hell! – They're playing some bloody fine game with me! Thought three: I'm *outside* the hexangle!

The drums are all around me now, beating the pedal notes, deep and rumbling. A giant organ shaking this tower like a rocket engine. I turn towards the barrier, to address the producer of the pantomime. She seems much brighter now. And the gaps between the planks are wider than they were a minute ago. Much wider. I yell: 'No more apparitions, please, Cymbeline. No more cardboard cut-outs. They're crap! They wouldn't fool pussy.'

Wheeling on the apparition at the window, I scream: 'Get away! You're not my father! *She* sent you. Get out! Get out of my world. Get out, you baaastard! GET OUT! GET OUT! GET OUT!'

My chin feels wet. I know I'm spitting blood.

The grip on my wrist slackens momentarily. I yank my body round. My wrist breaks free. In a scarlet mist, I scramble back to the centre. Safe at the centre. I crouch. Panting.

'Jimmy! Oh, Jimmy, please . . . Nobody sent me. It's *me*. It's your f—'

'I suppose you can fly now,' I yell at it.

'Fly? Sorry? What the . . . ? What do you mean, James?'

'I mean fucking *fly*! There's no ladder this high.'

More flames leap up – one, two, three . . . The deep voice cuts in: 'Hurry. She's going, sir.'

I laugh out loud. 'You can fuck off an' all,' I shriek at the other apparition.

'Here, officer, quickly. Quickly. Tell him. Tell him who I am. Tell him what this thing is. This contraption we're on.'

The fireman-apparition's head appears at the window. 'This here's a Bronto Skylift, son. She's sixty-six point two metres fully extended. Outreach twenty-two. Lifting capacity four-fifty K. Twin monitor. Internal plumbing. Three booms, one telescopic section. Four outriggers.

Mercedes chassis. In-cage and base control consoles. And, as far as I know, son, this gentleman's your dad. Now *come on*, lad.'

'There. You see, James? I *am* your father. And I'm going to tell you *everything*. No more secrets, I promise. That business with the mower . . . No one *murdered* anyone—'

My head is spinning, I feel hopelessly confused, but the pain from my wounds has dwindled to an aching throb. I feel sick, that's all, and badly need to lie down.

'How would you know?' I moan.

'You thought I was on the caravan telephone, didn't you, James? Well I wasn't. Just as I got to it, it stopped ringing. I saw everything.'

He saw it, I whisper. Sweet Jesus, *he saw* . . .

'I stood at the window, and watched. It was amazing. But you're right about one thing – it wasn't an accident. You *meant* it all right. You deliberately swung the thing round and aimed it. I stood there watching you grapple with that big old machine, up on your toes, hardly able to reach the handles. You looked like a demented cockerel to me . . . But no one was *murdered*, that's the point, Jimmy. No one even – hey!'

I feel myself rise and turn. Away from my father. I start down the four steps to the barrier . . .

I will pay now. In full. And serve me right.

'James! Where are you g—? HEY! Oh, no. Over here, James! FOR CHRIST'S SAKE! OVER HERE . . . !'

So, there was a witness after all . . . Unfortunately, it is hostile. No accident, he said. That's it then.

I am vaguely aware of my father shouting and raving – insane stuff – I catch the words 'messy' something, or some*one* – a girl's name, I think. It's all quite irrelevant now. The planks of the barrier dissolve before me

and there She stands,

blazing

Reflection

39

There's a cardboard cakebox on my bedside locker; flat, square white card with the confectioner's name in swirly green writing on the lid. Lawrence sent it. No cake, just all that remains of the Ghost.

I have to sleep now. I sleep a lot. I'm not angry with the firemen, but I hope to sleep for a very long time.

Auntie came. It might've been yesterday or the day before. She never says goodbye she just wasn't there any more. And there was a waterpistol on my locker plus a note saying, Get 'em Jim. See you tomorrow, Love Auntie.

The old man opposite has a heart-shaped gas balloon in pink and silver hitched to the bedrail. He told me the story of it even though I shut my eyes and pretended to be asleep. It seems the man who brought it in used to be his boyfriend; the balloon was a goodbye present because the boyfriend had found someone else.

I heard the old man crying in the night, and then yesterday the Registrar told him, either he gave up smoking or he'd be discharged without further treatment. And that meant he'd lose the other foot. Fuck you, sonny, said the old boy. Then he lit a fag and sent for his clothes. On the way out he stopped at my bed. 'Your auntie's a cracker, son, ain't she? If more women was like her, things might have been different for me.' He winked and gave me the balloon. When I wanted to know the secret of life, he told me, I just had to open the window and let go of the string.

My left arm is in a cast from wrist to shoulder, but it does not hurt now. You'd have thought it would. I can still feel my finger even though it's no longer with me. This morning I forgot; I tried to pick my nose; it really came home to me then.

Yesterday they took the bandages off my head. I asked the Irish nurse for a mirror but she pretended to keep forgetting. She tries to look at me normally but it isn't too convincing. She smiles but the eyes are wrong inside. Anyway, I can see by my hands what I'm going to be like. She's nice though. I think she would have liked me.

I sleep so much I don't know whether it's morning or evening, but the window by my bed faces north, at least I can tell that by the Cathedral. The window's so big I could almost be flying – apart from the hospital smell and the fug. Last time I woke the sky was so blue it was black at the top. There was one star, probably a planet, smack bang over the Cathedral – almost sitting on top of the tower, like a fairy on a Christmas tree. Three seagulls went over, high up, flying south. The underside of their wings were shining gold. The tower and turrets were dark grey, the four gold pennants barely visible. But the gulls were gleaming. I looked down the ward to the big plate window at the far end. The sky over the black treeline was greenish yellow. There was no sun for us yet. Even though this hospital is on top of St Thomas's Hill, there was no sun here.

One thing I've noticed: no more games, no more voices. All that's done with. I hope.

I've been watching them putting up the scaffolding. You

can see the whole Cathedral from here – down to the gutter line, I mean. It is big: it makes the ordinary houses look like Monopoly houses. There is less damage than I thought there would be. It is only the roof of the quire and the south-east transept and part of the south-west transept that have gone. There is no doubt which turret I was in; one of the windows is blacker than the others where they knocked two into one to get me out. I could do with a pair of binoculars.

She brought it in the end, wrapped in a teacloth with the bedpan. She didn't look at me; she just touched my arm and said, 'Take it easy, Jimmy,' and went. It took me all day to screw myself up for the peepshow. I kept thinking, Go on, it can't be that bad if the nurse can stand it. In the end I closed my eyes and held it out at arm's length. I thought I could open them just a crack, then shut them up quick if need be.

I was actually on the point of peeping when I heard the clump of Auntie's tough walking boots and her voice calling my name. She was coming straight to me, cheeks flushed, hair all over.

I hid the mirror under the bedclothes.

She put the cakebox on my locker then sat down on the edge of the bed. I heard the mirror crack but didn't say anything. Then she said: 'Truth time, Jim. Your father knows I'm here. And he knows what I'm going to do. He tried to stop me – I've got to tell you that – but I've had all the little white lies I can stand. And so have you; that's obvious now. So, if you're ready, mate . . . ?'

I don't think I even nodded, but she started anyway:

'Father told me what you said up there, about murdering your sister, Jim . . .' She picked up my good hand and held it between her two hands. 'The truth is, dear, Cymbeline died when she was still a tiny baby.' She looked

429

at me with her clear blue eyes, reading me. 'He says he's explained that already, but . . .'

I nodded – I couldn't smile back for the tightness around my lips. I was trying to read her eyes too – searching for signs of revulsion.

'That's something, anyroad,' she said, 'I thought perhaps . . . Well, I'm surprised, I must say. But I'm very pleased you managed to take that much in.'

I felt tired. I shut my eyes and nodded my head on the pillow.

'You weren't responsible for what happened, Jim, you were only a little nipper yourself, remember.' (I was too tired to open my eyes but thought: 'nipper?', I reckon you've slipped up there, Auntie.) 'You must try to understand, dear, an infant is an emotional warzone – just a sec.' Feeling the weight of her lift from the bed, I opened my eyes and watched her clump round to the other side.

Between me and the double doors was another old man. This one had a bag of clear liquid on a pole. He had no visitors of his own and I guessed Auntie had spotted him eavesdropping. She sat down between us, her back towards him now.

My eyes would not stay open so I gave in and let them close.

'Children of that age are just like wild animals inside; in fact the younger they are the more savage and uncontrollable their emotions. It's a stage we all go through, dear. And – I'm sorry to say this – but no amount of holy water will change that. No. Nor over-strict upbringing either; that invariably makes things worse.

'You did get some funny ideas in your head, mind. I remember one time you yanked your baby sister clean off mum's lap when she was happily glugging away at the breast.' I opened my eyes. Her face looked sad now. 'That was the first time you were locked down the cellar . . .'

Her eyes became unfocused as the memory took her off.

After a moment she said, 'I did try to warn him, but he's older as you know, Jim, and he never would take advice from his clever-dick sister; our dad was the same with my aunt.' She chuckled briefly. 'Another time you brought mum your little toy feeding bottle full up with milk – there was milk all over the kitchen of course, but you'd managed to fill it. I don't know exactly what was going on in that four-year-old head of yours, but whatever it was anyone could see that it scared you to death – not for yourself, for your Ma – anyone except Edward, that is. Edward was too busy congratulating himself on never having laid a hand on you. He didn't need to: he had other devices, did Edward, most of them far more effective than an old-fashioned clip round the ear . . .

'A docile and perfectly obedient infant is a terrible thing – terrible! How many times did I tell your dad that? But that's exactly what you became. It's nothing but a time bomb waiting to explode, I told him. He wouldn't listen, though. I'm sorry to say this, but your father—'

'Hang on, Auntie,' I said. I could not allow such a basic discrepancy to pass unchallenged again. 'I was hardly an *infant*, Aunt Mary,' I said, 'I was nine years old when she . . .' My voice trailed off.

My aunt was staring at me, her head shaking slowly from side to side.

'I thought you said Father . . . But he didn't. Of course not. I ought to have known.' She sighed and patted my leg. 'Well then . . . looks like your old auntie is left with the sticky end again. Never mind. She came prepared anyway, so let's get the job done.'

Still holding my eyes, she picked up the cakebox, opened the lid and held it out to me.

I shook my head, bewildered and more than a little disappointed. How could she imagine I'd be interested in eating?

She shook the box.

I shook my head.

'Take one,' she said.

I stared.

She stared back, insisting with her eyes.

I shrugged and reached into the box. What I drew out was a rubbery object, five inches across, like a small, thick pancake, matt black in colour apart from a network of cracks which showed through dull pink. I turned it over. It was pink underneath. I sniffed it. 'Soot,' I mumbled. I looked at my aunt. 'I can't eat that,' I said.

She smiled, set the box down on the bed and nodded at it. I craned my neck. Inside were three more pancakes and a lumpy brown envelope. 'Meet Cymbeline Bishop,' she said, smilling her lopsided smile.

The name came like an electric shock. I gaped. How *could* she joke about something like that?

She pursed her lips. 'You still haven't cottoned, mate, have you?' Then she lay down beside me, her head on my pillow, and she talked, and she talked, and she talked. She was still there talking when Staff came to turn out an hour and a quarter later. The sunlight had gone by then, and the ward lights were on, though I never noticed it happen.

Cymbeline's full and proper name was Messy Mary de Luxe, but I changed her name to Cymbydoll after christening her in the bath – full immersion. From that moment on, the doll and I were inseparable.

Auntie knew all about Messy Mary – they shared the same name after all – more to the point, it was herself, she said, who was sent off to buy the doll the day her sister-in-law left Maternity, Ma being anxious that her little boy should not feel left out.

Cymbydoll was eighteen inches of fully articulated flame-resistant vinyl. She did *everything*: she wept real tears, she fluttered her eyelids, she cried a real baby's cry when her tummy was squeezed, she had washable nylon hair – rooted of course – bottle, highchair, rattle, bib, dungarees, dresses, bonnets, a crib, but . . . the thing I loved best, so Auntie informed me, was the wetting; that had me in raptures. For hours I would sit feeding her water, then sitting her up so she'd wet herself. Then I'd shout, 'Bad gel, Thimby-doll, wet you nickies,' and roll about screaming with laughter. Then I'd do it again. And again. And again.

For a while life seemed good for my parents – Ma had the daughter she'd always wanted, Pa's business was thriving and, at least for a few months, my disturbance seemed pretty well under control. Then the disaster struck.

It seems that Ma simply could not accept that her baby had been crushed to death in a garbage truck. Rather, her *brain* could not accept it. The way her poor brain dealt with the shock was to transfer all her motherly love to my doll. To Ma, Cymbydoll *became* Cymbeline in every possible way.

When they finally took Ma away, Cymbydoll had to go too. Mother and doll could not be prised apart. To make matters worse it soon became clear that I had adopted the very same delusion, the absent doll had become sister to me. I was mortified by her removal, but that was how my child's mind coped with the terrible burden of guilt.

Despite Doctor Keylock's warnings, Pa subtly encouraged my delusion. When Auntie challenged him he told her he could not force me to accept the truth without risking my sanity, and, in the event of my spilling the beans, any chance of recovery for his beloved wife – of that he was utterly convinced. The shock would be too great, he declared. To my father, everything that happens in this world is God's will: my mother's delusion was God's way of protecting her mind, and my own delusion was the Lord's guarantee of his mercy.

Due to the peculiar isolation of the house and yard, wedged as it was in the no-man's-land between the lines, the marshes and the sewage farm, few visitors ever came.

As for me, I was always too clever for the liking of my schoolmates at Marshside Junior. I never once invited any of them home – there's not one that would have come anyway – and when I transferred to the big school I was too ashamed of my origins to invite anyone home. So that was it: Cymbeline lived on in hospital, in the form of Messy Mary. And when she came home . . .

We all know what happened when she came home.

As my aunt's account reached its end I experienced a sensation of extraordinary relief. Here was meaning. Here was sanity. Here was reason, albeit born of the most bizarre and shocking events. But beneath the relief a shadow still lurked which I could not immediately bring into focus.

I looked at my aunt. Her eyes seemed very moist. She took the brown envelope out of the box and handed it to me. I ripped it open. Two eyeballs, each blue and white, tumbled on to the bedspread.

I felt my whole body recoil. I stared at them in horror. 'Where—? Where did you find those?' I stammered.

My aunt smiled. 'Look at them, Jim.'

I forced myself to do as she bid me.

'No, Jim, I said *look*.' She picked up one of the eyeballs and placed it in my palm.

For a second the eye seemed to stare right through me, then suddenly it became what it was – a coloured glass ball.

'Where did you find them?' I whispered again.

She shook her head slowly. '*I* didn't. A friend of yours did.'

I gazed at her, remembering the grey shape vanishing into the shadows along the Shelf, remembering the hope, and the terror . . . 'You mean . . . Lawrence?'

She nodded. 'He'd been searching for you ever since you disappeared. The night of the storm, he went to the turret, to look for you there. As soon as he saw those bits of doll in the turret, he knew they were yours. He'd seen them before, in your old blue tool box, he said. Anyway, he waited as long as he dared, then he took them and hid them for you in a place he called the Bible store. "In case a Mamba found them," he said. It's silly, I know, but I have an idea that boy thinks you might have got yourself mixed up with witchcraft, Jim. Not that he said so, but—' She laughed and patted my leg.

'Anyway, after the fire he went back and searched among the ashes of the Bibles until he found them. He was up there on the platform you see; it was him who called the fire brigade; he told them he knew where you'd be; he seemed to know so much they decided to break all the rules and take him up with them. That's where I met him; not on the platform, of course; I was down with the engines; I came with your father, you see, Jim.' She squeezed my good arm. 'I understand why you wouldn't come out – of course I do, dear – but . . . it's all over now, you've no cause to feel that way any more, my darling boy. You've lived through a nightmare, it's time to wake up now.' She blinked at me in the deepening gloom of the ward. After a moment, she said:

'That friend of yours . . . he heard you tell Father how you'd murdered your sister. And he heard Edward's answer . . . He may be rough round the edges but he's no fool, that boy. He didn't understand everything – I'm not saying he did – but he did pretty well considering the truth of it. He put it together well enough to come up with these – four lumps of melted plastic and a pair of glass eyes. And I can't think how else I'd have got through to you. You've got a mate there, Jim. A *real* mate.'

I stared into memory. There had been a third shadow on the platform. Fancy Shag doing that, I thought, just for *me*. Then I remembered the hell I'd been through trying to solve the mystery of the relics' disappearance, and I made the mistake of smiling with my tissue-paper face.

My aunt was staring at me, as though willing me to remember everything.

After the barrier gave way . . . what then?

The awful vision . . . the vision drawn in lines of fire, of Cymbeline dancing victorious among the flames . . . and smiling . . . smiling . . .

Then what?

A blow in the back . . . in the small of the back, like a kick from a horse . . .

And after?

After that? . . . Nothing. I don't know.

'What happened then?' I asked my aunt, 'after the fire-man came? And Pa?'

Aunt Mary told how I'd walked away from my father, seemingly speaking to some invisible presence – though no one could understand the words. In desperation they turned the platform monitor on me, full blast. The jet flung me straight through the blazing barrier, through all the flames in the spiral, down fifty steps into the arms of firemen working their way up from below.

Meanwhile my father had snatched the fireman's axe, smashed out a pillar, leapt through the gap, only to be felled by a slab of falling stone. (Which explained his absence now.)

I looked again at the shapeless cakes of vinyl. How neatly everything fell into place now that the Big Lie had been blown away by my aunt, with the help of my friend, my 'real mate', Lawrence. At last all the incomprehensible details fitted, I didn't have to hammer them into place any more like wrong bits of jigsaw. Even the awkward bits like the way Cymby had cried when I squeezed her tummy while drying her after . . . after . . . (the shadow darkens) sweet Jesus – the things I did to that kid – NO, not *kid*, it wasn't a child – when would my brain accept this thing? – to that doll, to Messy Mary . . .

Even the enigma of Pa's indifference to the bloody mess on the lawn was explained. Why should he have cared? There was no *bloody* mess, just a mess – the blood was all in my mind. Dolls don't bleed. But, above all, it explained that awful omission: the absence of any kind of funeral. I might have hated her, but I never did accept that. Even a dog gets buried . . . 'But she wasn't a dog. She was only a *doll*.'

In my brain, the echo of a voice departed: *Only . . . ?*

'Is it wrong to say, Only?'

Something in my aunt's eyes told me I had spoken aloud. Her eyes seemed to shine in the yellowing gloom. 'You've asked now, that's enough.' She gently took my bandaged hand. 'I'll tell you a secret, Jim. However we are . . . is OK.'

She stood up. 'Shall I take these?' she asked, returning the relics one by one to the cake box.

I shook my head. 'She can stay,' I said. 'There is one more thing, though. If you don't mind, Auntie.'

I turned back the covers where she'd been sitting and fished out the two bits of mirror. My aunt held my eyes a moment, then, without speaking, she took the larger piece of mirror and turned it towards me.

What I saw was a pink face with skin both wrinkled and smooth, a face without hair, or lashes, or eyebrows – a child's face.

'See you,' she said. She stooped to brush my forehead with her lips. Then she turned and clumped away between the rows of white beds.

Today was my first walking expedition. I unhitched the balloon and tied it round the cake box. Then I took them both to the window . . . and let go. For a moment they hung there, perfectly balanced between the pulls of earth and sky. Slowly they drifted out over the car park, then rose sharply, on the updraught from the incinerator, I guess. They climbed high over the city, spinning in the breeze. Above the Cathedral the sun touched them, turning the silver to gold. Up she rose flashing pink, gold, pink, gold, pink, gold . . .

Beautiful ending, I thought.

I stood at the window while she dwindled to a speck.

When I could see her no more, headvoice whispered,
Rest in peace.

I had to smile then.